THE
KING'S
BEACON

To Alex,

A reminder of your very first public performance on the trumpet in St Catharine's School Brass Group — Chipping Campden Literature Festival, 2 May 2013 at 9.45 a.m

Congratulations

Terry

THE
KING'S
BEACON

TERRY DILLON

authorHOUSE®

AuthorHouse™
1663 Liberty Drive
Bloomington, IN 47403
www.authorhouse.com
Phone: 1-800-839-8640

Published by AuthorHouse   09/21/2012

ISBN: 978-1-4772-2992-7 (sc)
ISBN: 978-1-4772-2991-0 (hc)
ISBN: 978-1-4772-2993-4 (e)

CONTENTS

CHAPTER 1

PETER

It had almost escaped. Despite what appeared at one time to be his limited prospects, he was now what he had always dreamed of becoming.

As a teenage cornet player, Peter had, in his usual thoughtless way, succumbed to what was at that time the attractive possibility of a career in brass bands. Enticed by the prospect of using his talents in the local colliery band, he took a job in the nearby mine. It did not take him long to recognise his mistake.

He left the black debilitating dust and the daily dangers of the dark, low-arched underground tunnels, the hazards his father and those like him faced daily, within a year. The consequence, he knew, was that once out of the mines he was likely to be conscripted into military service like thousands of other young men in the 1950s who, for two of the most formative years of their lives, donned khaki uniforms, obeyed often futile orders, and on occasions were asked to fight for their country. He pre-empted conscription and the whims of the recruiting officers who nominated him for The King's Own Yorkshire Light Infantry, by using his musical talent and choosing to voluntarily serve for three years as a musician in the Brigade of Guards. The experiences he enjoyed convinced him that what he now saw as the hard and dangerous life of the miner was not his only option but that his dream of being a teacher, a person committed to educating young minds into realising their potential, could become more than fantasy.

Peter did his training as a teacher in London. His main subject was not music, as he had expected, but history, a love of his from his school days. Towards the end of his three years of training, he was delighted to be offered a post in what was regarded a first-rate school in London, a school in which he had done his teaching practice and impressed the headteacher. His instant response was to take it, but for once, he reined in his usual thoughtless and spontaneous reaction to a new opportunity; he decided to discuss it with his young wife, Catherine.

'It's very tempting,' she replied, 'but we can't afford to live in London. Houses are the most expensive in the country, and there's no way I want to live in another flat. I know we've been OK in this one, but we both saw it as only a start and not a permanent place to live. Anyway,' she added purposefully, 'I don't want to bring up children in London. Can you imagine what it must be like to be a child surrounded by lots of cars, buses, concrete, and people?'

'You're right, I suppose. I've enjoyed my time in London,' Peter responded wistfully, thinking about his own life in London—first as a soldier and then as a student. He thought about the range of experiences he had enjoyed, many of them with Catherine. The memories of the dances, the shows, the theatre, and the general excitement of gazing at the sumptuously adorned windows in Oxford Street, flooded his mind. 'We were at the right age to enjoy London, but I suppose you're right about being here as a young child. It would no doubt be somewhat different, I have to admit. In some ways, it's a pity to refuse the offer of a job, but you're right. It makes sense to look elsewhere.'

They both became pensive, sitting in their easy chairs, looking at each other without really seeing, eyes glazed with memories. And then, suddenly struck by a shaft of inspiration, rather like a streak of sunlight breaking between the tiniest of gaps in a closed curtain, Peter exclaimed, 'What d'you think about going back north?'

'I'd love it,' replied Catherine with enthusiasm. 'But that raises a few questions, too. There's the problem of finding somewhere to live, and then . . . .'

'And then all sorts of things,' interrupted Peter, 'but unless we take it on we'll get nowhere. I know it's not going to be easy to find a post, but I'll start looking in the *Times Educational Supplement* and other educational journals, and with luck I might spot a job.'

Catherine nodded her agreement, clearly more cheerful with the prospect of returning north than remaining in what to her would have been a characterless life in the foaming hubbub of a London suburb. And so Peter decided to look north, often allowing the thought to pull at his imagination and provide him with visions of a life so different from what he was currently experiencing.

Not surprisingly, his search eventually concentrated on Yorkshire. Both Peter and Catherine had been born in Yorkshire, they had married there, their parents still lived in the county, and now, reminded again of the happiness they associated with it, both felt a strong desire to make it their home.

For some time, it looked as though the dream was not to be fulfilled as Peter failed to gain nothing more than polite letters of acknowledgement from the schools to which he applied. Gradually, he felt the pangs of desperation growing as the realisation took hold that he may not find a school willing to employ him. It raised fearful questions as to how he would be able to care for his wife and children and how mistaken was the decision to turn down the London offer.

Throughout the uncertainty, however, Catherine's faith in him never wavered, and she regularly reasserted her belief, in moments of his despair, that all would be well. And then, as if at the last gasp, there arrived an invitation for interview as head of history at Weberton Secondary Modern School. Although it might not fit his ideal, he had no idea whether it was a 'good' school or not, he accepted the invitation without hesitation.

Weberton was an old market town. It sat in the Aire Valley, enfolded by moorland and overlooked by the famous *King's Beacon*, a landmark that dominated the surrounding area. It bore the name of *King* because of the way its flaming summit had warned the armies of Charles I of the approach of the Roundheads during the Civil War. An encased handle, the remains of a sword found in more recent years in the cave near the summit of the *Beacon*, was displayed in the museum at Weberton as a reminder of those fearful days.

The town bore other traces of its past with its medieval market hall, castle, and the imposing Yorkshire stone market hall. But it had moved into the industrial era with the building of its canal, woollen mill, and thriving businesses of the High Street. It was now more a commercial than an agricultural centre famous for its sheep market. The town was regarded as prosperous and, by those who knew of it, as a place to which those with enterprise were being drawn. This meant that most of the population earned a good living and enjoyed a lifestyle to match. For the more ambitious, the nearby cities of Leeds and Bradford offered even more attractive prospects, without the need to relocate. But at the bottom of the scale were still those who were unemployed and dependent on public benefits, or who were scraping a living by doing odd jobs.

The palpable disparity among the inhabitants of Weberton was reflected in the pupil population of its secondary modern school, though not in equal proportions.

On the day before his interview, Peter travelled north from London by train to stay with his parents. They lived in the small mining village, about 40 miles from Weberton, in which Peter had been brought up and where he had, for a short time, experienced life underground. He had arranged to stay overnight and then borrow his father's car to go across country for his interview.

Peter could not fail to be impressed by Weberton and its surrounds. Having driven through the industrial heartland of the West Riding, with its smoke-gushing factories and its seemingly incessant noise, he emerged into a valley of luxurious vegetation and rich farmland, which rose in gentle contours to open moorland. Following the directions he had been given, he entered the tranquillity of a country town, proceeded down High Street, past the gates of the imposing castle, and over the narrow boat canal. With *The King's Beacon* at his rear—he was yet to learn its significance—he turned into the school through the imposing gates and found a parking space.

He was impressed by his first sight of the school. Just on the outskirts of the town, its situation was idyllic. In front of him was what looked like an extensive public park, its trees offering shade to people sitting on the grassed parkland or by the canal. At the top of the park, he could see the usual swings and carousels that proved so attractive to young children. As he turned, his eyes followed the curve of the complaisant moor rising above the town to give the impression that it was snuggling Weberton within its open arms. Rising above was the *Beacon*, seemingly standing as king of all it surveyed.

He locked his car, entered the school, and reported to the office staff. Having been asked to sit and await his interview, along with three other applicants, in the corridor outside the headteacher's study, he was struck by the strand of tension that linked the four of them. The pressure to gain a position—there were only three weeks to go before the start of the new school year—was drawn across the faces of the young men and woman seated by the door imposingly marked, 'Headteacher.' Peter had no doubt that they, like him, were going over and over again the likely questions of the interviewers and the answers they should give. Their anxiety was cloaked in the supposition of confidence that they knew they would require once they walked through what had become to them an intimidating door. They sat in silence.

Peter had experienced interviews that he regarded as important as this one before. His reminiscences about one in particular, his interview for university, disturbed his thinking whilst he was awaiting the call. On that occasion, he had been shown into a room, far more imposing than his present location, which was seemingly imprisoned within shelves of books. They posed as if to remind him that university was about study and that it would be foolhardy to mistake its purpose. It had struck Peter that the sad- and tired-looking shelved books had not had the joy of being reached for, opened, and browsed for some years. Somehow, they seemed to be appealing to be read rather than expecting it, like sleeping lovers hopefully waiting to be awakened by a kiss. Peter had known that they were unlikely to be disturbed by those anxious sixth formers who sat passing the time away, looking up at them whilst waiting to be called into the inner chamber for their interview, pretending to themselves that they might one day have reason to take down and read similar books to those displayed before them. That most of the books were totally unrecognisable on that particular day was of no special concern.

Peter was brought back to reality when eventually a slim, grey-haired, small gentleman with kindly eyes opened the door to the headteacher's study and called him in. Peter was the second of the four candidates to be interviewed. The gentleman introduced himself as Mr Holdsworth, the headteacher, and then introduced the two governors. One was a woman of middle age with short, blond hair and rather plain brown sandals that Peter caught sight of under the table as he bent to take his chair. It surprised him to see sandals, and even more that he gave them any consideration, especially as visible above the table was a smartly dressed woman with a skull-hugging hat that sported a coquettish feather. She was clearly planning to ask him challenging questions.

The second governor was a man of about forty whom the headteacher introduced as the chair of governors. He was smartly dressed, wore what looked like a club tie, and sported a thin moustache. He put on his spectacles as Peter entered the room, as if to get a better view of the new candidate.

The headteacher opened the interview by informally asking Peter if he had had a pleasant journey north and whether or not he knew Weberton. Peter answered, 'Yes' and 'No,' and then the real questioning began.

'What experience have you had to date in teaching?' asked Mr Holdsworth.

'I was a student teacher for a year before I went to college. That was in the period that I spent at home after my national service. I'd been a musician in the Brigade of Guards. I had a year to wait before starting teacher training and so I thought it would be time usefully spent. I found that to be the case because it gave me some valuable experience, which helped me on my teaching practices in college.'

The head seemed pleased with his response, so Peter tackled the next question, 'Why do you think history is important to children?' which was posed by Mrs Arnold, with increased confidence.

Peter noted that Mr Megson, the chair of governors, jotted down something on his notepad as he began his answer.

'As for the value of history, I believe that knowledge of the past will help children to understand the times in which they live better. It will help them understand the concept of change and have some idea of how we've arrived at where we are. I think they'll be able to understand something of politics, they'll learn some moral lessons, such as the causes of war, and hopefully they'll recognise the importance of valuing other people, no matter where they come from.'

'And what about planning, planning to ensure that the pupils learn what you want them to? It's one thing to have the sort of ideas you have just outlined; it's another to get the pupils to absorb them. How important do you see planning and how would you set about it?'

This was the sort of question that Peter had prepared for and was not surprised that Mr Holdsworth asked it. With a confident smile, he said, 'The time I spent on teaching practice impressed upon me the importance of having a daily plan based on an agreed long-term plan. You need a good structure so that you know what resources are required, what questions to ask, and what sort of work would be best for the pupils. If you organise in that way, you can ensure that the lessons are coherent and interesting.'

Again, Mr Holdsworth appeared happy with his answer, and Peter began to see the possibility of a job.

'Now, what I think is a very important question,' said the chair of governors in a severe voice, 'the question of discipline and class control. How well do you think you will cope with that, and have you any techniques in mind?'

Peter recognised this as the trickiest question and one that tested an area in which he was least secure. As he answered, he endeavoured not to relax the confident manner he had adopted throughout the interview. 'I think it's important to have boundaries that children know and understand, and equally important to insist that they stay within them. I think it's also important that they know that there are punishments and that if they misbehave they will be imposed. But I think most importantly lessons need to be lively and interesting and involve the pupils so they are not tempted to become a nuisance.'

Peter knew it was a sort of classic answer that did not really say much. In his student-teacher days, he had met pupils who had an antipathy to school and took more pleasure in confronting the basic ingredients of learning than absorbing them. As a result, he had found it almost impossible to keep them focused on their studies, no matter what boundaries he set or how well he prepared his lessons. There was something in the psyche of such children, he had concluded, that made them impossible to teach. They brought furrows to his brow as he sought to ascertain what mysteries were so compressed in their minds that learning could not infiltrate. He did not really understand how he or anyone might deal with such pupils, but he believed that, just as the musician listens, practices, and explores before achieving quality in a performance, the same rituals would help him build on his experience and help him find the key to a solution.

The interview lasted around half an hour. Peter sat straight backed, his hands lightly pouched around thigh height, his knees uncrossed, and from time to time with his head slightly on one side in listening mode. These were tips he had learned through studying a newspaper article titled, *Success in Interview*. He went through the stock answers he had prepared with the calm and confidence that he had practised in the waiting room and rehearsed with Catherine. In fact, throughout the interview, Peter somehow sensed that Catherine had been willing him to say the right things and so convince his interrogator of his worth.

Eventually, he was asked if he had any questions, but as he had none, he was then asked, 'If offered the post, would you take it?'

'Without question,' was his response.

He was asked to wait outside whilst the remaining candidates were interviewed. His anxiety was such that he could not simply sit and wait. He had to move, and so he took the opportunity to walk around the school for a few minutes. The classrooms were empty, as the pupils were on their summer holidays, but Peter gained an agreeable impression of the atmosphere that no doubt permeated the bustling corridors and the rooms when full of expectant learners. He walked along the corridors, peered through doors, rustled his way through school magazines harboured at the entrance, and then went out to the playground, before returning up the stairs to his station outside the headteacher's study. He felt excited about the prospect of a job in Weberton.

Within minutes of his arrival back at his seat, the third candidate reappeared, her interview over. It was another ten minutes before the head came out and invited the fourth candidate into his study. As no one had been dismissed, it was clear that the panel wanted to offer the job and get a response that day. The anxiety continued as the corridor fell into deeper shadow; the windows could not transport themselves to match the movements of the sun's dusty rays. And so the wait, almost funereal in its absorption, continued. Peter's anxiety engulfed him in earnest when, after the fourth candidate's interview had been completed, the head reappeared and invited the third candidate back into his study.

Damn. It's all over, were his immediate thoughts. *They've decided to offer it to her.* He could not help but feel cold depression creeping over him and a sense of the difficulty he would have sharing the news of his failure with Catherine. *No point in waiting here,* he despondently thought to himself.

He was about to stand and leave the building when the head reappeared with the young lady, thanking her for her time and wishing her success in her next application. Mr Holdsworth then turned to Peter and smilingly invited him to go into his study.

'Take a seat please, Mr Delaney,' said Mr Megson as Peter entered and Mr Holdsworh closed the door. 'Are you still interested in the post?' The question was unequivocal and required a simple yes or no from Peter.

'Yes,' answered Peter, still not entirely sure as to why the question was being asked. He had difficulty controlling, however, the sudden surge in the expectation that began to beat in his breast.

'That's fine,' said Mr Megson. 'We would, therefore, like to offer you the post.'

Peter was flooded with emotion. He felt a tingle under the skin in his face and wondered whether it had changed colour. He managed, however, to control himself sufficiently to be able say, 'Thank you very much. I'm delighted to accept.'

What had happened to the young lady was no longer his concern. Whether she was offered the job and refused it, he would never know. And he would never care.

Mr Holdsworth came round the table, gave him a congratulatory handshake, and then left the room, presumably to inform the remaining candidates of the panel's decision. Peter had difficulty believing it, but at last he had a job and in one of the most appealing areas of his native county.

Peter's call to Catherine that evening was one of the happiest he had made. Catherine was away with her parents, as they had undertaken to take her, their newborn baby, Sarah, and their year old Katie, on holiday whilst Peter endeavoured to find a job. 'I got it!' was about all he could excitedly shout down the phone when Catherine eventually picked it up. 'It's a super place, and I'm really chuffed.'

'Oh, Peter, what a relief. Congratulations.'

The conversation continued with first Peter and then Catherine exclaiming their good fortune to the other. Peter eventually brushed away all the congratulatory talk to reveal what was becoming uppermost in his mind. 'Now we've to sort out somewhere to live.'

His search for a post had taken until August, three weeks before the start of the new school year in September. This gave very limited time to find somewhere for the family to live in Weberton or nearby. With Catherine still away with her parents, it meant that Peter was left to see what he could do on his own. It meant a visit to different estate agents in the town and his being offered the viewing of several properties.

When he was alerted to the availability of 29 Brent Road, he visited it with an old friend but without Catherine. In his keenness to acquire it, he put in an offer, which was accepted.

By the time Catherine was aware of what Peter had done, he had already approached the local building society for a mortgage and arranged a meeting for the exchange of contracts with a solicitor. When Peter shared the news with her, Catherine was stunned at the haste with which Peter had acted. Nevertheless, because she recognised that they would have been in dire straits if they had not found anywhere to live, she decided to hold her counsel. She was determined, however, that she would not let such a thing happen again.

If only she could have read the future!

Fortunately, when Peter and Catherine looked at the property together, despite some reservations expressed by Catherine, both agreed that it was the best they could do in the circumstances. The appointment with the solicitor sealed the sale, and together they signed the appropriate documents.

The house, a former council property on an estate, fell into the category of three up and two down. The two single bedrooms and one double bedroom upstairs provided well for their current needs. There was also a small bathroom. The loft above also offered plenty of storage space. Downstairs, the front door led straight into the sitting room, which was characterised by a large window overlooking the small front garden, a modern fireplace that would burn wood and coal, and three doors. One opened into the small pantry, another into the narrow, dark staircase, and the third into the reasonably sized kitchen, which also served as a breakfast/dining room. Once in the kitchen, Catherine and Peter could pass through a narrow passage, which also accommodated the toilet, into a back garden that was large enough for a vegetable patch as well as a small lawn.

The house was in a row of four similar houses towards the end of a driveway wide enough for only one vehicle. This remained a nuisance to Peter not only on the day that Bill, one of his old schoolmates, delivered what little furniture he and Catherine had collected or been given, but for as long as they owned the house.

Its one redeeming feature was the view from the sitting room window. Looking out across the front garden, Peter and Catherine had an uninterrupted view, through a gap in the two opposite rows of houses, of the moor rising in the distance with *The King's Beacon* at its apex. Peter's eyes often settled on the moor, its changes of appearance matching the seasons. It responded with glowing warmth to the caressing summer sunshine, with colour to creeping autumn, and gleaming white to the winter snows and frosts. Inevitably, the view stirred his desire for the independence it seemed to offer, but any thoughts of enjoying that freedom were like dreams that flutter through the night and become hardly a memory by morning.

The building society was happy to provide a ninety-five per cent mortgage on the £1,750 house. With an interest rate at around five per cent, Peter and Catherine, though aware that they would have to be cautious with their finances, saw 29 Brent Road as a manageable if not attractive proposition. With a teaching salary that did not stretch much beyond providing basic monthly living needs, and with two very young children, the possibility of acquiring anything more enticing had quickly dissolved. Although Peter had been the prime mover in the initial decision to buy the house, he hoped that it would be their home for only a short time. It did not take long for him to realise that he was to be reminded of his daily commitments by the presence on the estate of so many pupils from school and that he had a neighbour who seemed to breed mice that wanted to feed themselves in other people's houses. But until such time as he could afford something else, he knew he was tied into Brent Road.

CHAPTER 2

A DIFFICULT LESSON

And now, in his second year at the school, Peter was awaiting Webster and 1C, a class that not only he but also staff with much more experience described as something of a challenge. His morning had gone pretty well. Classes had listened attentively and worked industriously. This was how he had always imagined teaching to be: hard-working children keen to learn and to follow willingly the guidance of their teachers.

But his experiences with all his classes were not so positive, and there were occasions when he felt engulfed by the tide of apathy that swept over his efforts. He was annoyed with himself because of what he felt to be a weakness in his dealings with the most difficult pupils, particularly the likes of Joe Webster; and yet he knew that he had to find a solution if he were to stay in teaching. It had crossed his mind more than once that there must be less stressful careers and ones that were better paid, but his commitment to helping youngsters develop any potential they may have was strong. His memories of his boyhood friends committed to a life in the mines by their failure to take advantage of their education were a constant spur.

Peter knew that the eleven-year-old Webster was the eldest of four children and that he had two younger brothers as well as a sister, Martha. They lived with their parents in a house huddled among similar houses to Peter's on the largest council estate in Weberton. The house in which Webster lived had been freshly painted on the outside, as had Peter's just before he purchased it. But on going inside, the differences were marked. The tidiness associated with Peter's property had no place in that of Mr and Mrs Webster. Disintegrating, crumpled, lace curtains, once clean and new, now hung lopsidedly at the dirt-stained front windows from strings of wire that were aslant from age and neglect. The furniture was tired, overused, and ready for the scrapyard, and the old carpets with their congealed dust and dirt were well trodden. Whilst the interior of Peter's house reflected care and organisation, Webster's reflected the personalities and demeanour of the dysfunctional family that lived within.

To those who knew him, Webster looked the natural outcome of such a family. He was an unkempt child with little understanding of how to socialise or behave. He had a badly cut crop of hair that was rarely washed and which straggled untidily about his forehead and ears. Like his mother's, it was of a mousy colour. His dark-brown eyes seemed too close together, particularly when he was in a mood, and his sharply pointed nose, reminiscent of his father's, also seemed to be constantly dripping. His mouth hung agape, enabling him to respond quickly when the need arose.

He was a dishevelled figure, but to those of his age and younger he made a fearsome spectacle. Most saw him as someone to be avoided, and there were instances when children would take the long way home from school rather than walk by Webster's. To others, he was a paramount, a chief, one to be followed. These were the characters who supported Webster in his misdemeanours in and out of school. Indeed, it was his classroom antics that gave him and his supporters the feeling that he could manage the lesson better than the teacher could.

On this particular afternoon, Peter's lesson, an introduction to a project on Roman roads, had been carefully thought through, and he had made sure on his arrival at school first thing that morning that the resources required, which included the materials to create papier-mâché models, such as paper and adhesive, and paint and brushes, were ready. He had also rearranged the desks so that they were no longer in the traditional rows but clustered to enable pupils to work in groups. He knew that by the nature of the lesson, much of the responsibility for learning would be in the hands of the pupils and that success depended on their self-discipline and their cooperation with one another.

Peter knew that he had to dispel from within his mind any thoughts of likely problems in the lesson as Webster and 1C walked into the classroom, as any signs of hesitancy on his part would only encourage some of the pupils to be at their worst. However, his composure was quickly challenged.

As he entered the room, Webster looked in hearty mood, nonchalantly flicking the satchel off the shoulder of one of the girls so that it fell to the ground and caused the girl to trip. Her response, 'Stupid prat,' drew attention to her predicament and laughter from Webster and his pals.

'Come along and take care what you're doing,' Peter said sternly to Webster as he assisted the girl in regaining her balance, but he couldn't help but wonder what further opportunities for mischief the lad would find. Peter had heard from colleagues during afternoon break of Webster's antics that morning. He had managed to disturb a science lesson by 'accidently' leaving water to run across the top of a bench, dampening pupils' books, and ruining an experiment; and he had 'accidently' managed to spill some soup over another pupil at lunchtime. In both instances, Webster's proneness to 'accidents' had left him unpunished but admired by his mates.

The lesson started well enough, with a blackboard sketch of the approach to road building adopted by the Romans, which Peter explained stage by stage. He was careful to control his voice—neither too loud nor too soft but measured in speed—so that he could exude the confidence he was going to need to show the class that he was in control.

'The need for the Roman armies to move quickly around their conquered territories led to them replacing the muddy tracks that criss-crossed the country by good, passable roads. As a result, they sought to build stone-structured roads, fast and straight, so that they could move quickly. Their influence throughout Europe led to new roads and showed their understanding of the need to have a good means of transport. What sort of transport do you think they used?' he asked the class, partially for information and partially to identify which of the pupils were still involved in the lesson and committed to learning.

'Ferrari cars!' shouted out Webster, generating giggles from some of the class as others diligently put up their hands to indicate a willingness to answer in the time-honoured way. Ignoring Webster, Peter elicited from the sensible members of the class horses, carts, chariots, or simply walking.

Peter continued, 'Good, you've got the idea. In order to ensure that the roads provided what they needed, the Romans planned them with great care.'

Continuing to speak at a regular pace, he went on to describe how the Romans built their roads. He pointed, with the blue chalk he held between his fingers, to his sketch on the blackboard in order to illustrate the point. One of the pupils, Raymond Horbury, looking more closely at the diagram, asked with obvious interest, 'How did they get all the stones to where they were needed, Mr Delaney?'

'Well, Raymond, they had to be quarried in different areas, but they always hoped to use local quarries to save time and money. If they had no quarries nearby, stones had to be transported in the ways that we were discussing earlier, usually by horse-drawn carts.'

He pointed again to his sketch on the blackboard, which he had drawn with different-coloured chalk in order to illustrate the points he wished to make. 'Here is the ditch, the smaller stones, some larger ones, and then the top surface, which, as you might guess, was not as smooth as that on roads today. Are there any Roman roads left, do you think?'

Up went the hands again, but they were beaten by a sniggering Webster who shouted, 'Stacks in Italy!'

Webster rarely planned his outbursts. Indeed, he sometimes surprised even himself by their spontaneity. It was an aspect of his character that, it might be argued, could be traced back to his upbringing; and most people did. But there was something deep within him that, on the one hand, encouraged him to contest what others considered acceptable behaviour, and on the other spurred him to respond in the most positive of ways. His brief work on the school boat project, for instance, had provided a stimulus that brought out the hidden gifts unrecognised by many of those associated with him. His teachers had been amazed at his commitment, application, and skill during the couple of weeks he was involved with the project and believed that they were to have a new Webster sitting before them in class, keen to learn and to reap the benefits of their endeavours. Sadly, the apparition quickly passed. Once the boat project was finished, the old Webster, confrontational and truculent, returned.

This was the Webster at work in Peter's lesson, and his antics were irritating Peter, who could not help but fear the danger of being distracted from the calm, measured approach he had initially adopted. Constantly sweeping his eyes around the class with the peripheral vision he had learned was critical to good teaching, Peter could not help but see Webster leaning back on his chair and occasionally flipping bits of paper at his pal Ginger, who was returning the compliment. Aware that other members of the class were keen to learn what they could, Peter, with a voice betraying some of his anxiety, but still under control, called, 'Robinson, Webster, behave. And unless you have something useful to say, keep quiet.'

'I was only trying to answer the questions, sir,' came the cheeky reply as Webster, backed by the now brazen laughing of his mates, felt growing confidence in his ability to embarrass Peter.

Peter knew that these were the situations Webster loved. When quietly discussing Webster with his friend, Stan Wensley, in the staffroom earlier in the term, Stan had concluded, 'Oh, Webster isn't worried about the threat of one of the usual punishments, of being sent out of class, kept in detention, or ordered to go to the head's office. He seems to find it much more enjoyable to be a figure of attention and being a damned nuisance by disrupting the class with his inane remarks. To him, the risk of punishment is worth it.'

Peter had no reason to disagree with this view. He fully understood that, through his disruptive behaviour, Webster was trying to undermine his role as teacher whilst making himself a sort of hero among his mates. To Webster, the banal admiration of his adherents mattered more than anything he was likely to learn.

'Anyway, sir, who cares about Roman roads and who's bothered about how guys with shields and pikes got from one place to another?'

This brought more giggles and further exasperation for Peter. But he persevered, knowing that others were keenly interested in what he was doing. He wondered whether he should move Webster to the front of the class so that he was immediately in front of him, but he remembered Stan's comments and so desisted, continuing with the lesson.

'Once the Romans left England, their roads were allowed to fall into ruin and were rarely repaired. The routes of some are still followed by our modern roads—the A1 in places, for instance—and you may have heard of the Fosse Way.'

'I've heard of candy floss,' chipped in Webster. 'You get it at the seaside and it's all sticky, but it tastes great. In fact . . . .'

'That's enough!' shouted Peter, his patience breaking. 'Come down here to the front.'

Peter was annoyed with himself for losing his cool, but he realised that the irascible Webster was making the lesson he had prepared with such forethought a farce.

'Go on, Webster, do as you're told!' called out one of his aficionados in a mocking voice. He was joined by others who, in a barely audible whisper, took up the chant, 'To the front, Webster, to the front.'

'Quiet!' rasped Peter who was now showing genuine anger. The boys and girls who had been supporting Webster took the cue, went quiet, and with contentedly admiring eyes watched Webster nonchalantly sidle to the front desk.

Once some sort of order was restored, Peter went on. 'Unfortunately, after the Romans left Britain, many of their roads were allowed to fall into disrepair. It was only when people began to realise the importance of getting around quickly, especially at the time of the Industrial Revolution, that new roads began to be built and people like Blind Jack Metcalfe and Macadam began to devise new routes and road-building methods.'

'How did Blind Jack find his way about, sir?' quipped Webster.

This was the sort of question that Peter dreaded. Despite being trained as a history teacher, there were always questions that pupils found to ask that he had never himself queried or been helped to understand. A classic was, 'How much was a penny worth in medieval times, sir?' This one was of the same ilk, and Webster, with a mischievous grin on his face, was waiting for an answer. The best the inexperienced Peter could come up with was, 'He used a stick, and other people guided him as he walked, picking out the easiest way.' Fortunately, this seemed to satisfy for an answer, especially as the questioner had not the slightest interest as to why someone like Blind Jack would want to spend his time walking about behind a white stick plotting routes.

Peter moved on with the lesson, pointing the pupils in the direction of the artefacts that he had prepared and had put on one side to help them do the practical exercise on road building. He divided the pupils into groups of four, ensuring that Webster and his chums were split amongst the rest of the pupils. He indicated that during the lesson they should work out a plan by which they could build model roads of different types, roads that reflected the changes they could identify taking place through the centuries. Each group was given a map with various physical features so that rivers, hills, and areas of habitation, for example, had to be considered. His hope was that the task would provide problem solving that would apply not only to history but also to other subjects, such as mathematics, crafts, and possibly the moral issues likely to be faced.

The project had some success in that the groups quickly settled into discussing how to resolve questions related to road building at different times in history. One group in particular became involved in how to carry a road across a river, whilst another debated whether they should go over or round steep hills. Peter was delighted at how well the class as a whole was responding to the lesson. But before long, it was clear, and not all that surprising to Peter, that Webster's group was in difficulty.

Peter moved across to their desk and peered over shoulders to see what they were doing.

Webster was holding court with, 'That's rubbish; roads don't get built like that. If we do that, we will all get buried in sand.'

'Look, Joe,' said young Raymond, addressing Webster rather timidly, 'as we have to get across marshland, we have to put something down to support the road.'

To which Webster replied in no uncertain terms, 'OK, but once we've built it, you can go and run across the f—ing thing as it's your idea.'

Peter immediately spun round and clipped Webster across the ear with, 'Watch your language or you're straight to the head. Now behave and listen to what the rest of the group is discussing. Then perhaps you can make sensible suggestions.'

Webster's chums clearly enjoyed the scene, whether it was because Webster had had a clip around the ear or because he had further irritated Peter. What they did not see was Webster showing a closed fist, just below desk height, to Peter. There was only one interpretation. Here was an eleven-year-old threatening a teacher, but in such a way as the only two who realised it were Peter and Webster. Peter's reaction was to look at Webster directly in the eyes as if to say, *You dare lad.* The end of lesson bell brought to a close a likely confrontation that was beyond Peter's experience and probably skill to deal with.

Fortunately, Peter's lessons were usually much less fraught than his meetings with 1C and his relationships with his pupils more analogous with good learning. His classroom was welcoming, with desks normally organised to enable their most effective use, and any equipment pupils needed was ready to hand. The walls were adorned with a variety of illustrations, mostly the work of the pupils, but some were displayed by Peter to either encourage his pupils' interest or further their understanding. The drawings and accompanying descriptions of one set of work made Peter particularly proud, as it was the outcome of the very first out-of-school visit on which he had taken pupils.

The class had spent a half day in the nearby castle where they studied the defences, inspected the weaponry of the time, and walked through the various rooms used by those who had taken refuge within the castle as the Roundheads pursued their aim of deposing the king. The pupils learned how difficult it was to take a well-built and well-defended castle, but how uncomfortable it could be in the castle if supplies of water and food began to run short during a siege. They could also distinguish between the ostentatious rooms that accommodated the lord and his family and the hovel-like areas that were inhabited by those who served them.

In a crude sort of way, Peter, in considering what he thought to be the meagre circumstances of his own family's life, could not help but detect some similarities. He was always quick to put aside these rather perverse thoughts, but inevitably, the impression lingered and only re-emerged from time to time to excite the hidden desires for a life that he never expected to realise. This aside, he and the pupils had had a most enjoyable and fruitful day, to which the pupils' work bore ample witness.

Nevertheless, the recent lesson left Peter considering the important question as to how he was going to deal with Webster and others like him. Even though Webster was a relative newcomer to his secondary school, the reputation he had earned in his junior school days preceded him. It gave him a standing which meant that, although most pupils of his age stayed well away from him, there were others that would always be at his side. Predictably, there were boys at school older and bigger than he was, and the toughest of these, Trevor Makin, had to be shown due respect even by Webster. Nevertheless, Webster's tenacity in playground fights earned the respect of not only those of his own age but also of those who were older. As a result, he could relate to the likes of Makin and regard them as his mates.

Disconsolately, Peter made his way back to the staffroom. He could reach no conclusion, but he was sure he could not outline what he had just experienced in any sort of detail with his colleagues. He had too much to lose in professional dignity, and as a young teacher, this was important to him. He had to show to his colleagues that he was confident in what he was doing, that he could control a class, and that his pupils were making real progress in their learning. How he achieved these aims was not of particular concern to his colleagues, but that he succeeded was.

As he walked down the corridor, passing pupils who chirped, 'Hi, sir,' he was concerned as to how the last lesson might impact on his future lessons with 1C or any other class if the word got round that he was not a good disciplinarian. This was an issue that he knew he alone must resolve, and by means that left him with the standing he needed to be successful in his chosen profession. It was in moments such as this that the presence of his former tutor in education, to whom as a student he could put his questions directly and without apprehension, would have been invaluable. He was in little doubt that the welcoming 'blossoms of learning,' words that his tutor had used to describe to him the pupils he would meet, were not personified in the likes of Webster and his cronies. Peter was in no doubt that he had to find ways beyond the normal that would help him establish the respect from Webster that his teaching, to be effective, needed. *It's a pity,* he thought wearily, *that I'm not building a boat.*

CHAPTER 3

THE STAFFROOM

As Peter approached the staffroom he wondered who was likely to be there at that time of the day. Pushing open the door he knew that he would not find the usual busy hive, resounding to the buzz of staffroom activity. As he expected, most of the staff were in class, teaching, whilst he and three of his colleagues had what was termed a non-teaching period, ostensibly to give time for preparation and marking. On this occasion, however, with his mind pulsating from the stings recently inflicted by Webster and his followers, he considered the possibility that it could be used most beneficially as time for coffee, reflection and a chat.

Peter, still ruminating over his last lesson, could not help but think of his college lecturer's description of the ideal teachers he wished to train. He had also used the metaphor of bees, but of bees 'in search of the pollen of learning which they transported from pupil to pupil before returning to their hive to share with colleagues what success they had extracted from their day's efforts.'

It was a vision such as this that had sustained Peter through the hard graft of his training and through the first hard year of his teaching career. Somehow, the 'pollen' he was looking for and through which he might enrich the minds of all his pupils was proving difficult to find on occasions in face of the realities of his chosen profession. Despite the friendliness of colleagues and the willingness of the majority of pupils to learn, his ever present anxiety was his inability to spark the desire for learning among those pupils for whom the school offered a different agenda to his or to the majority of those with whom he came into daily contact. He had quickly come to the conclusion that to a small minority of pupils, schools were designed as entrapments for an audience before which they could display bravado, as well as a stage on which they could challenge the leading actors, their teachers, rather than a centre for learning.

These pupils saw no point in studying because for them it was unlikely to lead to a more meaningful life or to the job of their desires. They were the pupils, like Webster, who sought to make their own rules and refused to accept the restraints necessary for social harmony. Peter, as with many of his contemporaries, had had little practical guidance on how to deal with such pupils. As a result, he had to rely on his ingenuity and the odd snippets of advice he garnered from more experienced colleagues as he sought to plot his way through his early years in teaching.

Having entered, Peter placed his books on the large work table that dominated the centre of the room, a room that bore the marks of its past and as well as its present. He then made his way to the far corner where he stood putting instant coffee, boiling water and milk into his mug.

'Anyone for coffee?' he asked as he half turned to look at his colleagues. He saw that all had mugs and so he simply carried on making his own. As he did so his thoughts drifted from his recent lesson into considering his immediate surroundings.

The staffroom had, at one time, been an impressive sitting room in the country house of a worthy family in what was once the manor of Weberton. The corniced ceiling, with its large central floral garland that he thought must have been very attractive at one time, was painted a pallid white. Now, it almost failed to attract the attention of the wandering eye. For an instant, Peter tried to imagine what it would have looked like when it more closely reflected the natural colours of the flowers the craftsmen had painstakingly endeavoured to represent.

As he moved away from the corner, he surveyed, with an instantaneous movement of the eyes, the rest of the room. The high walls were coloured a pale green. One wall, at around table height, carried the fresh scars of its present use, the result of contact with articles of furniture and the paraphernalia of a working staffroom. Another wall, reflecting an earlier age, was adorned with a magnificent fireplace with marble pillars and an imposing mantelpiece. The mantelpiece had lost the allure of the fine porcelain that it must have once displayed. It now served as a resting place for a range of pens, pencils, untidy papers and the usual flotsam and jetsam typically found in rooms which were seen by occupants as places of work rather than rooms preserved for the display of aesthetic beauty and the affluence of those who occupied them.

The large French windows on the third wall, now rarely opened other than to give quick access to fresh air, overlooked what had once been expansive gardens. Responding to the needs of a school, they had now been ripped up to create a hard surface play area for the pupils in the immediate foreground, and converted into playing fields in the further distance. The fourth wall contained a large notice-board with its scattering of daily orders, messages for different staff and, by far the most imposing, the lesson timetables of the different classes and teachers.

Throughout, the room reflected more its new purpose than its past. It was a place of both work and relaxation. The tables along one side of the room, with chairs at intervals, were littered with books and papers, pushed to one side occasionally to enable a space for the marking of pupils' work or the preparation of lessons. The rest of the furniture included a leather settee and a pair of matching armchairs placed to allow ease of conversation. In reasonable vicinity was the fireplace, which, when lit in winter, gave the room a feeling of warmth and comfort. A number of hard-backed chairs that at first sight appeared to be scattered around the room haphazardly were actually arranged to provide different foci where staff with common interests could congregate and discuss matters, serious or frivolous. One corner, the one from which Peter had just turned, contained the necessities that enabled staff to make tea or coffee and enjoy a biscuit, or on festive occasions, such as a staff birthday, a piece of celebratory cake.

As a result of his previous lesson, he could not avoid the feeling of inadequacy worming its way like a bug into his confidence. He knew he still had much to learn about his chosen profession. Before his training for teaching in the late 1950s and early 1960s he had spent, as he had mentioned in his interview, time as a student teacher, a job open to those not yet trained. It had been a tough introduction to classroom practice. Although he was expected to be no more than classroom support, he had actually been given the responsibility of a class; and it was not an easy one.

Almost half the pupils in his class could hardly read or write and several were serving some sort of supervision order for activities in which they had been involved outside of school. In school, in the manner of Webster and his friends, they paid little attention to what was said, larked about with their friends or, the most portentous of all, directly confronted their teachers. Peter's youthful age had also presented a further vulnerability at that time, as it had seemed to tempt the more flirtatious young ladies of the class to take the front seats and follow his every move with transfixed eyes. He often found it difficult to concentrate on what he wanted to say whilst seeking to avoid their gaze, and wondered what it was like for a young, pretty female teacher to walk into a class which included a group of fifteen-year-old boys.

Peter had received little advice before taking on such a daunting task, one for which all knew he was ill-prepared. But the senior staff had appeared to believe that the strength of character they felt they had recognised in him would be sufficient to cope with such challenges; whether he was capable of teaching the pupils anything worthwhile or not seemed to be a side issue. Totally new to the situation, Peter had accepted their expectations, worked hard to keep the pupils seated in their places and taught them what he could.

As he completed making his coffee, he could not help but ponder on the question of whether or not he was better prepared now. In his years in college he had attended lectures on child psychology, behavioural patterns, and his specialist subjects of history and music. He had also spent several weeks on teaching practice in different schools developing his teaching skills. In theory, he had been successfully prepared for his new career. In truth, however, his training had not given him the key to understanding the range of attitudes encompassed within a cluster of pupils or how to deal with them. As a result, he was not finding it easy to deal with the problems engendered by the likes of 1C and his frustrations were real.

Despite his concerns as to what he recognised as his shortcomings, Peter took some satisfaction from what he was achieving with the great majority of his pupils. He felt that he had done well to gain a position in what he came to realise was a good school, and he felt that overall he was making an effective contribution to its work. The school catered for those pupils who did not pass the 11+ examination and gain a place at the much older and more prestigious local grammar school. As a result, they were regarded by some as failures. Peter found, however, that many of the pupils belied the alleged truths of the examination system as to their capabilities and showed themselves to be bright enough to achieve well. Most were a joy to work with and, despite his moments of difficulty, confirmed his view that he had made the right choice when he surrendered his cornet for teaching.

He made for a chair by the three other members of staff who were relaxing between their programmed forays into the classroom. They had settled themselves into comfortable seats, drinking their adrenalin-restoring coffee, and sharing that comradeship of conversation that cements relationships among colleagues.

John, the woodwork teacher, was discernible by the overworked brown overall that he wore. His hair had long departed the top of his head, leaving those grey-coloured tufts around the sides of his ears. They matched his bushy eyebrows which, when he wanted to show displeasure with the work of a pupil, would take command of his normally benevolent face. They would come together under a furrowed brow to express either amazement or disbelief at what he was observing. To John, wood was not a commodity to be treated lightly or to be wasted by the wrong cut of the chisel by a pupil as he searched to create matching joints. It was the malleable article through which could be conjured a work to be admired and one in which his young chargers should forever take pride.

At his side, on the old couch with its well-used sagging cushions, sat the much smarter Arthur, in suit and tie, to some the archetypal English teacher. To pupils he had no past or future, but simply appeared from, and disappeared into, a timeless mist. His dark grey jacket was of a smart cut, held a white handkerchief in its top pocket, and opened sufficiently to reveal a red waistcoat adorned with a silver chain and fob attached to a watch. He kept pulling it from his pocket to check the time to his next lesson. His hair, thinning, but still providing sufficient coverage to allow him to venture out into the sun hatless on hot summer days, topped a thin face which provided openings for his sharp blue eyes and smaller than usual mouth. His pointed nose dominated his face whilst his thin lips suggested his being a man of sarcasm. Certainly, many a pupil had suffered from the sharp wit of those lips over issues that were probably of little concern to them.

On one of the soft chairs sat Maxine, fully involved in the conversation and bringing a youthful joy to the proceedings through a wide smile that revealed beautiful white teeth. She was just 30 years of age. Her fair hair was combed back into a pony tail and tied with an attractive ribbon of blue silk. Her dress was of light cotton and wore the colourful flowers that designers like to use as mirrors of the summer garden. Her bare, gracefully crossed legs revealed the tint of days spent in the open air. She was wearing a pair of sandals coloured to tone in with her dress and the blue silk in her hair. There was an attractive uniformity in her appearance that reflected the care with which she had prepared herself for school that day and with which she approached her life in general. It would not take a great deal to see in her the art teacher that she was.

Peter had decided to take up residence in the other easy chair. He settled himself, his mug of coffee precariously resting on the chair's arm, and began to listen to what his colleagues were discussing.

Although Peter was now the proud father of two daughters, it was clear that he was a man who was at the outset of his career, struggling to make his way financially, but at the same time intent on responding positively to the importance of his calling. A shock of thick black hair betrayed his youthfulness, whilst his complexion bore a freshness that was not present in the faces of his older male colleagues. He had open honest eyes, which could quickly express pleasure or disappointment to his pupils. His nose, though straight, had a slight swelling at the top, the long-time mark of a cricket ball that beat his gloves and planted itself between his eyes when he was keeping wicket in a school cricket match. When standing, he was around six feet. He carried the broad shoulders of a sportsman. His generally smart suit and shirt were usually set off by a military tie that was a reminder of his days in the army, and the shiny-toed boots he wore, through the necessity of cost rather than preference, were also inherited from those earlier days.

Recognising that he was still on a steep learning curve, Peter often took opportunities such as this to talk through some of his problems with those more experienced of his colleagues who were prepared to listen and give what advice they could. In this instance, his colleagues were discussing a newspaper article that had stirred up a reaction and Peter could not resist joining them to see not only what he could offer, but more importantly, what he could learn.

CHAPTER 4

THE NEWSPAPER ARTICLE

It was obvious from the tone of the conversation that his colleagues had been disturbed by the article that had appeared in the newspapers the previous day. The headline in the *Daily News* had shouted 'Major Disruption in School', and described how a group of boys and girls at a school in a neighbouring town had enjoyed themselves throwing some younger pupils into the school pond. The newspaper had gone on to criticise the school for the children's behaviour, drawing attention to the danger and asking how it was possible for children to do such things when in the care of their teachers. It made great play on how parents entrusted a school with their children and expected them to be safe. This particular school, like others the journalist implied she knew, was letting down the parents and the children.

As Peter tuned in to what was being said he heard Arthur expressing his views in his usual forthright manner. 'Some kids are dreadful. They don't know how to behave.'

'Well, you might think that, Arthur, but as usual the press don't tell us the whole story,' responded John. 'They take a view and then pronounce it. They don't consider its likely effect on the school, or the pupils for that matter. I'd like to know more about what happened before blaming the teachers. You know what the press are like.'

'I understand what you say, John, and I accept that we only know the bit of the story that leads to good headlines, but you've got to admit that there are some characters here who, if given the opportunity, would be up to tricks like that. Remember those lads the police brought in one day because they had been caught chasing one another round the market when they should have been in school.'

'You're right, Arthur, but if pupils misbehave, is it the teacher's fault or have the pupils to take some responsibility?' Rather than answering, the strict disciplinarian Arthur just looked at Maxine with the sort of quizzical look that implied the pointlessness of her question. Maxine went on, 'To be honest, I think it's not simply schools and teachers who are responsible for controlling difficult youngsters.' And then, in a not untypical way for Maxine, she went universal. 'To my way of thinking much of the responsibility rests with parents and for that matter with society in general.'

'I agree, Maxine,' started John. 'It's not that long ago that people looked to one another for help and support, and often got it. Now, everything seems to be pointing towards personal material gain. The whole business of trying to get out of society as much as we can,' continued John warming to the theme, 'is downgrading social responsibility. The 'I'm all right Jack' approach is destroying relationships between people. How d'you expect children to be different?'

'I've to agree with both of you,' responded Arthur, who for once seemed to be in full agreement with his colleagues. 'I'll go even further. Parents not only have to raise their expectations, but they've also to set a good example, and show their children how to behave and respect the rights of others. I'm afraid we've some here who don't do that. Do you want some names?' His query received a nil response and so he carried on. 'I think the paper's right to draw attention to what happened in that school, but I agree with the possibility that the reporting has, perhaps, not been as balanced as it might. But even so, you can't get away from the fact, no names no pack drill, that some teachers are not as good as they should be. I could mention one or two that I have come across in my time even here,' he added.

The others looked at one another knowingly, realising that Arthur, if given the chance, would be on his hobbyhorse and rounding up for execution the weak teachers he believed he knew. Fortunately, he was interrupted by Peter. 'I've to admit that there are occasions when I'm uncertain as to what to do if a class is difficult. Take the class I've just had, 1C. They can be incredibly annoying and that Joe Webster is a real problem. He's always looking for chances to stir up the rest of the class and by God he seems to believe he can get away with anything.'

'I've sometimes found him to be a problem as well,' interjected John. 'It's simple for outsiders to argue that we should have more control over the likes of Webster. To the general public, the solution always seems easier than it does to those of us faced with the problem. The accepted view is that if we've clear rules, explain and implement them, everything should be all right. So the logic is, if children misbehave it's the school's fault.'

'You're right, John. It's such notions that lead to assumptions among the general public that the education system is failing them. Of course, the media see a good story in this and so they cultivate the idea. They don't seem to realise that they're undermining confidence in teachers and in the system generally, and so their reports, rather than improving things, are likely to make them worse.'

With that, Maxine stood and moved across the staffroom to make herself another coffee. 'Anybody want one?' she asked as she began to unscrew the lid of the coffee jar. John nodded 'Yes,' and so she made two cups, sipping her own as she made her way back to her chair.

Peter had followed the gist of the arguments, but he recognised that factors likely to influence the behaviour of a pupil such as Webster went beyond a simple description of misbehaviour. They were more complex to unravel. He could not resist putting his own view, based on what he had read and what he had often discussed at college.

'I reckon that with some pupils the problems are psychological.' This shift in the conversation captured the interest of Peter's colleagues as they focused their attention on what he was saying. 'Somehow, they need to show that they belong, that they're an integral part of a class or a group, but not in the usual way. They have the urge to be in charge and the desire for others to follow, and they believe that they can achieve that by misbehaving. They think that the worse they behave the more followers they will have. I reckon Webster fits into this category.'

Maxine continued the new theme. 'I agree. In Webster's case, I think it's closely linked to his looking for attention, no matter of what sort. As with other pupils I have known, there are occasions when Webster feels inadequate and lacks confidence in his ability to do things, especially when asked to do something new. I've noticed he's disconcerted and becomes difficult when I ask him to try to paint some figures in a painting. He seems disturbed by having to study people in any sort of depth. He's fine splashing on colour, but as soon as I ask him to add an animal or a person, because he doesn't seem happy portraying living creatures, he gets all uptight and asks why should he waste his time painting things he's not interested in.'

'That makes sense, Maxine,' said John after a moment or two of reflection. 'I noticed he was a bit the same with the boat. He seemed a lot happier working on the exterior than trying to figure out what would make comfortable seating inside.'

Arthur picked up the theme. 'Well, this is an instance in which you can say that the lack of good example from his family is the key. His mother is aggressive, doesn't seem to mix very well, and has failed to give him the loving care he's looking for. Just look at the way he turns up to school on some mornings.'

On that particular day Webster was wearing a dirty grey shirt, with the sleeves rolled halfway up his arms. His long trousers were soiled, revealing where he had sat and walked in days past. His pullover, once green, was a dull looking khaki, covered with grime and filth and containing the memories of several breakfasts, lunches and teas, though it was generally thought that three meals a day did not always figure in his diet. If his teachers were to lift up his feet by the ankle they would see the soles of the shoes he wore were holed beyond repair and that his socks provided only strings of cover for his skin. This was the Webster they all could recognise, the lad who was never seen in anything resembling school uniform.

John, who thought he knew Webster better than most, listened to Arthur, and then added, 'It's all right us discussing this, but I doubt whether Webster could explain why he does certain things himself. I think that deep down he wants to be liked, but he doesn't know how to go about it. If he'd some success in doing something he might be different. He knows most pupils are unlikely to admire him for what he is, and so I think he's decided to gain their attention by what he does. He recognises that he appeals to those who are game for a laugh. It's those characters that give him the sort of status that he enjoys.'

And after a further sip of his coffee, John continued, 'I'm sure he believes that if he shows them that he's afraid of nobody and doesn't shy away from trouble, they'll support him. But to be fair, he's the sort of lad who, when he has led others into trouble, then stands up and is willing to take the blame. He did that the other day when three or four of them were caught playing havoc on the netball pitch. He just said it was his idea and the others shouldn't be punished.'

'I think you're right, John,' said Maxine. 'I suspect he feels he couldn't be sufficiently successful in anything worthwhile to be able to win around himself such a body of what he calls friends, but who are really hangers on. The only occasion on which he seemed to be at ease in school, and probably felt wanted, was the very short period when he was working on the boat. Unfortunately, that experience was far too brief to convince him that being positive in his approach to something like that was the best way to behave. It would, I suppose, take something similarly engrossing, but capable of challenging him for a much longer period, to ensure that he was pulled in the right direction and able to recognise the benefits of putting behind him his less appealing self.'

Maxine's colleagues nodded in agreement, and then Peter, seeking to lighten the conversation commented, 'I don't know what you find, but there are pupils who try very hard and it's a pity that they're disturbed on occasions by the likes of Webster. They take great care with their work and deserve at least as much attention as those that, by being a nuisance, demand it.'

Again, there were nods of agreement but, as if to indicate that the griping was over, Peter's colleagues showed a disinclination to contribute anything further to that particular topic. They seemed content to sit and drink their coffee, absorbed in their own thoughts as to the cause of problems with different pupils. The reasons no doubt varied from one to the other, but each knew that there was no single solution. They recognised that different approaches better suited different teachers, and that the relationship between pupils and teacher, as sensitive as silk between the fingers, varied as much as the different colours of that same fabric.

And then, as if to distract attention away from his own problems, but recognising his lack of professionalism in saying it, Peter tentatively threw in, "At least, the general behaviour in my classes is OK. I can't, in all honesty, say that about everybody's classes. I've often wondered what's going on next door when I hear constant noise and the teacher's irate voice crackling louder and louder through the wall. It's as if the kids have no respect.'

Thank goodness, thought Peter, as Arthur at last spoke. He knew he was treading on dangerous ground criticising other colleagues. 'I know what you mean. I think some staff are too soft. When the same pupils come into my lesson they behave because they know if they don't there'll be hell to pay'.

Colleagues nodded, knowing that Arthur had a reputation among pupils and staff alike as a firm disciplinarian. Even though he was not popular with the pupils, he somehow had the knack of belittling them to such an extent with his sharp wit that they rarely misbehaved. The concentration and commitment that he also expected were, his colleagues recognised, among the reasons that enabled his pupils to get the very good examination results they achieved in English. Not everyone agreed with his methods, but none could gainsay the outcomes.

'They know the teachers they can manipulate and the ones they can't,' mused John. 'But you've to admit, Arthur, that it's better to get their respect. I reckon that if they see that all we're trying to do is help them learn something worthwhile they'll respond. Take for instance that group I had working with me on the boat'.

'You mean that venture you had that resulted in our having to remove windows to get it out of your workroom,' interjected Arthur.

He was referring to the boat that some pupils, including Webster for a couple of weeks, had built in his workroom. It had, Peter had heard from several colleagues, been a great success, until it came to getting it out of the room. It was then that John realised that he had not considered its size. The only option he had was to ask the head if he could remove the windows that formed almost one side of the workshop. And so, despite the achievement of building a first-rate craft designed to transport staff and pupils from time to time along the canal on the occasional educational or social outing, the outcome had not passed without some hilarity in the staffroom.

Undeterred, John went on. 'I think that's an example of work pupils did which they saw as being of advantage to them as well as to others. The fact they could see a positive end product, encouraged them to do what I asked without any fuss. What was great about that project, was that their attitude to work carried over into my lessons. I'm sure that, by working with them, they realised I was really interested in them. If you can create that attitude, the majority, the keen pupils, will influence the minority, who otherwise might be a nuisance. That troublesome minority, if given the chance, take the lead, distract the rest and begin to create the havoc we've been talking about. It's obvious to me that until you build up some trust amongst the youngsters, you'll always have problems.'

'I agree,' said Maxine. 'I've certainly found that through taking pupils to art galleries, on school trips, and running an after-school art club, I've established a positive relationship that carries over into the classroom. Once they feel you're on their side the whole atmosphere of a class changes.'

'That goes so far,' responded Arthur, maintaining his belief in discipline. 'But it's to be backed up by pupils knowing that there are boundaries, what those boundaries are and if they cross them they'll be in trouble'.

Peter listened with acute interest. His mind was responding as it does in situations where ideas emerge. First they are explored and then either dispelled or cosseted in that area of the brain from which they can later be lured to advantage. He was aware that he would have to resolve the issue of 1C, and he was prepared to listen to anything that might help. He believed that the answer to his problem might lie within the experience of the colleagues with whom he was currently sitting. He hoped, as those who are learning are often tempted to hope, that there was an easy solution to his difficulties and that it had been discovered by those around him, because of their experience and expertise. He was acutely aware of the possibility that they might share that mixture with him and so enable him to find a speedy answer to 1C.

'So what d'you think would be the best way of dealing with Joe Webster?' he asked, laying aside his earlier concerns about revealing his difficulties with the lad. 'It's difficult to keep him motivated throughout the full lesson. For parts of it he will be biddable, but for other parts he will challenge, if not by action, by look or by word'.

'Look, Webster is just at that age when many children develop what might be termed self-consciousness. At the risk of repeating some of our earlier comments, some youngsters seek to demonstrate that they should be taken notice of, but they're not sure how. They may still be of an age when it's not clear what gifts and talents they might have and where life's going to take them. They've passed through the infant's stage in which they probably didn't feel apprehensive or inhibited about the way they acted, and by the time we get them they've reached a new stage in their lives.'

'Carry on, Maxine,' said John, 'this sounds interesting'

'At the infants stage children invariably express themselves without reservation, heedless of the consequences. As we know, they change in secondary school when many enter a stage of uncertainty. It's only later when they begin to see something of their future that most gain in self-confidence and self-awareness. It's then that they begin recognise some positive purpose in what they're doing at school. We all know that we often see a link between how well children cope with their middle years in school and what happens later. For the likes of Webster, such a transition from one period of life to the next doesn't follow so easily. The path to adulthood isn't so well marked, and they have uncertainties regarding the next step. This can lead to them rejecting conventional values and life styles, and seeking to challenge those who are responsible for them. I've seen youngsters act in ways well beyond their natural age and others act below it. This can make them difficult at school and may influence them for a lifetime.'

'So what you're saying, Maxine, is that Webster fits somehow into one of these models. He's trying to find himself. Interesting,' commented Peter.

'I see,' said John. 'The logic is: his erratic behaviour indicates, perhaps, and I stress perhaps, that he could be further advanced on his way to adulthood, no matter how meaningless it might turn out to be, than most of his peers. That's why, you think, he is prepared to challenge accepted standards and try to take control.'

'That's what I'm trying to explain. Webster's concern is to show his friends that he's different. His saving grace, and I agree with you, John, is that, if found out, he's prepared to take responsibility for his actions and would not point a finger at any of his partners in crime. I am impressed with this aspect of his character and I'm sure it has an impact on his so-called mates.'

'That's fair comment, Maxine,' chimed in Arthur. 'He's a naughty lad for his age and he's got plenty of followers. In fact, I reckon he quite enjoys being picked out as something of a rebel in front of his pals.'

As John added to the discussion, Peter listened even more intently.

'It was only when he became interested in the boat project that he became really cooperative. This told me that when he becomes aware that his efforts are worthwhile and when what he's doing is genuinely valued, he becomes most cooperative.'

This last sentence, drawing together some of the points made earlier in the conversation, struck Peter as the most perceptive point made so far on the subject of Webster. It seemed to him that John's approach had a good deal of merit and was worth consideration as a means of coping with, and educating, the likes of such a lad.

For Peter, still inspired by his search for 'blossom', the challenge was to fulfil his own professional commitment, help pupils to improve the quality of their minds, and enable them to see what they could learn from the experiences of the past. He was now beginning to mentally formulate an approach designed to help the more difficult pupils share in that ambition. He could see that the more willing he was to engage with the pupils in and outside the classroom, identifying and nurturing their strengths and interests, along with ensuring that the pupils had a clear understanding of those boundaries that Arthur had been talking about, he should be able to create a classroom atmosphere beneficial to everyone.

Even though he had learned something worthwhile, Peter knew that he had another difficulty that he wished to air. 'My problem is made more difficult because I'm living in Weberton along with so many pupils. It's amazing how often I see them and they see me. I go shopping and I can guarantee somebody like Webster will be around, being as cheeky as he dare, and embarrassing me in front of others, some of whom are parents.'

'Why not shop somewhere else, Peter?' asked John, as though that was the obvious solution.

'It's not so easy. We've no car and few other options. I live on an estate a bit like one of those towns in South Africa you can read about. We, too, have only one entrance and exit, and even if we had a car, we couldn't leave the place without half the estate knowing.'

'Is there any chance of your moving?' asked Arthur.

'What a thought! With my current salary and mortgage I'll have to wait, oh I don't know how long, before that's possible. I'd love to move, but we've no options at the moment. It's not all bad. I enjoy playing with the town brass band, the rugger team, and mixing with a good many friends in and around the town. Fortunately, Catherine's making contacts in the neighbourhood and I'm sure we'll make out. But there's no doubt that a place up Willesley Road or in Branford, where you live Arthur, would make a difference.'

Peter was well aware that Willesley Road and Branford were situated in the most salubrious areas in and around Weberton, and were regarded as the right places to live if you were to have any status in the town. It was to these two areas that people gravitated once they felt that they needed the standing to match their growing economic well-being, and it was no surprise to his colleagues that Arthur, with his views of what was right and proper in the world, was living in one of them. The imposing detached houses of Willesley Road, built in late Victorian or early Edwardian times, reflected the display of grandeur associated with those days. The well-proportioned windows, hinting at the sumptuousness of the rooms that they lit, overlooked well-kept gardens and carefully tended lawns. On his way to school, Peter often took a route that necessitated his walking along Willesley Road and allowed him to absorb some of the self-indulgence he associated with the prestigious houses. No matter how he felt about the houses and the people who inhabited them, he recognised how much was to be gained by a move to Willesley from his present abode. Even the birds seemed to chirp more tunefully than back on the estate, and the noise between one house and the next was muted by their detachment.

The same tranquillity pervaded Branford. A village neighbouring Weberton, it hid its houses and cottages within oak, birch, larch and rhododendron, and only opened out to general view the village inn, church, and general store. It bore few marks of activity, but more of that pastoral life associated with contentment and tranquillity. Peter knew he could enjoy existence in such an environment, with its peacefulness and serenity, and that he would welcome the opportunity, if it ever arose, to transplant his family into such a tranquil setting.

Before Peter could explore his concerns further with his colleagues the bell rang, directing them back to the classroom. Arthur and John headed straight for the refreshment corner and quickly rinsed their cups before chatting their way through the door. Maxine paused by Peter as they shadowed the actions of their colleagues and quietly said, 'If you're interested, I may be able to help. I'm on outside duty at lunchtime and if you fancy you could join me and I'll tell you more.'

Peter, curious, agreed to the invitation.

As he walked towards his next class he reflected on what Maxine might mean and how she could help him with his present situation. He knew she came from a well-off family because of the things she talked about. Her themes seemed to be mostly about her horses, and the hunting and point-to-point events she participated in. She of all staff seemed to have a life outside school that was possibly richer and more important to her than that within, but Peter could not work out how any of that might be useful to him. He pondered on the various possibilities but kept coming back to the same conclusion—that Maxine had the sort of attractive lifestyle that he could never aspire to and that although she had often proved to be a good friend, it was only within the context of the school and the fact that she was another member of staff. To his mind, this did not give her any reason to invest any great time or energy in him or his family. In any event, she knew little about Peter and his family and he knew even less about her.

He finally satisfied himself with the thought that she was indeed a good colleague who wanted to help him find a solution to his current housing dilemma, but that she probably had little to offer him that was within his means to accept. However, because he liked her, and because she seemed so genuine in her intentions, he made up his mind to see what she had to say at lunchtime, although he admitted to himself that he could see little point in it.

As soon as he saw his first year pupils, 1A, lining the corridor by his classroom door, all thoughts of what Maxine might have in mind for him disappeared, and he resumed his role as teacher, a person of authority, able to lead this group of pupils into the classroom with an air of confidence and impart the benefits of his own learning.

CHAPTER 5

THE CONVERSATION WITH MAXINE

Peter's lunchtime conversation with Maxine was of greater significance than he could ever have dreamed.

'I thought, in view of what you said in the staffroom, that you might be interested to hear a story.'

'I'd be fascinated to,' said Peter almost jocularly. 'Why d'you think I'd be specially interested?'

'Well, it's about an elderly lady I knew who hadn't been very mobile for a number of years,' responded Maxine almost mimicking the tone of Peter's question. After a brief pause, she continued. 'Despite advice from different people who had been concerned about her ability to look after herself, she'd refused to move into neighbouring Binkley to be closer to amenities such as the shops or any kind of medical support. She'd no relatives in the immediate neighbourhood either, as far as I know.

Anyway, as a result of her increasing inability to drive, she had come to rely more and more on people taking her to town, perhaps doing some shopping for her, or simply dropping things in at the cottage. I did a lot for Ma' Winstone as she was called, as my daily horse rides across the moor took me past the cottage. Often I'd stop and chat, see how she was doing and ask if she needed anything from Binkley.'

'She must have appreciated that a lot,' said Peter, partially keying into the serious nature of what Maxine was telling him.

'I think she did. She used to like to talk. She told me a lot about her relationships with her family and how her brother and her sister rarely came to see her. It was this that made her so pleased that her friends in the village stopped by to help her. What she also said was that her relatives were expecting to inherit everything she had, and that they never failed to remind her, either openly or in veiled references, when they visited her. She wasn't a bitter woman, but she resented the expectations, especially in light of the little support they offered her. 'Anyway,' she used to say, 'the dogs don't like them!' I knew nothing of her intentions but simply sat astride Lester and listened, offering a comment from time to time and making sure she was all right and had everything she needed.'

Still more than a little surprised as to why she was telling him, Peter eventually asked

'It's all very interesting, Maxine, but why d'you think I'd be interested?'

They strolled on at a steady pace, rounded the hard surfaced playing area and made for the field, Maxine with her hands behind her back and eyes scanning the children as they played. When they reached the playing fields

Maxine was interrupted by a flying football that Peter just managed to shield away from her head. He shouted to the boys to be careful and then turned again to Maxine in order to understand the point of her story.

'When I first knew her she was pretty active about the cottage and the outbuildings. In fact, I used to see her from time to time, busy around the property or walking on the moor with her dogs. She seemed perfectly comfortable. But gradually, as she became less mobile, she spent more and more time inside, and in recent years she had taken to living mostly in her front bedroom. If I ever saw her downstairs, it seemed she'd only come down for food or to feed the dogs. It's a sad story, but I suppose she did what she wanted to. I passed the cottage most days and she was usually sitting at the upstairs window, reading or knitting. She was an avid knitter and one Christmas gave me a lovely woollen sweater to wear when riding. The postman seems to have been another regular who stopped to gossip for a minute or two, he through the window of his van and Ma' Winstone through the open upstairs window. The milkman was also a daily visitor. Her links with the church meant that she had an occasional visit from the local vicar. Sadly, she got to the stage that she rarely came out of the cottage, and the dogs seemed to have the run of the house.'

'Why would she want to live in what sounds such a remote place? What would have happened if she were ill? Did she have a telephone?' asked Peter stringing together a list of questions. He was beginning to show real interest in what he thought a sad story, though he was still trying to work out how all this concerned him.

'It's amazing how the locals kept a caring eye on her. It says a lot for the villagers. She seemed to love her contacts with them. As I said, she relied on several of us to do any shopping for her, or collect prescriptions or anything else she might need from the chemist. The doctor from Binkley is happy to make visits to the village if he's needed. She did have a phone, so she could always ring for help. I know she had one or two of her neighbours' numbers and on a couple of occasions she rang me; once when sheep had got into her garden and she needed someone to clear them out, and another time when one of the dogs needed to be taken to the vet. Anyway, all this led to me having a very close relationship with her.'

This prompted Peter to ask the obvious question. 'Was there any reason that the family wouldn't look after her?'

'None that she mentioned. She'd an occasional family visitor but nobody showed up on a regular basis. That's why she became so dependent on us. She had the dogs, of course. They barked a lot and seemed to run around downstairs or upstairs. They'd be at the bay window snarling if I visited or the postman delivered anything until she told them to be quiet.'

Peter could well imagine the scene. Dogs scurrying from one window to the other as though intent on defending what they saw to be theirs, and either the postman making sure that his fingers couldn't be nipped as he threaded letters through the letter box, or the cheery Maxine, astride Lester, nodding and smiling at appropriate intervals whilst the patient horse provided a welcome but silent audience to a lonely lady.

'She never said what she intended with her cottage when she died other than she made it very clear that she didn't want her family to inherit anything belonging to her. It was obvious that there were difficulties in the family. Sadly, she died a few months ago. There was a good turn out for her funeral in the parish church in Binkley. Apparently, in her younger days she'd been very popular and used to visit the different families to chat and offer help if she could. And the vicar spoke very highly of her contribution to the parish before she had become housebound. What I took to be members of her family sat in the front seats in church. No doubt they assumed they would get the cottage, which would allow them to make some money by selling it. They seemed the sort of people that were unlikely to want to live in what, to many people, would seem to be an isolated place.'

They had now crossed the playing field and were approaching the hard play area in front of the staffroom.

'Well, you'll imagine my shock when a couple of days after the funeral I received a letter from Ma' Winstone's solicitor telling me that she'd left the cottage and all its contents to me.'

Peter stopped and looked at Maxine for a moment. 'Phew. I reckon it must have been. Had you expected anything like that? How'd the family take it? Have they raised any objections with the solicitor?' he asked, responding to what must have been a dramatic incident in Maxine's life.

Peter could not help but be stirred by the spectacle of a dismayed family having no option but to watch Maxine walk off with the inheritance they had expected to be theirs. But even so, interesting as it was, there was nothing in what Maxine had told Peter so far to explain why she had asked to meet with him, and then talk to him about a sick old lady and a situation that did not seem to concern him.

'Well, yes. There was a good deal of fuss, I learned later. But the solicitor told me everything was in order and that Ma' Winstone's will was very clear as to whom she wanted to have the cottage. All the paperwork for the transfer of the deeds have now been signed and sealed and the cottage is now definitely mine.'

Maxine went silent for a while, seemingly to allow what she had said to be absorbed by Peter.

She then continued, 'It's left me wondering what to do with it. If things were different I may well have been tempted to go and live there myself. But I've no need. Although there's a lot about the place that I like, I don't really want to live there. I'm well settled with my mother and father. At the moment, I've no need to move and there are plenty of good reasons why it's better for me to stay where I am. To be honest, it's not much use to me. As I've said, I'm happy where I am and have what I need. My brother has left home recently and, although my parents are still relatively young, I know they like me to be about,' she added, as if to exemplify the difference between herself and the late Ma' Winstone's family.

Having picked up through the tenor of her voice the affection she had for her present home, Peter fully understood her feelings. It was obvious from what she'd said and from what he'd heard from colleagues that she loved spending what time she could in the open air, tending to her horses and being a general help to her father and mother. It was the sort of life that explained the tanned legs, rosy cheeks, and infectious smile that Peter had seen in the staffroom. It also explained the slim figure of an active woman who ate enough for sustenance and rarely more, and saw exercise as a normal corollary of a life in the country.

There was much to admire in Maxine; her general friendliness with all the staff and strong relationships with her pupils seemed to offer to Peter a model he might one day be able to emulate. Only the hands, larger and coarser than one might expect for such a pretty woman, hinted at the more unpretentious activities, such as cleaning the stables and brushing the horses, in which she engaged in the evenings and over the weekends when her school work was finished. Peter also knew, as a consequence of staffroom gossip, that Maxine was heavily involved with a young man from further up river and that the prospect of marriage may not be far distant.

Having negotiated their way around the school buildings, Maxine continued her story. 'Anyway, having had a look at the cottage and seeing how much needs doing, I've realised that it would be better for me to sell it. Mum and dad came round with me and suggested that I might be better with the cottage as an investment. Their idea was that if I sold it, I could hold the mortgage and so make it a long-term investment.'

Peter knew little of business matters but recognised straight away that Maxine could charge interest on a mortgage, ensuring her an income over the period that she set for the repayments. It struck Peter as a sensible idea.

'I've someone interested but I'm not sure that they'll really buy it. The reason I suggested having a chat is probably now obvious. When I heard you this morning in the staffroom talking about wanting to move, I thought that if you were serious you might be interested in the cottage. If you're serious about moving I could put you second in line, then if, as I expect, these friends of mine decide not to take it, you could buy it.'

Maxine looked at Peter quizzically as she said this, keen to see his reaction. If she had hoped to see a flush of excitement she was disappointed, as Peter managed to control his outward appearance. Inwardly, however, things were different. He felt a tingling in his arms and legs, and his stomach seemed to jump into his mouth before falling and resting again in its normal habitat. But it had done enough to set in motion a stream of inter-connected but haphazard thoughts about the opportunity that Maxine was offering and the issues it raised—the release from Weberton, the cost, the moorland, distance, a cottage, transport—which left his mind in a whirl. The best he could do was to utter, 'What sort of cottage is it?'

This was not as strange a question as it would appear to some. Peter had never lived in the sort of country that the word 'moor' characterised. His only knowledge of open country was vested in his experience of the wasteland around and between some of the towns he knew, places where travellers set up site, or where the Easter fairs would base their dodgems, their whirligigs and their amusements. He knew little of the wide expanses of the moorlands of North Yorkshire, for instance, as his experience of the country was restricted mainly to those areas of land, sometimes farmed and sometimes deserted, between the small industrial villages around his own that had been built in what had once been open countryside. He knew more of towns and cities dominated by industry or commerce in which people lived cheek by jowl than the expanse of a moor. To put before him the prospect of living on a moor did not immediately bring to mind the charms that such a life may have, and which might enchant so many other people.

Peter also wasn't sure what distinguished a cottage from a house. As he continued his circular tour of the school grounds with Maxine, making the occasional response to a pupil's enquiry or helping Maxine to intervene to ensure that pupils stayed within the school's rules, he puzzled whether it was to do with size, location, or how it was built?

Interpreting his question as a query as to the condition of the cottage, 'Well, it needs a little work,' was Maxine's hesitant reply, quickly followed by, 'but it won't cost much, and I think I can give you a good mortgage deal. I should have added that it has about ten acres of rough pasture land with it as well.'

'Ten acres of land?' Peter repeated aloud with a somewhat flabbergasted look on his face, and then to himself, *What would I do with that? I know nothing about farming. How do I cope with ten acres?*

Then, aloud, he asked, 'How much land is ten acres? I guess it's as big as a football field.'

'I think bigger, though I've never played football,' replied Maxine with a chuckle. 'The farms in and around the village tend to have a bit more, but not much more. So they've to rely on being able to let their sheep feed on the moor for most of the year.'

It was at that point that the bell signalled afternoon school and the two of them hastened towards their classrooms for registration. Inevitably, Peter found his thoughts wandering back to the offer Maxine had made him and he found himself constantly asking whether or not he was he doing the right thing even in considering it? Unusually for him, he was having difficulty in resolving the doubts that were invading his thinking, even though he was battling to resist them. More often than not, when he was presented with an opportunity as intriguing as this one, he would jump at it, ignoring the need to consider all the questions raised, and take risks that others might have balked at. On more than one occasion, Catherine had taken him to task over his impetuosity, warning him that he could not rely for ever on her acquiescence to his rashness. In this instance, fascinating as Maxine's proposal was, he continued rolling the negatives and positives around in his mind, confessing to himself that there had been worrying aspects in what had been said about the cottage that he could not ignore. As he and Maxine had wandered round the grassy verge of the school field, her question as to whether he would be interested in buying the small moorland cottage had taken him aback. It had left him pondering what Catherine would think and what his answer to Maxine should be.

He could not turn to his wife immediately for advice and he was not sure she could provide anything worthwhile on the basis of what he would be able to tell her. She had taken their children on a visit to see her father, grieving after the recent death of her mother. She was back in Hull and would be there for a few weeks more. The telephone was their means of daily communication and their evening calls were a great source of strength to Peter as he sought to fend for himself.

Not surprisingly, their conversations focused initially on how much they missed each other. In these early exchanges, Peter also took the opportunity to ask about how to prepare different dishes for meals or where Catherine kept things like dishwashing liquid. It never took long for him to begin to unload himself of the cares of the day and in particular to begin to share with Catherine his worries at school—what had gone well and what hadn't—and his concerns about 1C and Webster, especially on the days he had had a lesson with them.

Catherine would soothe and encourage, occasionally mentioning her own difficulties in endeavouring to console her father whilst also looking after the children.

Peter knew that introducing into the conversation the prospect of a move to a moorland cottage would be almost like throwing a hand grenade into a quiet living room in which the family was sitting at ease. He also knew that his ability to describe any of the challenges that might await the purchaser of the cottage was more than questionable, especially as he had not yet seen it. As a result, he decided to delay mentioning to Catherine anything about the cottage until he had something more definite to report, and so he determined to keep the tenor of his evening phone calls at their usual pitch.

CHAPTER 6

PROBLEMS IN
THE PARK

At the end of the school day, Peter took leave of his colleagues, nodded cheerfully to the caretaker, and set off on his walk home. He passed through the school gates and turned towards the park, his mind still churning over the issues that his conversation with Maxine had raised. Even though there was nothing she had told him that suggested that the cottage would be a sufficiently attractive option to his present home, his instinctive impulses, rather like a virus worming its way into a poorly protected body, were driving him to believe more and more in the possibilities. He could not avoid being tempted by the opportunity to escape from Brent Road.

Oh, what the hell. There can't be any harm in going to look at the place. I'll talk it through with Maxine tomorrow.

Peter's thoughts were suddenly interrupted by the sight of a group of boys at the far end of the park. Near the swings, they were making a good deal of noise, laughing, cheering and shouting. The phrases he was hearing were, 'Go on, Trev, ler' 'im 'ave it,' 'Dun't bi such a chicken,' and 'Up yours, son.'

Peter's concern about what was happening was such that he felt he had no option but to go and investigate. He was startled by what he could see as he walked across the grass. A group of boys from school, including Makin, Skelton, Conway, Robinson, and not surprisingly Webster, were having the time of their lives terrifying a young boy and young girl. Peter recognised the school uniforms of the children immediately. They were from the junior school across the road from the park. It took him only a brief moment to fully realise what was happening. The youngsters had obviously come into the park to play on the swings and the lads from the secondary school had seen an opportunity to have some fun.

Disturbed by the screams coming from the young children, Peter quickened his pace and was shocked by what awaited him once he reached the swings. The bigger boys were pushing the swings as hard as they could and making them go higher and higher, with no concern as to whether they were veering towards one another or likely to wrap themselves around their iron supports. The children on the swings were terrified. They were gripping as tightly as they could, screaming at each push, their eyes streaming with tears. They couldn't slow down the swings or find any means of getting off them. They were at the mercy of their tormentors.

Peter shouted, 'Stop that! You're going to hurt those children! Stop it!'

'What for? We're having some fun.'

'Don't talk rubbish, Makin. Those children are in danger. Stop it now.'

Peter got no response. The boys were clearly challenging his authority, the older ones like Makin setting the sort of example that was likely to attract the likes of the younger Webster. At least he, Conway, and Robinson lowered their eyes and showed some discomfiture at Peter's presence.

Increasingly concerned about the safety of the young children, who were still being pushed by Makin and Skelton, Peter again called upon them to stop it. All he received in return were disdainful looks and the comments from Makin. 'So what? What's tha' goin' to do abaht it? W' not in school na, tha' knows.'

Realising that his presence was having no impact on the lads' behaviour, Peter dropped his briefcase, strode up to Makin, and shouldered him. 'Makin, Skelton, do as you're told and stop it.'

As Makin tripped and fell to the ground, Peter set himself to begin to slow down the swings, calling to Skelton to do the same. Makin was furious and, having got to his feet, made as if to approach Peter. The other boys looked aghast, not sure what Makin intended to do but also aware of the folly of attacking a teacher. To irritate, to disobey, or to challenge by word were the norms for this group, but a physical confrontation was not in their repertoire. Webster had tightened a fist in front of Peter to show his exasperation in class one day but would never have done more. As they stood and watched, anticipating something extraordinary, Makin seemed to think better of his initial intention. Instead of heading for Peter, he went to join his mates.

Peter breathed easier as the swings slowed and the children's screams melted to sobs. Behind him, Makin turned away and headed for the park gates, followed by the rest of the lads, their fun having been brought to an unexpected end. As the swings stopped, he asked,

'Are you all right?'

'Yes, thank you,' the boy said between his sobs. 'We were just playing when those boys came up. They started pushing us. It was very frightening. My sister's really upset, and I've got a tummy ache from jerking up and down. We couldn't do anything.'

The children's faces bore the signs of their ordeal. Flushed, they had tear stains down their cheeks and their eyes still mirrored fear. Peter took out a handkerchief and wiped the face of the little girl, who was about seven years old, and then that of her slightly older brother.

The tension they had been displaying gradually disappeared, and Peter was able to comfort them further. 'Well, you're all right now. Where do you live?'

'Just down Willesley Road,' said the boy. 'Once those lads have gone, we'll run home. I'll tell my mum and dad what happened.'

'That's all right. I'll come with you to make sure that you're OK. What are your names?'

'I'm John, and my sister is Jane.'

'How are you feeling, Jane?' Peter asked as he went up to her, lifted her down from the swing, and leant down to check that she was all right. Jane clung on to him for a moment as though he was a friend she had been searching for, and then she let go and let out further sobs.

'Come along then, let's take you home.'

Peter took Jane by her left hand while John stood to his right. He then picked up his briefcase and the three of them headed for Willesley Road.

When they reached number 94, the children's home, Peter, still holding Jane's hand, put down his briefcase and rang the bell. The door was answered by the children's mother who showed surprise at seeing her children holding hands with a stranger. Both John and Jane ran towards their mother, who bent with open arms to receive them. As Jane broke again into sobs, Peter introduced himself and explained what had happened in the park. Mrs Jameson, clearly thankful that there had been someone willing to help her children, thanked Peter profusely and then invited him in for a cup of tea.

'Please come in, Mr Delaney. My husband is in the sitting room, and we are just about to have a cup of tea.'

'That's very kind, but—'

'No, no, you must come in. We really need to show you how much we appreciate what you've done.'

Holding the door ajar, she made way for Peter to enter the house and then led him, once the children had disentangled themselves from around her legs, through the hall to a door on the left. Never having been in one of these Willesley Road houses he had passed so often, Peter went in expectantly.

He was not disappointed. The front door opened into a vestibule that was large enough to accommodate a beautifully veneered antique table topped with a tastefully decorated jardinière bursting with the yellow, blue, red, and violet colours cascading from the carnations, roses, and lilies. On the wall above the table was a gilt-framed mirror. The vestibule also contained a free-standing rack for coats and hats and an umbrella stand decorated with more flowers delicately painted on the sides.

Leading out of the vestibule on the right hand side was an impressive staircase, its highly polished wooden handrail ending in a flourishing curve. As they moved farther into the house, Mrs Jameson opened the door on the left, which led into the sitting room. Glancing quickly, like any visitor viewing a house for the first time might, Peter spotted ahead another door, which he assumed to be the dining room, and then to the right of that, beyond an alcove, was an arched entrance through which he glimpsed a large, well-equipped kitchen.

'Brian, this is Mr Delaney. He's a teacher at the school by the park. I invited him in for a cup of tea. He has just rescued the children from a gang of teenagers who were causing problems in the park.'

'Pleased to meet you, Mr Delaney, and thank you very much,' said Bill Jameson as he rose to shake hands.

'The name's Peter,' said Peter as he shook hands. 'Good to meet with you, though the circumstances could have been different. Nice property you have here.'

'We like it. Now tell me what happened.'

The children, who were by this time standing on either side of their father's chair, excitedly proceeded to describe what had happened. Mrs Jameson went into the kitchen to make tea and Peter took the opportunity to glance around the room.

His imagination had not let him down on those mornings when he had passed the impressive windows of Willesley Road. The high-quality armchairs and sofa, the tasteful Welsh dresser, the thick carpets, and the ornate fireplace all deserved to be lit by the impressive chandelier hanging from the centre of the ceiling. The couple of paintings on the walls also looked, from where Peter sat, like genuine oil paintings, though he could not read the names of the artists.

'Here you are. Sugar and milk?'

'Just milk, please,' replied Peter.

Mrs Jameson had put the tray down on a small coffee table, and as she poured, she once again thanked Peter for what he had done. Her husband took up the same theme and then asked, 'Do you know the boys?'

'As a matter of fact, I do. I'm embarrassed to say this, but they're from my school. They're known troublemakers. I'll certainly make sure that I'll make plenty of trouble for them tomorrow.'

'D'you think we should report it to the police?'

'That's up to you. I know the school'll take a tough view on their behaviour, whether the police become involved or not. As I say, it's up to you.'

A few more words were exchanged, with Bill trying to get as much detail about the incident from Peter as he could, before Peter finished off his tea, stood, and said it was time for him to go. Mrs Jameson, continuing to thank him, led him to the door.

As he walked down the road and made his way home, he could not help but reflect on the differences in his own house in Brent Road and Jameson's. If he had needed a further incentive to go and have a look at the cottage on the moor, he had just experienced it. The ambience of Jameson's house, its interior character and its exterior setting, had impressed him greatly. And so, even before he had arrived home, he had convinced himself of the importance of making a visit to the cottage. He determined to make arrangements with Maxine on the following morning.

Before he could do that, he knew he had to see the head and report what had happened in the park.

CHAPTER 7

THE COTTAGE ON THE MOOR

O n arriving in school on the following day, Peter went straight up
to the head's study and gave him a full account of what Makin,
Webster, and their friends had done on the previous evening. The head,
shocked by what he heard, thanked Peter for taking the action that he
had and said he would now deal with it.

Peter left the office believing that he had done all he could to ensure that
the boys were reminded that their behaviour had been disgraceful and
would not be tolerated. He had mentioned to the head Mr Jameson's
query about police involvement, something that he knew the head was
keen to avoid. Peter knew that, as always, he would be anxious to keep
what could be seen as bad news about the school out of the public
domain and would take any necessary action to avoid that happening.

Peter learned later that day that Mr Holdsworth had contacted the
Jamesons to apologise about the behaviour of the boys. He had also

managed, with the good name of the school in mind, to dissuade them from going to the police. As for the boys, he had caned them before sending them home for the day with a letter for their parents saying that they would not be allowed back until the parents had been to see him. He had then contacted the chair of governors to inform him of what had occurred. Nobody in the staffroom believed that the head's actions would have much effect on the boys' general attitude to school, but neither could anyone suggest a better solution.

Peter's second job of the morning was to make contact with Maxine, which he did at the first break.

'Maxine, I thought a lot about our conversation yesterday. I'm really interested. Can you take me up to see the cottage?'

'That's good news. I'd love to take you up there. We'll sort out the details at break.'

The pair of them continued their discussion over mid-morning coffee. 'Saturday morning would be ideal for me,' said Peter.

'That would be fine. What time do you think you can make it for?'

'Well, that's a problem. I have no transport. Somehow, I need to get a lift.'

'Perhaps I can help. I could pick you up by the old abbey if you can get a bus to there. What do you think?'

'That's great. I know there's a bus around nine, which would get me there for about half past. Would that be OK?'

'That'd be fine. I can have my morning ride and then nip down to pick you up. That's agreed then.'

On the Saturday, Peter could not be but impressed with the way Maxine handled the climb, which snake-like took them up the hill towards their destination. She demonstrated her driving technique by approaching bends at speed but taking them with care as the road twisted towards its hidden summit. Moving through the gears with the expertise of an experienced driver, she was able to sustain the momentum needed to climb the one-in-four slope without the ornery complaints likely to be directed at a less expert driver from what could have become an underpowered engine.

As they climbed higher, the trees thinned and the rich, arable land fell behind to be replaced by a more austere, though still engaging, landscape. It was characterised by undulating country seemingly disturbed only by impressive drystone walls that stretched way into the distance to areas it seemed that man could not reach, the clumps of tufty grass that even the sheep did not deign to eat, and the purple heather. Occasionally, what appeared to be disused barns or sheds, also in stone, stole into sight as they marked the road's winding route over the moor.

Peter began to anticipate with excitement the first sighting of the cottage. It was hidden by the same roadside walls that also offered a shield to each of the houses that Maxine identified. These scattered, mostly traditional farmhouses with adjoining barns, fashioned in their solid Yorkshire stone, were what Maxine described as the village.

Driving still with enviable skill, she gave, in her usual jaunty manner, some of the background to life on the moor. 'There's about a dozen families living in the village. Almost all of them farmers. There are one or two, like my own family, who work either in Binkley or Leeds or Bradford. Generally, the farms are only small, I suppose with rarely more than 20 to 30 acres. But the farmers have rights on the moor and so they can let their sheep roam the moor for food. They usually use the land around their houses for cattle. Most of the farmers sell milk. A tanker comes up each day and calls at the various farms to collect it. The fields around the farms are also harvested for hay for winter feeding.'

'How would we get milk?' Peter asked in a sort of absent-minded way as he continued to take in the scene through which they were passing.

'One of the farmers has a milk round and so he calls at some of the houses in the village on his way to Binkley. If you want milk, I'll give you his phone number.'

'Let's see how things turn out,' replied Peter, still trying to decide if he had been given the option as to whether or not he wanted to bring the family to the moor.

'The other thing is, and I suppose you'd expect this, the farmers make weekly visits to Weberton. They go to the auction, hoping, I suppose, either to sell or buy animals. As far as I know, their wives go and do some shopping, because for some it's the only time they can get into town. Living on the moor can be hard for them. For those of us who have other jobs, the moor allows us to get away from the pressures of our everyday work.'

Whilst Maxine continued her description, Peter's thoughts drifted to wondering how he and Catherine would be able to get to and from town, how he would get to work, and how lonely Catherine might feel. Only half listening, Peter heard Maxine saying, 'You can't believe how much I enjoy getting rid of my school clothes, putting on my casuals, saddling the horse, and getting out onto the moor and into the fresh air. Even in winter it's great.'

The joy of horse riding was not a pastime known to Peter, but the phrase *'to get away from the pressures of everyday work'* still resonated within his mind. The prospect of finding an escape from Brent Road rather than the difficulties that the moor might pose dominated his thinking as the car swung round another bend. Maxine kept it close to the overhanging wall so as to leave as much space for any oncoming vehicle as might be needed. As for Peter, he could not completely turn his mind from wondering again about the wisdom of the venture he was likely to become engaged in.

'I don't know much about farming, but I remember spending some time picking potatoes for a local farmer at about five shillings a day when I was eleven. I also helped occasionally to clean out the animals and stack harvested crops on Saturday mornings. My dad also had hens, and so I sometimes had the job of looking after them. That was the way things were done in my village in the early post-war days,' he added nostalgically.

'Well, other than for household gardens, there's no crop-growing here. I reckon one look around will tell you why.'

Maxine was right. Even without a country background, Peter could see that the land lacked the fertility of the richer soils that had been left behind. There had been no evidence since they turned off the main road and onto the moor of the fields of corn or vegetables that he associated with Weberton and its immediate surrounds.

'Now this is where the land belonging to the cottage starts. You see the corner of this wall, well, that's the boundary, and it leads right up to the gate of the cottage.'

As yet, Peter could not see their destination because of the height of the wall, but as the road straightened briefly, Maxine pointed while saying, 'There it is.'

The cottage stood alone, to some viewers isolated but to others in beautiful harmony with its backcloth of moorland, which rose up towards *The King's Beacon*.

As they approached the cottage, Maxine slowed and asked, 'Well, what do you think?'

The best Peter could conjure up was, 'It's different to what I expected.'

Maxine had now pulled up in front of the cottage and parked the car. The journey had brought the pair upwards of a thousand feet from the road below and over a steeply rising hill that featured many sharp bends. Although the road up the hill and through the village was occasionally too narrow to allow vehicles to pass, which had not gone unnoticed by Maxine's passenger, it was in good condition and very different from the non-macadamised roads that one might have imagined for such a moorland location.

Once out of the car, Peter looked around. He could see, northwards, the moor rising towards the *Beacon*, its predominant feature, offering a rising view that was covered with the purple heather as well as protection from the cold winds. To the south-west of the cottage, the views stretched for miles over the valley of the River Wharfe, which wound its way through some of the county's most beautiful countryside.

As for other properties, the nearest was a white-painted small farm with an adjoining barn. It was at least a quarter of a mile away. The smoke from behind the house signalled activity but no evidence as to what it might be. Across the fields, farther towards the *Beacon*, Peter spotted two other farms, concealed from view from the road by the contours of the moor. The one looked as tidy as Peter would have expected of country folk, with what appeared to be a well-kept house and carefully tended barn and fields that characterised the paintings of country artists. The other, surrounded by the paraphernalia of an untidy farm with its old tractor, plough, and several other pieces of disused machinery piled by a barn with a sagging roof, gave quite the opposite impression. Peter wondered, as he stood looking around the environs of the cottage, what other differences the diverse appearances of the two farms embodied.

Once he had completed a fleeting look at the setting of the cottage, he brought his eyes to rest upon what might one day be his home. It was surrounded by a warm, contemplative air of restfulness and calm, a direct contrast with the exhilaration of the drive up the hill. His instant reaction was that this promised more than he could have expected or dreamt of. He was sorry Catherine could not be with him and share in this first-sight experience that almost amounted to exhilaration. He was captivated by what he saw and what he imagined. Images nourished by his love of history began to press upon him as he tried to visualise tracks rather than macadamised roads, carts instead of cars, and farmers in dress-like smocks herding their animals across the moor.

'Let's go in.' As she said it, Maxine pushed open the gate and felt in her pocket for the key.

They followed the short path towards the door, passing a rather incongruous window, which bore the hallmarks of a twentieth-century amateur rather than those of a skilled craftsman of earlier times. Fitting the description of a poorly made bay window, it protruded in straight lines from the stone walls of the cottage. Its top was covered with a coarse felt whilst the wooden frame, painted like the rest of the woodwork in a creamy colour, showed the signs of wear, with the flaky wood being revealed from beneath the peeling paint. The door, constructed of panelled glass, was relatively new and made of hard wood that offered the strength clearly lacking in the window frame. To the right of the door, Peter saw another window of the same ilk as the one to the left. Above were three other windows set into the walls of the cottage in a style more consistent with older cottages such as this.

His mood changed somewhat once he entered the cottage. Identified as built in the seventeenth century, it bore all the hallmarks of its age. Once Maxine had unlocked it, the front door creaked as Peter used his shoulder to break its resistance to being opened. As it yielded, he was met by that musty smell that he associated with old and dirty.

'I'm afraid the place was not cleaned or painted very often. I must say I was shocked when I came in first,' said Maxine as she followed Peter through the door.

Peter scanned the room into which he walked and saw peeling walls, filthy carpets, and evidence of spiders in almost every corner. His gaze was drawn upwards to the original massive oak beams and joists, laced with the dust of woodworm. This appeared to be a dining room from which an open staircase led to the bedrooms above. It was about two-hundred-and-fifty square feet in size. On the exterior wall, to the right, was a fireplace encased in dirty grey concrete with three square recesses of red tiles presumably for holding ornaments. Currently, they held nothing but a layer of undisturbed dust. In the centre was a small electric fire. On the far wall was a wooden door that he guessed might lead into a kitchen. Directly ahead of the door that Peter had entered rose the open staircase, with a rickety banister looking well beyond its usefulness. He could not imagine how the previous occupant, if she had been in any way incapacitated through age, could have found it of use.

'Perhaps it was the reason for her staying upstairs in her bedroom,' he childishly murmured to himself.

To his immediate left was a door, the lower half being of dark, unidentifiable wood with peeling paint and the upper half being of encased clear glass. Through the glass, he could see what looked like a sitting room. The thick oak beams, supporting the floor above, continued through from the dining room and, along with the linking oak joists, offered a home for even more spiders and the dead flies they had left hanging in their webs.

'This was the sitting room,' declared Maxine, 'though I rarely saw her in it. The room seems to have been given over to the dogs, though they were in the dining room and upstairs as they pleased, it seemed to me.'

The sitting room was slightly larger than the dining room. It had an old stone fireplace with a stone chimney breast and a dog grate with a metal canopy. The large, south-facing bay window, which he had seen as he approached the house, provided the natural light sufficient to enable him to see everything clearly. Worn furniture, well past its use-by date, consisted of a settee, an armchair, and an old wooden stool. All faced the fireplace. The couple of small pictures hanging from the walls offered little in the way of decoration or art. Wherever he looked, he saw the evidence of the dogs that Maxine had mentioned. The legs of the furniture had been gnawed, and strewn across the floor were scraps of food, now dried and withered through time. Dog hairs were visible everywhere.

'She didn't have a cleaner, then,' Peter said as they moved towards the kitchen.

His glib remark earned no more than an upwards flicker of the eyes from Maxine and the comment, 'What do you think?'

The kitchen was small and cramped, little more than three feet wide and twelve feet long. It contained a stone sink and a free-standing cupboard, which, as Maxine pulled open a door, bore the smell of rotten eggs and the must of waste. She amusingly gripped the end of her nose between her thumb and forefinger while uttering, 'Cor, what a smell.'

Hanging on the far wall were some kitchen utensils. The only redeeming feature was the window over the sink, which offered a view of the open fields to anyone washing the dishes. The external views were about the only appealing feature that Peter had seen since he had entered the cottage, and they sparked in him a flash of the possibilities that the cottage might offer.

'Upstairs will be interesting,' said Maxine as she led the way up the bare wooden stairs.

At the top of the stairs, a door to Peter's left led into the first of three small bedrooms. This one was separated from a second by a flimsy hardboard wall that was sagging away from its fixture in one corner. Together, the two bedrooms matched the size of the sitting room that was directly below their wooden floorboards. The ceiling again featured beams and joists typical of the cottage, with a white-painted plaster finish between the joists. The second bedroom, with its well-used bed and narrow-doored wardrobe, was obviously the room from which Ma' Winstone conversed with those who had some concern for her well-being, and this was confirmed by Maxine.

'This is where I normally saw her at the window. She was usually in what seemed to be a dressing gown and a sort of a scarf. How she managed, heaven alone knows.'

Across the landing was the bathroom with a panelled bath, WC, and pedestal washbasin. Their condition was not too bad, and the enamel had remained firm. The room also contained an airing cupboard with the immersion-heated cylinder providing hot water. It was on seeing the bathroom that Peter began to wonder about mains facilities for water and gas. There was certainly electricity—he confirmed this by switching on the landing light—but as to the others, he remained unsure but sceptical.

Maxine led the way to the end of the landing and the third very small bedroom, capable of taking a single bed and not much else. *It'll do for one of the children,* thought Peter as he squeezed past Maxine into the room, though he hardly dared think as to Catherine's reaction.

The windows in all the bedrooms and the bathroom were low, but from all of them, once he stooped to peer through, Peter could see the beautiful scenery that so attracted him to the place. The greyish Yorkshire stone of the walls that threaded between the smallholdings concentrated the eyes on one view after another as though they were picture frames enclosing an artist's brushwork. As the eyes followed the rising moor, the land became less nurtured than that closer to the farmhouses and less restricted by the stone walls. It rose to what was its natural summit: *The King's Beacon.*

Maxine, cheerful as ever, although aware of the cottage's shortcomings, seemed unfazed by what she was revealing, but Peter quickly recognised the reason why she thought she would be better staying with her mother and father. In response to her question, 'Well, what do you think?' Peter was surprised, almost shocked, to hear himself using the estate agent's one-liner, 'It certainly has potential.' They both laughed, Maxine clearly amused by the comment, Peter more from the nervous realisation of what it meant for anyone who bought the cottage.

The back door opened onto a small walled area and then to the first of the three fields he might own. Outside, the picture was much more encouraging. A substantial barn about four-hundred-and-fifty square feet in size, an outhouse, and a mistal, once used for cows, adjoined the house. As they walked round the barn Maxine, pointing in the general direction of each, said, 'Those are the fields. I've seen animals grazing in them from time to time, but I've no idea who, if anyone, uses them now. I've never thought to ask whose cows or sheep they were. I know that any farmer would be glad of them simply to be able to increase his stock. As for the barn and outhouses, I've not been aware of their use for years.'

They walked around the back of the barn and through the field gate that led out onto the road. It brought them to the front of the cottage again, where Peter noticed for the first time sheets of glass, seemingly intended as a conservatory of sorts, straddling the corner created by the wall of the barn and the outhouse. In its useful days, it probably offered protection from any breeze whilst garnering what it could from the sun. Now it sagged dangerously. Making sure to avoid it, Peter peered into the outbuildings. Straw was still strewn about the floors and in one of the outbuildings stood the stalls in which cows had once been milked, clearly by hand. On the outside of the mistal, at the far end, stood a very large butt made of ringed aluminium for collecting water from the roofs of the barn and outhouses.

By now, Peter and Maxine had circled the cottage and seen what it had to offer, both inside and outside. Peter's head was in a whirl.

One minute, his mind said, *This is ridiculous. How can you bring Catherine and the children to live here? How will they cope? What's going to happen about transport?*

And the next, it was saying, *This is a great opportunity for you. Yes, it's a challenge, and yes, it'll present some unimaginable problems, some of which you've not yet even thought about, but when will the chance to live in an environment such as this come again? The place affords tremendous opportunities for the children to play, to learn about the country, and actually come into contact with the living animals they enjoy looking at in their picture books. Once you have enough money for a car, you have a ready-made garage in the outhouses. Beyond the barn, you've ten acres of fields to do with what you wish.*

He was abruptly brought out of his reverie by Maxine. 'Is there anything else you need to know?' she asked as they wandered around the buildings. Reality dawned.

'I was wondering about mains services. Good water and sanitation are pretty important, especially when you have young children.'

'Well, there's mains electricity, but there's no gas, as you've probably noticed. As for the rest, come with me and I'll show you.'

It was in the highest field that Maxine showed him the house's water supply. It consisted of a deep pit, covered with an ill-fitting concrete slab, which Peter deduced collected water that ran off the field and, he assumed, from the surrounding moorland. Through the gap left by the cover, which, like an open grate on the roadside, seemed to allow anything to drip in from a wet field, Peter could see that it was just about full. A small outlet pipe on the downside clearly led to a duct that took the water into the house. It was a header tank with a difference. The extent of its likely impurity entered Peter's head, as did the likely consequences of a dry summer, but they were dismissed speedily as he sought to convince himself of the cottage's attractions.

'And what of sanitation?'

'Well, that's in the lower field, where there's a similar tank. All the waste feeds into that.'

'Is it what they call a septic tank?'

'I'm not sure, but I think so.'

The dampness spreading into the field below the tank's cover suggested the answer. Any sewage from the cottage was piped into what was a large, covered hole in the ground and then allowed to seep in its own time into the lower end of the field. Peter's limited knowledge of all things technical left him without a question as to its fitness for purpose.

They wandered back to the cottage, Peter becoming increasingly bewitched by the ambience of the area within which it was set. The majesty of the *Beacon* entranced him. He wondered how arduous the climb was and whether, if he ever had the opportunity, he would be able to negotiate the stone buttresses at its peak. He could just make out the stony path made by the hundreds of walkers who had already had the joy of sitting atop the buttresses in the sunshine and enjoying, westwards, the valley with its fields and houses hugging the river. Eastwards, the open moor teemed with grazing sheep.

As the time for the end of the visit approached, Peter found himself in a quandary. He was aware that the shortcomings of the cottage were obvious to anyone who cared to walk through it. Nevertheless, he was so tempted by it that he was already formulating in his mind how he was going to describe it to Catherine, so that she would agree with his purchasing it.

The main thrust of his case had to be the price of the cottage and the likely mortgage. At twenty-five hundred pounds, it was more than their present house, which had cost only fifteen hundred a year or so ago. However, the interest on their current property was almost double what Maxine was asking for the cottage. What made the cottage even more attractive was that Maxine was not asking for a deposit and was suggesting a small, manageable mortgage well below the five per cent they were currently paying to the local building society. In addition, he could draw attention to the amount of land surrounding the cottage, the prospect of extensions into the barn and the outhouses as the family income increased, more a hope than a certainty, and the opportunities for a life in the fresh air for the children. The problems, which he steered to the back of his mind, could be glossed over as the need for a good clear-out of the rubbish and a lick of paint.

Once they were back in the car, he turned to Maxine, saying, 'I'm very interested in the cottage and the deal that goes with it. I have to speak to Catherine about it before I can make a definite offer, as I'm sure you will realise.'

'No worry. Somebody else is interested, but I'm not sure that they will take it. They currently live in Leeds and have a feeling that they would like a second house in the country. Once they've seen it, they may decide it's not for them. They're coming to look at it tomorrow and they've promised to let me know by the end of the week if they want it. But I've another couple wanting to look at the cottage and so I'll need to have an answer from you by next Tuesday.'

Peter realised that he was going to have to reach a decision whilst Catherine was still away, something he had hoped to avoid. He wrestled with what to do, but then, almost without realising it, he said, 'I'll let you know by Tuesday.'

CHAPTER 8

THE PHONE CALL

That evening, when he arrived home, he was tired and concerned. He had two major problems that were thwarting an excitement about the cottage that otherwise would have been all consuming. One was Webster, a problem he had failed to resolve and one that would be with him in each of the two lessons a week that Webster turned up for history. Even though his day at school was over he could not put this concern behind him. But a more pressing challenge, one that had now pushed thoughts of Webster to the back of his mind, was selling the idea of the cottage in as honest a way as he could to Catherine, convincing her that a move to the moor would have some significant merits.

His need to impress upon her that a decision had to be made by the following Tuesday, as after that date the opportunity for purchase may have gone, further heightened the tension. He had practised his arguments, both for and against, whilst he had been preparing his tea. Having eaten his cheese sandwich with bread that was someway past its sell-by date, he picked up his coffee and a biscuit and ambled across the sitting room to look wistfully at the moor and its *Beacon*. The dipping sun, throwing its fading rays across the highest point, did nothing to diminish the excitement of his visit to the cottage. After a while, he turned and dropped into one of the armchairs. He sat munching his biscuit whilst staring into the empty fireplace, reflecting on his relationship with Catherine as he awaited the appropriate time to ring.

Peter knew Catherine well enough to realise that his task of convincing her of the attractions of the cottage would not be easy. Catherine had the ability to ask the searching questions that sometimes foiled his best answers and prevented him from wriggling away from her probing. But he also knew that their mutual trust, knowledge, and understanding of each other had been the basis of their relationship; a relationship thriving on a loyal commitment to one another and their marriage vows.

An intelligent woman, Catherine had done well in her final school examinations but instead of going on to higher education she had left school at eighteen and taken a vocational course leading to physiotherapy. It seemed normal to her, and many like her in the early 1950s, for a girl to move on to what was considered a worthwhile job rather than continue into higher education, no matter how well they had performed in their final examinations. She had resisted her parents' entreaties to go on to university and with another school friend had decided on a different career path. Peter never knew whether she ever regretted not going into higher education. She never talked of what might have been, or undersold the work she did as a physiotherapist.

When in discussion, the points she would make were embodied in the expectations of the times through which she had lived.

A Peter in his younger days would not have found Catherine's decision to opt out of the opportunities presented by higher education strange. But now, as he sat quietly thinking, he felt confused by the reasoning that had resulted in many able women readily seeking a career outside one related to that of academia. Peer expectations in the early 1950s were of a different measure to what society was now, some ten years later, beginning to experience, and he recognised that as they changed, he, like many men, had had to adjust his own.

Peter had been brought up in a working-class environment that assumed different social and economic roles for men and women. Women were expected to take on the responsibilities associated with family and home, thus limiting their progress in any other career, whilst their menfolk looked to support the family by making their way in whichever career they had embraced. This explained, as far as Peter understood it, why men usually took the lead in the professions and the difficulties that women had in making their way to the most senior posts in business and commerce. In his youth, Peter had unthinkingly fallen into the trap of seeing this pattern as normal.

It was only as he matured and met women of talent that he began to question the validity of such a social structure. During his days in college he came to believe strongly in the value of learning in terms of broadening intellectual experience and challenging the mind to explore new ideas. He came to see the sense in encouraging those, whether male or female, with the capacity for advanced study to seek what higher education and beyond had to offer. It was not surprising, therefore, to find him in the profession he loved.

Even so, Peter was aware of his own feelings of insecurity when it came to study at the highest levels. He had not read widely as a child, but had preferred to join others in the streets of his village, playing games such as kick out can, hide and seek, and hopscotch, as well as participating in the key sports of football and cricket. He had also spent many hours each day practising his cornet. Although he did reasonably well at school and more or less kept pace with his contemporaries, he knew that because of such activities he did not give sufficient priority to his studies. He put it down to an immaturity that did not take him out of his teenage years easily, nor allow him to move to that responsible, almost adult, response to the challenges of his studies that was required for success. When he looked back on those days he wondered whether he was that much different to many of the youngsters he was now teaching, including Webster, and to what extent their interests outside study explained their presence in the town's secondary modern school.

On the occasions he went through the reasons that he believed justified what he had done in his life, his thoughts would turn to Catherine and his good fortune in noticing such an attractive girl across a crowded ballroom. Peter never understood what attracted one person to another and saw it as a facet of human life difficult to explain. He accepted that perhaps the anthropologist and the psychologist could, but for mere mortals such as him, the impulse of desire that one person has for another remained a wonder of nature. He was mystified by the fact that certain features of the opposite sex did not appeal directly to all in the same way, and even more by what attracted one particular individual to another. In some inexplicable way an attraction was recognised, whether it was because of a person's personality, their features such as the sparkle in their eyes and the becoming smile, or primarily what might be termed a sexual attraction. No matter, he recognised that in circumstances where a mutual attraction was recognised, whether it was instantaneous or an emotion that had developed over a longer time frame, terms like adoration, devotion and worship, concepts usually associated with the divine, became an integral part of the communication between the lover and loved and helped to cement their relationship.

Peter knew, from his own experience with Catherine, that in these and similar ways people expressed the depth of feeling that their love for another engendered, rarely questioning why it was for the particular person of their desire and not for another. It had always amazed him that even for those he would have described as philanderers, the same urges existed, no matter how spontaneous and short lived. They too, at particular times, centred their desire on one person rather than another.

Peter looked up at the clock. It was still only half past six. Another thirty minutes of reflection and anguished waiting. Peter wondered what Catherin's response was likely to be. He knew her to be resolute and a person capable of taking on a challenge. He admired the determination and courage it took for a nineteen-year-old girl, having worked for a short time in her native Hull, to move to London with a childhood friend. She had shown no fears of a dissolute London, about which her parents had warned her, hidden beneath the bright lights. As it was, Catherine and Margaret settled in Kensington. They adjusted to their new life, following a pattern that reflected their moral upbringing whilst taking opportunities to enjoy some of the pleasures that London had to offer.

Catherine took up a post in a nearby hospital. Her immediate superior was a young woman of some social standing who enjoyed social life more than working and who sought to offer tips on life in the capital. She informed on the best shopping centres, the clothes to wear, the good but inexpensive restaurants, and the safest places for pleasure. All had some bearing on the way Catherine settled into London.

Even so, Catherine was a girl with her own ideas on what would make life interesting and did not hesitate to make up her own mind. It was not surprising, therefore, to find her exploring various parts of the city not mentioned by her supervisor. A chance visit to Hammersmith Palais with Margaret on an evening when Joe Loss and his band were swinging, found her dancing with a young man who was also from the north. A second and then a third dance followed and without any pre-intention, the spark of attraction struck and was fostered. Peter's and Catherine's romance had begun.

For a young couple, especially one from the provinces, life in London had much to offer in the 1950's. Visits to one of the Tate, the National Gallery or museums such as the Imperial War Museum and the Natural Science Museum could fill a day. The evening offered theatre, cinema, and opera in places as different as Leicester Square and Covent Garden. Indeed, Peter's first introduction to opera was through the head of Catherine's department who was wealthy enough to invite his staff and friends to Covent Garden on the occasion when the world famous Swedish tenor, Jussi Björling, was to sing in La Boehme.

It was to be a new and testing experience for Peter. At Catherine's instigation, he took great care to dress well. A clean white shirt was the order of the day, as was his best suit and smart tie. His shoes had the sparkle of the guardsman on parade. The journey by tube brought Catherine and Peter to within easy walking distance of the Opera House and for Peter an introduction to Mr Felston, their host. Peter's nerves quietly rumbled in his tummy as he was unsure as to what to do or what to say. Catherine, meanwhile, was in her element. Wearing a smart evening dress with a sparkling diamond brooch her father had bought her as a going away gift on her departure to London, she was thoroughly enjoying meeting with work colleagues and introducing Peter.

'Mr Felston, Peter, my boyfriend.'

'God evening, Peter. I hope you enjoy your evening.'

'I'm certainly looking forward to it. Many thanks for inviting me.'

'It's a delight to have you with us,' replied Mr Felston in English slightly tinged with a foreign accent as he turned away to welcome more guests. His bow tie, evening suit, and his brushed-back hair matched the surroundings. His sharp eyes took in all that Peter's appearance had to offer. What Mr Felston made of him Peter never knew, but his host was quickly distracted by the need for further introductions. Catherine joyfully circulated amongst her colleagues, introducing Peter as and when appropriate.

Meanwhile, Mr Felston returned from the foyer bar with drinks and Peter began to feel a little more comfortable. Even so, as he looked around, he was intimidated by what he witnessed. His nervous self-consciousness and appearance contrasted sharply with the evening suits, the jabbering voices, and the obvious ease with which regular opera goers mingled. Mr Felston displayed an enviable social confidence as he astutely played the role of master of ceremonies among his guests. Peter wondered if he was observing a charade or whether those with whom he was now temporarily associating lived their lives in this way. He had only seen such scenes in films and had never imagined himself to be part of one. *What would my Dad think of me now?* he wondered.

The pre-performance gathering slowly began to disperse at the sound of the first warning bell and groups began to move to their seats. Peter, more comfortable alongside Catherine, followed Mr Felston along a corridor displaying photographs and prints of the stars of the past, through a curtain held back by a smartly dressed lady usher, and into a box which overlooked the stalls. The seats offered to Catherine and Peter were in close proximity to the curtained stage, giving them such a privileged location that it startled Peter. It took him a while to adjust to the fact that, on his first visit to Coven Garden, he was in such an eye-catching position.

And then a shock for the audience, and the evening seemed destined to lose its sparkle. The opera house director appeared from behind the curtain just before the opera was due to commence and announced, 'I'm afraid I have some disappointing news. Jussi Björling is ill and unable to perform this evening. He sends his apologies. Of course we all wish him a speedy recovery. Lancelot Winstone-Smith will deputise. He is a singer who has performed here and on the continent to impressive acclaim. I am sure you will have an enjoyable evening.'

The exciting anticipation, noticeable amongst the audience, was suddenly replaced with a deep disappointment. It infected the box in which Peter was sitting. Mr Felston turned to his guests, obviously disappointed, and even though the situation was not of his making, apologised.

But then, totally unexpectedly to the people already in the theatre, unheralded, the Queen Mother, Elizabeth, and her entourage arrived. In a silver tiara and white dress she looked resplendent as she took her seat in the box opposite to the one in which Peter was sitting. He couldn't believe what was happening. He had seen members of the royal family when on duty but like everyone else in the theatre he was taken aback by her arrival. Along with the rest of the audience he stood in respect and joined in the clapping. Within a couple of minutes the director appeared again from behind the curtain and bowed towards the royal box.

'Your Majesty, ladies and gentlemen, I'm pleased to announce that in light of Your Majesty's unexpected, but most welcome attendance, Mr Björling has agreed to perform. He asks for your patience in respect of his performance, because of his illness, but he feels it a great honour to be performing before you.'

The announcement was greeted with further clapping and a royal wave of thanks in the direction of the stage.

Within a few minutes the opera began and to Peter's ears, Jussi Björling performed wonderfully well. On occasions he needed to grasp the back of a chair or lean on a table as he took up his positions around the stage, but his performance led to standing applause. The end of the opera brought the whole cast on to the stage, and with hands held, they turned and bowed respectfully to the Royal Box. The Queen Mother responded with a wave of her gloved hand, first to the cast and then to the audience. As she turned to leave, the applause broke out again.

It was quarter to seven and there were still fifteen minutes before the phone call. As Peter waited to pick up the phone, these recollections flooded through his mind, leaving him thinking tenderly of his wife, their life together, and the noteworthy occasions they had shared. He rose from his chair to look again through the window at the splendid view of the moor, as if to gain strength from the reason for his anxiety. Peter always felt his stomach churn a little when so close to speaking to Catherine, but in this instance it outdid all other occasions.

Catherine was an extremely good looking woman, only a half inch shorter than Peter's six feet, a tall girl for those days. She carried her height well, her back straight and her head held at a proud angle. Her brown hair was cut just below the ears and ran into waves that surrounded her evenly proportioned face. Her large brown eyes matched the complexion of her skin, which looked slightly more tanned than most. The line of her firm breasts was accentuated by the relatively slim waist and long shapely legs.

In her absence, Peter could not help but feel the pangs of need which had been stirred by their first embrace. But he knew that such delightful moments sometimes become overtaken by the realities that surround the living, realties that seek to force themselves disproportionally across the boundary lines of tenderness and affection.

Eventually, seven o'clock arrived, the agreed time for the phone call, and the time when Catherine would have the children ready for bed.

Peter imagined her sitting with the youngest, Gregory, in the crook of her arm so that he could gurgle into the phone and so say what he had to say, in words which only he understood to his 'Daddy'. Katie and Sarah would no doubt be standing by their mum's side, ready to say, 'Hello, Daddy,' at their mum's prompting.

The 'brrr, brrr' of the phone went twice before the receiver was taken from its hook and, 'Hello,' was transported through the wires to Peter. As usual, it stirred anticipation in him and a longing that the familiar voice could not fully satisfy. Nevertheless, he understood the reasons for their current separation and shared with Catherine the feelings she had for her father. He knew that at critical times in life. as this was for Catherine's father, support was essential and it was natural for him to look to his only daughter for sustenance. It was this mix of thoughts in his mind that encouraged Peter to begin with the usual niceties that characterised such conversations. Though commonplace, they are the essential questions that put minds at rest.

'How are you? How are the children? Is your dad OK?'

To his questions, Peter received, happily, midst the gurgles of Gregory, their newest born child, positive responses.

'We're missing you Peter. I'm really looking forward to coming home. The children are also keen to be back in Weberton.'

'The same here. The house doesn't feel like home without you,' responded Peter, looking around the sitting room. 'It's all neat and tidy,' to which he imagined Catherine smiling. She knew too well that the distinction between tidiness and untidiness in Peter's language meant very little.

'Well, I'm going to quote something I read in the paper today,' Peter added. 'I have to admit it's about someone else's house but you could imagine it's this one. It says, and I'm reading, 'this is a house which bears the aura of being valued', so what do you think to that?'

He could not help but laugh out loud and Catherine seemed to share the joke with, 'I don't think so.'

More seriously, Peter added, 'But I have to say it's missing you and the children. It's like being at an empty rugby club. If there's no team there isn't much point in having a ground,' he added, as everything around him seemed to be paling into insignificance. At the forefront of his mind was a vision of the cottage.

This was Peter. The ease with which he could desert reality for a dream, or distance himself from one situation so as to make room for the next, was part of his charm. Catherine had learned this and had had to adapt to it throughout the time she had known him.

Trying to keep in check his excitement about the cottage, Peter continued the conversation for a short time on matters that he knew Catherine would expect. 'Young Webster has been giving me problems again,' he said, 'and I'm not sure how to deal with him. D'you know what he did?'

'Obviously not. I'm in Hull, remember?' Catherine said with a provocative laugh.

'You're lucky. I'd to cope with him tearing up a page of his exercise book. I'd written that he had do his homework again as it wasn't good enough. The page was in such a mess I could almost tell what he'd had for his tea. You can imagine how I felt. I managed to settle him and get him to collect the bits of paper and then, after the lesson, I kept him behind for half an hour.'

'How did he react?' asked Catherine.

'The fact that he wasn't going anywhere until he sat down and did his homework again, convinced him to get on with it, and so I think I won by a head. On top of that, the Local Authority adviser was in to see how I was doing. It seems that the head gave her a good report and when she visited my first lesson I was lucky enough to have 4A, a really good and well behaved class. They worked beautifully and did all I asked without a murmur. It was great,' he added enthusiastically. 'They produced some really good work in their books. The adviser was impressed with the wall display and as she left the room to speak to the head again said to me 'well done'.'

'That's really good news, Peter.'

He went on to explain how the adviser had been pleased with what she had seen around the classroom and with the responses she had had from the pupils about how much they enjoyed history.

'Anyway, the really good news is that she passed that on to the head and it can only do good for my career. She was the same inspector that saw me teach last year and recommended me for full qualified teacher status. You can imagine how I feel.'

'I think I can, and that's great news Peter. You should have a beer on it,' responded Catherine laughingly, still unaware of the even more enthralling news that Peter was desperate to reveal, and thinking that the most important message had been shared with her.

Indeed it was important, because like all teachers, Peter had to satisfy the powers that be that he was a capable teacher. Without the recommendation of the Local Authority, the likelihood of his being able to further his career would be a distant dream.

He went on, 'I'm doing OK at home, though shopping, cooking and cleaning are not my strong points as you know.'

It was at this point that he could contain himself no longer and blurted out, 'I've been looking at a super property today which I think we should buy.'

CHAPTER 9

NEWS OF
THE COTTAGE

Peter's words about the cottage did not come out in the calm and measured way he had intended, but at least he had given the news and stated his position with conviction.

'Oh,' came the hesitant response.

Peter realised immediately that his news had unsettled Catherine. He could almost feel the phone vibrate under her quivering fingers and tell she was seeking to control the tremor in her voice as she asked, just audibly above the gurgles of their newest child, 'What have you been doing since I've been away? You haven't made any rash commitments have you? What sort of property are you talking about?'

It was obvious to Peter that her thoughts had sped once again to the rapidity of change in her life since she had been drawn to him, and his propensity to make decisions without thinking through the consequences. 'Peter, I was hoping that we might find time to get fully bedded in to Weberton and build on the friendships that we've established. I know there are issues about the house but people are far more important, as you've found in the band and the rugby club. Please tell me that we're not going to move again.'

At last she hesitated and gave him the opportunity to speak. He appreciated Catherine's concern about moving again after so short a time, and that any suggestion he might make implying that would be sensitive. Although he had convinced himself of the advantages of a move to the cottage, he was aware he had much to do to get Catherine to the same position.

Peter recognised his tendency to make snap decisions and on occasions he had been forced to rethink them as a result of the response of others, sometimes wisely, but sometimes in circumstances that he later regretted. In truth, he often relied on Catherine's own breezy approach to life when he reached what to others may have appeared suspect decisions. He believed it was what was within her own soul that explained the fortitude with which she could accept his unpredictability. Had she not told him that it was his spontaneity, hidden to most of his associates by his seemingly dependable reliability and constancy, which had been one of the features that had first attracted her? He knew, however, that this aspect of her love for him would in no way have prepared her for the momentous news he was now sharing with her, or, indeed, the obvious demands that would be made by a life in the cottage.

'Catherine, this is a great opportunity,' he stated in his usual forthright way. Without giving Catherine any opening to interrupt, he began to spell out those things he regarded as positive selling points. 'I've looked all around the place and feel that we could make it a super home for the family. There are sufficient bedrooms and a bathroom upstairs, and downstairs there's a separate dining room, kitchen, and sitting room, which is one up on our present place. Not having a dining room is a real problem, especially when we have friends round for a meal.'

In Peter's mind that was one point scored.

'There are also lots of opportunities for extensions, as there's a barn and some outhouses. And guess what.' Without giving Catherine time to guess, he went on, 'The cottage has ten acres of land. The cottage itself is situated just under *The King's Beacon*, within beautiful moorland. It will bring back some great memories of your days in the Lake District.' He added the last as further inducement, because he knew how much Catherine loved the mountains and lakes.

All went quiet at the other end of the phone line.

'Well, what do you think?' More silence followed. 'We need to let Maxine know by Tuesday.'

This was clearly the last straw for Catherine and opened the floodgates to all the questions and doubts that Peter had been having himself.

'Peter, what are you thinking? I haven't even seen it yet and it sounds miles from anywhere? We don't have a car. What will we do for transport? What if one of the children is ill? How will I get to the shops? What do we do about schools?'

'We'll work it out somehow, Catherine. Now that I have an improved salary we might be able to run a car. The old lady that lived there previously used to get lifts down to the shops from the neighbours.'

'Oh, so there are neighbours then?' Catherine said with a touch of sarcasm, and then, after a slight pause to allow the point to sink in, 'You hinted that it needs a bit of work. What exactly does that mean? We've three small children Peter! You have a full-time job, plus the band on Wednesday evenings and rugby at the weekend. How on earth are you going to find the time to do any work on it?'

'Yes, I know all of that, but I think some of the lads from the rugby club'll help us out with one or two jobs. Catherine, we've to put this into the context of our lives. We're currently living in a nice house, admittedly, but one in which we don't want to live forever. With our present and likely income it's difficult to see how we're going to be able to afford anything else, as far as I can see. The cottage offers us a way out, and Maxine seems to be able to help us financially.'

'So you say, and that's all well and good, Peter. But we have to be practical, too, and maybe now, with the three little ones and you only just settling into your job, isn't the best time to be doing this. I'm sure something else will crop up when we need it. I know you, Peter, you'll always go your own way, but for God's sake please consider this one very carefully.' She hesitated for a moment and then continued, 'I have to go now as Gregory is causing a fuss. Let's talk about it again tomorrow . . . . but please see if you can hold Maxine off at least 'til I get back.' The plaintive 'please' disturbed Peter, but at the same time strengthened his resolve to find a way of convincing Catherine of the benefits of a move to the cottage.

'Well, I could ask Maxine for an extension, but she's pretty determined about Tuesday as the deadline. I don't really see much chance of holding up the decision. Catherine, it'd be a lovely place to bring up the children . . . . open fields in which to roam, sheep and cows to see, and farmers' children to play with. Honest, it's fantastic.'

'Peter, the more you say the less you're convincing me that this is right for us. There's no way we can live in the situation you describe. I refuse to be stranded on a moor miles from anywhere with young children. You'll be away at school all week and I'll have nobody to turn to if I have a problem. If you go ahead with this before I come home and we've no time to discuss all the implications fully, I'll never forgive you.'

With that, Catherine slammed down the phone.

Peter was at a loss. Should he ring back and try to persuade Catherine again? Should he tell Maxine that he did not want the cottage? Or should he go ahead and take the risk of Catherine's ire when she returned? She had made it quite clear that to say, 'Yes,' to Maxine was to put their relationship at some risk, an outcome he had never considered. For the first time, Catherine was saying, quite deliberately, 'If you buy this cottage do not forget that you made the decision and that you are putting in danger the trust of your wife and children.'

Peter was only slightly mollified by the thought it was unlikely, despite her obvious chagrin, that Catherine would disappear into the streets as she had done on a previous occasion before their marriage, forcing him to lose a night's sleep in his search for her. She was now married to the man she loved, had three children, and bore the responsibilities of a mother.

Peter's night in bed was disturbed by his tossing and turning and by the tortuous twisting of his mind as he went over and over again Catherine's words. His own thoughts about the cottage were unchanged and he remained sure there was benefit in accepting Maxine's offer, but the question, *Dare I do it?* found no ready answer. Monday morning came and, as he awoke from yet another bout of fitful sleep, the question still remained without an answer. His call to Catherine on the Sunday had been no less disturbing than that of the Saturday and he suspected his call this evening would be of the same ilk. With Tuesday looming large in his mind, he realised he had to be in a position to give Maxine a reply. He could see no way of calming Catherine's aversion to the idea of a move, and so decided that it was better to let Maxine know a decision as soon as he could and not delay until Tuesday. His walk to school was not made any pleasanter by the clear sky and warm morning sunshine. Somehow, he thought that storm clouds and rain would have been more fitting.

Back at school, Peter looked towards the last couple of weeks before the summer holidays with less excitement than he might have expected. Whatever decision he made about the cottage was likely to cause him some grief. If he said yes, he would have to face Catherine, and her tone on the previous evenings was designed to leave him in no doubt as to the seriousness of her misgivings about his purchasing the cottage. If he said no, he could look forward to heaven knows how many further years of discomfort in 29 Brent Road.

He coasted through his first couple of lessons, relying on tasks written on the blackboard and to be completed in the children's books. This was a useful ploy that enabled him, when other things arose that he thought were more pressing and more important, to avoid introducing a new topic with the need for careful preparation, introduction, and explanation. His lesson after break brought 1C through the door. He had used the break to set up the project on road building they had already started in a previous lesson and, as they entered, they naturally went in to their group positions. After a brief introduction, in which each group leader outlined what their group was doing, they set to work. To his astonishment, all the groups, including Webster's, settled into discussion, trying one solution and then another, before agreeing how best to design their road to reflect the limits of the historical time period they had been given. When the bell went for the end of the lesson, equipment was stored tidily and the class filed out with a semblance of order. The experience left Peter somewhat flabbergasted.

It was only during the lunch break when chatting with one of the pupils from 1C in the dining room that he learned that the class had fallen foul of his friend Stan, who had sent for the head because of their bad behaviour. The head had delivered the most serious of warnings as to their future behaviour and its likely consequences, and had caned, in front of the class, Webster and two of his pals. Webster, as usual, put on a brave face, though he couldn't help but wince when the fourth stroke struck. The other two boys showed less fortitude and both were in tears by the time the head had finished. For once, the class and the difficult individuals within in it, had taken heed and Peter had been the beneficiary.

It was also during lunchtime that Peter had intended to talk with Maxine about the cottage. He was still in a quandary as to what he dare do and was relieved to find that Maxine was not in the staffroom; she was in the art room helping some pupils finish off their work. It gave him a little more time, but he realised time was no use to him. He knew what his own view was, but he also knew what Catherine thought. He realised that decision making was what was needed and that to go through all the various arguments, weighing the pros and the cons, would get him nowhere. It was Catherine's opposition to the cottage that was a critical factor and which was playing the most important part in the tentativeness of his resolution.

Even though none of his colleagues knew of his dilemma, those who sat close to him in the staffroom during break were aware that he was not the Peter they all knew. Normally, he entered into conversation with some vigour, expressing views and listening to others in a way that made his company enjoyable. Today, he was not contributing to the stories being shared but, to his colleagues, seemed immersed in his own thoughts. His coffee was held in the right position to enable him to be freely involved in the group, but the tapping of his fingers on the chair arm and the vacancy that crept into his eyes from time to time told those around him that his mind was wrestling with something he had not shared.

'OK, Peter, what's bothering you?' asked Stan. 'You've been fidgeting most of lunchtime and you don't seem interested in anything any of us has to say.'

'Nothing,' said Peter, trying to sound unconcerned. 'I was just thinking of the family and how many more days they're going to be away. I keep working through the diary.'

'Oh, of course, they're away, aren't they,' said James, the religious education teacher. 'I'll bet you're keeping the house nice and tidy. I remember when my wife went away for a while . . . .'

As he continued, Peter again drifted into his own thoughts and allowed what was being said to pass him by like some untouchable mist that enveloped him but did not penetrate. He clicked in again as James was concluding, 'God, I got into bother when she got home. I hadn't done any hoovering or cleaning. I had dirty clothes spread around the house, the bed was unmade, and wherever she went her finger found dust.'

His colleagues laughed as he pointed his index finger and pulled it across the nearby table, turned it towards him and then pulled it towards his face, now contorted in mock disgust, as if to inspect it thoroughly, mimicking the action of a woman when judging the cleanliness of a room. 'She went ballistic.'

At that, as if recognising the word 'ballistic', the bell went and it was time again for registration and classes. Peter went back to his room with some relief. He had not yet had to finalise a choice. However, he knew that by four o'clock, he had to have made up his mind.

Afternoon lessons progressed well. Form 3B showed keen interest in the advance of Napoleon on Moscow, a fatal decision that had Peter thinking of his own plight, and 1A became interestingly involved in seeing what the story of Caedmon told them about the early monasteries, and in particular about Whitby. A double lesson with 5A on the Industrial Revolution and the movement of whole communities into the towns and away from the sort of life he was now seeking to create for his family, brought teaching for the afternoon to a close. With sheets of paper for more marking under his arm, he locked his classroom door and, with his mind still wrestling with the issue of the cottage, he walked casually towards the staffroom. He knew that the inevitable had to be faced.

He met Maxine on the stairs as they were heading back to the staffroom at the end of school.

'Hi, Peter, how are things?' was her cheery greeting.

'Fine. Look, Maxine, is there any chance of delaying a decision about the cottage until Catherine gets home at the end of the summer holidays? She's pretty keen to see it before we have to decide on whether or not to buy it.'

Maxine drew back her lips in thoughtful mode, half closing one eye as if in hard thought. After a brief pause she replied, 'I'm afraid not, Peter. As much as I'd like to, I have someone else who's really keen and awaiting an answer from me once I've heard from you. You can understand that I want the worry of the place off my hands as soon as possible.'

Peter realised he was cornered.

'I thought that might be the case,' he said as they neared the staffroom. He then went quiet, trying to delay a decision for as long as possible. Once inside, Peter found a space for his papers on the work table and then together, he and Maxine moved across the staffroom to make coffee, nodding to, or exchanging a brief word with, different colleagues. They made their coffee, found a seat, and then Maxine put the inevitable question to him, 'Well, how's the thinking going on the cottage?'

'We'll take it,' came the reply, more as an impulsive reaction than a considered response.

Peter actually felt relief as he said it, though a deep sense of self-reproach lay just below the surface of his answer. He knew he was yet again challenging Catherine to follow him, rather than his listening to the good sense of her reasoning. His immediate thoughts, even fears, became concerned with how she would react. But to ask the question, he recognised, was as pointless an action as anyone could take.

'That's great. I'll tell you what. We could call in at the solicitor's on our way home from school, and if he can see us we can tell him that you're buying the cottage and ask him to draw up the papers for signing next week. What do you think?'

Peter felt he had no option but to agree that the sooner things were signed and sealed the better.

The solicitor's office was a short distance from the school and Maxine gave Peter a lift in her rather sporty Porsche. The ride itself was a pleasure for Peter, but less pleasurable because of the weight on his mind about what he was doing, was finding that the solicitor, a friend of Maxine's father, was available. They were shepherded into his rather dusty office. He was seated behind a large oak desk, which was so crammed with papers that he had had to make a space down the middle in order to talk to his visitors. Behind him, the wall supported a bookcase that displayed a variety of legal books and journals, whilst on the floor by his desk were other books and folders that had not been able to find a resting place on the shelves. In front of his desk were two straight-backed wooden chairs, placed conveniently to enable Maxine and Peter, once they had seated themselves, to look down the central aisle he had created on his desk.

The solicitor took off his rimless spectacles and listened intently as Maxine explained the proposal. He briefly checked on Peter's credibility and warned him that there would be a fee. Clearly satisfied with the responses he received, he undertook to draw up the documents. Maxine was true to her word and confirmed a mortgage at extremely generous rates. She also agreed not to ask for a deposit.

Everything was done so simply that the anxieties Peter had experienced on his way to the solicitor's seemed to melt away. The details of the sale were eased considerably by the fact that Maxine did not have to delay in order to find another property for herself, and Peter was able to purchase without having to raise a deposit through the immediate sale of his own house. As it never entered Peter's head to ask for a survey of the cottage, the solicitor willingly undertook to speed through the process. Peter confirmed that he would re-visit the office in the following week along with Maxine to sign the documents.

For years to come he would mentally thank Maxine for the opportunities the purchase of the cottage opened up to him. It was not that he was totally unhappy in Brent Road, for, as was well known to his friends, his own upbringing was in the terraced house of a small mining village, which even lacked some of the amenities of his present house. For instance, he and his older sister, Veronica, and their parents had to cross the back yard to use the lavatory that had no flushing water, and, for lighting, the house was dependent on gas mantles. The lack of electricity also meant the absence of gadgets such as a fridge, a washer, or a telephone. But his life had changed as a result of his education and through his marriage to Catherine, and so had his aspirations.

However, there was still the call to be made to Catherine to let her know of his decision!

CHAPTER 10

PETER IS GIVEN A NEW RESPONSIBILITY

The evening's phone call did not go well. After the usual pleasantries, Peter declared, 'Catherine, I've told Maxine that we'll have the cottage.'

'What?' exclaimed Catherine, loud enough for Peter not to need a phone to hear her response. She then slammed down the phone.

It was only after another three attempts to get through to her that she eventually answered again. Distraught, she let him know her feelings.

'What have you done? Why didn't you wait until I came home? Have you been so stupid as to forget that you've got three children? I still can't believe you've ignored what I said the other day.'

All Peter could do was listen, hoping that time would heal. Eventually, Catherine broke into tears, and as Peter tried to calm her ire she put down the phone in obvious frustration. Peter decided that the best thing to do was to leave it at that and give Catherine time to settle. On the days that followed, the phone conversations were no more encouraging for Peter, the cottage was not mentioned, and there were occasions when he was in despair.

Catherine's absence meant that he had to live with his decision in a sort of vacuum. He could not talk it through with her. His only option had been to discuss it with his good friends, Roger and Stan, over a pint in the local pub, The Dragon. Such meetings had helped him to manage his feeling of loneliness because his family was away, but they did not help him to live easily with the realisation that what he had done could have serious repercussions for his marriage. He found it difficult to put Catherine's hurt to the back of his mind.

Of course, the prospect of moving house did not relieve Peter of the responsibilities he had at school. In fact, it gradually dawned on him, and it is unbelievable that he had not thought it through earlier, that the distance of the cottage from school was likely to increase pressure as he continued his efforts to do the things he currently did, particularly those that were after school or on Saturday mornings. These extra-curricular activities were an important part of what he saw as his contribution to the education of the pupils. He saw unpaid involvement in sport, school productions, visits to places of interest, and trips abroad as a normal part of his role. It was the provision of opportunities for pupils to participate in these activities that substantially added to the satisfaction that Peter gained from teaching, and which he felt compensated for the differences in financial rewards that he knew some who had chosen a different career path were enjoying. Such involvement with pupils in experiences outside the normal school curriculum, he had to agree with John and Maxine, helped create relationships with pupils that supported good teaching and learning.

It was on the Tuesday after his critical decision and his revelations to Catherine that he was asked to go and see the headteacher. Having no idea as to the reason for the call, he went up to the head's study circumspectly. There could be all sorts of explanations but until the head revealed what he had in mind, Peter could not even surmise a reason.

As he climbed the stairs, midst ruminating on the decision he had made about the cottage and some of the likely discomforting consequences, Peter thought about his family. As he had matured as a father, he had sought to help his growing children understand respect for others and the importance of working towards the greater good. He had learned that, even at home, it was important to set standards of behaviour for his children and encourage in them positive attitudes towards others. He also knew that these expectations were to be applied consistently if the right response was to be achieved, but not at the cost of ignoring the differing sensibilities of his children.

He was aware that Katie was already showing the signs of the bossiness that singled her out as the future leader of the other children. She liked playing with a little porcelain tea set that Catherine's mother had bought for her, and would love to play mum, warming the pot, putting in the imaginary tea leaves, and adding imaginary hot water. She would then pour out the invisible contents into the tiny white china cups decorated with transfers of blue bells, before insisting that the other children, even the tiny Gregory, drank it. Peter and Catherine knew that she could, even at this stage in her life, become somewhat obstreperous if the ritual was not properly followed, and so they had to be ready to intervene to quell any childish fuss.

Sarah, he recognised, could at one moment present the innocent charm of a rising two-year old and the next spin off into a tantrum for no apparent reason, kicking and screaming. When she behaved like this in public, Peter was aware that, no matter what he did, he could not avoid the disparaging looks of others who no doubt had cast aside their own memories of going through a similar experience as a parent. Nor could he guarantee finding a quick solution that did not lead to even more tantrums or, worst of all, his own abject surrender to the wishes of a child who felt aggrieved. Gregory, at just 3 months, was a big beaming boy that gurgled contentedly, and didn't really give many clues as to what his personality might eventually be. Peter hoped that he retained his relaxed, untroubled demeanour, as he was sure it would stand him in good stead. What Peter dared not visualise was Gregory, or even any of his children, becoming so frustrated in life that they became imitations of some of the children he had to deal with at school.

At least, he reckoned that if any of them were difficult children, he would be able to cope with their behaviour within the privacy of the family, which was different to his situation in school. There, his belittling before a class of pupils could do harm to his reputation across the school and, with so many youthful mouths to spread the news, very quickly.

The stairs seemed longer than on previous occasions, mainly because Peter had no idea as to the purpose for the call. He did not even try to find a reason as he entered the head's PA's office, which presented orderliness and diligence. Anne, the head's PA, asked him to wait a few minutes as the head was on the phone. She was a likeable person, popular in the staffroom. She took her responsibilities to the head very seriously, and was always willing to converse with a member of staff or help with some photocopying or typing if she had the time.

'How are Catherine and the children?' she asked. She was aware that Catherine's mother had died and that she and the children were away.

'Fine,' replied Peter. 'They're in Hull at the moment, as I think you know. Catherine's dad is taking time to get over her mother's death.'

'It's a terrible shame,' Anne said as she placed both elbows on her desk and rested her chin on her joined hands. It looked as though she was settling for a longer conversation and an opportunity to indulge in some chitchat away from her normal duties. But she was interrupted by the phone. 'The head's ready to see you,' she said, lightly nodding towards the study door.

Peter knocked on the head's door. The little buzzer sounded, 'Enter,' and he went in.

'Hello, Peter, sit down.' The head pointed to one of the chairs by the low table, normally used when he spoke with parents or other visitors. It was circled with low, matching chairs designed to make those who came to see him feel at ease.

'I wanted to have a word in readiness for next term. I understand that you play in the local brass band.'

It was as much a question as a statement, judging by the questioning look he gave Peter.

'Yes,' replied Peter. 'I've played with one band or another since I was about nine. My father and his three brothers were bandsmen and so I simply carried on the tradition.'

'Well, as you know, we've a couple of lads who play brass instruments. They're currently receiving weekly lessons from a peripatetic teacher.' He looked at Peter who nodded his assent.

'You may also know that it is the Local Education authority that encourages the school by sending us a variety of peripatetic music teachers. Quite a number of pupils have taken up the opportunity to learn an instrument as a result. I must say, I'm very pleased they do. We've a group of string players, some on woodwind and a couple are learning the piano. I have to admit, I really enjoy being able to help in one way or another. Anyway, the reason I have asked you to come to see me is that, unfortunately, the brass teacher is leaving at the end of this year. Apparently, he's a top trumpet player and is going on to play with the BBC Symphony Orchestra, which is based in London. As things are, the Local Authority doesn't have anyone in mind to replace him. I think it'll be a pity if the two lads can't continue. I spoke to them earlier today and they said they're very keen to keep playing. Certainly, the reports the teacher gave me of their progress have been very encouraging.'

Peter appeared to be sitting patiently, listening to the head and awaiting the point of the conversation. He gave the head, who still thought he had a surprise in store for Peter, no indication as to what he was thinking. But in fact, Peter's mind was working at full velocity as he had quickly perceived where the conversation was going. The questions shooting through his mind, which he felt were likely to need quick answers, were, *Is he interested in helping the boys? Does he have the time with all his other responsibilities? What effect does the work required in the cottage have on any further responsibilities he is likely to take on?*

'I was wondering if you'd be prepared to take on the responsibility . . . . The school would be able to make a small payment for the extra work; I also think it could be of importance to your career in the future. I'm sure that a successful outcome to your efforts with the pupils would have a positive impact on any CV you wrote. I know you've helped with football and cricket and that Stan has been appreciative of the time you've given. This, I think, would open out other opportunities for broadening your experience.'

Any doubts being explored in Peter's mind did not really expect to be considered with any seriousness; they seemed to know how Peter's thinking worked. Almost immediately, with hardly a gap between the head's proposal and Peter's answer, came, 'I'd love it.'

The questions that had been buzzing about in Peter's mind were not surprised at the spontaneity with which Peter had answered It was common practice for questions to be raised but then dismissed before they had time to consider or register a response. Peter often wondered how many people were affected in the same way. And why? *Is it because they have no answers to the questions? Is it because they fear that if they ignore an answer that emerges, the effects might come to chastise them at some time in the future? Or is it because, when they are asked, there is too little time in which to search all the implications of the questions and find the right answers?*

Peter had experienced many occasions on which he did not seem to want to consider his response logically, especially when an unexpected or an exciting proposition was put forward. He had heard that before some climactic occurrence, all the significant experiences of a lifetime rushed through a person's mind, as bright and as memorable as the day they happened. The realities of the past, deeply hidden in the individual's psyche, suddenly emerged as if to better prepare him for what was about to happen. The images came and were gone in a flash. Peter wondered whether what was happening to him as he sat quietly twiddling his thumbs in front of the head was something of the same nature. Whilst seeking to take in what the head was saying, his mind was being exposed to visions of his past, of his first days on the cornet, the hard practice, his joining his first band, his military experiences, the joys of concerts, successful contests, and the satisfaction of mastering skills. As quickly as they had arrived, they were gone, but they left him with the feeling that his response, 'I'd love it,' was exactly the right thing for him to have said. Little did he realise, as he sat before the head that morning, the significance of the answer he had given.

'You're sure?'

'Yes, definitely. Thank you for asking me. It's something I would love to do. I've thought on several occasions that I'd like to help other youngsters play, as I was helped when I was young, and I'm sure I could give them what they need. I've not heard them play and so I don't know at what level they're performing, but if they're as keen as you seem to be suggesting, I'm pretty sure there's something worth working on. Presumably, I can speak with them before the end of term to discuss how we'll proceed when we come back after the holidays?'

'Of course. It would help if you spoke to their teacher as well, but that may be difficult as we are so close to the end of term.'

'I'll see,' said Peter.

The head was clearly satisfied with Peter's response and wished Peter well as he rose and left the room. The circumspection with which he had entered the head's room had now gone, to be replaced with a measured exhilaration. It reflected an inner feeling that the head's request indicated more than simply asking him to help the young brass players. It was, to Peter, a further sign of recognition that his first years had gone well, and that he was now being seen as a fully-fledged member of staff, one who could be given extra responsibility, and one whom the head clearly thought had a future in the profession. What more could a young teacher look for at the end of his second year?

And then he remembered Catherine and the cottage.

CHAPTER 11

PETER GETS TRANSPORT

Catherine was due to come home for the start of the school year at the beginning of September. Her visit to Hull, the outcome of the sad loss of her mother, had been totally unexpected. In fact, the initial plan had been for her mother to come to Weberton to look after the family whilst Catherine was in hospital bearing her third child, and then for the following few weeks whilst she was recovering. Gregory had been expected in May and did not disappoint. Unfortunately, his gran' had died in the same month, with cancer the victor, despite all the efforts of the National Health Service.

Both Catherine's mother, Elizabeth, and her father, William, were born in Yorkshire. Her father had been a merchant seaman, as had been his father before him. Both had captained tug boats that ferried coal and other commodities down the River Ouse and along the coast to London and other East coast ports. The family was originally from Leeds, but had moved east as a result of the experience of Elizabeth's grandfather in the First World War. He had served in the navy, fallen in love with the sea, and established himself as a coastal skipper.

Naturally enough, Elizabeth was living close to the Humber estuary when she met William and married him. William was a smart young customs official, with brown sleeked hair, a carefully manicured moustache, and a slim figure. He had been posted to Goole for a couple of years to broaden his experience before returning to Hull, the city which was to become his more permanent station. His father edited the local paper in Hull, and some said that William had inherited some of his father's writing skills. He occasionally published a piece of poetry or a commentary in one of the local civil service journals.

The couple moved into a first floor flat in a quiet street on the outskirts of the city. The flat had two bedrooms, a sitting room, dining room, bathroom and kitchen. It was in no way ostentatious but served their purpose well and they seemed to have no desire to move to anything grander. Having survived the war years in one of the cities so heavily targeted by the Germans, they led a quiet life, mixing easily with long-term friends.

When Catherine was growing up her mother worked in the office of a technical supplies company once involved in the arms industry. Both Catherine's father and mother had introduced her to the children of the different families with whom they were involved. The relationships worked well, and Peter could draw on memories of photographs he had seen whilst visiting the flat, of Catherine with friends of her mother's at a work's party, and at a customs officers' dance sitting on her father's knee. Catherine's friendship with Margaret, her flat mate in London, was the outcome of those early days.

With retirement approaching, mother and father began taking their annual holidays in foreign holiday resorts, usually in Italy. Both were smokers, which was no doubt a factor in Catherine's mother's cancer and death. Despite the increasing evidence from research indicating the dangers to health of smoking, and the attempts of the medical profession to point out the dangers of nicotine, people continued with the habit. The perpetual myth that inhabits the souls of men, *It will not happen to me,* could be one explanation as to why people persist in smoking and seem unable to desist from the foolishness of the practice. Friends of William and Elizabeth, who had tried to stop smoking, found all sorts of reasons to take it up again, and few managed to give up the practice permanently, despite the coughing and spluttering that seemed to accompany the draw of the cigarette.

Although Catherine's mother had suffered for some time, depending on cortisone injections to enable her to live in some comfort, the news of her death came as a great shock to Catherine. Catherine was too close to pregnancy to attend the funeral and was distraught. Peter was unable to get paid leave from school and so nobody from Weberton could to go to Hull to provide support for Catherine' father at the funeral. As a sort of compensation, and she recognised that this was all it could be, Catherine decided to go across to her father's for a few weeks once she was fit enough to travel. It would be tough with the three young children, but there was no question that the visit was essential. Catherine knew that her father, who was more reserved than her mother and less likely to look for the social support offered by friends, was struggling with his loss and needed the love of someone near to him at this particular time.

Catherine's absence had some blessings for Peter and the cottage. Having made the purchase, he could now give time to considering how best to smarten it up and make it look at least liveable before Catherine returned. Fortunately, he had the six weeks of the summer holidays in which to tackle some of the issues, particularly those that could be quickly resolved, such as brightening the interior by removing the old furniture and splashing the walls with new paint. As to the more serious problems, such as the water supply and the drainage, much more time and money would be needed.

One of the trickiest jobs Peter faced was actually getting to the cottage. It was not possible until Peter had transport of his own, and he knew that funds were limited. He became dependent, therefore, on Maxine. Fortunately, whilst school was still in session, she could give him the help he needed. She was prepared to transport him to the cottage and stay to help in any way she could until such time as he decided to leave. She was then prepared to run him to a convenient bus stop so that he could get home. He knew, however, that he needed to get his own transport as quickly as possible.

He then had a piece of luck. He heard of a second hand van being for sale, cheap. A friend of his at the rugby club, Billy Smith, was a mechanic. He offered to go with Peter to look at it. When they saw it, to Peter's unskilled eye, it looked superb. Green, a steering wheel and four wheels were the first things he noticed. It also had an engine which started at the turn of the key. He thought, *What more do I want?*

Billy was more circumspect. He interrogated the salesman with questions such as, 'What year is the van? What's the van's history? How many previous owners has it had? What mileage has it done? What's its service record? What condition are the tyres in? Can I see the log book?'

The salesman had clearly been expecting such questions and answered with confidence, '1954 Morris Minor van. One owner. 54,000 miles on the clock. Serviced regularly, as the log book shows. The tyres have been changed recently.'

Billy looked around the van, opened the bonnet, and investigated what was underneath, a marvel of modern science in Peter's eyes. Having taken out the dipstick, Billy satisfied himself with the colour of the oil. He then perched himself on the driver's seat, switching on and off the lights, trying the brakes and seeing how easily the seats adjusted. After he had contented himself, he suggested a test drive. He and the salesman disappeared down the road and around the corner some hundred yards beyond the garage, returning about fifteen minutes later. To Peter's relief, all seemed well and the deal was done. The family had wheels!

Having dropped off Billy with many thanks, Peter decided to drive to the cottage, facing the four-in-one slope and the tight bends. The van, with its green paint blending wonderfully well with the colours of the moor, behaved admirably, and he made good progress. That was until he was on the steepest part of the hill and he met another car descending the rather narrow road. Reacting quickly, but without sufficient care, Peter steered to the left to allow the car to pass. But he steered too far, was too slow to adjust, and before he realised what was happening the nearside wheel mounted the grassy verge and ended up in a ditch. Desperation! Repeated attempts to reverse out failed. He was stuck!

He pondered a good while, going through his options, of which there were few. It was obvious that he was not strong enough to lift or to push the van free; he had no means of contacting anyone he knew to come and tow the van onto the road; and his knowledge of those who lived in the village meant that he was likely to be seen as a stranger and a nuisance if he asked for help. Even so, this was his only recourse.

Fortunately, he could see the speckled grey and brown slates of the roof of what appeared to be a farm, as if hiding tortoise like in a cluster of trees across the moor to his right. It looked to be at the end of a rough, non-macadamised path. Even if he could get over his embarrassment and go and ask for help, he was not sure that he would get the response he looked for. *Why should he?* he asked himself. He knew nobody other than Maxine and her family, and he suspected that the quiet, reserved life of a moorland smallholder bred a suspicion of the unfamiliar face.

Peter recognised that this was no time to be circumspect, however, and made his way down the track to the farm. His nervous tap on the door was eventually answered by the farmer's wife, a younger woman than he had expected, and one who had a prettiness that was not hidden by her working pinafore and rather dishevelled hair. She was clearly a young woman used to hard work and the demands of life on a small farm. Her hands, no doubt once small and delicate, now showed a roughness indicative of the work expected of her.

Peter, expressing his apologies for bothering her, introduced himself, explained his situation, and asked if there was any chance of help. He could see from the twinkle that brightened what had at first sight seemed saddened eyes, that she was amused by his predicament, but her sympathetic, 'Wait here a minute while I speak with Colin,' gave him hope.

'Thank God,' muttered Peter, 'the farmer's in.'

In a couple of minutes, Colin was at the door. 'What's thee problem?' he asked, peering at Peter with a steady eye. He held the door ajar, revealing his strong hands and muscular arms.

In a rather strained voice Peter answered, 'Well, my van has ended up in a ditch. I was coming up the hill when I met another car. I avoided it, but went too far and I'm stuck. I can't get the van back onto the road.'

'And so what's tha' want?'

Peter was a bit surprised at the question as he thought it would be obvious what he wanted, but he went on, 'Well, I wondered if you could use your tractor to drag me out. I think that's the only way I can manage to get on my way. You probably know I'm moving into the cottage on the bend just beyond the next farm,' added Peter hastily.

'I, I think I've sin thee,' he said, and then, to Peter's relief, added, 'A'l get mi' coat on and gi thee a hand.'

Peter walked back to the van, leant his back against it with some relief, and awaited Colin's arrival. The welcome sound of the tractor disturbed a couple of crows that had settled on the path, startling them to flight, whilst announcing a saviour for Peter. Colin assessed the situation quickly, jumped down from his tractor, and soon had a rope fixed to the rear bumper of the van. He climbed back on his tractor saying, 'Thee ger int' van, start it up and I'll pull thee art.'

An accelerating tractor engine, a tightening rope, a sharp jerk, and within seconds the van was safely back on the road. The effusive thanks were received but the offer of payment refused, and Colin and the tractor disappeared across the fields to do more fitting work.

Peter headed for the cottage thankful for the generosity of Colin. He hoped to be able to repay him some day.

On his arrival at the cottage, Peter conducted a thorough assessment of what could be done to make it look a more attractive proposition to Catherine on her return from Hull. It was obvious that it had to be cleared of the old and damaged furniture and carpets. There was also the food that had wasted and rotted in cupboards; eggs, cheese, bread and variety of lidless pots containing different jams. A range of condiments that looked as though they had inhabited the cupboard for years also had to be removed. Once the cottage was clear, he could see that a good deal of scraping, painting, sweeping and washing would have to follow, so that the cottage took on a new appearance and a more welcoming ambience. He listed the tasks in a small notebook, also itemising what assorted paraphernalia he needed for sprucing up the property.

He was fortunate in having extra time, one of the blessings of the extended summer holidays of a teacher, and the support of his two friends, Maxine and Roger. It took him several days to clear the cottage and when he was joined by Maxine and Roger, his rugby club friend, the washing, scraping and painting, followed by further washing, scraping and painting, were tackled with lively enthusiasm. If he were to avoid the worst of Catherine's wrath, the cottage had to be presented as attractively as possible, so that she would fall in love with it as had Peter. At times, he thought he was going to fall short of even the limited targets he had set, but he persevered. It helped that his two co-workers were very good friends and had a sense of humour. They sang, told stories and laughed, not being fully aware of how much they were achieving or of how important their efforts were in ensuring that Catherine left Peter with no more than aching ears. The basic objective was clear to all three, however, and they were prepared to do what was necessary to achieve it.

Peter had had to buy paint and brushes, Maxine had produced cleaning materials, and Roger had been happy to do what was asked. The old oak beams, original and beautifully adzed, were cleaned, and the sawdust, the residue from the hard working woodworm's activities, swept away. The old cupboard, emptied of its foul, redolent contents, was brushed and washed so that the indescribable filth left little or no trace. It took plenty of fragrant cleaning soaps to get it to an acceptable state, one which may not discourage Catherine from using it until such time as it could be replaced.

The paint was a rather nondescript colour but covered the walls and gave a light and airy appearance to the rooms—at least at first sight. A closer look told a different story. It revealed how temporary the work was likely to be and how much more would need to be done to ensure the quality that Peter knew Catherine would expect. The thick walls, typical of old seventeenth century cottages, had been rendered with a yielding, spongy plaster. In parts it was so soft to touch that it felt it would crack and fall at any moment. When bits parted company with the wall during the painting, they seemed to contain something of the nature of horsehair, which the enthusiastic workers assumed was part of the mixture that went to make up plaster those many years ago.

The fragile nature of the plaster in some areas was a worry, but it survived the painting; Peter hoped it would survive well beyond the first inspection. The walls did not have the luxury of skirting boards and the plaster zigzagged around the rooms, sometimes touching the floor, sometimes not. Despite their best efforts, the 'decorators' were unable to disguise this fact with the paint that they spread generously along the edges, and the unevenness remained. Around the two bay windows, one in the sitting room and the other in the dining room, were what appeared to be window seats. The removal of the dirty, dog-haired cushions, revealed the bare stone of what could become a useful seat, part of the thick old walls into which had been inserted the rather ugly square-fronted bay windows.

The floors creaked as the painters began their task upstairs, but the thickness of the oak beams and joists supporting the floor guaranteed their safety. Little could be done with the dividing wall, ostensibly separating two of the bedrooms, other than to re-nail it to the cross beam. Painted, it looked presentable, but made, as it was, of a sort of hardboard, it did little to hinder sounds passing between the adjoining rooms. Neither room was very large, just about big enough to take a double bed, and in Peter's mind would sleep Catherine and himself on the one side and the two girls on the other.

The third bedroom was even smaller and, as Peter had noted on his first visit, incapable of housing other than a single bed, or, if the need ever arose, a bunk bed. The window was of rotten wood which flaked as Peter began preparing it for painting, and it was clear that it offered an easy entrance to winter draughts. It did little to lighten the room, although when Peter leaned to peer through, it provided a captivating view of the moor and its inhabitants, as well as a sight of the occasional vehicle that swung round the rather sharp bend on which the cottage was situated.

The bathroom contained, to Peter's eye, all that was needed. The old soap was quickly removed and replaced with a sweet smelling bar of new soap, and the dirt and filth of the sink and bath washed away with a commercial cleaner. The floor had been covered with linoleum, now old and cracked, which would have to stay until Catherine passed judgement on it.

The saving grace of the upstairs was the beautiful scenery that could be seen surrounding the cottage. In what was to become the main bedroom, the view climbed up to the *Beacon*, taking in on its way the rocky outcrops, the heather, and the sheep mown moor grass. Other windows stretched out a view across a landscape of open fields, distant farm houses, and rugged walls. On the beautiful days of high summer, as the decorators moved from room to room, they were presented with different scenes as the moor adapted to the sun's passage.

Without the help of his friends Peter would have had little hope of achieving what was done. Some old furniture, which included a grandfather clock, the value of which Peter realised only when it was too late, had been moved into the barn. Other belongings of the previous owner such as jewellery boxes and the like also found their way into the barn. A couple of old cupboards were moved outside and chopped up for firewood, and some old furniture, including a broken bed and what pretended to be a carpet, was carted away by Maxine's father to a nearby dump. As a result, the cottage floor could be swept, the painting completed, and the windows cleaned.

In its emptiness the cottage appeared almost inviting. Peter felt more confident in his ability to demonstrate to Catherine the advantages the move offered, certainly when compared with their present situation. The potential for development of the cottage, with its outbuildings and land, had to be a real bonus, something that the family could work towards without the interference of neighbours. Similarly, the constraints of living on an estate would be replaced by an openness that could be enjoyed, in whatever way they wished, by the whole family. And to top it all, this would be a wonderful and exciting adventure into a life different to any they had previously experienced.

In addition, he could make much of the fact that the moor overlooked Binkley. The town and its environs were attractive and for centuries were a centre for those who sought fresh air and cool, healing waters. Scenically settling next to the River Wharfe, it provided a range of shops distinguished by their individuality.

There was also the ubiquitous supermarket, in which Peter was to spend more time in the years to come than he could have imagined. The weekly visit to town for shopping, and the frustrations of watching women pacing the supermarket shelves, were experiences that Peter would avoid if he could. It was beyond his understanding why shelves so captivated women. Men would stand with the steadily filling basket as their womenfolk slowly moved from one stopping place to another, like hunting cats prowling in the early morning along a hedge, stopping every now and then, still and silent, peering with a piercing focus that would allow nothing to escape. And then, with a sudden movement, out went the hand, like a cat's paw grabbing a mouse, to snatch a tin or a bottle before placing it in the basket. To Peter, women's concentration on the shelves was almost matched by his own concentration on the checkout point, and its growing queue spitefully prolonging his stay on the wrong side of the shop door.

The town also had a wide range of facilities for children and adults. As Peter had pointed out to Catherine when seeking to convince her of the merits of the cottage, 'There's a large riverside park with plenty of swings and roundabouts as well as sports facilities. I've seen people playing tennis and cricket and there's a good rugby pitch. I've seen golf and swimming advertised as well. I also saw advertised on a notice board at the town hall pictures that were being shown at the local cinema, which I'm sure you and the kids, as they grow older, would enjoy. There are also literature, art and music festivals at different times. The place seems to be alive with activity. A big plus is that there are buses and trains to Leeds and Bradford, as well as to Weberton. The fact that it's also near to my aunt's, who you know is always helpful when we need somebody to look after the children, is also a factor worth bearing in mind.'

In searching over all the positives of the move up onto the moor, Peter continued to hide all the unresolved issues that were still burrowing away in his mind. These would have to wait until Catherine had had a chance to see the cottage. He dare not raise issues related to schools and how the children would get to them; talk about the simple problem of shopping when there was no bus service across the moor; or refer to the need to resolve the essential issues concerned with the supply of good, clean water and adequate drainage. Another factor that remained nestling in its hiding place was the likelihood of Catherine, a sociable, garrulous person, being lonely. Even though they now had the van, she could not drive and would have to go through the whole process of passing a test to gain a licence. The more Peter allowed himself to think about the obstacles, the more they took on an intimidating force. In his excitement about the cottage, Peter had buried them deep in his sub conscious. As was his normal practice, that is where he hoped to keep them; yet he knew they would eventually surface and have to be resolved.

What Peter was also to learn later was something he had not foreseen. The white-housed farmer, on what was clearly a very small holding, kept a few cows, sheep, and pigs, as well as hens to provide eggs for his own use. Once settled into the cottage, Peter and the family learned that living to the east of the white house and in direct line with the prevailing westerly wind, meant that they suffered at certain times of the year from the rancid smell of pig 'muck', being spread by the farmer across his fields as manure. On those particular days, every corner of the cottage seemed to be infused with the smell, reminding the family of how farmers had to make use of everything that the country presented. Fortunately, after a couple of days it was gone, to be replaced by that pure fresh air and quietness so prized by both inhabitants of, and visitors to, the moor.

CHAPTER 12

A HOLIDAY INTERLUDE

During the summer holidays Peter made regular journeys up to the cottage, but he also had to keep an eye on things at home, as well as go in to school from time to time to prepare for the coming academic year. On occasions, he met Stan in the staffroom and together, over coffee, they took the opportunity to exchange ideas about what might make a worthwhile impact on the children. They recognised that the links between geography and history were strong, and that both had something to gain from exploring how they might capitalise on them. Both believed strongly that making connections across subjects was an excellent way of reinforcing pupils' learning.

It was Stan who came up with the idea of using the canal by the park.

'Look, Peter, I've been thinking about this idea for some time but never really found the right occasion on which to discuss it with you. Why don't we do a joint project on the canal? In geography, I could use the route of the canal to enable pupils to learn about the physical features through which it has to pass, while in history, you could use it to further develop pupils' understanding of the Industrial Revolution. It would even be possible to take the class out to the canal to look at the locks and talk about why they are needed and how they work. We could go further, and discuss with them the strengths and limitations of canals and what led to the coming of railways and the impact they made on people. I think we have the ideal visual aid.'

'That's a great idea. I'm all for it. I also think that Maxine would be interested. The possibility of sketching parts of the canal and its environs would appeal to her I'm sure. I'm seeing her up at the cottage tomorrow, and if it's OK with you, I'll raise it.'

'Fine by me. Tell you what. As it's such a fine day, let's go and have a look at the canal and work out in a bit more detail how we could use it.'

With that, the two of them rose from their chairs, put down their mugs, and made for the door.

'Hang on a minute. One of us needs a pad so that we can record our thoughts.' Peter turned back, went to the table and collected the notepad in which he had been doing some preparation for lessons earlier. They then left the staffroom, went through the front door of the school, round to the back of the building, through the gate, and in to the park.

It was one of those balmy summer days that attract people into the open spaces, determined to make the best of summer. Sitting in pairs and small groups, several had fridge boxes or baskets, indicating their intention to linger for some time on the grass and then take refreshment. Others were walking along the paths, admiring the flower beds blossoming with different coloured roses, the vivid petunias and rich begonias. Another attraction was the canal and the path along its bank. Here, a few young couples were strolling, taking advantage of the heat wave. Suits and ties suggested that some had taken a break from work, while others, the women in flowered summer dresses and the men in sports shirts and occasionally shorts, were clearly out for the day. From time to time, the two teachers, chatting about how best to use the canal, looked up to respond to the, 'Hello sir,' of pupils taking the opportunity to enjoy their holidays in the summery park.

Stan and Peter, aware of the sun's warmth, had left their jackets in school and both were in shirt sleeves. Therefore, despite their intended business, they matched effortlessly the scene through which they were walking. They made first for the lock at the far end of the park in order to see how they might use it to help the pupils understand its purpose. They were fortunate enough to find a couple of boats manoeuvring their way through and they stood to watch. Peter noted on his pad the actions of the boatmen in opening the lock gates and the time it took for the water to sink to the appropriate height to allow the boats to sail on. Both he and Stan began to formulate the sorts of questions they could ask the pupils about the lock and about this stretch of the canal.

Satisfied that they had gained enough from their observation of that section, they set off along the path in the direction of town and the bridge that would enable them to cross to the opposite bank. Peter became quite excited about the prospect of being able to raise questions about the impact of the canal on the economic development of Weberton in the nineteenth century. He also saw the opportunity of showing how it changed from a purely agricultural centre, famous for its sheep and wool, to one that developed industrial enterprises. He could then go on to demonstrate how, as the canal became outdated with the coming of railways, it became less economically viable. He was hoping that there would be some evidence around the bridge and on the edge of town that would allow him to demonstrate the changes.

They were still discussing the advantages of walking the pupils along the canal when, as they neared town, they saw a group gathering and pointing across to the other bank

'What's going on?'

Stan had asked the question, but Peter had the same query in his mind. It didn't take long for them to find the answer.

'Hells bells! It's that idiot Webster and his mates.'

On the opposite bank of the canal, Webster and a couple of his friends were jumping in and climbing out of the water. They were all stark naked! Stan and Peter knew all three, and all of them had reputations. Spiky Conway, notorious for never seeming to comb his hair, which, as a result, rather than lying flat on his head stuck up straight from the crown, was known as a close ally of Webster. Ginger Robinson, another member of Webster's clique, seemed to spend as much time standing in the corridor as he spent in the classroom because of his antics. They lived in adjoining houses on the Avenue, and frequently emerged from their homes to walk alongside Webster, their hero, to school. They were the type of boys who willingly joined with Webster in his exploits, but who rarely had sufficient ingenuity to do other than follow their idol. He was regarded by them, and several others, as their leader.

'Is that one of his young brothers and little sister standing watching?' asked Peter.

'Looks like it. I'll bet he's supposed to be looking after them. Blood and thunder! What's going to happen if they decide to jump in? We'd better get over there quick. Not only must they be breaking at least two laws, swimming in the canal and being naked in public, but they're all in danger. Don't they realise that a barge or a boat could come along at any minute? I've never seen anything so stupid.'

Peter signalled his agreement and the pair of them quickened their pace towards the bridge. Once across they headed back towards the boys and reached them just as Webster was climbing out of the canal.

'What are you doing, Webster?' was the best that Peter could muster.

'Havin' a bit a fun, sir. It's so 'ot we thought we'd have a swim.'

The lad seemed unabashed as he stood facing his teachers without a stitch of clothing on. Stan and Peter seemed to feel the embarrassment more than he did.

'Don't you realise you're breaking the law, that you're offending visitors to the park who didn't come to see you naked, and, I suppose most worrying of all, you're putting yourself and your brother and sister in danger? How would they get out if they decided to jump in? Do you think you'd be able to help?'

The tone of Stan's voice portrayed his anxieties but Webster appeared totally un-fazed.

'Dun't see a problem. Anyway, we're on 'olidy, so what's it to you?'

'You'll get what's it to us. Get yourself dressed and away from the canal, and hope nobody has reported you to the police.'

The mention of the police seemed to stir Webster and his friends more noticeably than had the arrival of Stan and Peter. They rubbed themselves down quickly with an article of their clothing and dressed. It was as he was about to leave that Webster turned to the people across on the other bank, gave them an obvious V sign with his fingers, and called, 'F . . . . k off.'

He then took hold of his sister's hand and ran off with his mates.

All Stan and Peter could do was to look on, shocked at the lad's behaviour. They realised there was no point in chasing after the boys and they were not sure what sort of punishment they could inflict even if they could catch them.

'All we can do is make a note of what has happened, how disrespectful the boys have been, and then report it when school re-starts after the holidays' said Peter as he began to write in his notebook.

'I agree, but to be honest, it's importance will have so faded with time and we'll be so taken up with preparing for the new term, that I suspect no one will be interested.'

'You're right Stan. Anyway, I've made a note of the date, time, place, and the youngsters involved, just in case.'

With that they began to retrace their steps. They crossed the bridge as those who had observed the whole spectacle were re-commencing their stroll. Embarrassed by the whole affair and knowing that among the watchers were parents of children at their school, Peter and Stan lowered their heads and endeavoured to look as though they were in deep conversation, simply enjoying their walk through the park. In as dignified a manner as they could, they made their way back to school.

The new school year was not due to begin for another couple of weeks. Stan and Peter agreed that by that time, memories of Webster's canal adventure would have faded and so it would probably be better to let the incident rest. They recognised that there would be matters that were of more importance at the start of a new term, and that to try to get much of a reaction from Mr Holdsworth or his deputy over something that had happened during the holidays was most unlikely.

CHAPTER 13

CATHERINE SEES THE COTTAGE FOR THE FIRST TIME

It was Friday morning. Peter found himself standing alone on Weberton station, waiting for Catherine's return from Hull. He was filled with excitement and a good deal of trepidation. He had missed her and the children, and on occasions, in spite of the unforeseen events that had occurred in their absence, had been overcome with feelings of forlornness and dejection. He always felt the same when away from Catherine, and now this included the children. In the evenings, or even during the day, when he was quiet, time seemed to stretch out, interrupted on occasions by his preparation of lessons for the new academic year, the occasional book, a visit to the supermarket, some preseason training at the rugby club, and the occasional band practice. But from time to time, he would feel the need to stand for a while at the sitting room window with hands in his pockets. He would look across the deserted street at *The King's Beacon*, complemented as it was by the surrounding moorland that encircled it like the ruff of a stately lady of a bygone age. After his purchase of the cottage, the scene had taken on a new and more pertinent meaning.

The intervening weeks since the fateful phone call announcing the purchase of the cottage had been more poignant than usual, because he knew that he had deeply upset Catherine. Knowing Catherine as well as he did, he had imagined her talking through with her father the implications of what he had done, on the one hand blaming Peter of thoughtlessness, and on the other, through her love for him, trying to find the justification for his decision. He knew her father, as sensible fathers do, would no doubt listen, nod, and *hmmm* at the appropriate times but would keep his counsel. Peter knew him well enough to know that he would not be drawn into interfering in the relationship of his daughter and son-in-law and would value both of them sufficiently to avoid wishing to be seen to take sides. This had always been his way. He displayed it never more obviously than on the momentous occasion of Catherine's marriage to Peter in a Catholic church. Despite his general antipathy to Catholicism, he maintained that same stoic approach. Peter had recognised the hint in his manner that indicated, *I've my own view on this matter, but it's not my business to interfere. They've to live with the decisions they make, and I'll let them make them. If they specifically ask for advice, I'll give it. Otherwise, I'll do as asked.*

At last, the train arrived.

Peter followed the carriage in which he had spotted Catherine and the children so that he would be on hand to help them down on to the platform when it stopped. For their part, as soon as they saw him through the window, Katie and Sarah began to wave excitedly, smiles

148

spreading across their faces. He waved back, mirroring their smiles as the elation at their return spread through him.

When the train stopped and the carriage door opened, he lifted the two girls off the train, returning their hugs with fond kisses. Katie animatedly began to tell him what they'd been doing at their grandpa's, but anxious to help Catherine, Peter disentangled himself and reached up for the luggage. He then helped Catherine, still holding Gregory, down from the train. She looked tired, her pale skin emphasising the dark circles under her eyes. She showed signs of worry. His own exhilaration at seeing his family again was somewhat dampened, especially when Catherine did no more than offer her cheek for a welcoming kiss. He rightly inferred that she was determined to let him know that she was not happy.

Once out of the station, Peter led the way to the van. 'What d'you think?' he asked as he opened the door, hoping that the sight of their own transport would ease the tension.

'Hmmm, I suppose it's better than having to walk from the station. Come on. Let's get home. We're all tired. In you go, children. Peter, where are the back seats?'

'Oh, I forget to mention it. It doesn't have any because it's designed to carry goods in the back. That's one reason why it was cheaper than I expected. I thought it would be OK, especially while the children are small, because we can put cushions in the back for them to sit on.'

'Huh,' muttered Catherine, raising her eyebrows skywards, implying that she was witnessing another shambles.

By this time, Katie and Sarah had eagerly scrambled into the back of the van and were waiting to be taken home. Peter held Gregory while Catherine climbed into the front seat and passed him over to her. He then rounded the front of the van to take his place in the driving seat. With one switch of the key, the van started and they were away.

The edginess did not cool on the journey or once the family had arrived home. No mention was made of the cottage.

The two girls were as frisky as ever. After Peter had helped them out of the van, they ran down the path to the front door and excitedly waited for it to be opened. Once inside, they dived into their toys, and in minutes the floor was as it always seemed to be: covered with children's playthings. Meanwhile, Peter carried the cases and the pushchair into the house and Catherine took in Gregory. The relationship between husband and wife remained tense, and Peter did not dare be the first to mention the cottage.

Eventually, the children were fed, and together Peter and Catherine put them to bed.

It was only when they had finished their own supper and were about to relax that Catherine let Peter know what was in her mind and what she thought of his actions. The tirade went on for some time, and as Peter's attempts at defence did nothing to appease Catherine, he simply sank into an apologetic package in his chair. From the moment he had given her the welcome-home kiss as she alighted from the train, Catherine had been unable to give Peter the smile that he anxiously looked for. There was no softening of Catherine's attitude now they were in 29 Brent Road. She was upset, and Peter had to know it.

Even in bed, Catherine discouraged Peter's advances, and she made it clear that she would not offer the intimacy that usually characterised their relationship when they met after days apart. The only thing that they agreed on was that a visit to the cottage had to be made as soon as possible. It was clear that Catherine wanted to see the outcome of Peter's actions. They decided that a visit the following day would suit her purpose.

Exchanges remained frigid next morning as Peter and Catherine discussed the visit to the cottage. Peter could not go until the afternoon because of a preseason meeting at the rugby club. When he returned for lunch, he ate almost in silence. He was anxious about the forthcoming visit to the moor and his anxiety intensified as Catherine, unusually, also hardly said a word. She wanted him to know that she was not going to excuse his behaviour easily.

Even so, hiding it very well from Peter, she could not avoid that tingle of excitement that affects everyone approaching the unknown. In Catherine's case, the descriptions that Peter had given her of the cottage had raised her curiosity and expectations, but there had been enough gaps in the information he had given that it had left her with doubts she could not dismiss.

Whilst Catherine dressed the children and prepared for the journey to the cottage, Peter walked down the driveway to where he had parked the van. Having organised the interior to ensure everyone's comfort, he backed up to the front door of the house. First, the children climbed into the back and organised the cushions to their requirements, and then Catherine sat next to Peter with Gregory on her knee.

'Everyone ready?' Peter asked jokingly as though a guide on an official tour, trying to lighten the atmosphere. He pulled the starter and released the handbrake.

As they approached the moor, Peter's confidence began to wobble. The vision of the cottage and its surrounds that had been imprinted on his mind and had supported him in his conversations with Catherine were fading. Somehow, the fields did not seem as inviting as before and the walls did not hold the same fascination they had on earlier visits. The sky seemed lower. Its billowing clouds were resting on the hills as though tired rather than flitting across the sky and leaving space through which they could present the sun in scene after scene of joy. The cottage, instead of harmonising with its surroundings, now looked buried in a hollow into which it had sunk since his previous visits.

In his nervousness, he wondered what Catherine was thinking. He was beginning to rely more and more on the love and trust that they had always placed in each other. It was these two elements that helped them rebuild the structures designed by their love that looked to be crumbling when any disagreements or actions threatened to drive them apart.

What Peter did not know was that, despite her annoyance with him, Catherine was beginning to feel a curious expectancy as she sat by his side in the van. He glanced at her from time to time to try to judge her reaction. But he was not to know that, as the van left the main road and began to climb across the moor, she was being affected by the tranquillity of the landscape and the innocent welcoming of an environment provided for the needs of the wide range of creatures which lived contentedly off its nourishment. Neither did he know that the journey was bringing back to her some of her most endearing memories of her hiking days in the Lakes and that she had begun to feel, creeping upon her, an affinity with what she could see through the van window.

Meanwhile, the children sat relatively quietly in the back of the van, playing with the toys that they found there and totally unaware of the tense atmosphere in front of them. Too young to understand what was happening, they had no idea of their destination.

And now it was in sight. The steep hill and the challenging bends had been successfully negotiated before Peter said, 'There it is.'

There was no word from Catherine as she got out of the car and approached the door. Taking Gregory from her, Peter wondered what was going through her mind. Had he known, he would have felt more optimistic than he did.

Catherine was enjoying what she saw. Holding back any outward sign of her thoughts, she could see what had attracted Peter. The setting was idyllic. She loved open spaces and was enthralled by the richness of the perfumes that emanated from them like the scent of good wine in the glass. On her summer vacations in the Lake District, Catherine had come to enjoy the freshness of the mornings as she set out on her daily treks across the mountains and the mellowness of the evenings as she returned to the hostel. To say that she was enraptured by what was now before her would be to underestimate its impact on her imagination. Like darts flying through the air before striking a board, visions of what pleasures the cottage's surroundings offered to the family flashed into her mind.

As they approached the door, she could not restrain her feelings any longer. 'How did you manage to be offered such a super place?' she asked.

Peter's expression freshened and the pace of his speech quickened. 'I was lucky to be at the right place at the right time,' was his relieved response. 'Maxine was in a bit of a quandary as to what to do with the cottage. I'd mentioned to her that I was unhappy in Weberton and then the whole thing came together.' After a slight, telling pause, he added, 'You can't believe how glad I am to hear you say you like it. I've been living in misery, terrified of your reaction, since I made the decision to buy. It's great to hear you say you like it.'

But he knew that there was still the interior to come. He wondered what impact it was likely to have. As they entered, Catherine became a little more hesitant. She noticed that the door did not open easily and that the square bay windows were somehow incongruous, set as they were within the grey stone walls. Once through the door and into the empty dining room, she began to survey with the eyes of a wife and mother.

It was a while before she spoke, a time during which all Peter could do was watch and wait. For their part, the children had taken off, like gambolling lambs, in search of different experiences in and outside the cottage.

'At least it's clean and looks to have been freshly painted. It looks as though someone's been busy,' she said with a smile.

'You betcha,' replied Peter, thinking back to the long days he and his friends had spent trying to get the cottage presentable.

Peter followed Catherine as she led the way through the cottage whilst the children played outside. They toured the downstairs and then the upstairs before going through the back door to take a quick look at the outbuildings. They then returned in to the cottage so that Catherine could take a more focussed look at the interior.

As was her wont, she was quickly planning, seeing things that Peter had not had the inclination to consider. To him a room was a room, but to Catherine it became a space that provided infinite opportunities for her creativity. She was already placing different pieces of furniture in the dining room and sitting room, imagining which carpets would go where, how the photographs would best be placed, and what could be done in the kitchen. As they climbed the stairs, she said, 'Hmmm, we need to do a lot up here.'

Peter could only agree.

'Nevertheless, I'm pretty sure I'll have plenty of time,' she added with a hint of cynicism that let Peter know that he was not yet fully forgiven, but also betraying a growing commitment to what the cottage and its surrounds had to offer.

Peter was now beginning to feel more optimistic about Catherine's reaction. For him, the clouds had lifted, the sun was smiling, the cows were mooing, the sheep were bleating, and the birds were singing. Welcome was in the air. Peter was beginning to get strong vibes as to the success of the visit. By the time they reached the third bedroom, even he was making suggestions, willing to add his own ideas as to how the cottage could be converted into a place worthy of his family. After peering through the window, Catherine turned to Gregory, who was still in Peter's arms, gently pinched his cheek and said, 'And this is your room, little fellow.'

As yet, the really tricky aspects of the purchase which niggled away at Peter and could ruin what was going so well, had not been touched upon. The less they were raised, the more chance there was of Catherine remaining positive about the cottage and the new opportunities it seemed to offer the family. There was no chance that they could be avoided indefinitely, however. Once raised, answers would be difficult to find.

The reference to a school bus eased the tension.

'No problem there,' he told her. 'A taxi comes round the village every day to pick up and deliver the children who go to school in Binkley. It works well, according to the locals.'

However, this was the only question he could answer with any confidence as the questioning began again. 'How do I do the shopping? What do I do when you are at school? How do our friends come to see us if they don't have a car? What's it going to cost to move here? What are you going to do with ten acres of land?'

He shared what answers he had, but they did not add up to much and he knew that they lacked the precision that would have given Catherine the sort of comfort she was looking for. She was not surprised by his failure to respond, as she knew that his thoughts often circled around his own needs before finding time for those of others. In fact, she had been surprised by his knowing about the school bus.

Peter was also aware of his selfishness but could not resist it, even though his actions might have an adverse effect on the lives of others. He was often angry with himself for surrendering to it but realised that the spontaneity of his decision making usually meant that his struggle to contain it often occurred too late to enable him change direction. As a result, while his decisions could bring a quiet feeling of achievement to himself, they could dismay others. In this instance, he had become increasingly aware that his decision to buy had serious implications for Catherine and yet had only a limited impact on his own life. He foresaw that he would continue almost as always but with the new dimension of making the cottage habitable.

It was strange that he recognised it in others as well as in himself, and he wondered what it was in human nature that enabled it to persist. Whether it was an outcome of spoiled childhood or the offshoot of teenage desire to have, sometimes despite the consequences, he was unsure. His intuitive understanding of human behaviour suggested to him that it was a universal trait and one that from time to time spawned dissension in human relationships. He could find some solace on occasions by regarding his motivation as self-interest rather than selfishness, less iniquitous to his mind in that it did leave some space for giving thought to the needs of others.

Peter's first recollection of a significant occasion when selfishness surfaced in his own life was when, while still a very small boy in post-war Britain and rationing was still in force, a good lady had been distributing cakes on Bonfire Night. He had already had enough when she offered more and he could not resist. After one bite, he could eat no more and threw what was left away. This did not go unnoticed by the good lady, the mother of his friend, who pounced on what she described as his greed and selfishness. His feeling of guilt was real but seemed to have little impact on him other than to raise his awareness of his weakness.

On several occasions through his life, the same urge of desire had arisen and more often than not he had surrendered. Although he recognised moral issues in his behaviour, he had grown to prefer his weakness to that of others who seemed to have an opposite propensity. These were people who displayed a generosity that was beyond any expectation, but it was a generosity that reflected, to his mind, a desire to either control another or win some sort of undeserved approval or favour from those it affected. To Peter, this demonstrated a different and worse form of selfishness.

Even so, Peter could not avoid recognising that his own weakness had often taken command of his desires and actions, and no matter what explanation he found for what he had done, he was aware that he had again overstepped natural expectation. He knew he was asking of Catherine what would be seen as impossible by many, and he felt the guilt, but it had not changed his desire. Despite the many obvious difficulties, he was prepared to persuade her to see what an exciting new start this could be to their lives. Loving as she was, Peter believed that Catherine was more likely to accept the possibilities rather than the negatives. Consequently, he felt she could be swayed into acceptance by his words and by the excitement displayed by the children on what to them was a new playground. While Gregory sat in his father's arms, Katie and Sarah frisked around the cottage and into the field then back into the cottage, buzzing with delight and expectation. To them, the cottage and its environs were already becoming home.

For her part, Catherine, having completed her first cursory inspection, was walking hither and thither in the cottage, indicating to Peter, though not expecting much of a response, which piece of their furniture could go against this wall and which would be better against another. Back in the dining room and looking at what appeared to be the framework of a large fireplace, she said, 'If that were uncovered and it was what I think it is, it could become the central focus of this room and, perhaps, will help it recapture some of its former glory.'

'I agree. It'll provide for a good fire, especially in winter. I'm pretty sure we'll need one up here.'

Together they identified the adjacent room as the sitting room, which would take the easy chairs and the couch that Catherine's parents had bought as a wedding gift some years previously. Things began to fit into place as easily as they always seemed to do when Catherine took charge and Peter stood back to offer only a token commentary, usually in support of what was suggested. The cottage was to become Catherine's domain and Peter a willing serf who was asked sometimes for affirmation of what was being planned. This had always been the accepted strategy since the early days of marriage and to them was a natural routine of their relationship.

Certainly to Peter it was. He had seen his parents operate in the same way and, as far as he knew, it was the way every other family operated in the street in which he had spent his childhood. Where the marriage went awry, in Peter's mind, was if the husband did not strive to ensure that the family had a worthwhile income, or where the wife failed to provide those comforts that were expected. As his thoughts raced over the implications of such a relationship, one that he had come to doubt as the years unfolded and attitudes changed, he still could not help but recognise the responsibility he had for ensuring the well-being of his family. He had recognised some time ago that if he was to stay in teaching, a job he loved, his only way of meeting the new challenges of marriage and family was to impress his superiors and earn promotion. He delighted in feeling that his end-of-term meeting with the head had set him on the first important steps.

'When do you think we can move in?' was Catherine's first question once they were back in the van and on their way home.

Peter had no immediate answer. 'We need to put our house on the market. A lot then depends on how quickly it sells. My concern is that it is not in the most attractive part of Weberton and that some renovation is required if it is to attract a buyer.'

'Do you think we'll get as much for it as we paid?'

'I'm sure of that. House prices have gone up, though former council houses still tend to be relatively cheap. We're lucky in that we are under no real pressure to sell, as Maxine will be patient now that she knows we intend to buy. She's not asked for a deposit and says we can start the weekly payments once we move in. So, for the time being, it means we can continue to pay the mortgage for Brent Road without any extra pressure.'

Catherine replied, 'We'll need some extra cash for even the basic renovations that are needed before we can move the children up into the cottage. You realise that, don't you?'

'I suppose so. The best thing will be for you to contact the estate agent on Monday and ask him to give a price and get it on the market.'

'I'll do that. Perhaps we can begin to move some things in the meantime, so as to be ready?'

'Will tomorrow be soon enough?' Peter joked as he turned into the estate and began to look for somewhere to park, a perennial problem where the houses were so closely knit. The open spaces of the moor seemed ever more appealing as he parked some fifty yards from the house and had to trundle down the narrow street with the children and their belongings. As usual, they felt the eyes of those he taught following their every move. But there was a jauntier step in Peter's walk than had been the case when he had left in the morning. Catherine's obvious enthusiasm for the cottage was encouraging him to believe that in purchasing it he had made the right decision.

CHAPTER 14

THE NEW SCHOOL YEAR

Peter approached his responsibilities now as a teacher with some experience. Initially, as a rookie, he had been like most newly qualified teachers, unsure of the responsibilities he would have or of the colleagues with whom he would be working. Now he had the confidence of a teacher with two years' experience under his belt and he was, seemingly, recognised by his headteacher as having a promising future in the profession. In addition, he had colleagues with whom he had established positive relationships. With some, Peter and Catherine had become very good friends, delighted to share an evening at one or other's homes. A regular had been Stan and his wife Marjorie. They lived some ten miles from Weberton but were happy to go across to Brent Road for dinner, to join Peter and his family in the local park, or occasionally accompany them out to dinner. Both Peter and Catherine regarded such friendships as important in establishing them in the town and, when added to the friends that Peter had made at the rugby club, such as Roger, and in the local band, they extended their relationships beyond their immediate family circle.

On this first morning of the new year the staffroom was buzzing as colleagues exchanged stories of their vacations. Arthur had enjoyed a fabulous month in the Alps, John had been camping in the South of France, and Maxine had found time to visit friends on the Isle of Wight. Their stories and those of others who had been fortunate enough to spend time in distant and, presumably, exciting parts, were tossed around as staff began to organise themselves for the year's work.

The same could not be said for Webster. Peter was disappointed to hear that he had been in trouble for a second time during the holidays. He had linked up with two of his friends, Trevor Makin and William Skelton, and run foul of the police. It was the deputy head, Tom, who told Peter and a small group of colleagues sitting in the corner of the staffroom the story.

'I gathered from a neighbour the other day that Webster had been defacing the bus stop in front of the co-op with two of his mates, young Makin and Skelton.'

'That pair. So Webster has got mixed up with them again. Why is it that rogues seem to find rogues, even though they're not of the same age? It's not good for a youngster like Webster to be associating with them. They're a couple of years older than he is.'

Tom nodded, agreeing with Peter's assessment. The two older lads were well known in school, and particularly so by Peter. He had come across them just before the holidays, bullying a younger boy and trying to get money from him. Makin was a tall, strong looking young man with cropped hair that finished with a black fringe on his forehead. His mean face had a hardness that spoke, *Take care,* to any other boy who might wish to challenge him. He bore himself as a leader, and having fought and beaten the best in the school expected to be followed. It was this that attracted Webster to him. Skelton was a smaller lad but equally combative, capable of holding his own in a fight. He had more the attributes of a follower than a leader, however, which made him good fodder for the likes of Makin. Both of them had been responsible for a good deal of trouble at school and provided a model for Webster to imitate.

'Anyhow,' continued Tom, 'a police car was passing and stopped. Apparently, before the lads knew what was happening, they'd been collared. They were taken to the police station where they were given a severe warning as to their future behaviour.'

'Were they released?' asked Peter, perhaps showing a little more interest than his colleagues.

'Yes, but, apparently, only after their parents had been in to the station and promised to ensure that the boys would behave in future. Statements were taken and had to be signed and the police apparently went through all the trappings of the law, as much to frighten the lads as anything. Apparently, the Websters refused to go at first, and young Joe had to wait an extra couple of hours until they eventually turned up.'

'How typical. But it serves him right,' said Stan. 'For me those hooligans are not worth worrying about. Peter and I had the joys of meeting Webster in the holidays swimming naked in the canal with some of his friends. They were cheeky to members of the public and deserved a good rattle.'

'Have you drawn it to the head's attention? It's the sort of thing that he should know about in case he gets some queries from the authorities.'

'Didn't think it was worth worrying him, Tom. He's enough on his plate. Anyway, what's he going to be able to do? They were on holiday.' Stan had sufficient status in the staffroom to be able to say this and have it accepted by Tom as a reasonable response.

With that, the group had to break up and join other staff in preparing for the new term. Some were checking with the office to find out if books they had ordered for the new term had arrived, whilst others were at the stockroom, requesting new exercise books, pencils and pens in readiness for the needs of their pupils. The timetable was also of key interest as teachers compared with colleagues how they had fared. One perennial was how many non-teaching periods each had and why some had more than others.

Tom, who constructed the timetable, found himself at the centre of discussions as he tried to explain the outcome of his holiday task. Only he knew how many different coloured pieces of paper had littered his spare room floor as he had endeavoured to fit in four periods of English and mathematics for every class, schedule different classes in a given year in such a way as to allow teachers to organise pupils into ability sets, and ensure that no teacher was overstretched. Above all, he had to avoid clashes on the timetable that would lead to the chaos of pupils going to the wrong rooms and teachers having two or more classes arriving at their room at the same time.

Peter had found through experience that it was wrong to assume that the design of a timetable fell naturally into shape. In his time at school he discovered that the first days rarely passed without some unexpected hitch. The calm he had expected was disturbed by rougher seas, and he learned that despite the long hours spent by Tom, his manual jigsaw habitually perished during the first week back at school.

Peter picked up his timetable from the office and to his relief did not see 1C, but his joy was quickly dispelled when he realised that Webster and his friends would now be in 2C. *Am I teaching that class?* flashed through his mind like a meteor with nowhere to rest until it was absorbed in the stratosphere. Further relief, as 2C did not appear on his timetable. It was with a more buoyant spirit than he had expected when he sat down with his colleagues to listen to the head's introduction to the new academic year.

The head, who had entered the staffroom almost unnoticed, took his place behind a table that had been conveniently placed for his use. He started by sorting his papers and then proceeded with, 'Welcome to everyone. I trust you all had a good break and are now ready for the new term.'

There were several ironic chuckles around the room as he said, 'ready for the new term', but this hid the fact that for most it was good to be back at school. They were to restart what they had been trained to do, educating the future generation.

The head, as was customary at the start of a new academic year, took the opportunity to introduce new members of staff. On this occasion there were two: a rather pretty young woman, with all the attributes to make her the centre of male interest, to teach physical education; and a tall young man, with early thinning hair, whose subject was mathematics. The meetings were also used by the head to draw attention to any changes in school procedures and policies, and to any National or Local Authority directives that were likely to affect the staff or the school. Nothing much attracted Peter's attention, as little had changed and it seemed as though his third year would progress much as had his last.

'Now we've made one or two changes in classes. You'll remember that last year we had some forms that were problematic, mainly because of the mix of pupils. Tom and I've been discussing this over the holidays. We decided that rather than keep classes the same, there'd be some advantage in splitting up some of the groups.'

Peter's ears pricked up. Where was this leading? He certainly knew of one class that had proved difficult and had without doubt an insalubrious mix of pupils.

'Normally, we move pupils to ensure that the brightest are together, and we've continued to do this. So Bill Parker, who came on a lot last year, has been moved from 3B up to 4A, and Jenny Roberts from 1C up to 2B, in the hope that they will continue to make the good progress they made last year. To split some difficult groups, we've decided to move Jane Wallace to 4C and Michele Barlow to 4B, hoping that they'll settle away from their closest friends. Webster is to move to 2D'.

A quick glance at his timetable confirmed Peter's worst fears—he had 2D. He could not help a dry smile, especially as his good friend Stan looked across at him with what could only be described as a beam, as though he was enjoying Peter's obvious discomfort at the news.

When the head had finished what he had to say and answered questions from the staff, he left the staffroom with Tom and returned to his study. The meeting broke into chatting groups as teachers discussed what had been revealed, collected bits and pieces, and then made their way to their rooms to prepare for the arrival of the pupils on the following day. Peter recognised that this period in school, before the arrival of the pupils, was a critical time. Free of distractions, he could organise his classroom thoughtfully, taking into consideration the likely demands of the plans he had been preparing over the vacation, and ensuring that he had sufficient appropriate materials with which to support pupils' learning.

Peter knew that many of his colleagues had spent much of their six weeks break preparing lesson plans, re-organising their resources and stockrooms, ensuring that the appropriate equipment was available, and enhancing their teaching space with appropriate displays. Although he had spent many days in the cottage, he had also, like them, been in school from time to time preparing for the new term, and had been working hard in the evenings to modify his schemes of work and his teaching plans. He was keen to ensure that each class he taught had challenging learning pitched at a suitable level for the range of ability within it. Like a bird preparing its nest, he had spent time in and out of his classroom, carrying and distributing those things necessary to make it welcoming accommodation for those who were to use it. To Peter, the classroom was a learning environment which could, if properly prepared, provide a worthwhile return on his efforts through the interest it could stimulate in his pupils.

On the following day, once the pupils were back in school, it was clear that Tom had done a good job with the timetable. A few problems arose, some pupils going to the wrong room and some joining the wrong class, but the school quickly settled into its usual routines. Peter felt he had a good balance of classes, with some of high ability and others in which pupils' literacy and numeracy skills were known to be below standard. He knew he had 2D and Webster, but reckoned it would be a lesson or two before Webster found his feet in his new class. He even dreamed that the change might encourage Webster to shake off his bad boy image.

The first week was taken up with issuing new exercise books for pupils' best work, and rough working books for note taking. Peter also took time to remind pupils of class rules and impressing upon them what he expected in terms of ruled margins and dated exercises. Only in the second week did Peter get into the more serious phase of teaching the history he had planned.

It was also in the second week that Peter eventually made contact with the budding brass players. From the first note, it was clear that they had been well taught. He saw the stretch of the lips, the sharp intonation as the tongue struck, and the movement of the diaphragm as they took in breath. However, he was quickly aware that the cheeks became puffed, as they failed to control the air with their stomach muscles. This allowed the air into their mouths with a force that pressed against their cheeks, seeking a quick exit. He knew from his own experience that this could restrict the ability to control the flow of air or to reach the higher notes with comfort, as, like the wasted force of a badly tuned engine, the power of the muscles in the lower body was being squandered.

His first few lessons, therefore, were spent encouraging Arthur and Alan to think about controlling their breathing and refusing to allow the cheeks to inflate. Not surprisingly, they found it difficult initially, but gradually they grasped the essentials of the technique. The main target that Peter set them in the short term was to bring more control to their breathing whilst practising a couple of tunes from their *Tune A Day* book, and this they did with admirable perseverance. Peter was thoroughly enjoying the sessions and could see how he might help the boys over the coming weeks.

News of Peter's involvement with teaching brass gradually spread to other pupils and then to the school as a whole, when, just before half-term, the boys opened a school assembly by playing, as a duet, *All Through the Night*. Peter had discussed with Mr Holdsworth the possibility of the boys playing in assembly, and the value of setting a date to give them a target to aim for. The head had agreed to the last assembly before half term, which gave Peter and the boys three weeks of regular practice in order to reach an appropriate level of performance.

Even so, he was not surprised that they were extremely nervous when called onto the stage by the head. The head explained to the rest of the pupils, 'Arthur and Alan are receiving weekly lessons as part of the school's policy to encourage as many as possible of you to take up music. They've worked very hard and are making excellent progress. There are also other pupils in school who play different instruments and, as I look around, I can see a violinist, someone who plays the flute and also . . . . Jane Rogers, who we all know plays the piano. Jane, you will remember, played for us at the end of last term. I hope we'll hear all our different instrumentalists as the term progresses. But first we are going to listen to Arthur and Alan.'

With a smile, he nodded to Peter who had been waiting with the boys in readiness to start, once the head had finished his introduction. To Peter's delight, the boys rose to the challenge, were disciplined in their approach, and achieved the quality he was seeking. They made a precise start, which was followed by well-articulated controlled playing. Their nervousness quickly disappeared as, like young ducklings taking their first dip in water, the further they progressed the more confident they became. By the time they had finished, Peter had the impression that they would have loved to continue.

The expression and tunefulness of the playing impressed staff and pupils alike and was a topic of conversation for the next couple of days. The head complimented Peter on the boys' performance, Stan said he'd been delighted, and John, with a knowing wink, said, 'That's the way to show them it's all worthwhile.'

The interest it stirred led to Peter being approached by other pupils who expressed a desire to learn to play. The problem, he explained to them, was lack of instruments, but if they could find a way of acquiring their own they could join the group.

It was not long before a further two pupils turned up at the sessions after school looking for tuition. They had persuaded their parents to buy them cornets. Peter was impressed by their keenness and by the speed with which they adapted to the new skills they were learning. The duet was now a quartet. There were still other interested pupils, however, who could not become involved because of the lack of instruments. And then, by coincidence, Peter learned that a works band in the next town had gone defunct because the factory had closed down. As a result, all the instruments, sheet music, uniforms, and other equipment were to be auctioned. Peter thought this might present opportunities to extend the number of players, and he went to see the head about the possibility of being given money with which to go to the auction.

The head was enthusiastic to the extent that he said he would go along with Peter. This was more than Peter expected, but as he had no capital himself and did not know what the school could afford, he thought it might turn out to be beneficial to have the head by his side. No way could he have foreseen how beneficial. The head became engrossed in the auction, willing to bid for anything that Peter suggested would help the young musicians. He successfully bid for an Eb bass, two tenor horns, a euphonium, a baritone, a trombone, a couple of cornets, and a flugelhorn.

Peter could not help but be slightly embarrassed, wondering what his colleagues back at school would think. They usually made do with minimal resources for their subjects, even if they knew of more suitable learning materials on the market, because of what they thought were limited school finances. Here, in front of Peter's eyes, the head was spending well beyond what anyone dreamed was available. It was as though the head had been impulsively sucked into the competitiveness of the auction, rather like a novice paying his first visit to a bookmaker's shop might be tempted to bet beyond his means. He seemed to have been taken over by an incomprehensible urge to compete successfully, and an unquenchable desire to outdo competition.

At one point, Peter almost cried 'Enough', but the head seemed to be in no mood to listen. He would wave his registration number in response to that of any other bidder once he had decided to buy, without seemingly giving thought to the amount. Luckily, the instruments were bought, according to Peter's reckoning, at reasonable prices, as most of those present were dealers who were rarely prepared to bid beyond what would not give them a worthwhile profit on a resale. The seeming aggressiveness of the head's approach no doubt worked in his favour. By the time he was ready to leave, he had purchased enough to give Peter the basis of a brass band. Peter was overwhelmed.

On the drive back to school, Peter thanked the head profusely. Already, plans for the future of the instruments were taking shape in his mind. He was not daunted by the prospect. His experience in banding over many years gave him the confidence to believe that he could help youngsters progress and, in doing so, repay the head's generosity.

The following day, Peter announced in assembly that there were some instruments available and anyone interested should stay behind for a few minutes so that he could take their names. His intention was to ask the ones he chose to come to see him at break in order to go over in more detail what would be expected of them. The whole process seemed very straightforward. As pupils filed past, those interested gave him their names, which he added to his list. Then, the shock. The name Webster was called out.

Peter looked up with a start. The lad had eventually found his feet in 2D, gathered around him his supporters and begun, once again, to make Peter's lessons problematic. On one occasion the class had been disturbed by the banging of a desk lid every time Peter turned to the blackboard, started, he guessed, by Webster, but taken up by others at intervals. Unable to identify the culprits directly he could do little other than to warn that if he caught anyone they would be heavily punished. What he dare not do was guess as to who was the culprit and punish the wrong person, or threaten to punish the whole class. He was in this situation because staff had been advised by the head at morning staff meeting that a whole class should not be punished for one or two miscreants, as he was dealing with parents complaining that their innocent children were suffering as a result of the practice. As a result, Webster and his followers went largely unpunished.

Had Peter known what Webster had been up to on that morning whilst on his way to school, he would have been even more circumspect about entertaining his desire to join the band. Webster was finishing off his sandwich breakfast, when he came across young Ron Smethurst, sitting on a wall awaiting his school friends. Webster was in low spirits as he thought of desks, pens, books and, to his mind, too-demanding teachers. As soon as he saw Ron, his mood lightened.

Young Smethurst was nine and still at primary school. He was a quiet lad and popular with his contemporaries. He was wearing a clean shirt, pullover and smartly pressed short trousers. His shoes had been polished that very morning. His appearance was in direct contrast to that of Webster. If he hoped that Webster would carry on his way and he would be left in peace to await his friends he was to be disappointed, because the bullying Webster saw a good chance of a little sport and the possibility of brightening his mood.

As he approached, he called, 'Hi, Ronny boy. What's tha' doin' 'ere sittin' s'quietly.'

'Waiting for Mick and Frank.'

Seating himself next to Ron, Webster, talking through a mouthful of sandwich, started disarmingly, 'And so what's tha' bin up to, Ronny?' As if he had not expected an answer, he continued, 'As t' bin to t' pictures lately? Mi' mates say there's a good cowboy film on at t' Plaza.'

'No, I only go to t'pictures on Saturday mornings when they put special films and cartoons on for us kids. Everybody I know gus. They show good films on Saturdays.'

'That's for little kids that stuff. Got so bored last time I went up there I gor into a fight and was turned aht. Never bothered going back since. You wanna come up to t'Plaza of an evening an' see a good film.'

It was just at this point that Webster saw Mick and Frank approaching in the distance. Suspecting that their presence might hamper his designs on their friend, he stood up and nonchalantly taking the half-chewed sandwich from his mouth, rubbed it into Ron's face.

'Enjoy that, Ronny boy,' he said as he moved off, laughingly, in the direction of his school.

Ronald was left in disarray and almost in tears as he wiped the remains of strawberry jam and crumbs from his face and clean shirt. By the time Mick and Frank arrived he had almost finished. They sympathised, but not one of the three expected anything else from Webster and none of them was brave enough to challenge him.

This was the Webster who was feared by most of his contemporaries; the Webster who, having discomforted Ronny, felt more pleased with himself than he had when he set off from home. Then he had been somewhat downcast, the victim of his mother's tongue. Now he had had fun with Ronny, and he felt better for it.

Webster! Peter's antenna was out quickly. How could Webster believe that Peter could entertain him as a musician? Peter's thoughts raced. *What am I to do? Am I justified in refusing him a chance to learn an instrument? What will the head say if a pupil who has shown willing has been refused, when he himself has been prepared to go beyond expectations with his financial commitment to brass music?*

Peter felt he had little alternative. His list had all the names he needed for the instruments he had but for one, and here was Webster.

'How lucky for me,' thought Peter, as, biting his lip, he added Webster's name to the list.

CHAPTER 15

THE MOVE TO THE COTTAGE

It was a month before a genuine purchaser, accompanied by the local estate agent, arrived on the doorstep of 29 Brent Road. From that moment, things moved quickly and within three weeks the deal was done.

Whilst the sale was going through, some smaller pieces of furniture were moved up to the cottage. The Morris Minor, reliable but basic, provided the transport. Billy had chosen well. He had supplemented his professional advice with a free mini-service, which meant that the van ran with a smoothness belying its age. It had two seats in the front for the driver and passenger, the latter being what was called a 'bucket' seat, which meant it tipped easily. It provided a convenient entry point for the two girls to climb into the back of the van, where they could take a position in readiness for the pitching and lurching that typified their journeys. Without seats or grips of any sort, they relied entirely on Peter's ability to give them a smooth ride, something he could not always guarantee, particularly as they climbed the hill to the moor and rounded the sharp bends to the cottage. Nevertheless, it made for lots of laughing from the rear and much fun.

By the middle of October the family was ready to move in earnest. On his mentioning to one or two of his rugby friends that he was moving, they stepped in and said they would help. They said there were enough cars and vans to transport the furniture and household belongings, and they would not hear of Peter hiring a removal firm. On a fine Sunday morning, a row of about half a dozen vehicles took turns to manoeuvre, one after the other, up the narrow driveway to load with furniture before moving off on the trip from town to country.

All went smoothly, or so Peter thought. And then one of the cars limped into the parking area by the cottage with a displaced bumper and shattered front light. A mishap with another vehicle on one of the sharp bends was enough to spoil a day that had promised to be among the most exciting enjoyed by the family. Brave faces and talk of insurance helped to soften the feeling of guilt that Peter and Catherine shared, but the damage was done.

Despite the disappointment, and the obvious pain for the owner of the damaged car, the helpers continued with their work, and before long all the vehicles arrived and were unloaded. Under Catherine's guidance the interior of the cottage began to take shape.

Catherine's call from the kitchen, 'Anyone for a cup of tea and a sandwich,' was greeted with enthusiasm and provided time for friends to begin to observe and pass judgement on the cottage. Some comments were passed by those who, joining in the usual camaraderie of rugby players, saw a joke at Peter's expense and made just the sort of quips that Peter wished to avoid in front of Catherine.

'What on earth made you want to come and live out in this Godforsaken spot?'

'Are you sure we're in the right place?'

'What did you say it cost? Whatever it was it was far too much.'

'How are you going to keep in contact with the rest of the world—by parachute?'

Fortunately, others were more positive, drawing attention to those aspects that had attracted both Catherine and Peter. These were the friends who, sitting with their cups of tea in front of the cottage looking across the moor and to the valley below, discussed the merits of the cottage in more serious mode. They commented on how enriching living on the moor could be for a family, and especially for young children, and how the land and outbuildings offered such exciting opportunities for development. As it happened, they did not have far to look to see how keen the children were to start their new life on the moor. Indeed, at one moment, Katie's and Sarah's curiosity led them to stand by the path leading into the cottage in a sort of wonderment to watch as things were carried beyond them and through the door, and at the next, they would run in and out of the outhouses in their excitement, already inventing the games they could play.

Whilst appreciating what Peter and his friends had done, Catherine was determined to put her own stamp on their new home. As a result, for some weeks after removal day, the family lived in conditions in which the smell of paint pervaded everything, even their clothes. First, the living room was repainted with the traditional white paint of the country cottage. Cleaner windows and the fitful sun bouncing off the walls at least lightened the room and gave it a freshness that it had lacked for many years. The dust and spiders were attacked once more, to be replaced by a human family.

The next room to be tackled was the kitchen. Again, white paint was used, this time to give a sense of the airy ambiance that Catherine wished to achieve and now, partially, could, as the old smelly cupboards were long gone. The back door was sufficiently loosened to open more easily and the stone sink spruced against any likely germs. By the time they had finished, the swept floor, the walls painted in white, the new cupboards, and the clean cooker presented a small kitchen that was workable if not stylish. The sink was big enough for the children to be seated in for a quick wash down after their explorations in the fields and across the moor, always within earshot of the cottage. Underneath, there was space for an old white bowl, used for washing pots and pans. The quality of the water was still an issue, however, and remained so as neither Peter nor Catherine could as yet think of a solution. It was something they had to put to the back of their minds. They were amazed, when they looked back some years later, that they had dared to put their young children at risk with the impure water.

The dining room had to wait. It had been painted by Peter and his friends in the first flush of activity after the purchase of the cottage. It was reasonably presentable, and would have to do until the upstairs had been thoroughly cleaned and repainted.

As the interior took shape, Peter and Catherine were able to dip into what little money remained from the sale of their previous house to buy carpets and rugs for the floors and some other essentials of furniture to give a sort of comfort. It was far from perfect, and there was more to do, but it was liveable, and it meant that any visitors could at least be welcomed and feel that the family was getting settled.

But as was her manner, Catherine continued to attack the cottage with enthusiasm, sorting, ordering and straightening. Peter helped in the evenings and the part of the weekends that he was not playing rugby. Eventually, the day came when the couple looked at one another and agreed that they had done what they could. They agreed that what they needed was time to sit and discuss how they could organise their finances, so as to begin to make the more substantial changes that were required if the cottage was to be the home they desired.

One Saturday evening, as they sat watching Laurence Olivier in Henry V on television and exchanging ideas about how they might develop the cottage further, a shadow crossing the window was followed by a knock at the door. Standing there in a white shirt, a tie, and what appeared to be a 'best' suit topped by the usual flat cap, was Mr Helme, the neighbour from across the field. To date, they had exchanged only the occasional pleasantries such as, 'Morning,' 'How are you?' 'Nice day,' and so on across a boundary wall or when he had passed on his tractor. This evening was clearly a more formal occasion for which Peter, in his loose-fitting slacks, slippers and sweater seemed ill prepared.

'Come in,' he said shaking hands with Mr Helme.

Peter closed the door once his visitor had passed through, and led the way into the sitting room. Mr Helme, taking off his cap but still holding on to his crook, followed.

'This is Mr Helme from the farm at the bottom of the field, Catherine. My wife,' said Peter, introducing Catherine as Mr Helme moved across to shake hands. As he took the seat that Peter indicated, Catherine was quick to offer a cup of tea, but it was politely refused.

Peter was delighted to have a visitor because he was keen to establish friendly relationships with his neighbours. He saw this as a way of quickly settling on the moor and showing that he was willing to become fully involved in the life of the village. He also knew from Maxine, that Mr Helme was one of those priceless neighbours who was always willing to help, and with a good heart. She had told him more than once how Mr Helme was one of those neighbours whose practice it had been to do shopping for Ma' Winstone, and after knocking on the door or shouting up to the upstairs window, would leave the shopping on the step for Ma' Winstone to collect at her leisure.

Peter could not help but notice that his visitor took the opportunity to look around the sitting room and hoped that he was impressed with the difference between what he was looking at now and what he would have seen previously. Peter knew from what he found when he first visited the cottage, that Mr Helme would have been fully aware of the state of the place when they moved in. His face, however, had a dour expression that gave nothing away. Neither did it appear there was any time for the pleasantries that those in towns often become accustomed to. Mr Helme, clearly, was not for social talk. There was no expectation of Catherine or Peter to ask about family, about how well the farm was doing, or how long he had lived on the moor. For their part, no questions were fired at them as to how settled they were or how the children were adapting to their new surroundings, and so, by the time Mr Helme was ready to leave, he was still Mr Helme, and neither of the parties was any wiser than they had been of the circumstances of the other.

'Mr and Mrs Delaney, good evening. Mi' name is Jack Helme,' began the visitor. 'As yer probably know, I live across t'field and keep sheep and cows. I have abaht twenty acres. I know you have abaht ten acres and I wondered what yer intended doin' wi'em.'

'Well,' began Peter, 'we've not given it much thought as yet. We're still trying to settle in.'

'I thought yer might be interested in letting 'em.'

Peter was somewhat taken aback. The thought had only vaguely crossed his mind as he and Catherine had, on occasions, exchanged the odd view about what they might do with the land. They had reached a point at which no feasible solution seemed to be emerging. In some ways, the presence of Mr Helme and his question offered a solution the intricacies of which they had not yet fully thought through. Peter and Catherine exchanged glances and wondered.

'A'm willin' to pay fifty pounds a year. A'l look after t'walls an t'land as well.'

Peter didn't not know what to say, such was his surprise, but he glanced across at Catherine, whom he knew would be as taken aback by the proposal as he was. Nevertheless, he saw the prospect of some income, which would be very welcome. He also saw the possibility of some expert oversight of the fields and walls. The man looked and behaved like one who could be trusted. After a thoughtful pause, Peter responded, 'Mr Helme, thanks for your offer. Will you give us time to consider it?'

'Aye,' he replied. 'Well a'l be off then,' and without much ado he stood and headed for the door.

Peter and Catherine were somewhat stunned by his brusqueness, but he had come on business, the business was done, and now it was time to leave. Why waste time on other things, seemed to be his approach.

Peter was fascinated by the meeting. First of all he recognised the possibility of establishing a relationship with a local farmer to whom he might, in the future, be able to turn for advice and help. Secondly, it raised for him visions of the relationships between landowner and tenant he had studied in history. This was not exactly the same situation, but it had some undertones which gave him a strange feeling. Was his status now one of landowner? Had he moved into a world within which he was regarded as a man of means? He was somewhat bemused by the turn of events, but knew he had to consider how he was likely to deal with it. He turned to Catherine, 'What's happening? What should we do? Are we really landowners able to have a tenant?'

He noticed Catherine smiling at his predicament, something he should have expected as she knew him so well.

'Surely you foresaw this. Within your grand design, you must have recognised some of the consequences. Now you're a man of means, you're likely to be courted by all sorts of people who, a couple of months ago, wouldn't have given you house room.'

Peter knew she was amusing herself at his expense, but could not help but smile with her.

'Ok, so it seems a bit of a joke that I might become a landlord, but blimey, Catherine, what are we going to do? We both know that without stock, the land will be a waste. And we both know that I'm no farmer.'

'Why not?' interjected Catherine. 'I never saw myself as a farmer's wife, but the idea is becoming quite attractive.'

She was still having fun. It was not untypical of Peter to join her in her playfulness; it was one of the features that had cemented their relationship from its earliest days.

'I have to say that it'd be great to go to school and tell Stan and the others that I needed to get home early in order to sort out some issues with my tenant. I'd love to see their faces.'

Catherine rose from her chair, walked across to him, gave him a kiss and, 'I think I'd enjoy that too, but I'm a bit tired right now to sort out all the issues it probably raises. I need to sleep on it and I'm sure you do. Come on, it's time for bed,' and she headed for the stairs.

Peter sat for a few moments engrossed in thought. He began to think about how his life had been turned upside down. His concern about 29 Brent Road was its situation and its reminder of the unappealing streets of his childhood. But he had not been unhappy as a child, indeed the very opposite. Nevertheless, he had been aware that there were those who for one reason or another had more control over their lives and what they did as a result of what they owned. They were the people who did not have to join the clip clop of clogs and metal toe-capped boots down the length of the street as the miners headed for early-morning work, awakening for a second, children, who, like Peter, were snuggled in their beds.

Mr Helme's visit had brought his awareness of the influence of those who owned land into sharp relief. It left Peter wondering how he was to respond to the new situation in which he found himself.

The move to the cottage was such a break from any of the experiences in his former life that he had not foreseen the measure of personal adjustment that was likely to be necessary. The visit of Mr Helme, rather like the crack of the starter's gun concentrates the minds of the athletes, had concentrated his mind on an issue that he had hardly begun to ponder; that was the likely impact of his now owning ten acres of land.

As he made his way up the stairs to join Catherine, the questions he going through his mind included, *How am I going to cope with this? What does it mean to be a landlord? Is there anything I'm likely to have to do?*

Like it or not, there was little doubt that the evening's visitor had unwittingly raised the bar in respect of what Peter considered his social and economic status.

CHAPTER 16

WEBSTER AND THE TROMBONE

'Guess what,' was Peter's first comment to his friend Stan next morning at school. 'I had a chap from a neighbouring farm visit me last night. He was enquiring about the land I've got around the cottage.'

'I wondered that myself when I visited you during the summer holidays. You said you'd about ten acres. That's a fair amount.'

'It is, and me and Catherine had not really had much time to talk about what we were going to do with it, before this chap knocked on the door last night. He's a very upright sort of bloke, clearly not used to visiting or becoming involved in social chatter. In no time he came to the point. He wanted to rent the land and was prepared to give me £50 a year rent. He'll want to keep sheep and cattle on it, I suspect. But I reckon of even more importance for me, is that he also offered to look after the walls and do any other maintenance associated with the fields. Looking after that lot had begun to worry me.'

'It seems good to me, though, as you know, I don't know all the circumstances. Have you decided to take him up on it?'

'Well, I'm still thinking about it. I don't know all the angles. If I let it, does it mean I can't get him off if I want to, for instance? Another thing that I've to bear in mind, I suppose, is I never know what's likely to turn up and whether I may need the land for something else at some time.'

Stan nodded in agreement. 'That's a good point. You'll probably have to talk to a solicitor about that. I suppose you'll have to have a written agreement. Perhaps Maxine will know. Look, she's over there at the table looking at some drawings. Let's go and have a word with her.'

The pair of them moved across the staffroom to where Maxine was sitting.

'Maxine, sorry to disturb you, but I need a bit of advice. Mr Helme came over last night and offered to rent the land. It's got lots of attractions, but I'm not sure as to what liabilities I will have. Have you any ideas as to where I might stand in relation to a tenant?'

'I'm no expert, my Dad sorts out all the legal issues related to our place, but, as far as I know, it's essential to agree a letting for one day short of a year, otherwise the tenant could claim a permanent lease and then you can't get him off the land without a lot of fuss.'

'Interesting. It's things like that which I need to know. It's a good job you've told me. It's fortunate that I didn't agree to anything last night. Thanks for the advice, Maxine. I think I'll do as Stan suggests anyway, and have a word with my solicitor.'

'That's got to be the best thing, though David Helme is a good bloke and I don't think he would try it on. He only has a small farm, possibly a little more land than you, and he may have rented the fields in the past. I'd be surprised if he didn't know about any legal rights. I'll have a word with my Dad as well. I'm pretty sure he'll know the ins and outs.'

Their conversation was disturbed by the morning bell's call to registration and lessons. Collecting the things they needed from their designated areas of the staffroom, they followed the procession of colleagues through the door and to their different bases, Maxine to the art room and Peter upstairs to the history room.

As Peter moved down the corridor and up the stairs, always on the left, pupils passing on his right chirped, as usual, their lively, 'Morning, sir,' as they headed for their form rooms. Registration was a straightforward affair, with the calling of names and the denoting of those present, absent or late. Peter went through the process in the time-honoured fashion until he reached the name Williams. The 'W' brought to his mind Webster, and his decision to offer him the trombone. Peter's knowledge of where, and therefore potentially how, Webster lived made him wonder about the safety of any instrument that was entrusted to him. He was also concerned as to the seriousness of Webster's commitment. What Peter did not want was to have Webster acting the fool in the band and then deciding he wanted to quit, having wasted Peter's time and that of the other pupils.

After registration, Peter ushered his form out of his classroom towards the school hall. The hall was large enough to accommodate all the pupils of the school, but standing rather than sitting. If they needed to sit it had to be on the floor. At the front was a raised stage. It was here that Alan and Arthur had entertained the school with *All Through the Night* and from which, during assemblies, the head addressed the school from behind a plain wooden lectern. Below the stage, to the right, was the piano at which Miss Andrews usually played some classical piece as the pupils quietly entered, and then led the hymn-singing. Down one side of the hall were curtained windows, ceiling high, which looked out onto the playing fields. The opposite wall contained photographs and posters related to the school's successes, and Peter's eyes often strayed to the reference to his Under 14's victory in the local school's football competition. It had been with great pride that he had watched them collect the cup and posed with the team for the photograph that now took its place among the other school successes. At the back of the hall were the doors to the school kitchens where the lunches were cooked. They were ideally situated as the hall also served as a dining room.

As was customary, the form teachers brought their classes into the hall, stationed them in the correct place and then stood close by, overseeing their behaviour. Peter took his class into what was a normal morning assembly. The deputy, Tom, was on the stage ensuring that classes filed in smoothly and quietly, and Miss Andrews was at the piano playing *Fur Elise.* Once all the pupils were in place, Mr Holdsworth walked on stage and bid the school, 'Good morning.'

190

'Good morning, sir,' responded the pupils and staff and then Miss Andrews began to play the hymn *Lord of All Hopefulness*. The pupils sang rather half heartedly until the head stopped the singing and urged them, with some success, to sing with more enthusiasm. As if to show that he had heeded what he had just said, he made sure his own voice could be heard at the back of the hall as, with reddening face, he sought to engender commitment from the pupils. After the hymn, a pupil read a short Biblical text and then all joined in the Lord's Prayer, led by Mr Holdsworth. As usual, a list of notices followed and then the pupils filed out to their lessons, the piano seeming to sound the retreat.

Peter knew that he and the pupils had just experienced a daily ritual that was followed by the great majority of schoolchildren across the country and one that, as far as he knew, was unique to schools in England. He had heard that even in European countries that might be termed Catholic, for instance France and Italy, the dominantly secular nature of their education systems meant that there was no place for the type of religious assembly that still persisted in England. Peter wondered to what extent it reflected the influence of the Archbishops and Bishops in the unelected House of Lords, where such matters might be discussed, or simply the inborn belief in an Almighty amongst a public that was ostensibly materialistic.

To Peter, a Catholic, the school's daily morning routine, incongruous as it might seem, did the worthwhile job of reminding many of the participants that there were still those who called themselves Christians. The actual impact on their lives, he deemed, was likely to be slight, although he recognised that some of the moral issues raised by the headteacher in assembly probably did penetrate. For instance, issues raised in assembly related to the treatment of one person by another often surfaced in lessons, especially in history, or when children were being disciplined. When challenged around such issues, pupils often showed a surprising maturity in their perception of right and wrong, and Peter could not help but believe that school assemblies played their part.

At the end of assembly, as the pupils filed out of the hall, Peter took a position by the door from which he could intercept Webster. He had come to the conclusion during assembly that he needed to speak to him and resolve the question of the brass group. Webster turned nonchalantly as Peter called him across.

Assemblies or not, how will this lad ever learn respect, thought Peter as Webster casually made his way towards him through rows of other pupils, sometimes pushing another pupil aside to break a row at the appropriate place.

'Webster, I have been thinking about your request to join the brass group. How serious are you?'

'I'd love to join, sir. I've always wanted to play. I heard of a bloke called Tommy Dorsey in a music lesson and thought the music on his record was great. I think it'd be great to do what he does.'

'Well, I think Tommy Dorsey plays a bit better than we're likely to do in the brass group, but I admire your ambition. I hope you realise what hard work it has taken him to reach the standard he has. You'll have to work just as hard if you're to become the next Tommy Dorsey.

Understood? If I give you an instrument will you look after it, keep it clean and in good order, and not let anyone else play about with it. D'you think you can keep it away from your brothers and sister?'

Peter had seen them about town from time to time and come to the conclusion that their behaviour reflected that of their older brother. Having seen the mischief they could get up to, he couldn't help but pity any musical instrument that fell into their hands. He was also concerned about the likely conditions in Webster's home, having seen the personal appearance of Mr and Mrs Webster on their visits to school. If the care they took with themselves replicated the care they were likely to expend on the trombone, he realised there was little chance of it avoiding serious damage. He knew he had to have some agreement with Webster, as his concern for the well-being of the instrument had to be his first consideration.

'No problem, sir. I'll mek sure nobody touches it,' was the lively reply.

Peter had heard the pitch of that voice too often in class when Webster was being troublesome to feel immediately comfortable with the reply. 'And what about practising? You know it takes a lot of commitment to become as good as Tommy Dorsey.'

'I know that, sir. But 'am willing to practise, 'cos I really want to play.'

'And will you do as you're told?'

'Yes, sir.'

Peter's questions were answered and, although he did not attach a great deal of credibility to them, he could not see any option but to give Webster the chance.

'Come to see me in my room straight after school and we'll sort something out. Off you go to class now. If you are a little late, tell your teacher that you've been seeing me. Who is it by the way?'

'Mrs Hargreaves.'

'OK, off you go. Chop, chop, a bit quicker than that lad.' With that, Webster was on his way while Peter headed for his class, still doubting the wisdom of his decision to have Webster in the brass group.

Shortly after the end of school, Webster was at Peter's classroom door. Having dismissed his class, Peter called him in and showed him the trombone he was proposing to let him have.

'Now this is just like the instrument that Tommy Dorsey played. One of your first jobs is to learn the positions of the slide to get the notes you want. This is the slide, and as you can see you move it to different positions. Now this is the mouthpiece. It fits in the trombone here. This is what helps you make a sound. You put it to your lips like this.' Peter put the mouthpiece to his lips and as he withdrew it said, 'In doing this you create an embouchure. What's the word?' he shot at Webster.

'Emb—something.'

'Embouchure,' repeated Peter.

'Emb . . . . embe . . . . embe . . . .'

'Embouchure.'

'Embechur'

'Good, that's not bad. Now remember it because it's something that you'll develop the more you play. OK, put the mouthpiece to your lips where it feels comfortable . . . . is that it?

'Yes,' said Webster, returning the mouthpiece to his lips.

'That's fine,' said Peter. 'Now I want you to take the mouthpiece away from your mouth. I'm going to stick this piece of paper to your top lip, and then I want you to blow it away.'

Webster began blowing, only disturbing the bottom end of the paper and failing to achieve what was intended. He blew harder with little more success.

'Now, Webster, try using your tongue, like this.'

Peter proceeded to stretch his lips, rest the tip of his tongue on the bottom of his inner top lip, and then quickly withdraw it as if spitting. Webster watched quizzically and then tried himself. Overdoing it, he sprayed small dribs to and beyond the paper. He increased the intensity of his spitting action, still keeping his tongue as instructed, and suddenly the paper flew off his top lip. Peter enjoyed the look of achievement and pleasure that passed across Webster's face.

'Do you get the idea?' Peter asked and Webster nodded that he did. 'What happens is you create a flow of air. This goes through your lips, which then vibrate or quiver on the mouthpiece. The air and the vibrating lips, along with the instrument, then make the sound. The better you carry out the technique for producing a note, the better will be the sound, or what a musician calls the tone, from the instrument. Do you follow?' Peter had explained in detail in order to ensure that Webster understood.

'Yes,' said Webster, as he again used his tongue to spit air and whatever else came out of his mouth.

'What I want you to do is put the mouthpiece to your . . . . your what?'

'Embouchure,' responded Webster.

'Well done,' Peter said, realising that this was the first time he had complimented Webster for anything.

'Anyway, put the mouthpiece where it's comfortable and go through the same process with your lips and tongue.'

Webster followed the instructions, creating an indistinguishable, crabby sound. He tried again and again, and Peter admired his persistence. And then he got it right. His tongue struck his top lip precisely, his lips vibrated, and a recognisable sound emerged from the mouthpiece. 'Well done. Now you're getting the idea,' said Peter. 'I want you to take this book home with you and learn the notes and positions. I'll test you on it next week. I also want you to take home the mouthpiece and practise what you've been doing,'

'Can't I take the trombone, sir?'

'Not yet,' said Peter.

'Oh, sir. What's the point if I've no trombone?'

Peter began to recognise the Webster he knew in the pushiness he began to display.

'Webster,' Peter uttered with some frustration 'what's our deal? You promised to do as asked and to behave.'

Webster flushed as though having some inner battle and then muttered something to the effect of, 'OK then'. He picked up the book and mouthpiece without ceremony and left. Peter, foreseeing problems ahead, wondered how he might deal with them and half hoped that Webster would soon lose interest and find some other activity.

The next morning, early, Webster was at the staffroom door.

'Could I see Mr Delaney, please?'

Peter heard and recognised the voice. His immediate hope was that Webster had decided that learning to play the trombone was too difficult and wanted to quit. As Peter moved across to the door and opened it wider, his gaze fell on a shy and apologetic Webster.

'Sir, I've lost mi' mouthpiece,' he mumbled with a look of abject misery and eyes fixed on the floor.

'What?' exclaimed Peter. 'How can you lose the mouthpiece in one evening?'

Webster collected himself and explained what had happened.

'Well, I went home on mi' bike after school through t'park. I'd put mi' mouthpiece in mi' pocket, but when I got home it had gone.'

Peter's dismay was obvious. Where was he to get a replacement mouthpiece, and why was Webster so stupid? 'Look,' he said. 'Come back at lunchtime and I'll go with you down the park path to see if we can find it. What were you doing riding in the park anyway? There's a sign that says no bike riders.'

Webster, who seemed to recover quickly once he had broken the news, smirked 'Well, everybody does.' Peter shook his head in disapproval.

At lunchtime, Peter managed to gather four other brass players and together with Webster they started the search for the mouthpiece. They were lucky. Within five minutes one of the boys shouted, 'Got it.'

Peter's relief was obvious. He took the mouthpiece and gave it to Webster. 'Next time will be the last'.

Webster seemed to learn from his experience and for the first time Peter saw a chink of promise. The boy came to him during break the following day saying, 'Sir, I think you're right about the trombone. 'Am not sure about teking it home. 'A think it might get busted. But 'a need to practise. Would it be OK if 'a practised before 'a went home and sometimes in the mornings before school?'

Peter was impressed. He felt that at last Webster was recognising responsibility. This was an ideal, if surprising, solution. 'That's a really good idea, Joe. I'm sure we could organise that.'

Webster did what he had promised and Peter often heard him after school in the music room making the most frightful sounds. He also attended individual tuition, where his progress indicated, as Peter shared with his closest colleagues, and to their amusement, that he was trying to be another Tommy Dorsey. All agreed, however, that if one of the intentions of allowing him to take up the trombone had been to encourage him to be more responsive in class, it was not working. The regular comment that brought a laugh at break times, especially from those that had just had Webster, became, 'I wonder what Tommy Dorsey was like at school?' Peter had to agree with the regular answer, 'Tommy Dorsey must have been have been a damn nuisance!'

Over the next few weeks members of the brass group responded well to Peter's tuition and made progress. Most pupils quickly began to sight read the music in *Tune a Day*, and learned the fingering for the different notes. Within a month, the group could make a reasonable sound. Arthur and Alan led the way, providing the sort of example that brought the best out of the others. As a result, Peter's early attempts to get the group to work successfully together as an ensemble were proving successful. Unfortunately, within the group, Webster's conduct often reflected his behaviour elsewhere.

Peter had developed a programme whereby he would spend some time with each individual boy or girl, helping them to improve their technique and setting them challenging tasks as a sort of homework. He would then, about every couple of weeks, call the group together to see what they could achieve as an ensemble. He would arrange pieces they had been practising, ensuring that each part matched the capabilities of the pupil who would be playing it. Even so, Peter was pleased he was not making any recordings, as the sound produced was more like the discordant cawing of rooks as they return to their nests high in the trees, rather than the tunefulness for which he was searching. Nevertheless, Peter persevered, and, having in his mind the sound that he was trying to cultivate, he patiently gave encouragement and guidance.

The members of the group, also keen to improve, worked hard to follow and do as Peter asked. But not Webster. His frustration when playing false notes or being checked for playing in the wrong places often led to a burst of expletives, as well as a stomping out of the room with the trombone and its case under his arm. In the very early sessions, Peter would call after him, 'Webster, sit down,' but, as it had no effect, he eventually gave up.

To Peter, the most important objective was not to control Webster but to get the group playing harmoniously. And so, Peter and the group learned to live with such eruptions and simply carried on practising. Unable to collect followers in the way he had in class, and aware that his behaviour made him look a fool, Webster, still feeling within himself the desire to be the new Tommy Dorsey, usually returned after a short while and tried to get things right.

These sessions taught Peter a good deal about Webster. His desire to be noticed and to be the centre of attention was the fundamental trait that somehow powered his behaviour. In class, others who shared his disinterest in what was being taught were happy to be drawn along by his example. This was not happening in his sorties with the trombone. Even he took what he was learning seriously, though he could not always escape his normal self. When having individual tuition, Peter found he responded well and made impressive progress, whilst in the brass group he was surrounded by pupils, some older and more mature that he, who were committed to what they were doing, and were not to be deflected by anything he did. As a result, such antics only produced antipathy towards Webster rather than the attention he desired, and to Peter's delight, the group showed to Webster that they were determined to persist and ignore his efforts to disrupt practice. This took him out of his normal comfort zone, and Peter could see that he was beginning to recognise the importance of teamwork and to play by the rules.

As time passed, the improvement in the quality of playing was marked, and it reminded Peter of something that had been said to him in his early days as a player, *'With the persistence of waves rolling on to a shore, you will erode weaknesses under a developing melodious sound, the result of your concentrated practice.'* He was not sure who said it, and no doubt he thought it rather fanciful at the time it was said, but it aptly described what he felt was happening to his young musicians.

Occasionally, at weekends, Peter invited different sections of the group up to the cottage for extra rehearsal and for drinks and cakes. He would pick them up in town and a couple of hours later drop them back. Catherine loved to see them and thought they were charming children. Even Webster impressed, and relationships between him and Peter improved. It seemed that Webster felt he had found people who were interested in him and, although he could not always resist the temptation to give in to his least appealing traits, he responded more positively than Peter had hoped.

As Peter took these weekend groups through their paces, Catherine would sit with the Gregory on her knee swaying and humming to the different tunes. Katie and Sarah paid interest to what was going on for a while, but, as little children do, they soon wearied and found playing with different toys, chasing the hens, or having fun in the breaks in practice with the pupils, much more to their taste. Peter was aware that his musicians also relished these sorties into the country. They enjoyed the drinks, the cakes, and the meetings with the children; the girls loved to play with little Gregory in particular. The musicians also had the opportunity on occasions to ramble across the moor, being startled by the grouse and observed by the munching sheep.

Occasionally, Peter decided to take the different groups up onto the crest of *The King's Beacon*. They had asked about it so many times that it seemed a natural thing to do. Picking their way carefully along a hardly distinguishable path, they eventually reached the rocks at the *Beacon*'s base. Here, Peter pointed out the entrance to a small cave.

'That's where the watchers at the time of the Civil War used to shelter, so that they would be ready to give warning of an approaching enemy if need be. It was from there that the Roundheads were spotted,' added Peter as he encouraged his pupils to cast their eyes over the valley and imagine what they might have seen those many years ago. 'They then climbed to the top of the *Beacon*, lit the fire and so gave warning to the Lord Fairfax's men, who were fighting for the King. And so it got its name.'

Not surprisingly, all the pupils had to take their turn to go into the cave, some uttering, 'It's creepy,' others, 'I wouldn't like to have stayed here at night,' and the rest taking in what they were observing without comment.

Peter could see that to his pupils these outings were idyllic and did much to cement together the band as a unit. He had no doubt that the delights of their visits would linger in their minds for years to come. It became clear that even Webster enjoyed these outings and that he became increasingly comfortable within the family as his trust in Catherine and Peter developed. Equally important was his growing attachment to the coterie of musicians, as his recognition of a common interest grew.

CHAPTER 17

THE FAMILY SETTLES ON THE MOOR

Peter wondered how people came to live where they did. For many, it was a simple matter of economics. They needed an income so were drawn to those places in which they could find paid work. As he knew, the stories of the Agricultural Revolution and Industrial Revolution in Britain clearly spelled out this fact. The towns offered work, work provided money, and money offered a life. The rows of houses huddled as close as possible to a factory or a mine were the outcome. The rows stood as if on parade, not unlike the ranks of troops on a march at Trooping the Colour in Horse Guards Parade. The red brick, topped with black roofs, progressed through the village like guardsmen across the square in their red tunics and black bearskins, the puffs of smoke from chimneys distinguishing each row, as a plume distinguishes each regiment. The pomp and splendour associated with the celebratory scenes in London were not replicated in the industrial towns and villages, but they had a soul that London, Peter knew, could not match.

The fondness with which Peter looked back on his early days had more to do with the living community than with its surroundings of red and black. It was his friends and their families that created the atmosphere of comradeship and trust, so important when people lived and worked cheek by jowl. Below ground, men were willing to risk their own lives for others not because they knew what they did would be reciprocated but because this was what one did. They did not take oaths and make pledges, as was the custom in male societies above ground. The invisible bond did not need to be recognised by ceremony. None of these things were needed. Peter had grown up in a village among friends who played together, mostly in unison, occasionally in spitting rivalry, but always with the understanding that they belonged.

But there was another aspect that weighed on his recollections of his young life in his mining village. These were the memories he had of the opportunities for play and exploration in nearby woods, fields, and streams. Those experiences were different to what the moor offered. The moorland terrain was often wilder, and stretched over a much wider area. Nevertheless, his boyhood experiences could not be ignored as being some sort of preparation for the life he was now leading.

Peter could not escape the fact that the tightly knit industrial setting in which he had been brought up had provided only the beating heart of the strips of countryside that surrounded it and in which he and his friends loved to play. With them, he had been able to find space in the evenings and weekends away from the industrial huddle and meet up with the insects, birds, fish, and other animals that enriched their lives. The morning hunt for mushrooms in the damp fields of early autumn, the search through bush after bush for bird's nests, and the dangling of string with its attached bent pin into a stream or pond in anticipation of catching a fish, were memories that still lived within him. He could not help but think that such distant childhood experiences had unconsciously impacted on his desire to move to the moorland cottage.

And so it had never crossed Peter's mind that the family would have any difficulty settling into life on the moor. He knew there were some significant physical difficulties to overcome, but their importance faded in face of his enticing prospect of open moors and country life. He could not imagine a scenario in which Catherine and the children would not enjoy life on the moor as much as he knew he would.

Peter's vision of moorland life was relaxing in the cottage or garden, and wandering quietly over the moor, imbibing the sights and sounds that he imagined only moorland can produce. He looked to enjoy his new environment. The singing of skylarks, as they hung high in the early morning sky, provided that entrancing backdrop he knew could never be present in a town. The moor, as he had anticipated, revealed a living milieu for the family that would be difficult, if not impossible to replicate, if only for its birds: the nervy, plump partridges and grouse that startled walkers as they rocketed with rapidly whirring wings from under booted feet and headed low across the grass, alternating between noisily beating the sky and silently gliding; the pewits with their harsh call; and a wide variety of smaller birds, such as the musical blackbirds, the thrushes, vibrant and full-throated, the various tits, and the chirping sparrows. They all sought food in and around the garden, singing to their hearts' content and nesting in their chosen locations. He also envisaged seeing swifts swirling around their nests under the eaves of the cottage, and brambling, with their red, white, and black feathers decorating the garden trees in winter.

Sadly, he was also aware that there was another side of life in the country, one that he would have to become used to. He was always disturbed at the sound of gunshot as the so-called 'hunters' sought their prey. The ease with which they could find their targets, driven as they were by the beaters across the moor, made a mockery in his eyes of the term *hunter*. With the waving of flags and shouting that had the secondary purpose of forewarning any innocent ramblers on the moor, the beaters drove the startled grouse whizzing towards or adjacent to the barrels of the guns and their painful deaths.

Peter was to learn that it was the gamekeeper's job to ensure that the breeding months were productive of the reddish-brown birds to entertain those willing to pay a goodly sum for the pleasure of shooting them. From what was described as the 'The Glorious Twelfth,' the biggest misnomer there could be in his view, the shooting season got under way. He also discovered that, even though his land was private, custom, established in past times, allowed the marksmen to collect the shot birds that landed on it. Tradition also demanded that the landowner, whether his land had been soiled by the boots of the 'guns' or not, received compensation. In Peter's case, this usually meant a brace of grouse left hanging by his door at the end of the day's shooting.

It was the romance of the moor, however, that was to win the hearts of the family and ensured that they settled into their new life happily. The full sky and the distant horizon on the days when the sun shone were not interrupted by bricks and mortar, or the undulating landscape hidden by their shadow. On such days, the moor seemed to sing a welcome to those who wished to step onto its thick carpet, with its conversing animals and birds, uninhibited by the moor's serenity and undaunted by fear of intrusion. Even when hidden beneath a white cloak in winter, the moor charmed. Its all-encompassing tranquillity was undisturbed even by footsteps, which simply left a silent imprint, and even the sounds of the inhabitants of the moor were inexplicably muted.

The doubts that Catherine had expressed on that ill-fated phone call to Hull about buying the cottage had been dispelled as soon as she saw it. Her walking experiences in the past helped to hook her into the different harmonies of the moor. She was used to the calls of the birds, the cows, and the sheep mingling with the sighing of wind, common at moorland heights. She had also experienced the hardships of life with limited amenities as when she and Peter had camped through Holland, Germany, France, and, more recently with baby Katie, in the field of one of Peter's rugby-playing friends. With neither Peter nor Catherine realising it, these adventures, because that was what they were, had helped prepare them for what they now faced.

The allure of the country captured them as they set about enjoying what it had to offer whilst tackling with energy what needed to be done. They were determined to make their move to the cottage a success.

They lived their days enveloped by nature. From the cottage situated at the foot of the *Beacon*, they could see the extension of the moor across the valley of the Wharfe, which stretched in the direction of the mill towns of Keighley and Bradford. And they could follow the highs and lows of the seasons as they drifted or gusted through the valley and across the hills, bringing frisky springs, long summer days, autumnal glows, and crisp, white winters. They were able to follow the course of nature as they observed the routines of the farmers. Lambing in springtime, sheep shearing as summer approached, and haymaking as it was about to depart, and the gathering of cattle in the barn in preparation for the winter, became signals of the changing activities in their lives as they responded to the seasons.

Peter also came to realise that he and Catherine had to react to nature's moods. Good weather provided opportunities for improvements outside the cottage and enabled improvements to the front and rear gardens to be implemented, whilst inclement weather encouraged further improvements inside before it became too cold to move away from the open fire of the living room.

The children, unconcerned about any of the challenges that faced their mum and dad, played around the cottage and made the best of the roaming in and about the various outhouses. As children do, they found ways to make their days memorable, from attacking with an axe and hammer what might have been a valuable grandfather clock that had been left in the cowshed to chasing the newly acquired hens in all directions.

Just as Peter and Catherine built up relationships with others in the village, the children too made useful contacts. Once Katie started school, she quickly made friends with other children from the village, and their meetings on the school bus gradually developed into visits to homes, where Katie and Sarah would play with the John and Julie Thomas or Mary, Sandra, and Jenny Gillam. On other occasions, these same children would come to the cottage, giving Catherine the opportunity to meet with their mothers. Eileen, who lived at the farm just across the first field, also became a useful contact. She looked after the children on several occasions when Catherine and Peter had evening engagements, and these gradually extended into her taking them out from time to time, the most memorable trip for the children being to a local agricultural show.

As they became more confident, Peter was pleased to see that they began to visit the different farms, especially if they saw anything happening that they thought was of interest. They would come back to the cottage and tell Peter and Catherine what they had been doing and what they had seen. Katie was the usual narrator, but Sarah was always ready to add or correct.

'We've been farming with Mr Helme today. We like him. He tells us funny stories and he always makes us laugh with what he says to us. Mrs Helme gave us a biscuit. D'you know what we saw today?'

Before anyone could even say, 'No,' the garrulous Katie was answering her own question.

'We saw some little lambs. They were really little—about this size,' she said, indicating with her fingers.

'They were a bit bigger than that,' interrupted Sarah as she spread her own fingers a little wider than Katie's.

Katie looked doubtful. 'Are you sure?'

'Course I am.'

'I don't think you're right. Anyway, one was so small after it'd just been born that Mr Helme carried into the house and put it in the oven for a bit. I think it was cold and needed to be warmed.'

'No, it wasn't. Its mummy had died. He put it there to feed it with milk.'

And so went the report, Peter and Catherine enjoying the story as well as the interplay between the children.

On another occasion when the girls came home, they explained how they'd helped with the haymaking.

'We had to put the hay to make it look like a wigwam. It was really funny. Mr Helme told Sarah off for running in front of his tractor. She was doing a dance like an Indian.'

'It's true, Dad. I was running in and out of the rows like an Indian chief, hopping on one leg and then the other like they do in my book,' added Sarah as she laughed.

One evening, as Peter arrived home from school, Catherine, with Gregory in her arms, greeted him with, 'You want to see what they've been up to today. They were playing in the barn. As you know, there's some old straw on the floor. Well, they decided to tidy up. They came in for a brush and asked if they could use the rake, and then off they went. About twenty minutes later, Sarah walked in holding a dead rat by the tail. She wanted to know what it was.'

'Gor . . . . what did you do?'

'What do you think? I chased her outside and told her to throw it somewhere. Anyway, it's out the back, waiting for somebody to bury it.'

'I suppose it's been in the barn for ages. At least I hope so. I don't fancy rats running around the place. I've never got to cleaning out the barn. Heaven knows what else we'll find.'

Peter went outside and found the rat where Sarah had left it by the barn door. It was almost like a print on paper, with just the skin and bones stretched tight. It had been dead for a long time. He buried it and then went back into the cottage and washed his hands, all the time feeling shudders run down his spine. He was often amazed at how when he was young, like Sarah and Katie, rats, mice, strange-looking beetles, and other creepy-crawlies were bodies to be investigated, whereas now the sight of a moving mouse or rat sent alarm coursing through his body. This explained the reason for his investment in a couple of cats, which spent their lives in and around the outbuildings.

Unfortunately, Peter's commitments at school and elsewhere meant that he missed a great many of the children's exploits, but, as in this instance, Catherine was always ready to update him or to prompt the children into relating the rest of their day's activities as they prepared for bed.

Typically, as they donned their pyjamas and dressing gowns in front of the fire, Katie took the lead. 'The hens were funny today, Daddy. They went through the gate onto the road. Sarah and me had to help Mum get them back in. They ran all over the place, and we thought they might get run over.'

'I got Sadie,' said Sarah.

'What do you mean "Sadie"? Do the hens have names like children?'

'Yes, Daddy. Katie had the idea.'

'Well, what other names are there?'

'We have Jenny, and who else is there, Katie?'

'Well, there's Nora, Anne, and Ada. And they know their names. They come if we call them, don't they, Mummy?'

'Of course they do, love. Now come on, off you go to bed.'

Peter held out his arms and encircled the children as they gave him a kiss on each cheek before Catherine guided them through the door and up the stairs to bed. After tucking them in, she crossed the landing to take a peep at Gregory, whom she had put to bed a little earlier. He was still sound asleep face down, with his thumb in his mouth and his legs tucked under his raised bottom. He always slept in this seemingly uncomfortable position, and both Catherine and Peter marvelled at his elasticity.

Catherine went down stairs to find that Peter had made a cup of cocoa for the pair of them. Peter adjusted the radio to get rid of interference, and then, with the smooth music quietly playing in the background, settled next to Catherine on the settee.

'The children seem to have had a lovely day,' Peter said in a half-questioning manner.

'They did. They loved rounding up the hens and calling them by their name.'

'Do the hens respond?'

'What d'you think?' she said, and then they both laughed.

'There was an interesting discussion in the staffroom today. And it made me think how lucky we are. It revolved around when a young married couple should have children. The overwhelming view seemed to be that it made good sense to delay having a family until a couple was well established with secure jobs, had a well-furnished house, and possibly a car. Fortunately, I didn't get too involved, but I had to smile when I thought of our situation.'

'I'm sure you did. If you had, you'd no doubt have tried to educate them in what marriage is really about,' said Catherine smiling cheekily.

'Well, yes, I suppose I would. And looking at that lot that have just gone upstairs, I suspect we've demonstrated it. As you know, I've always argued that marriage is about family. I know that you can't ignore money in the whole equation and the need for somewhere comfortable to live . . . .'

'Here, here,' chirped in Catherine looking at some of the flaky plaster on the walls.

'But for us, don't you think, to have children was one of the reasons we got married. It's about the commitment we made when we married, and though it's a struggle, how else could you get hens with names so early in your life?'

'How can I argue? Here we are, married just over four years and with three children. Katie was a honeymoon baby and the rest just seem to have followed. I don't think we're in much of a position to agree with what your colleagues might have been arguing for.'

'No. Thank goodness we aren't. We have three lovely children. They're happy, and so are we.'

As if to confirm that, Peter turned and kissed Catherine fondly.

'You know while you were upstairs, I was thinking of Ma' Winstone. It seems she had a pretty lonely life in her later years. I wonder how it happens. There's a time in life when everything is hustle and bustle, just as we are now. It seems worth living. There's plenty to do day by day. What happens as people get older? I know when I was about six, a lady a couple of doors from us used to teach me to read. She was old, at least she looked it to me, but still lively and interested in what was happening around her. The thing was that some of the stories I read included grandmas and granddads, and they always seemed to be kindly, indulgent, and good-humoured, as though old age was a stage of life in which one could enjoy the fruits of one's earlier labours. Ma' Winstone doesn't seem to fit that picture. Rarely do the books, if I remember them rightly, refer to the aches and pains and the isolation that she seemed to suffer. Because we've never been old, I suppose it's difficult for us to imagine how it is for someone like her. You see such people, recognise their situation, but don't place yourself there.'

'Good point, but not one I want to even think about too much. We've enough problems, young as we are,' said Catherine, jokingly prodding Peter in the chest with her finger. 'Anyway, we decided we'd do another 'recky' at some stage and look around to see what we could do to improve our own lives here in the cottage. We know we can make this a special place for us and for the children.'

'No doubt they will grow up and move on, as we did, but links to a cottage such as this should always provide that unfathomable sensation that wells up in you when you think of the happiest moments of your childhood. Don't you get those feelings?'

'I do,' said Catherine, 'because I know I was loved. It's the warmth of that love that I want to pass on to the children.'

As she finished her sentence, Peter encircled her with his arms, pulled her towards him, whispered in her ear, 'And what about me?' and then kissed her.

Catherine lingered before pushing him away with a broad smile. 'Get away with you. You know what I mean,' she said as she headed for the stairs. Peter switched off the lights, closed the living room door behind him, and followed her upstairs, reflecting on how different things now were to that day when Catherine and the children alighted from the train after their sojourn in Hull.

CHAPTER 18

DRYSTONE WALLING

Outside the cottage, a good deal of progress was being made. Peter had taken down the ugly looking pergola of glass that had been erected in the corner of the barn and mistal. It had clearly been created by previous owners so that they could enjoy the sun and avoid the persistent westerly breeze. No doubt, at the time, it was a good idea, but now the supporting wood was rotten and some of the glass sheets had cracked. It presented a danger.

Peter also cleared a good deal of the rubbish from in front of the cottage, as well as an old wooden seat that was too wasted to sit on. The clearance provided almost enough room for Catherine's plan to establish a flower garden, but, for this to be a worthwhile project, further space had to be created in front of the cottage. The agreed solution was to link the end of the outhouse, which had now become a makeshift garage, with a new wall to meet the one that created a border between the garden and the moor. This would provide an extended garden and also space for a good-sized gate to replace the very small rickety one that currently provided the only entrance for visitors into the front of the cottage. Peter was enthusiastic about the project, but was left with the question, 'How do you build a drystone wall?' He needed some help.

He decided to go and ask Jack Helme for advice. Jack was now renting the three fields. Peter had made enquiries with his solicitor about the terms of rental and established that, so long as he did not commit to more than three-hundred-and-sixty-four days each year, he could always get the land back. Jack had had no problem with the agreement and so they both went to the solicitor and signed the necessary papers.

A visit across the field to his 'tenant', he liked the sound of the word, to ask for advice about walling led to the offer of some physical help. Delighted, Peter accepted.

A couple of days later, Jack arrived to help Peter complete the dismantling of the original wall and prepare everything for the new one. He said he could only give a couple of days but this should be enough to enable him to give Peter the basics of drystone walling.

'First, tha' needs to dig a ditch wide enough for a couple a' big stones and any fillings that wi' might need so as t'ensure that we have a solid base.' Peter set too and dug a trench so that the base of the wall stood on hard, firm clay and had a good width, sufficient to support the wall as it grew in height. Whilst he was doing that, Jack proceeded to dismantle the old wall with 'Na, we need to complete tekin' t'other wall darn, mekin sure that we keep t'building stone and small stones for t'fillings separate.'

They worked hard through the morning, Peter listening and learning. It was not long before he began to perspire and his back began to ache, but he had to continue his efforts if the job was to be completed. He had made a wise decision to wear leather garden gloves to protect his hands from the coarse, jagged stone, but could not but be impressed by the way in which Jack's roughened hands grasped stones of all shapes and sizes and placed them with care in readiness for later use. By lunch time, the original wall had been dismantled, the base for the new wall had been prepared, and they were in a position to contemplate the building. Jack went back across the field for his lunch while Peter surveyed their efforts. He eventually went inside where he was able to explain to Catherine what they were doing. The enthusiasm he had started the morning with had waned to some extent through his tiredness, but the prospect of building and seeing something grow from his efforts had him looking forward to the next part of the project.

When Jack arrived after his lunch, he explained how they would need to tackle the wall. To start with, Jack was to build and Peter was to hunt out appropriate stones from the nearby pile.

The first task was to establish a firm foundation. The wall was to contain a double gate to allow ease of access, which meant that Peter had had to dig out two stretches of trench about ten feet long, and leave space at the end of each for a post onto which the gate could be fixed. Jack was satisfied that the trenches were wide enough and provided the clay-based foundation that he said was required. He then went on, 'Fi'st, tek' the biggish stones and fixt 'em in t'channel, mekin' sure that they reach t'same height, and mekin' sure that ther' is a gap between the two lines of stone that can be filled wi' small stones that we call t'fillin's. So tha' works at makin' two lines of stone at same height, wi'll use this string to give us a guide.'

Jack then proceeded to fix the level of the first layer of stone wall. 'Dun't worry if they dun't fit exactly, we will just 'ave t'work 'em in.'

Peter proceeded to bring across the bigger stones and watched as Jack fitted them together. He admired the skill with which Jack chose the stone, slotted it alongside another, and followed both the ditch and the line of the string. For Peter, no two stones seemed the same size, but, somehow, Jack had the knack of jointing them into an even height and width. Very occasionally he did what the farmers hated doing, and chipped a bit off the end of a stone to keep his level, saying to Peter, 'Dun't do this often 'cause it wastes thi' stone. All'us try to manoeuvre it and then use t'fillin's to mek' t'wall solid.' Peter carried and watched as the wall grew. It was slow, backbreaking work, which made Peter wonder how the miles of drystone walls that snaked their way across country through Yorkshire and into other northern counties had been built. He no longer underestimated, if he ever had, the time, the energy, and the skill required, nor the seeming covetousness with which the farmers he observed in the fields now cared for them.

Eventually, Jack said, ''Ere, thee have a go.' Peter hesitated, contemplated for a moment, and then changed places with Jack. He quickly realised how difficult the task was as no stone seemed to fit with another, and the precision with which Jack managed the growth of the wall was beyond him. 'Tha' needs to tek' more time to manoeuvre t'stone—and bi' patient. If thy' 'as three or four stones at thi' feet tha' can mek' a choice, but dun't keep pur'ing t'stones darn and goin' to look for others or tha'll never be finished.' Jack came across to Peter and gave him a fairly large stone saying, 'Na' mek' it fit.' Peter saw that he had to make sure that the stone crossed the gap between the two adjacent stones that were beneath so as to provide the binding, just as a bricklayer did with bricks. However, the lack of cement meant that the stones had to be even more carefully balanced and fitted together to give the wall solidity as it grew in height. Peter was patient, worked the stone to fit the need, got, 'Well dun',' from Jack and made progress.

Sometimes Peter changed a stone, and very occasionally he chipped, but always under the guidance of Jack. He began to take satisfaction in the way the wall was developing and in his increasing ability to match stone with stone. His work was not as neat as that of Jack, but it would satisfy the untrained eye. The appearance of Catherine from time to time with words of encouragement and a cup of tea, contributed to the progress being made. The wall increased in length and height as the two lines of stone crept closer and closer to their goal, and the gap between the lines, packed with small stones which found their way into various nooks and crannies, ensured the wall's stability.

Another important element was what Jack called, 'T'thru' stone.' This, Peter learned, was the stone long and large enough to be placed across the two lines of stone at regular intervals, strengthening the binding of the stones and increasing the wall's sturdiness. In addition, there were the coping stones, which sat across the top of the wall, closing any gaps and providing a neat finish with enough 'spike' to discourage jumping sheep.

This job of drystone walling appealed to Peter, and, though it was hard and time-consuming work, he began to take a great deal of pride in it. After Jack left to tend to his own affairs, Peter continued the work and by the time he was called for tea he had what he thought was a substantial piece of wall. He continued with the project, and with visits and advice from Jack when he could give the time, Peter managed to raise the wall to the target height of four to five feet. It was then given a finishing look with the coping stones, which, standing on end, gave further height to the wall. The double iron gate, fixed to wooden posts, linked the two parts of the wall into a secure barrier. Peter stood back often during his endeavours to admire his work, and to see where he could provide finishing touches to a build that was to serve a purpose rather than become a prize-winning asset. It was not difficult to see where Jack had finished and Peter had started!

The wall was important. It declared to the animals of the moor that this was the end of their territory. Peter hoped they understood. His growing knowledge of the country told him that cows were unlikely to challenge a wall or a fence. They tended to accept their environs, grazing within the limits set for them. The moorland sheep were another matter. They were notorious for their persistence in finding ways to access fields, gardens, and buildings that were designed to be out of bounds to them.

Peter had had trouble in the past when a flock had found its way into the front garden, disturbed part of the wall, and decimated what they could find. Their flock instinct ensured that if one found a means of access, the rest would follow. Coping stones and more from the tops of walls would be brushed aside to provide a gap through which others could lumber, and then anything edible became their prize. Peter was constantly surprised by the resolve of the sheep when opposed by a wall as compared with the languorous way in which they grazed across the moor. Even when disturbed, a couple or so skips to distance themselves from the intruder seemed as much as they could muster, especially if it brought them into the shield of the rest of the flock.

Cows, he had come to accept, were different, but for some reason he came to see them as animals blessed with a great curiosity. He could not walk through one of his fields in which his tenant's cows were grazing without their looking at him with what appeared to be great inquisitiveness, as if his every move had to be observed. It was rather like moving through an airport in which patient passengers, waiting for their flight, spend their time observing those who pass, mentally noting their attire, the way they walk, and any luggage they might be carrying. What else was there for them to do? The cows gave Peter a similar feeling. With heads lifted to just above their shoulder height, lower jaws moving from side to side as they continued to munch, their seemingly languid eyes would balefully follow Peter as he took each step. It was as if, like the airport passengers, they were formulating an opinion as to the sort of person he was from the way he conducted himself.

Peter came to believe that he had some sort of adrenalin that attracted the cows, because from time to time they would follow him. Whether they thought he had come to feed them, or simply to fraternise with them, he was not sure. No matter, their actions made him feel uncomfortable, leading to a quickened pace matched by the cows, and occasionally a healthy nudge on the back with a blunt forehead, as he tried to keep his nerve. On one occasion, anxiety led to an increase in the pace from walk to hurry, from hurry to jog, and finally from a jog to run. The cows went through the same phases only more quickly; it was only the gate that provided an escape and gave him the time to ponder his embarrassment. 'After all, they are only cows,' he muttered.

Despite his inexplicable nerviness when in a field occupied by cows, he knew they were harmless. They tended to stay in the areas into which they had been herded, happy to graze, to stand, and to peer, grazing across a field slowly. Occasionally they squeezed up to each other, as if for company, or simply settled on their haunches in the shade chewing their cud.

It came as a shock to Peter, therefore, when, on one occasion, he found a cow in his hen hut. Previous owners had left it and it stood near the cottage in the first of the three fields. Peter had decided to clean and renovate it, and, in agreement with Catherine, he had purchased half a dozen hens, his measured gesture to his connection with farming. These were the hens that had now been named by the children. They clucked and clucked from early morning, always to the delight of the children. As was to be expected, the cockerel, which for some unknown reason the girls had called Nora, was the first to announce the start of a new day.

Luckily, the herd instinct of the domesticated cows was not quite like that of a flock of sheep, and other cows had not attempted to join their buddy on her foray into the hen hut. As a result, the hen hut was threatened by only one horned invader and not the herd. For some unknown reason the cow had made its way through the open door and become stuck. The door was only just wide enough for it to squeeze through, and once inside it had found itself trapped. Those that know these things say that cows will not back out of a space once its haunches touch any sort of impediment. How was Peter to know this? What he did know was that the stamping of feet was doing no good to the wooden floor, and the cow's growing panic indicated worse to come. The tail, still stuck outside the door, swished vigorously and the mooing began to take on the cry of anguish. The cow was spooked and so was Peter. This was a cow with horns and the last thing Peter wanted was to find himself stuck on the end of them. He looked, he thought, and he uttered words like, 'Come on then, let's have you, here girl, here girl,' but all to no avail.

Things were going from bad to worse in the wooden shed, whilst the hens, unaware of the drama, happily clucked and pecked their way through the titbits they were finding on the ground surrounding their home. Peter realised that his only solution was to get back into the cottage, pick up the phone, and ask his tenant farmer yet again for help. He thanked his lucky stars that Jack was able to come over straight away and seek to resolve the problem. Once again, Peter had to recognise his shortcomings as a moorland dweller and his dependence on those who were better equipped to deal with the challenges of the moor.

On arrival, Jack assessed the situation quickly, and came to the conclusion that he had to go into the hen hut and somehow turn the cow around. There was no way that it could be persuaded to come out backwards; as soon as it touched the sides of the hut it stopped and bellowed. Peter looked on aghast as Jack squeezed past the cow's buttocks and entered the hut. He grabbed the cow's horns and using all his strength forced the cow's head down and round. The straw and the muck left by the hens whirled around the hut as if in a cyclone, covering Jack and the cow, and nest boxes crashed to the floor. But in some miraculous way, Jack managed to concentrate all his weight onto the cow's horns whilst turning its head towards the doorway. Once it saw daylight, Jack released the horns and the cow was through the doorway and off into the field mooing and swishing with uninhibited relief. The crisis was over, though the hen hut bore the marks of the cow's visit.

The danger of the action that Jack had taken whilst manoeuvring the cow left Peter shaken.

'Thank goodness, Jack. I was terrified as you got hold of the horns. Anything could have happened.'

'Dun't worry, lad. It wa' my cow and I suppose mi' own responsibility. It wa' better than having to shoot 'er. Anyway, farmers ar' alus takin' risks'.

With that he headed for home across the field. Peter stood in wonder, as well as in admiration, for what Jack had said in his off-hand way about farmers. Peter knew the dangers of the mines, he had seen enough men in his village walking with sticks or bearing a plaster cast on an arm, but he was now learning that life in the country could be equally challenging. What he had just witnessed presented a danger as threatening as most he had seen back home.

CHAPTER 19

SNOW ON THE MOOR

Sitting quietly and listening to the wind whining around the cottage, as if prepared to break through the wall and discomfort the occupants as they sat warmly before the fire of wood, was something that the family quickly grew used to. As time passed, such sounds went largely unnoticed as Peter, Catherine, and the children became more and more accustomed to the varying moods of the moor, and adapted to its sounds and rhythms. The shared calmness within the living room was rarely disturbed by what was happening outside, as the thick walls of the cottage helped to cloister those within, cutting them off from extraneous disturbances.

It became something of a family joke when, one evening, Peter, was disturbed by the incessant drone of wind emitted by the television. He and Catherine, with the children playing at their feet, were watching an excerpt from the Bronte novel *Wuthering Heights*, when, and in some frustration, he commented, 'How ridiculous. Only in poor weather is the wind as bad as that. The sound effects man has overplayed his hand. He's no idea what it's like to live on a moor.'

To demonstrate how wrong the production team was, Peter turned off the television, went to the front door, opened it, and listened for the expected silence. To his astonishment, despite the relative pleasantness of the evening, the whining wind continued, seemingly more persistent than when on the television. The outburst of laughter as the rest of the family realised what was happening drowned the external howling. It also heightened the realisation that the moor had still much to teach the family, and that some people, such as the producers of the Haworth drama, might have grasped its teaching more quickly than they had.

Such occurrences served to demonstrate to Peter and Catherine how life on the moor continued to be a learning experience; and the process of learning continued the longer they lived on the moor. The relative isolation of the cottage in its moorland setting, and the vagaries of the weather, meant that they had to adjust quickly to cope with extremes of change, about which they were unaware when they first moved to the cottage. This was particularly in winter. Rain on a cold morning in the town below often meant sleet or snow on the higher hills. A covering of snow below, meant at least a foot around the cottage, and at its worst it could be as high as the drystone walls. To be caught away from home during such a snowfall meant it was unlikely that a car or van could make it up the hill, despite the town and country tyres, the wheel chains, or the four-wheel drive vehicles favoured by some of the farmers and the wealthier moor dwellers.

Peter's first experience of such inclement weather found him wondering about his chances of getting home from school as he took his afternoon classes. At four o'clock he managed to get to a phone.

'Hi, Catherine. We've quite a bit of snow here. What's the weather like there?' He realised it was a stupid question as soon as he asked it.

'As far as I can see, it's still snowing,' came the reply.

'Are the roads covered to any depth? I need to know whether you think I can make it home or not. What do you reckon?'

'To be honest, I can't see out of the window because of the snow. It's been snowing most of the day and so I suspect it'll be pretty thick.'

'Can you just go and have a look outside then?'

After a longer space of time than he expected, Peter heard, 'That was a stupid thing to ask. When I opened the door the snow blew in and I had a devil of job getting it closed again. I'm wet through. You can forget getting home today.'

'Oh,' uttered Peter, only half aware of what Catherine had met once she opened the door. With his anxiety growing, he sought solutions through throwing questions at Catherine, such as, 'Does that mean I've got no way of getting home? What do you think about my driving along the main road until I get to the turn off for the moor, parking the van and then walking the couple of miles up to the cottage? Do you think there's a chance that the snow may stop so as to give me an opportunity later this evening?'

His mind was racing with options, but he couldn't escape the fact that none of them seemed to offer a solution. His concern for Catherine and the children was growing as each idea came and passed. He shared them with Catherine, who could do no other than to confirm his worst fears. 'You won't be able to get home tonight, and I don't want you to take any silly risks either. Trying to drive looks impossible and thinking of walking up the hill would be even more stupid. You need to find somewhere for the night and let's see what tomorrow brings.'

'But what about you and the children? How can you manage?'

'We'll be all right. The children were sent home early this morning, just as the snow began to fall. All the village children are home safely. I suspect it will be a day or two before they get back to school. I've a good fire and plenty of coal and wood to hand, and we've got food. I've no need to go out of the cottage, so don't worry.'

As the conversation progressed, Peter became increasingly confident in Catherine's ability to manage the situation in which they found themselves. Around him, his colleagues were preparing for home, those having to drive discomforted somewhat by the expected hazards of coping with the snow-covered slippery roads. The lie of the snow was just sufficient to create a thin slush, which was manageable, as long as the wheels did not hit a harder crust and go into a skid. Fortunately, a number of the staff lived locally and so they could leave their cars at school and walk home. It meant a walk through the thickening snow, but at least they would be home for the night with their families.

There was a time when Peter would have been able to do the same, but since his move to the cottage it was obvious that this was no longer going to be possible. As the staffroom slowly emptied, with some staff taking the gamble to drive, while others put on winter coats, scarves and headgear intending to walk, Peter began to consider his options and explore ways in which he could successfully cope with his predicament.

There were hotels in the town, but he was left wondering at what cost; he could contact one of his rugby friends and request a bed for the night; or at worst he might be able to sleep somewhere in school. These were the alternatives he was considering when the head came into the staffroom.

'Tricky weather. I'm pleased we got all the children off. Those who come by bus from the villages just got away before the worst of it. How are you getting home?'

'Unfortunately, it doesn't sound as though I am. I've just rung home and learned that the snow is already over a foot deep on the moor. It's still snowing so hard that Catherine can't see out of the window.'

'So what are you going to do?'

'Well, I'm torn between trying to contact some of my rugby friends to see if they've a spare bed, or trying to find a room in one of the hotels or pubs in town.'

'Look, why don't you come and stay with us? We've a spare room. I'm sure Celia would love to have you. Give me a moment and I'll go and ring her.'

The head was back down in a couple of minutes. 'The family will be delighted to have you, if you wish. I've spoken with Celia and if you're happy to come, all will be ready.'

Peter's immediate problem was solved. He had a bed for the night. This did not ease his concerns about Catherine and the children, but at least he could assuage any worries she might have about his situation. A quick telephone call appraised her of developments.

'That's great,' she said. 'Hopefully all will be well for tomorrow. Lots of love and sleep well.'

Peter was made very welcome at Holdsworth's. The head's wife was a charming woman, and their two children, Matthew, aged fourteen, and Anne, aged sixteen, also showed how pleased they were to welcome Peter into their home. Matthew took him to his bedroom. He showed Peter where he could find things and also how to work the shower in his en suite bathroom. The head's wife sent him up some pyjamas and towels and also an unused toothbrush and toothpaste. Everything was done to make Peter comfortable. He was as impressed with what this house had to offer as he had been on his previous visit to a house in Willesley Road.

Once Peter had sorted things out he went downstairs, where he had supper of a bowl of tomato soup, ham with salad, and a cup of tea with home-baked cream cake. He wondered whether this had been done specially because of his visit, but, observing the ease with which the children tucked into what was offered, he came to the conclusion that something of this sort was a regular feature of the family's early evenings. Once the meal was finished, Peter turned to Mrs Holdsworth, 'Thank you so much for putting me up. Can I help with clearing the table and washing up?'

'Of course not. You sit with Michael and watch TV. I'll sort out the table.'

'Are you sure? I feel guilty not doing something.'

'Get away with you. Go and make yourself comfortable.'

Peter did as instructed. The children carried some of the crockery through to the kitchen and then went upstairs to do their homework. The head and Peter chatted around some inconsequential matters to do with school, their day, and especially about snow and its impact on school life, before the head switched on the TV to watch the nine o'clock news. Reports gave a good deal of time to the disruption caused by snow, especially in Yorkshire, with scenes of blocked roads and stranded vehicles, but the weather forecast that followed the news promised better for the following day, particularly in low lying areas.

After the news, Peter felt it was time to excuse himself and leave the family to get on with their normal business. He thanked Celia, for that is what she had insisted on his calling her, for a pleasant evening, wished the head a goodnight and retired to bed. It was not long before, despite his concerns for Catherine and the children, he fell asleep.

He awoke to the sound of movement downstairs, made use of the bathroom, dressed and went down to the living room. Celia had already prepared breakfast, which he ate along with the rest of the family. On looking through the window, he could still see snow on the ground, although it looked as though the weather may have improved slightly overnight. When he joined Mr Holdsworth to walk to school, they commented to each other that the roads were still dangerous, and Peter's call to Catherine when he reached school confirmed that there were still problems on the moor.

At lunchtime, Peter called Catherine again. She was able to report, 'The section of road that I can see from the cottage is passable, and, in fact, a couple of cars have been through already. A snow plough came by earlier. I suppose the tricky bit will be the steep hill from by the Abbey. Why don't you try coming up the Binkley way. It's more protected and I can see that the plough has been that way.'

'Makes sense. I'll try that.'

Peter was aware that a local farmer was hired by the council to keep the roads as clear as possible and from what Catherine had said he had been in action by mid-morning. It was generally accepted that he couldn't begin his attack on the snow any earlier because of his need to complete his morning work around the farm.

Leaving school promptly at the end of the school day, Peter made his way cautiously along the valley bottom. The snow gritters had been out but motorists, recognising there was still danger, drove at a pace designed to ensure that they kept control of their vehicles and were able to respond to any unforeseen incidents quickly. As Peter began to climb towards the cottage, he mentally blessed the farmer for his work, though the road still harboured rutted snow and on more than one occasion he felt the steering become very light under his hands as the front wheels momentarily lost their grip. The winter tyres at the rear, however, did a marvellously steady job, gripping as they were supposed to, and helping to ensure that he stayed on the road.

Had he had time, he could have marvelled at the scene through which he was driving. What he would have seen if he had not had to concentrate so much, was that beyond the road and across the moor the snow lay still and unscathed; it created a continuous white sheet rising upwards towards the *Beacon*, and levelled the normally corrugated look of the moor, hiding its dips and inclines. As he climbed higher, he would have become aware that the walled sections close to the farms held clusters of sheep, which had been brought in to the safety of the folds as soon as a heavy snow warning had been issued. There were no such refuges for the birds and wild animals of the moor, and the grouse, rabbits and hares, like other moorland creatures, had to rely on their own innate shrewdness to see them through the worst of such winter weather. He dare not look to right or left for fear of losing concentration, and made no attempt to distinguish any signs, whether through a movement or a track, indicating there was any life on the moor. In fact, only if he could have burrowed beneath the snow would the life of the moorland he had become accustomed to, be revealed.

As Peter progressed up the steep slope and tackled the tight bends, the intensity of his concentration produced a sweaty feel to his hands and brow. He had to be particularly careful as he entered and left the very sharp bends that signified he had reached the top of the climb and was passing the few farms that lined the way to the cottage. Maxine had spoken to him on several occasions about driving in ice and snow and he was now thankful for what she had taught him.

'Be extra careful. Try to avoid using the brakes on a bend, and compensate by early gear changes. The big danger is meeting something unexpected and having to brake hard. That's when the car is very likely to skid.'

He respected Maxine's driving, having been impressed when she told him, 'I used to test myself once upon a time by trying to see if I could get down the hill without touching the brakes. The longer I stayed off the brakes, the better I knew I was driving.'

Peter was now intent on trying to outdo her, driving with particular care on the trickiest parts of the road. The snow was banked up to about three feet on the sides of the road, leaving just enough space for one vehicle. Every now and again he came across a small bay that had been cut into the snow by the plough to allow vehicles a passing place. Fortunately, throughout the trip, he did not have to make use of any, as he was unhindered by other road users.

At last he was climbing the small incline to the cottage. There was no hope of putting the car in the garage because of the height of the snow at the door, and so he left it where he stopped, with the bonnet facing the gate and the rear just sufficiently clear of the road to allow other vehicles to pass. He was able to push back the gate wide enough to gain a passage. He was delighted to find that Catherine had spent the day to some purpose, creating a snake like track following the line of the path to the front door, and then moving enough snow to create sufficient gate-width to allow a person to enter.

The relief was indescribable as Peter opened the door and entered the cottage. The children were round his legs and knees in an instant, whilst Catherine, with tears freely flowing, flung her arms round his neck and kissed him as though never to stop. Peter realised, not for the first time, how significant was his spontaneous reaction to Maxine's offer of the cottage. He could not help but ask himself, *Have I really put the family at such enormous risk simply to satisfy my own ill thought-out inclination?* He could not prevent an imperceptible shudder as he returned Catherine's kisses and the children's hugs. If nothing else, the experience had been an acute reminder of the totality of country living and perhaps, although he even now found this difficult to admit, of thoughtless decision making.

Once the family's excitement had settled, the children were back at play, and Peter and Catherine were comfortably seated, the stories of the previous day's experiences, some of which had been exchanged earlier over tea, were continued. Peter had described in some detail his stay at the head's, the warm welcome he was given, and the supper he had enjoyed. He also described the sitting room and his bedroom as best he could, because he knew the interest that Catherine took in such things.

When it came to Catherine's turn, the story she told confirmed the wisdom of his staying overnight.

'This morning, the milkman, Roy, had tried to do his daily milk round. As you know, he has customers not only in the village but across the moor and down into Binkley. It seems as though his round was going pretty well, despite some early morning snow. He has a four-wheel drive and apparently he also puts chains on the rear tyres to help ease his path through the snow and ice.'

'That seems a wise move. I didn't have any chains, but the winter tyres seemed to do a good job.'

'Anyway, just as he had started on his downward journey and the snow was thickening even more, he skidded, slid off the road and hit a gate post. From what I've heard from Carol, who rang to see how you were, the jolt threw him forward, and he banged his head on the steering wheel so hard that it knocked him unconscious.'

'Wow, that's bad news. How is he?' asked Peter with concern.

'Well, he was unconscious. According to what Carol told me, he was in that state for some time. It was only when David Grenston, from the farm just beyond the cattle grid, found him that they managed to contact emergency services and get him to hospital. Fortunately, he seems to be OK now.'

The story heightened Peter's anxieties for his family. Without a means of transport, and with the nearest cottage being at least half a mile away, it was obvious to anyone that they could quickly become at risk, especially in emergencies such as those created by inclement weather. Peter was fearful of making too much of the issue with Catherine because he felt it could only add to some of the worries she had raised when he first told her about the cottage. Instead, he took refuge in the celebrations that welcomed him home. He could not avoid the fact, however, that the experiences of the past twenty-four hours had revealed how the different moods of the moor presented their different challenges, and that they had to be respected. He was left wondering what the morrow would bring, especially as the news promised more snow.

Again, the forecast was correct, and when Peter rose to go to school on what was a beautiful, cloudless morning, he could see deep snow covering the road and the moor. The scene struck Peter as being idyllic, ideal for the photographer or the artist. The tranquillity stifled, rather than accentuated, the usual sounds of the moor, and the songs of the birds and the baaing of the sheep were unexpectedly muted. Much of what he loved about the moor was encapsulated in what he felt as he pulled open the door and stepped outside. The bustle of the town, the pressure of work, and the foibles of the likes of Webster, were no more than mirages which disappeared as he focused on such a blissful scene. His doubts of the previous evening were ousted, replaced by the more desirous reality he now faced. His good fortune was that he was still at home and not elsewhere down in the valley, and, to his delight, the prospects of either him or the children getting to school that morning were nil. The vision of snowmen and family sledging replaced the anxieties of slippery roads and, he inwardly admitted, Webster and his friends.

CHAPTER 20

FURTHER COTTAGE IMPROVEMENTS

There is little doubt that the family's experiences on the moor alerted Peter to the twists of life. If Peter thought that the family's existence would settle to the steady pace of the country he had read about in books or had visualised in his dreams, he was mistaken. The moor revealed too many eccentricities.

Matters were not helped by the fact that the cottage remained in a poor state, and it needed a good deal of work if it was to be made respectably inhabitable. His concerns for his family's safety, as well as for their comfort, were matched by those of Catherine. They recognised that they could not do anything about the changes in weather other than prepare for them, but they knew that they could and should continue with improvements to the cottage. Improving the accommodation, which would provide comfort as well as protection from the worst of the weather, had to remain a priority, and Peter, despite his own selfish desires for involvement with a life beyond the moor, realised that he had to find the time to work along with Catherine to achieve it. When Catherine once again insisted that they had to agree a plan of campaign, he recognised the sense of what she was saying and agreed.

'It's clear', Catherine said to Peter, 'we need to take one room at a time and see how we can improve it.'

'I agree, but where d'you think we should start?'

'Well, we've to see what we can afford. It's obvious that we can't do much upstairs at the moment because of the limited space. The only solution to that is some sort of extension that'll allow us to have another bedroom. It'd be ideal if that also included a kitchen, to replace that apology for one we've got at the moment. But we can only do that in time, we both know that. We've also the problem of getting rid of the waste, and also ensuring we have fresh water. To sort that out is likely to cost us a bomb. We haven't enough money in the bank to get us very far, and if we have to rely just on your salary that isn't going to get us very far either.'

Not wanting to get into any sort of discussion about his thoughtless decision to take on the cottage, Peter, trying to be as cheerful as possible, responded, 'I think all we can do is some further decorating downstairs to brighten the place up a bit more. Like you, I've no idea how we're going to get the money to carry out any major changes, or to do any new building. Even if I got promotion, the increase in salary would be so little that even that wouldn't give us what we need.'

They looked at each other feeling trapped by their lack of finance, even though Catherine had dreams of what she would like to do with the cottage. A new large kitchen, topped by a double bedroom, was high on her list of improvements, though both she and Peter knew, that for the foreseeable future, such a development was out of the question.

And so Catherine could do no other than to agree with Peter. With paint being the cheapest option, all that could be done inside the cottage was to continue brightening it through decorating. What had happened outside with the walling and creation of the garden had cost little more than hard work, the re-use of the available stone, and the support of an expert. But that sort of self-help was not going to achieve all the renovation or development projects that both had in mind.

Some essential jobs had already been undertaken, even before they moved in, but always at a cost they could ill afford. They had found it difficult to manage through those early days.

One important job that had to be done before they could move into the cottage was have it fumigated against woodworm. They had hired a self-advertised expert from a neighbouring village to go in and treat the beams. They recognised that this was essential if they were to be free of the dust and the fear of the flying mites at the beginning of spring, as they picked out fresh chewing grounds.

Peter had visited the cottage daily during the clearing process and had been greeted by a pungent smell, as the workman bored into the hard oak.

'T'worm would never have eaten away this wood,' was his comment as he sweated away. 'It's real solid oak that's bin here for years. T'worm would never ha' conquered it.'

'Why are we bothering doing it then?'

'Well, if you leave it, t'worm would get to your other stuff, and you'd soon know why you're doing it.'

A price had been agreed for the job on the basis of the expert's estimate of the projected time it would take, but Peter became suspicious at the speed at which the work was moving to conclusion.

'You seem to be making good progress,' he commented on one of his visits.

'Aye, I've been working hard,' came the reply.

'I thought it was going to take about a fortnight?'

'Well, it should be finished by t'end a t'week.'

'Does that mean it'll be cheaper?' asked Peter, as money conscious as ever.

'Well, no. It's still taken a lot of materials to do t'job, and I gave you a good price to start wi'.'

'It still seems a lot for a week's work. Surely, you can cut a bit off. I've no doubt that you'll be starting another job next week and so you'll be getting the equivalent of two week's pay for one.'

'You 'ave to be joking. D'you know 'ard this work is?'

'Anyway, I'm not paying all that, no matter. It hasn't taken you anywhere near the time you said.'

'Well, thy is and I 'ave a solicitor that'll tell thi' so,' replied the workman as he packed his tools, cleared his steps into his van, and drove off.

'Oh,' thought Peter, dismayed at the outcome of what he would have liked to have described as his firm business approach. But he remained unsure as to whether, despite the smell, sufficient had been done to rid the cottage of woodworm, and so he persisted in his determination not to pay all that was being asked.

Fortunately, Catherine agreed with his sentiments when he arrived back in Weberton and told her what had transpired. They agreed that they had possibly made a mistake taking on a one-man business for the job, but his price had been impressively competitive, and he had been able to start immediately. It had seemed to be a good move, but now things looked different. They looked even worse when, a few days later, a bill arrived asking for the original fee.

Peter wrote back almost immediately to say that he was not willing to pay so much and to say what he thought was a reasonable fee for the work. To his mind, just over half the sum demanded by the bill would be about right. A couple of days later, a solicitor's letter arrived setting out the costs involved and the price to be paid. Peter and Catherine were at a loss. This was outside their experience, but they still felt justified in resisting the full payment. The only thing to do was to get in touch with Peter's friend at the rugby club, Roger, and ask his advice.

A local solicitor, Roger was happy to help. A few days later, he informed Peter that, after some discussion with the workman's solicitor, he had agreed to settle for a figure between what he had asked and what Peter thought he should pay. Advised to take what was on offer, Peter and Catherine settled, and decided to take their chances with what was left of the woodworm. Fortunately, the thickness and strength of the oak was to prove too big a challenge for any worm that had survived, while careful observation, year on year, of other worm-tempting structures meant that the threat of irreparable damage never materialised.

They were chastened by the experience, and determined to do as much as possible by themselves. Consequently, they agreed that the only sensible thing to do was some rather more tasteful decoration downstairs than had been achieved by Peter and his friends in the earliest days. They recognised that this took them nowhere near their intended goal for the cottage, but was as much as they could do in the short term. As a result, they visited the paint shop in Binkley, looked through the different books for the appropriate shades, and together agreed the colours.

They decided to tackle the dining room first, then the sitting room, and follow by decorating what Catherine had begun to call 'the hole', the kitchen. It was as they were moving the furniture in the dining room into a central position for ease of painting, and taking up the carpet for the same reason, that they came across another unforeseen problem. They discovered what they believed to be rising damp on the east wall. Peter investigated the problem, and quickly clarified the reason for the green stains that were discolouring the lower part of the wall—the earth outside, the continuation of the slope from the moor, was banked up against the wall. As a result, it was continually saturating it with what was left of any water from earlier rains.

'I'll have to sort this out before we start painting. Even with two or three coats this stain will continue to show. I think the solution is to dig out a channel by the wall and so let the water escape into the back garden.'

'Seems to make sense,' Catherine said encouragingly. 'When are you going to start?'

'At the weekend.'

And so in enthusiastic innocence, Peter spent the first part of the weekend removing earth and barrowing it to a part of the field at the back of the house that had been designated as an extension to the back garden. The work was strenuous, but he took some enjoyment from his success in achieving what he had set out to do. By the time he had finished, there was a clear gap running by the side of the wall, capable of carrying away any excess water. He was sure that the damp would now be cured.

He had failed to take into consideration, however, that, in the process, he had exposed the very cracks in the lower wall and foundations that were granting access to the damp. His error was discovered on the evening after the completion of his work when further rain came. Most of the water fortunately followed the channel Peter had dug, but some, instead of appearing as rising damp, began to seep slowly through the wall into the dining room, forming an ever extending pool just inside the offending wall. Something had to be done quickly, 'If', as Catherine said, 'your work is not to finish like a scene from a Charlie Chaplin film.'

Catherine was commissioned to stem the spread of water with cloth, mop and bucket, whilst Peter worked outside in the rain to cement the tiny cracks that had appeared between the lowest stones in the outer wall. Fortunately, their efforts were successful and the water was eventually diverted, the floor dried, and a real disaster averted.

'That's wasn't such a great success,' commented Catherine once Peter had finished.

'Nope,' was his glum response. 'Never thought of that happening. I'm afraid there are more cracks higher up and along the wall that pose a similar risk.'

Catherine and Peter looked at each other with an air of disappointment but said nothing. They both recognised a problem, and subconsciously added it to their list of priorities. But Peter was concerned about the immediacy of the wall's weakness and his response was to jump into the van as soon as the shops were open, and head down into town to buy bags of cement and sand. His craft skills were not one of his strengths, but he knew enough to be able to mix the cement with water, create a malleable paste, and fill any holes in the wall that he could see. He crossed his fingers and hoped—discovering over time that his hope had not been in vain.

Having dealt with the rising damp, the couple decided that, before they started painting, it would make sense, no matter what the risk, to attack the fireplace in the dining room to see what was behind the concrete. The stone pillars surrounding it suggested something more interesting than was currently visible, and so they decided to chip out the concrete around the small electric fire to uncover what was hidden. They speculated that there was something more in keeping with the style and age of the cottage, but, if not, they agreed that it could always be re-covered.

As the hammer and chisel went to work, Peter and Catherine became more and more excited. The more cement fell to the floor, the more convinced they became that they were doing the right thing. Suddenly, a large piece of cement fell, revealing part of what they had hoped they would find, an old ingle nook fireplace. The pace of the hammering quickened, the chisel seemed to get sharper, and in no time the full extent of the hidden treasure was revealed. A superb inglenook fireplace emerged. The darkened, burnt-covered stone base looked up to a wide opening which provided an outlet to the stone chimney. To the right, behind the fire, was an entrance to what Catherine described as a small salt cellar. She had heard that in the past it was customary to keep the salt dry by storing it close by the fire. There was no doubt that there was a space big enough for such a purpose, whether her explanation was right or not.

Protruding from the two stone pillars, which supported the now uncovered mantelpiece, were what looked like two stone seats. As both Peter and Catherine stood back to view what they had exposed, they looked with shocked amazement at one another and almost simultaneously exclaimed, 'How could anybody do that?'

'That's shocking. To cover up such a superb fireplace. What on earth were they thinking of?'

'I'm as astounded as you are Catherine. I mean it's such a superb historic piece, a feature that would be a talking point for any visitor. It still needs a lot of work to bring it back to its best, but it will be well worth it.'

'We'll have to get a proper iron grid and cover, and as usual there's a cost. But you never know, we might get a secondhand one that will look better than anything new. I'd love a spit. Can you imagine what it would be like at Christmas with a turkey turning on it? The kids would love it.'

Once the fireplace had been cleaned of its covering cement, Peter and Catherine cleared up the rubble and swept the floor. They washed down the walls, painted in Peter's first rush of cottage improvement, and followed by wiping the recently stained beams and the staircase with a damp cloth. By mid-afternoon on the following day, the painting, off-white to help accentuate the impressive dark coloured beams and joists, had been completed. The stone flagged floor was an attraction in itself and matched what was around it. Swept and scrubbed, it provided an ideal base for the dining room furniture, as well as for the colourful carpet runner that led from the front door towards the kitchen.

The sitting room presented an easier task as the stone fireplace, simpler and smaller than the inglenook next door, was already in use. Cream coloured paint was applied to the walls, and the carpet and its under felt, which had served the family well in Weberton, were cut and shaved to fit the concreted floor. Once the three piece suite, stools for the children, the oak dresser, the television, and the two water colours prized by Catherine, were rearranged and suitably placed, Peter and Catherine surveyed a sitting room that did much to fulfil their immediate needs.

The addition of new curtains for the windows, cushions for the window seats, and one or two ornaments spread throughout the room, added to its feeling of comfort.

The kitchen presented an altogether different problem.

'I'm not sure we can do much with the 'hole'. It's such a mess. It's tiny and you can hardly move in there.'

Peter was left in no doubt as to Catherine's frustration with a room in which she spent much of her time preparing meals for the family.

'I know what you mean. A totally new build is the only solution, but that has to wait until we can afford it, if ever. All we can do at the moment is to give it another good clean and re-paint it in a colour you would like. You're certainly right about it being small. It's hardly possible for us to pass when we are in there together. But I must say, I get a thrill when we try,' he said fetchingly. 'Do you want to try now?'

Peter's humour did not strike a chord with Catherine, who, with a sweeping brush in her hand, felt as far from the nub of Peter's imagination as the prospect of a new kitchen was from reality.

'The only ones who can find their way in and out of that place with any sort of comfort are the children. If they want attention and I'm busy in there, they always seem to be able to find enough space to fold themselves round my legs as I'm standing at the sink. They'd probably be disappointed to see it go. Come on, let's get on with sorting the place out.' Catherine thus made it clear that there was no time for the pastimes that Peter had been hinting at.

There was no doubt that by the time they had swept, cleaned, and painted the kitchen, it presented a much better work place for Catherine than 'the hole' she had become accustomed to. The kitchen cupboard they had brought from Weberton fitted well once the right position had been found for it, and meant that Catherine had to hand most of the things she needed. The cooker fitted safely in one corner and a small shelf, fitted by Peter, provided further space for storage.

It was with such small steps that Catherine and Peter tackled the cottage. As each of their planned targets was accomplished it became customary for them to celebrate with a glass of wine, a kiss, and sometimes more.

CHAPTER 21

A SURPRISE ANNOUNCEMENT

It was a cold February morning, with a sharp wind tugging at the landscape and blowing loose grass and straw across the fields, when Catherine, pulling Peter close to her, whispered in his ear, 'I'm pregnant'.

Peter gulped, reacted, and enthusiastically pulled Catherine even tighter towards him. 'Blimey, when's it due?' he asked.

'Sometime in October. I've had the usual symptoms, and so when you dropped me in Weberton the other day I took the opportunity to see the doctor, who confirmed it.'

Peter's gulp had been his spontaneous reaction to the anticipated joys of fatherhood. He couldn't believe that they were to have another child. But then the economic implications pushed to enter his thinking. Financially stretched as he and Catherine were, the prospect of another baby was, in that momentary instant of the announcement, somewhat unnerving for Peter. The thoughts, which came and went as lightning flashes in the sky, signalled cost, but were then overwhelmed by the same elation that Catherine was feeling.

'That's great, Catherine. Why didn't you tell me of your suspicions earlier?'

'Well, you're never absolutely sure to start with, but it dawns gradually. I thought I'd wait until it was confirmed by doctor Michaels. He's a super chap and, despite the distance, he's willing to keep me on his books and visit me here if need be. I think that's great, don't you? I'd love to have him continue as the family doctor.'

'He's been very good to us in the past. He's delivered one of our children so it makes sense that he delivers a second. How many more d'you think he'll have to deliver?'

They both laughed.

Peter was impressed by the fact that such a popular and busy general practitioner was willing to travel to the cottage if needed and maintain a relationship that had become very close since the family had moved into Weberton. It was through the anxieties associated with Catherine's high blood pressure and need to enter the hospital for observation two to three weeks before the actual birth, that the doctor had become more and more involved with the family.

Pregnancy, birth, and after-birth, had never been easy for Catherine and never failed to create issues for Peter. The one benefit of those early

1960s thought Peter in later years, was that he was not expected to be present at the bedside when any of the babies were born. The custom of people flying half way round the world, and even missing important events such as playing in a Test Match to be with their wives during the birth, had not yet become the fashion, much to Peter's predilection. Neither did Peter have a desire to see Catherine in pain, even though he did empathise to some extent with the view that to be present was to share, in some way, in that pain, as well as being able to share in the joy resulting from the appearance of a new soul in the world.

He remembered well the birth of their first child, Katie, though more as a result of what happened around it than actually being present with his wife during the birth.

He was still at college when Catherine went into hospital. She had developed high blood pressure and, as happened in later pregnancies, she was admitted to hospital two or three weeks before the symptoms of imminent birth began. Thus, the anxieties of the late rush to hospital were removed, but it did mean a daily bus journey, a walk across the small park, and then a pause in the waiting room before Peter could come to Catherine's bedside. Once in the daily routine, the visits became straightforward, and Peter was able to go and return without any major concerns. And then, one evening, he arrived, went to the bed which he had become accustomed to thinking of as Catherine's, and found it empty. Consternation!

Where is she? Has something unexpected happened? Is she safe? A myriad of questions and disturbing answers, a customary reaction of Peter's when he faced something new, jumped through his sub-consciousness. He went to the nurse on duty, an efficient looking young lady, asking,

'I'm looking for Mrs Delaney. She's usually in the bed just along the corridor, but she's not there. Can you tell me where she is please?'

The nurse looked bemused. 'What was the name again?'

'Delaney. Catherine Delaney.'

The nurse flicked through the pages of the duty book. 'I'm sorry, but I've no record of that name,' she said hesitantly, recognising Peter's anxiety. 'Are you sure that she was on this ward?'

'I've been visiting for the last week and she's always been in that room and in that bed,' responded Peter, his voice reflecting his growing alarm. 'What's going on?'

The nurse looked through her records again, opened a second book, and then, to Peter's great relief, said, 'Ha, here it is. She has been moved to the upstairs ward.'

Without more ado, Peter turned, found and quickly climbed the bare stairs. To his delight, he saw Catherine. 'What are you doing here?' he blurted out.

'Why?'

'Well, I went to the usual bed but you weren't there, and the nurse didn't know where you were. I was desperate. I didn't know what had happened to you.'

'They moved me this morning.'

'Did they give a reason?' he asked, fearing that something unusual had happened to her condition.

'No. I think they just needed the other bed for someone else.'

Peter looked perplexed, but the crisis was over. His anxiety subsided to allow him to give Catherine a loving kiss and then to settle down to talk with her, starting with the usual questions, 'How d'you feel? Have there been any developments? Are they treating you well?'

In her usual sanguine way, Catherine answered his questions, knowing that there was nothing neither could do at this stage to change nature's course. The conversation flowed between the two for the next hour. Peter embraced and kissed, and then made his way back to his digs.

The following evening Peter was able to delight Catherine with the news that his training as a teacher was going well, and that his lecturers had intimated that he was likely to get distinctions in a couple of his subjects at the end of the year. It was, they both agreed, an exciting foretaste of the joy they were anticipating in the birth of their child.

During the second week of Catherine's stay in hospital, in addition to visiting daily, Peter began to ring each morning, to check how things were going. At last he got the news,

'It's a girl, and your wife and baby are both well.'

He was a father and Catherine was a mother. This was the message he shared with his family and friends and all shared in some part of the new parents' euphoria. That evening, the journey into the hospital was one of excitement and anticipation. This being his first experience of parenthood he had no idea what to expect other than that he was going to see his new baby daughter.

He entered the ward to a smiling Catherine. His first action was to take Catherine in his arms, hug her closely and then kiss her with the fond affection they always shared. Only then did he take his first view of the baby, who was in a cot at the side of the bed. What he found shook him to the core. Wrapped as the youngest babies are, with only the face uncovered, all he could see were horribly bruised eyes. He felt sick and did what he should not do, slumped back onto the side of Catherine's bed.

'What's the matter?' Catherine whispered, as she turned her head towards where he was sitting.

Peter did not know what to say but eventually, 'Look at the bruises around her eyes. And her forehead. It has dents. The sides of her forehead are dented.'

Peter's shock had no obvious effect on the satisfied looking Catherine.

'Don't worry about the bruises. She's beautiful,' said Catherine, with the depth of feeling that only the newest of mothers is capable of mustering.

Eventually, Peter collected himself and asked, 'What happened?'

'Well, it was a difficult birth and they had to use tongs. They say it'll take a day or two for her face to heal, and then you'll see how beautiful she is'.

This was Peter's first experience of having a child, and one that he was never likely to forget. He managed to control his anxiety sufficiently to turn to Catherine with a smile, trusting that what she said about the bruises would come to pass, and that the beautiful baby he had anticipated would eventually shine through. Catherine had not deceived him, because as each day passed, the bruises faded and gradually the dents that Peter had seen began to disappear. By the time Catherine brought Katie back to the flat, Katie was as beautiful as Peter had expected to see her on that first day.

The next two babies created fewer problems. In both cases, however, Catherine had blood pressure and was in the hospital early. Peter remembered the baby Sarah being much darker skinned than he had expected, causing him to ask Catherine jokingly if she was sure he was the father. He also remembered Gregory arriving home in Weberton with his mum, just as he was preparing to leave to play rugby. This was the way it was at that time as far as he understood it. Babies were born and looked after, but it was mainly the concern of the mother. He was to learn that such a macho approach would not be tolerated in years to come, but that was the custom of the time as he understood it. Gregory's birth came at a particularly poignant time, however, and the joy that should have surrounded his home coming was subdued, as it coincided with the death of Catherine's mother.

Thinking back on these experiences Peter hoped that the new birth would pass more smoothly. It was no surprise when, during late September, Catherine developed blood pressure and, as usual, went into hospital several days before the expected date of the birth. Not surprisingly, anxiety began to invade Peter's thoughts, as Catherine had been quietly advised by her doctor after the previous birth that it would be unwise to have another child. Peter did not know the reasons for the advice but neither Catherine nor he could totally dismiss it, even though they continued to follow the teaching of the Church with respect to birth control. To use contraceptives was never an option, despite the doctor's words, but the innate concern that Peter now had for the safety of his wife and child raised for him questions that were common amongst his friends in the staffroom; questions that he had often had to rebut, as he sought to defend the position of the Church, as well as his own, in the face of others who challenged him to explain why he followed what to them was such an archaic teaching. He never found it easy, but remained committed to the Church's guidance on the importance of husband and wife having mutual respect for their bodies, and how this respect cemented a partnership in the tenderness of the love needed to properly fulfil the Sacramental commitment they had made during their wedding.

Peter's aunt looked after the children whilst Peter was at work, and her presence also allowed him to make his daily visits to see Catherine. Fortunately, everything went smoothly, and nothing seemed untoward until one night Peter was disturbed at two o'clock in the morning by the phone. Still half asleep, he rightly assumed that it may concern Catherine. With some trepidation he picked up the phone to hear, 'It's a boy. Congratulations. Both are doing well.'

'Fantastic. When can I come and see them?'

'Not too early in the morning because we've to deal with other matters first thing on the ward, but about ten o'clock should be all right.'

Peter went back to bed, and despite his inner excitement closed his eyes and slept. He woke next morning believing that he had had a dream, but he was not entirely sure. Typically, he first sorted out his breakfast, and then thought he ought to ring the hospital to check. Burr, burr; burr, burr, 'Hello?'

'Oh, its Peter Delaney here. I'm not sure whether I received a call last night about my wife or whether I was dreaming, but do we have a son?'

His question was greeted with laughter, and then, 'Of course you have. How could you think you were dreaming?'

Peter, also seeing how amusing his phone call must sound, laughingly responded, 'Hurray. I'll come in to see them both at about ten if that's OK?'

When he arrived at the hospital he could not conceal his embarrassment, which was further tested as he walked through the ward between the two rows of expectant mothers. As if by design, Catherine was in a room at the furthest end of the ward. As a result, he had to run the full gamut of clapping, laughing, and singing, which continued long after he had reached his destination. The expectant mothers, delighted that one of their number, having strained through the agonies of labour, had eventually reached the joy of birth, were in festive mood. Having heard of Peter's morning phone call, they welcomed him with the words of an appropriate song, 'Beautiful Dreamer.'

'Beautiful dreamer,	*Sounds of the rude world*
Wake unto me,	*Heard in the day,*
Starlight and dewdrops	*Led by the moonlight*
Are awaiting thee.	*Have all passed away.*

Beautiful dreamer,   *Gone are the cares of*
King of my song,   *Life's busy throng,*
List' while I woo thee *Beautiful dreamer,*
With soft melody   *Awake unto me.*

Thankfully, all was well with baby and mother. Still smiling embarrassedly, Peter bent to take Catherine into his arms and give her a thankful kiss. She was fine and so was the baby. Catherine couldn't resist a smile, too.

'What on earth d'you think you were doing? Dreaming! You don't change, do you?'

'Not much, I have to admit. But honest, I just didn't know whether I'd heard or not, and so, when I got up, I had to ring in to check. That aside, it's fantastic to see that you're both well. Everything is OK at home, but we're all looking forward to you getting out of hospital. When's that likely to be?'

Just as he finished asking the question, the baby found the energy to gurgle as though ready for lunch.

'Pass him to me and I'll feed him.'

Peter did as asked and watched as Catherine fed the little fellow. As she finished, Peter indicated it was time to go. He kissed Catherine and the baby, put him back into his cot, and took his leave. He managed to escape through the ward without attracting too much attention, and made his exit without further singing.

At the allotted time, Catherine returned to the cottage. Peter's aunt provided plenty of support through the early days of her return. Catherine grew in strength and, as if to outdo his mother, the baby developed ever stronger lungs. He shared Peter's and Catherine's bedroom and did what babies do, kept them awake a good deal of the night. They loved having him and he provided the family with the symmetry, two boys and two girls, which was to be one of the most interesting features of their life together as the years rolled by.

For Peter, his relationship with his aunt took on a new significance during these days. Only when Peter and Catherine had become engaged had he revealed that he had been adopted. To Catherine it was of little consequence, but, as the tale unfolded, she was struck by its incongruity. It emerged that Peter's aunt was his natural mother, but whilst he was still a babe in arms she had deserted her husband and family for a lover. Initially, Peter was looked after by other relatives, but once it became clear that his mother was not going to return, Peter was officially adopted by his natural mother's sister and her husband, and a new life had begun.

Peter did not know that he was adopted until he was about ten or eleven, and then not from his parents, but from a friend of his who had overheard a conversation between their two mothers. Whether his parents ever intended to tell Peter of the situation he never knew, but once he had faced them with the question, they told him as much of the story as they could.

Peter had never met his father. He had left the village a short time after the breakup of his marriage and, as far as Peter understood, the family lost contact with him. The fascination for Peter was that his natural mother and her sister had remained very close and consequently, as a child, he often visited his natural mother without knowing of the relationship. As a result, he related to her well, loved her as an aunt, and never saw any signs of antipathy between the two sisters. Everyone had seemingly accepted the situation and moved on. To Peter it was a remarkable story. His aunt, whilst always being on hand for Peter and Catherine if needed, never sought to undermine what had existed for many years, and even after the deaths of his adoptive parents continued to act as the supportive aunt. For his part, Peter never castigated his aunt for what had happened and he had never put to her the question, 'Why?'

Peter and Catherine very occasionally spoke about the situation, and both wondered sometimes as to what had actually happened to his natural father. Through a high commitment of loyalty to his adoptive parents, and perhaps of thankfulness for being given a happy childhood and family life, Peter had never made enquiries about his natural father or asked his aunt about him. He had been led to believe through family chatter that there was some Jewish connection, but he was never sure. He was clearly not interested in opening up old sores or creating tensions within his own life or that of his family. His relationship with his auntie and his adoptive parents was important to him and not to be disturbed. Perhaps it was this which also dissuaded him from sharing such sensitive information with his own children. What he failed to realise, however, was that his children had rights, rights of grandchildren to know who their grandfather was. It was much later that this was brought home to him by Gregory, who, speaking on behalf of the rest of the children, expressed his unhappiness at not knowing from whom he was descended. Peter's realisation of their concern raised his own unease about his past, and the thought that one day he may look for the answer.

It had become natural for Peter to visit his aunt regularly, spend annual holidays with her, and see her simply as a loving aunt. For him, she offered regular fish and chips, she ran a fish and chip shop, and the opportunity to meet with like-minded boys in the park opposite where he learned the basics of rugby and cricket. There was, therefore, a certain understandable naturalness about the ease with which Peter could look to his aunt for help with the family if needed, and the relaxed relationship between his aunt and the children, even though it was only after their aunt's death that the children learned something of their father's family history.

Although Peter could never understand how his mother could leave him as a baby, even if it was with her family, he never really allowed himself to be embittered. He had loving parents and a supportive aunt throughout his early life, and this gave him a security that he felt others who had been adopted may not have had. He did ponder often, however, on how successfully the whole family, which included his natural mother's lover, had remained close. They never allowed, what he had to accept was a strange situation, to impinge on what he saw as a happy family life.

As for Catherine, the situation hardly impacted on her relationships with Peter's relatives. She wondered, however, about the effect adoption might have on a child and in particular on Peter. She had seen the insecurity of children who had been taken from their families, as in the case of evacuees who had come into her village during the war. The often outward signs that those children gave of having come to terms with their situation and all that surrounded them, gave those who cared for them or played with them the feeling that all was well. Only occasionally had Catherine seen a refugee deliberately divorce herself from the group, and for a short time look adrift and forlorn.

As she grew older, Catherine realised that such behaviour reflected the fact that these children had brought with them the loss of family and friends, and the uncertainties associated with their changed circumstances. They anticipated being away from their parents and homes only temporarily, though the lack of a clear date for their return no doubt left them in an indeterminate state, little understood by those with whom they were spending their early life. The best of them worked at surviving, whilst a few had a tendency to lose their equilibrium if put under pressure, to react in unexpected ways, and to disconcert those who regarded them as temporary members of their families.

In Peter's case his separation from his natural family had been permanent and from time to time Catherine wondered if this could be a factor in the way he behaved. She had heard of adopted children occasionally reacting in ways reflecting an insecurity that, for much of their lives, lay hidden and only occasionally surfaced. Though the couple rarely discussed Peter's parents, her consciousness of his background encouraged her to look for any signs of any unsettling effect on his behaviour, or the extent to which it might explain a reaction that appeared out of character. Not surprisingly, she interpreted his tendency to make snap decisions, which did not fit in with his usual sound, loyal, and committed disposition, as an outcome of this. For Peter, the rarity of incidents that required him to draw out explanations for behaviour that might be related to his adoption, led him to ignore its consequences, and confirmed his view that the extended family life afforded to him by its peculiar circumstances had worked in his favour.

In quiet moments, Catherine would ruminate on how the two sisters related to what they surely perceived as Peter's unusual circumstances. An important aspect of parenthood, as she understood it, was to have the responsibility of introducing a child into the world and helping him to develop what his parents regarded as worthwhile attitudes, behaviour, and values. Her experience, especially through her contact with parents and children in her work in hospitals, led her to recognise that different parents interpreted these traits in different ways, and that their expectations of their children's response to various situations differed. To one parent, the freedom of a child to express itself in any way it chose, even screaming for attention in public, was regarded as acceptable and normal. To another, tight boundaries of what is not permissible would be set to ensure that such behaviour was unlikely to occur, and a child would be made aware of the parent's displeasure if it did. Catherine acknowledged that these examples were extremes, and believed that the expectations of most parents would lie somewhere within such a grid.

Nevertheless, she knew that parents did have different ways of bringing up their children and would often express views on the different approaches of other parents. When in this thoughtful mood, Catherine sought to put herself in the situation of the children's great-aunt. She would have observed Peter as a child and seen how her sister and brother-in-law treated him. She would have grown to recognise the boundaries set and what characteristics were praised or punished. To what extent, thought Catherine, did she agree with the expectations placed upon him, and how different would they have been if she had not deserted him in infancy? How did she cope when she saw things happen with which she did not agree? Did she feel the stress and frustration associated with wanting to interfere when Peter's parents acted in a way contrary to that which she would have espoused? Did she ever interfere, feeling the right to protect Peter, who, after all, was her own child? And how did she view her grandchildren?

Catherine also wondered how different a person Peter would have been if he had not been adopted, or if his mother and father had been his natural parents. To what extent would his personality have been so appealing to her if he had stayed with his 'aunt', rather than having been taken in by his parents to imbibe those qualities that made him so attractive to her? Did he have some characteristics with which his natural parents endowed him, and others that had been developed through the careful nurturing he had received from his foster parents? Was the selfish and often spontaneous response to issues of concern to himself genetic, and so partially the responsibility of his aunt, or developed through experience, and so the responsibility of his foster parents? These questions about Peter's circumstances did not unduly trouble Catherine, but they enthralled her when she found her mind wandering in their direction.

The occasions on which she pondered such questions also led her to consider the impact that she and Peter were having on the lives of their own children. Peter often referred to the experiences of his young life in a mining community, and how this had affected his approach to life in general, as well as in the way he related to his children. He told the children, with great pride, about the qualities of the miners and their wives, their honesty, their support for each other, and their underlying loyalty. He also outlined the many areas of success that those who had been born in such communities had registered. He related stories of athletes, of musicians, of writers, and of politicians, all of which he hoped would help to broaden the children's understanding of the different facets of their ancestry and of life in general. When added to what she also shared with them, about life in wartime childhood, the importance of her mother's and father's work during the war years, and about the dangers of living near a seaport, Catherine trusted that the children had, as the old adage indicates, 'an insight into the tapestry of life.' Her's and Peter's commitment to helping the children understand their heritage would help them, she believed, form attitudes and views, just as they would influence the values they developed.

Nevertheless, Peter did not share with them the fact that he was adopted or of his special relationship to their aunt. Catherine respected his desire for discretion in this matter, and was never tempted herself to say anything to the children about it. The good sense of their approach was observable in the lovable way the children continued to treat their respective 'Gran' and 'Auntie', and the fact that they were not torn between loyalties that they were probably too young to understand.

CHAPTER 22

THE PROSPECT OF
A CONCERT

Peter became used to the drive from the cottage to school and back. Coping with the steep hill and the sharp bends became second nature to him, and he prided himself on manoeuvring the van with the skills which he had first seen Maxine employ. He never forgot his experience in the ditch, no doubt his embarrassment had been enjoyed among the coterie of farmers who inhabited the moor, and he always took particular care if he saw another vehicle approaching.

As his teaching career progressed he also came to manage more effectively some of the difficulties he had experienced in his first couple of years. As he developed techniques based on his own experience and the experiences shared with him by his colleagues, his control of a class became second nature. He learned that the more settled and confident he looked, the more responsive the pupils became. He also realised that the same applied when he could demonstrate that what he was teaching was important to him as well as to them; in a strange sort of way, they became rather like apprentices, keen to grasp what was being taught by someone who had knowledge they wanted to share. As a result, they were prepared to ask questions, challenge, and investigate, to get a more accurate picture of what they were engaged in.

He was particularly pleased with the response of a fourth form class to a lesson on the First World War. It was a lesson following up previous work on the same topic. Peter briefly explained, 'As you know, the Battle of the Somme took place in 1916. It lasted for just over four months and involved a joint French and British force seeking to break through the German lines. It was a major battle in the First World War. I want you to use the books, maps, illustrations, and the photographs that I've put on your desks, to answer the questions on the board.'

He pointed to the questions and then asked the children if they understood the task. As they had no questions, Peter indicated they should get started. He was impressed by the way they settled down and the determination they showed in seeking answers. The group discussions were lively and the children made excellent use of the resources. Peter was also impressed with the searching questions the pupils asked him and how often the different groups combined without his intervention to discuss the information they were collecting. By the end of the lesson, the pupils had made marked progress.

That is not to say that everything went smoothly. Peter still had Webster and one or two like him to deal with. Webster was now taller and stronger than when Peter had first come across him. He could, therefore, be a far more difficult customer to deal with. The closed fist that he had shown Peter in an earlier year, which had been neutralised by Peter's look of, *Don't try it son*, would now pose a far trickier threat than it did at that time. In some respects, however, Peter found him more cooperative than previously. This surprised Peter a little, as Webster was now at that teenage phase of his life when he could be expected to become more rebellious, disobedient and at worst intolerable. He was at the stage of his life when the reputation he had established was likely to tempt him, even more than previously, into conflict. Like the children who followed the Pied Piper, he might have been expected to disappear more and more from a life of normalcy. But this had not happened.

Peter persuaded himself that the improvement he had noticed in Webster's attitude was related to his links with the brass group. Despite the predictions of some of Peter's colleagues, and also of his own fears, Webster had persevered. He continued to attend private lessons with Peter, group sessions with the rest of the band, and to practise in the music room after school. His inexplicable spontaneous behaviour continued, however, with the occasional outburst of expletives, 'This f . . . . ing instrument won't play the right notes,' or the quick exit from the room, only to return a few minutes later. Peter, aware of his own propensity to spontaneous actions, was less amazed than most at how he managed to control himself and allow Webster to continue in the group after such outbursts.

He believed that his patience was paying off. Although the boy was still tempted from time to time to try to create some mischief, his overall approach in the classroom had become much more positive. Peter began to feel that he was beginning to create a tentative bond of trust with the lad. Webster was prepared to put up his hand to answer questions, and on occasions to ask serious questions for clarification. His former sidekicks also seemed to have sensed the change and had found another leader, a pupil with little of the craft or imagination of Webster, and so, much easier to handle.

What was even more satisfying for Peter was the progress that Webster was making on the trombone. He really did want to be the new Tommy Dorsey or even Glenn Miller, another name he had come across, the result of a film he had seen. When Webster was quietly warming up in readiness for a group session, his *Little Brown Jug* was, thought Peter, worth catching.

Peter had had to give up his own position in the local brass band once he moved to the cottage. Disappointed as he was, he knew it made sense. He was daunted by the time he would have to give to attending rehearsals and the occasional concert when there was so much to do in the cottage. He was delighted, on the other hand, to hear that two more of his cornet players, young Whittaker and Smithson, had gone along to the band, had an audition, and had been accepted as second and third cornet players. He was sure that this would help raise their standards considerably and also give further encouragement to his group, which was, he happily told everyone, making good progress.

The band was now meeting once or twice each week after school. It was and during one of these evening rehearsals that Peter was surprised to see the head standing at the back of the hall. He was obviously listening to the band as they played through, tunefully, Peter thought, a piece entitled 'Negro Spirituals'. Peter felt that this style of music, as well as the melodious hymns the group often started rehearsals with, would help develop the rich tone and well-balanced sound he was searching for. He remembered, from his own days as a young musician, a new conductor coming to his own band and starting every rehearsal with a series of hymns. The result was a band with outstanding tonal qualities that went on to win the British Open Championship. Peter didn't quite foresee such an achievement for his brass group, but anyone listening to his young players over a period of a few weeks would certainly notice the improvement in the quality of their playing. The bass, euphonium and horns supplied an effective foundation upon which the melodious cornets and trombone could express their skills.

As the group finished their rehearsal, and began to pack away their instruments, the head approached Peter.

'How are things going?'

'I'm really happy with the progress several of them are making. Some, as I suppose you'd expect, don't give enough time to practice. But because I arrange the parts they're playing in the group at a level at which I know they can cope, they are able to make a positive contribution and get some pleasure from it.'

'So you do all the arranging?'

'Well, I have to, because some of pupils would struggle with some of the parts that are in the professionally arranged stuff.'

'Interesting,' said the head. 'I must say, standing at the back of the hall, I was impressed with what I heard. They make a lovely sound, and young Whittaker on the cornet played his solo parts beautifully. I thought Webster did OK on his trombone, too, in 'Deep River'.'

'You'll be interested to know that Whittaker and Smithson have joined the local brass band. They're very keen and I reckon they'll make very good players. Joan Jameson on flugelhorn, Bill Dodds on euphonium, and young Webster are also making good progress. In fact, Webster shows real talent, and, if he could control his behaviour more consistently, I think he'd also be a welcome addition to the town band.'

Peter was delighted that the head was taking such interest and was showing such pleasure in the band's progress. He knew the head had spent more at the auction than he had anticipated, without being totally sure as to how well Peter, a young and inexperienced teacher, would cope with the responsibility.

'I'm delighted to hear what you say about the way the pupils are progressing. I'm aware that you've spent a lot of time. From what I've just heard, they're doing so well that I'm sure they'll do what I hoped, that is broaden their own experience and enhance the school's reputation. On that matter, I came down to ask you something.'

The head looked pointedly at Peter, knowing that what he was about to ask would have important repercussions for the band and for the school. 'I've been contacted by the local town council. They're keen to develop links with schools and give them what encouragement they can. They also want to show to the locality, what schools such as this can do for their children. As you know, we live under the shadow of the grammar school, which isn't good for our parents or pupils. Anyway, the council's heard of the brass group. Apparently, the father of one of our pupils, Maureen Smith, is on the town council. Maureen told him about the group and how well they play in assemblies. Her father took a chance, brought it to the notice of the council, and they were interested. They've asked if you can give a concert in the town hall before the end of term. They'll make all the arrangements and also make a contribution to the band's funds.'

The head had said all this with hardly a change in his expression, and determined to make it look as though the request was as normal as his asking for Peter's lesson plans. Peter's reaction was somewhat different. His puffed out cheeks were followed by a quiet explosion of air, announcing the word, 'Phew. That's a tall order. A concert in the town hall? I'm not sure.'

'Well, while you're thinking it over, there's been another request,' the head said, now with an amused smile, as he observed Peter's obvious but, he hoped, temporary discomfort. 'The parish church wondered if you could accompany some of the carols at their annual carol service.'

Peter looked at the head as the last of his musicians disappeared through the hall door with a quizzical expression. 'You must be joking.'

The head didn't bother to respond, but simply watched as Peter twiddled his baton, stared into the distance thoughtfully, and then added, 'I'll have to discuss it with the pupils. Heaven alone knows what they'll say. When do they need answers by?'

'No hurry, I understand. You talk to the band and then let me know. I hope they're as taken by it as I am. I have every confidence in you and them. I'm sure they'd put on a good show.'

Peter wasted no time in sounding out his musicians. After assembly the following morning, he called them together and told them of the requests. The three girls, with flushed cheeks, bright excited eyes, and self-conscious smiles, looked at each other as if unsure of what to make of the request, whilst the boys looked more stunned than quizzical. Eventually, young Michael Smithson verbalised what everyone else seemed to be thinking, 'What the heck are you talking about?'

'That's exactly what I thought when the head asked about this yesterday afternoon. But I've had time to think about it and my guess is that with some hard work and extra practice we could do it. Any thoughts?'

Joan Jameson, having recovered from her first rush of excited anxiety, like a fledgling bird that had suddenly found it had wings, exclaimed in a strong confident voice, 'We should do it. What's the point of doing all this practice if we don't play anywhere?'

Having been given a lead, the others chimed in, almost all of them expressing support for the idea.

'Excellent. But that means more practice, more rehearsals, and an extension of our repertoire'.

'What's a bloody repertoire?' muttered Webster to Smithson, just loud enough for Peter to hear, but with an insufficiency of force to suggest that he did not want Peter to catch the phrase.

Saying he would let them know of the extra rehearsals, Peter sent them off to their classes. He went along to his, stimulated by the buzz he was getting from the anticipation of public performances. He knew there were challenges ahead, and he also knew that the extra rehearsals would conflict with what still had to be done in the cottage, but he recognised how important, in different ways, a performance in the town hall would be. Peter was going to have much to do. First, he had to organise a programme of music, and then spend time arranging the music so that all the pupils could participate with confidence. He was also aware that some of the instrumentalists needed a lot more practice if they were to perform to the level required, and this meant more commitment from him. He recognised his good fortune in having the likes of Alan, Arthur, and Joan, who would provide an excellent lead to the rest of the group. He knew which pupils would relish the opportunity of playing a solo, an essential ingredient in any concert. And he also wondered about Webster? He had probably made more progress in the last few weeks than any of the other pupils. What contribution could he make to the concert?

Peter loved the sound of the trombone. He had been raised in a home which had resounded with its sometimes mellow and sometimes sharp tones as his dad, a player of some repute, went through his paces. He used to love to hear his dad play 'Panis Angelicus', which for him suited the qualities of the trombone like no other piece. He and his mam used to sing along with the music, Peter the words, his school Latin giving him the pronunciation and meaning, and his mam humming.

'Panis angelicus	(Bread of Angels,
fit panis hominum;	made the bread of men;
Dat panis caelicus	The Bread of heaven
figuris terminum:	puts an end to all symbols;
O res mirabilis!	A thing wonderful!
manducat Dominum	The Lord becomes our food:
Pauper, servus, et humilis.	Poor, a servant, and humble.
Te trina Deitas	We beseech Thee,
unaque poscimus:	Godhead One in Three

Sic nos tu visita,	That Thou wilt visit us,
sicut te colimus;	as we worship Thee,
Per tuas semitas	lead us through Thy ways,
duc nos quo tendimus,	We who wish to reach the light
Ad lucem quam inhabitas.	in which Thou dwellest.
Amen.'	Amen.)

He knew that audiences loved to hear the trombone classic, *The Acrobat*, but for Peter it displayed more the benefits of the trombone slide rather than the intrinsic virtues of the melodious tone of the instrument.

He wondered whether he dared offer Webster a solo spot with *Panis Angelicus*. It didn't take him long to make up his mind, as he dismissed any likely problems. He knew it was a risk as time was limited, and he knew it would be hard work getting Webster up to standard, but he felt the risk was worth taking and decided to go ahead and offer him the spot.

Webster received the news with a look of disbelief. His mouth opened in such a way as to show his top teeth. Lines appeared from the ends of his lips to the bottom of his nose, and the tight wrinkles which appeared around his eyes forced them into a squint. Whereas Peter's other two prospective soloists had accepted his proposal with equanimity, and possibly a fleeting hint of pride, Webster could not withhold, 'You've got to be kidding. There's no way I'm standing up in front of a crowd of people to make a fool of mi'self, and if tha' thinks so, tha's gor another think coming.'

The startling, and to Webster clearly disconcerting, news provoked him into the slang of the playground. It also spurred him into rising from his seat, and with his trombone and case tucked under his arm marching through the hall door. It was five minutes before he self-consciously rejoined the rehearsing band.

After practice, Peter took Webster to one side and impressed upon him the seriousness of his proposal. 'Look, lad, I know my suggestion came as something of a shock.'

'You're bloody right it did,' mumbled Webster, head bent towards his shoes.

Peter ignored the expletive and went on. 'You must know that you've made the best progress in the band. You've a good range, you've that mellow tone that trombone players seek, and, despite your outbursts, I know you've confidence in what you can do. I know, because I've followed your improvement very carefully. Don't you remember when you could not read a note of music or know where to put the slide to play even the easiest tunes? Now you can do all those things and more. You started with *Tune a Day*, simple little exercises designed to introduce you to the instrument. Now you're working through *Arban's Tutor*, tackling some really tricky routines. Don't you realise how good you are?'

Still unimpressed, Webster retorted, 'That's not the same as standing in front of people and playing. Anyway, what d'you want me to play?'

That Webster had asked what he might be expected to play was taken as a sign of encouragement by Peter. 'I've given this some thought, and I feel you could manage *Panis Angelicus*'.

'What sort of bloody pan is that? I thought I was playing the trombone,' blurted the prospective soloist.

Half turning his head, and covering his mouth with his hand as if to sneeze, Peter just managed to avoid laughing out loud. 'You'll see when we start practising it. I'm seeing Alan and Joan, the other two soloists, once a week, but I think it will be helpful to see you a little more often at the beginning. When you've got the hang of it, you can spend more time on your own. What d'you think?'

Peter saw a flicker of interest in Webster's eyes, like a dawn beginning to appear in the eastern sky, an interest that Peter hoped would ripen into enthusiasm as the dawn matures into full day. Peter recognised the signs of Webster's emerging perception that this might not be a bad thing after all. He guessed, rightly, that Webster was beginning to have some fear of the practice required and how he would cope with it. But on the other hand, it did not escape the lad that there was the status to be gained through performing in front of a crowd of people. He even began to think of the pleasure that it might possibly bring his family, particularly when they saw that the evenings he was late home from school were not all wasted by his getting into mischief, but that some had been spent profitably.

'That's settled then. We'll start tomorrow evening looking at the piece I think will be suitable. It's always useful to learn the words of an aria that you are going to play and so I'll copy those out for you. They're in Latin. Will that be OK?'

Peter found it impossible this time to hide his laughter as he saw the stunned look on Webster's face.

'Only joking,' said Peter, deciding in his own mind to give Webster both the Latin and the English translation, though neither would mean much to him.

Peter felt the talk with Webster had gone well. The lad's initial suspicion of what Peter was offering had certainly disappeared and, as he left Peter, he looked quietly pleased with himself. Nevertheless, Peter knew that the idiosyncratic Webster was never likely to allow him to feel completely comfortable.

CHAPTER 23

THE CONCERT

P reparations for the concert progressed well. Peter found time, despite his many other commitments, to give each of his instrumentalists extra tuition where it was needed. His soloists required special attention because for all three it would be the first public performance. Alan had chosen to play *'Il Bacio'* (*'The Kiss'*), a piece in which he could show not only his aptitude for the melodic but also his flair for the more intricate skills required by a maturing cornet player. Joan was to tackle the tuneful *'Danny Boy'* on the flugelhorn. She had practised conscientiously, and Peter knew that she was prepared to give up to two hours a day to master the instrument. It was extremely gratifying for him to see how confident she had become and how, in her own way, she had developed into a leader in the brass group. If Peter wanted a good example to help encourage others, he would turn to Joan. Similarly, most other pupils would go to her if they had any problems with their instruments or any difficulties in reading some new music they were preparing to play.

She also became very much the spokesperson for the group. Peter was not surprised, therefore, when, with the band well into its preparations for the concert, Joan approached him. 'Sir, d'you think we're doing all right?'

'I've certainly been very pleased with the response of all the members of the band, Joan, and I think we're making super progress. As you know, none of us was very sure when Mr Holdsworth first asked us to play in the town hall, but the fact is I'm now really looking forward to the concert. Aren't you?'

'I am, and I know the rest are. But one or two think you're asking too much of us. They wanted to know if you could have fewer band practices.'

'D'you thinks it's becoming a problem?'

'I do, sir. When we add the time for individual practice, it's not leaving us much time to do the other things we need to do for school.'

Wisely, Peter listened. He looked carefully at the programme he had planned and realised that there was justification in what Joan had said. He resolved, therefore, to ease the burden on the musicians. His strategy was to ask for fewer rehearsals and reduce the time in rehearsal on occasions. He continued to monitor progress and was satisfied that with his more flexible approach, the band was still likely to reach the standard of performance he was hoping for.

As for Webster, things inevitably remained tricky. He continued to practise and make impressive progress, but his temperament occasionally got the better of him, and when corrected, he performed his disappearing act. Fortunately, he would return, settle, and do his best to contribute effectively to the band's efforts. His custom of practising in school rather than at home worked in his favour, as Peter often had a few minutes to pop into the music room and give him some serious tuition. The lad showed real talent as he came to understand the varied attributes of his instrument and his own skill in exploiting them. Other pupils in the group also recognised this, and it was clear to Peter that this was one of the reasons they were prepared to put up with his erratic behaviour. There was no doubt that when he first rehearsed 'Panis Angelicus' with the band, impressed by his teenage mastery of the piece, the group as a whole raised the quality of their own playing.

Despite his progress in the band and the close association he now had with Peter, Webster's behaviour in class and around the school remained problematic. Peter did what he could to speak up for him in the staffroom when more of his misdemeanours were highlighted, but he knew from his own experiences that there was no ready solution. At one of the regular pastoral meetings, when teachers discussed concerns about the pupils within their particular year, Webster's name cropped up.

'Webster. I see he's been in trouble again,' was a usual refrain of Stan, who was now the head of year, with special responsibility for pupils' welfare in Webster's year group.

As one of his teachers, Peter, always looking to mollify the criticisms of his colleagues, sought the positives in his contribution to the discussion. 'I agree Webster can be a nuisance in class and around the school, but I find he's a much more amenable lad with a trombone in his hands. You can't believe the difference. And I feel, as a result, things are a bit better in my lessons, though I know he can be very obstinate when faced with a bit of criticism.'

'I've a feeling he needs the help of a psychiatrist. Do we know if the head has a view on this?' asked Arthur.

'I'm not sure,' replied Stan. 'It's a matter that I could take up with him, if you feel it could be worthwhile.'

Arthur was in quickly, 'Well, I do.'

Others sitting round the table indicated their agreement.

'I'll raise it with the head then. Is it OK if I suggest that he call in Webster's parents to discuss it? I'm pretty sure it's been raised with them before, but they don't show much interest. Without their permission, we can't do much. We can recommend it to them and seek the advice of the education authority, but without the support of his parents, I'm pretty sure we won't achieve much. I understand that the new descriptor on the block is attention deficit disorder. Whether there is such a thing or not, it's pretty obvious that Webster has some of the symptoms.'

There were nods around the assembled staff and it was generally agreed that the parents should be called into school.

As the meeting broke up, much amusing discussion took place around attention deficit disorder, with jokes being made about staff who obviously suffered from it. To Peter and his immediate friends, it was those who walked off with other colleagues' pens, failed to make more than their own cup of coffee, or when first to school did not bring in the morning milk from the front door.

Peter continued his preparations for the concert and provided some variation with a few carols that the band had been asked to play at the parish church carol service. His easing of pressure on the pupils had no obvious ill effects, and the pupils grew in confidence, tackling the half dozen pieces with increasing expertise.

On one occasion, when going through the pieces on the programme for the concert with the band, as a shot at humour and a sort of get his own back on Webster, he called across, 'Worked out what a repertoire is yet, Joe?'

He got what he expected—some giggles and a contemptuous look from the trombone section.

Once he was sure that the pupils played the pieces accurately, keeping to a minimum any mistakes, Peter moved on to working on articulation, tonal light and shade, and the meaning of words indicated on the manuscripts, such as *rallentando*, to ensure sensitivity and mood. He used his baton, arms, and voice to draw from the band the right response, stopping on occasions to repeat and improve. As the practices progressed, the quality of the playing developed and each pupil's belief in his or her ability spread through the band to provide it with that resonance of sound that only a well-practised and confident band could produce.

With things going so well with the brass group and with school more generally, Peter was disappointed to hear that the Websters had been into school and during a rather heated meeting had refused to have anything to do with any sort of psychiatry.

'We know that Joe can be a problem. We've had to come up to school too often not to know that. All he needs is a clip around the ear and that'll be the end of it.' Taking the lead, his mother went on. 'Just let me know if he's been a problem and I'll sort it. The psych . . . . whatever it is you want will not be half as effective as a good wallop.'

Apparently, that was where the meeting ended. Nothing was resolved, and in truth, no one expected anything different. Webster continued in his customary ways, often being a nuisance in class and causing mayhem on occasions outside. If there was any sort of pupil disturbance on the field at break time, it was almost guaranteed that Webster would have something to do with it.

Then disaster. Two weeks before the planned concert, Webster and three of his chums had been caught by the caretaker despoiling the downstairs boys' toilets by kicking in the doors. These were not the first toilets to be damaged by pupils—even the girls were known to spread graffiti across walls—but this was the first time that the culprits had been doing so much damage and had been caught red-handed. Peter agreed wholeheartedly with his colleagues that punishment should be severe, but his views on what it should be were tempered by the concerns he had for the likely impact on his concert preparations. Others expressed strongly their view that exclusion was the only way. Peter was in a quiet panic once he heard such a solution being discussed.

The head dealt with the matter swiftly. He called the boys into his office, impressed upon them the seriousness of their behaviour, and told them that he was suspending them immediately. He then sent the boys home with a letter requesting their parents' presence at school as soon as possible. The letter read,

Dear Mr and Mrs X

I have, once again, to draw your attention to your son's misbehaviour in school. On this occasion, he was responsible, along with two other boys, for causing serious damage in the school toilets. The matter is important enough for me to consider expelling him from school. Before I take such a crucial decision, however, I should like to discuss the matter with you. I am sending him home, where he should stay, until you have been in to school to see me.

I trust you will impress upon him the importance of respecting the property of others and following diligently school rules.

I look forward to seeing you in the very near future.

Yours faithfully,
Mr Holdsworth (Headteacher)

When Peter heard of the exclusion and the contents of the letter, he feared for his concert programme. No Webster meant no *'Panis Angelicus'* and no trombone section. If the exclusion lasted more than a couple of days, the momentum of preparation for the concert as planned would be seriously hampered, and he would have to work hard to find alternatives. In class, in the staffroom, and at home, though he tried hard not to, he showed his despondency.

For once, Webster's parents answered Peter's prayers. They were to school first thing the morning after they had received the letter. Whether this was because of their concern for their son's education or because he was too much of a nuisance at home was of no matter. The important thing was that they were talking with the head.

The outcome was as Peter wished. Webster was allowed back in school the following day. His parents had promised that they would contribute to the repair of the broken doors and that their son would help clear up the rest of the mess that the boys had made. Suitably chastened, Webster and the other boys, whose parents had also responded quickly, did as they were told. The following day, they started on the second instalment of their punishment by patrolling the school grounds at break and lunchtimes, ensuring that there was no untidy litter.

Peter's relief was unfeigned. The head had left, whether deliberately or not, space for Webster to continue his musical activities—not that the boy wanted to when Peter first spoke to him.

'I'm fed up with school and everything to do with it. Ah' just want out. Why the 'ell do we have to come to school anyway? I'll never pass any exams, and all that'll 'appen is I'll be stuck trying to find a job when I leave.'

'What about the trombone? Don't you think school has helped you to learn that?'

'That's about all it 'as done. I spend most of mi' time being told what and what not to do, and I'm fed up.'

'Well, there is a great week coming up. Remember you are a soloist at the concert, and a good performance there will put you in a different light. Lots of people love to see those they think are wasters suddenly doing something exceptional, especially if it's something they themselves can't do. What do you think the mayor or Mr Holdsworth will think when you stand up and captivate them with *Panis Angelicus*? I know how proud I will be of you.'

This seemed to chime into Webster's inner brain cells and produce a more willing sparkle in his eyes. Chuckling to himself at the very thought, the words, *Am I striking a chord*, passed through Peter's mind. He had, because Webster, with his head bowed and eyes looking towards his shuffling feet, said, 'OK then, but I'm fed up with this bloody school.'

He then turned and headed for his next class without giving Peter the opportunity to reprimand him for his bad language.

Peter knew that there were different views on success. Some people loved to see others fail, because by comparison it implied that they themselves, without any effort or noticeable gifts, succeeded. They did not expose themselves through trying to achieve something different. Neither did they risk falling below the normal expectations of one human for another. In short, they insulated themselves within the safety of their cocoon; they played by the rules of conformity, and measured their success by their ability to live within a world of approval, secure from criticism, ridicule, or failure.

Others identified success in what they could achieve. It could be in anything, and for some at a very minimalist level. To them, it was not enough to sit back and wait for others to fail so that they themselves could feel comfortable behind their shield of rectitude. It was important to be able to say, 'Well, this is what I have done and this is what I have achieved.' It could be as modest as learning to skip as a child or balancing on a bicycle, or it could be as significant as winning an Olympic gold medal. To such people, taking on the challenge was success. Sometimes, they failed and as a result had to live with disappointment, but to have tried was for them a form of success. They recognised that, without trying, there could not be achievement.

Peter knew that in Webster's case, his performance at the concert would create such a dilemma. If Webster failed, there would be those who, taking their places at the table of righteousness, would say with self-satisfaction, 'I told you so.' There would be others who would count Webster's efforts, no matter how limited, as being success, as being indicative of his willingness to put his head above the parapet and try. To the likes of Peter, Webster's progress as an instrumentalist, whether he was the budding Tommy Dorsey or Glenn Miller of his dreams or not, was a measure of success and an outcome of his willingness to try, no matter what the consequences. Peter admired the lad because for a while he put aside his failures in life and tried to develop the gifts that nobody believed he had. He had taken on the challenge. By simply performing at the concert, Peter managed to convince Webster that he would demonstrate that he was an achiever.

At last, the great day came. Peter and the band were freed from lessons for the afternoon and allowed to go down to the town hall for a rehearsal. The school bus was made available so that they could take all their equipment, including instruments, to the concert venue. As far as Peter knew, none of them had been in the town hall before, and he hoped that they would not be too intimidated by its high, vaulted ceiling, its long windows shaded with expensively adorned flowing curtains, its walls lined with the names of dignitaries, and its impressive high stage. He was reminded of his own feelings in the intimidating ambiance of the book-lined town hall as he waited for his interview in his teenage days. He hoped that the outcome of this visit would be more successful.

'Are we playing in here, sir?' This seemed to be the anxious question all the pupils were asking as they were shown into the auditorium, the floor of which was already covered by two to three hundred chairs for those expected to be at the concert. Peter did not rush things, but allowed the performers to drift into their huddles to exchange views and acclimatise to their surroundings. Eventually, he suggested that they should go up onto the stage and warm up for practice.

The empty hall echoed the first note blown, startling those present like the sound of a falling rock in clear mountain air might disconcert the unsuspecting. Once the sound had run its course and the pupils' amazement had passed, more notes were produced. It became a competition as each instrumentalist endeavoured to elicit a more resonant echo than the others. Again, Peter wisely permitted the pupils to test the hall's acoustics, knowing that the more comfortable they became with the sound, the more effective would be their playing. For his part, he busied himself setting up his stand, ensuring he had his baton, distributing the music, organising the band's seating, and generally preparing for practice.

Eventually, he called the band to order, and once they were all seated began the process of helping them to accustom themselves to their surroundings. He knew that even the best of musicians needed an opportunity to test out their concert hall, whether it was the Royal Albert Hall or a less distinguished town hall. To his delight, the band responded well, and he was impressed with the precision with which they played the various passages he had chosen for practice. The soloists, too, displayed heartening confidence in the excerpts they played from their pieces.

Peter then took a little time to train the pupils in terms of posture, how to enter and leave the stage, when to stand and when to sit, how to respond to applause, how to congratulate the soloists, and even how to hold their instruments when resting. He had done some of this work in the preceding week back at school, but the circumstances were now so different that he had to make sure that the pupils were fully conversant with concert procedures.

After practice, the pupils were invited to look into the council chamber and were taken along to meet with a couple of councillors who happened to be around. They told the pupils how much they were looking forward to the concert and wished them well. The pupils were then taken into the café area and given drinks and cakes, after which they had free time until they met again three-quarters of an hour before the start of the concert.

Peter spent his time nervously checking and rechecking and generally worrying about what lay ahead. He managed to get sufficient copies of what he thought to be well-produced programmes for himself and the band. They contained a little history of the band and the names of the players as well as the pieces to be performed. After he had done all he could, he took some refreshment, had a quick word with Catherine to tell her how things were going, and then spoke with the head who popped in to wish the band well.

As seven o'clock neared, Peter's nervousness increased, but he worked hard to avoid showing it to the pupils. For their part, they seemed to have gained strength from the camaraderie generated by their experiences in their band practices, playing together in school assemblies, and their daily comradeship around the school. He had the feeling that they were genuinely looking forward to the experience as they quietly blew into their instruments to warm them and chatted amongst themselves. Even Webster seemed at ease, and since arriving at the town hall had been as well behaved as any of his peers. Peter began to believe that his hopes for Webster were at last being realised.

Five minutes to go, and a healthy hubbub from the hall indicated that a goodly sized audience was gathering. Then the master of ceremonies nodded to Peter and walked onto the stage as the curtains were drawn back.

'Good evening, ladies and gentlemen. I'm happy to welcome you to the concert given by Weberton Secondary School Brass Band, under its conductor, Mr Delaney. Your programmes will tell you that we are in for an enjoyable evening. I'm sure that we're all looking forward to it and that we'll show our appreciation of their efforts when the time comes. This reminds me of the story of the wife whose husband had just retired. To show her appreciation, she had a desk brought into the sitting room at home and encouraged him to sit behind it with his feet upon it. The words written on the desk were, 'As a reminder and in appreciation of your many years of hard work . . . . to a dear desk.'

With people still amused by the joke, he went on, 'And here is the band with their conductor. Over to you, Peter.'

Peter's heart jumped. The time had come. He pulled back the side curtain and gestured the pupils onto the stage. The audience received them in silence as they settled, and then Peter took his position, with his raised baton demanding attention. With eyes on their music and the baton, the musicians waited for the signal. In this hushed moment, images of the hours of practice, the prayers for inspiration, the dedicated commitment of his pupils, and the highs and lows of the past few months passed through his mind.

Is this what it has all come to? Are we actually going to amaze our audience with what we have achieved?

Then the baton fell and the band struck up with 'Colonel Bogey.' Peter's mind was back on track immediately as he heard the precision of the start and the confidence with which the pupils played. He could almost hear the tapping of feet amongst the audience to the well-known march. And when, at the appropriate time, he turned to the audience and encouraged them to whistle to the accompaniment in the manner of the film, *Bridge over the River Kwai.* He had immediate response. The mums, dads, and friends loved it. The concert was off to a great start.

Peter knew that his pupils were not among the stars of brass banding as those were who played with Foden's, Black Dyke, or Carlton Main

Colliery. And his trained ear also identified weaknesses of technique in the playing, the occasional wrong note and the rare bit of un-tunefulness, but for twelve-to fifteen-year-olds, he was immensely proud of the way they tackled their first major performance.

The Negro spirituals that followed the march settled the mood, and then Alan won warm applause for his *'Il Bacio.'* The English folk songs set some listeners humming, and when Joan played *'Danny Boy'* as lyrically as he had expected, Peter knew that the concert was a success. All it needed was a good performance from Webster and then the final March, 'Slaidburn'.

At the appropriate time, Webster took his place at the front of the band in a blazer and trousers that Catherine had bought for him, reflecting the positive relationship the two of them had formed during his visits to the cottage. For once, he looked as smart as a young gentleman should, with a school tie and shining shoes. He cleared his trombone of any excess water and then nodded to Peter that he was ready. He looked calm and confident, and as he put his trombone to his lips exuded belief in the quality of what he was going to produce. His strong, melodious tone interspersed with sequences of angelic quietness, announced that here was a boy of real talent. The confidence with which he tackled the range of notes in the piece, never losing the rhythm or sensitivity of the music, drew a response of high quality from the other musicians. Wondrously, thought Peter, the playing brought a true climax to the hours of practice that Webster had committed to preparing for the concert. The audience showed their appreciation with their applause, none more so than those members of staff who were present and aware of the problems Webster caused in school.

Surely, all thought, *such a performance and such a reception could only lead to better things when he's back in school.*

Once the concert was finished, members of the audience were invited for a cup of tea and biscuits by the mayor. Peter expressed his admiration and thanks to the band and then sent them out to join their parents. For Webster, this was not an option as his parents had not been at the concert, and he could not hide his disappointment. He left in a hurry having had, Peter noticed, a quick word with Joan.

Peter checked that everything was left in order and ready for collection to go back to school on the following morning and then merged with the throng of people for refreshments.

He was overwhelmed by the positive vibes that he picked up about his young musicians, and for the next half hour enjoyed the congratulations. Then it was time for him to leave and drive back to the moor and the cottage. He took leave of the head, the mayor, and some of his closest colleagues, and with Catherine drove back to the cottage.

When he arrived, he was able to describe for his aunt, who had willingly looked after the children, the evening's success and related how all the effort that he and his pupils had made had been worthwhile. She had heard of Webster from Catherine and expressed her delight that he had done so well.

CHAPTER 24

CATHERINE GOES INTO BUSINESS

During the months that Peter had been working hard in school and developing his young musicians, further progress had also been made in the cottage, and the family had continued to settle in to their new life.

For his part, Peter helped around the home, kept an eye on the children from time to time, and fed the hens. The family had also acquired cats which also became Peter's responsibility. The cats took up residence in the barn and only one cat, which became very much the family pet, was allowed into the cottage. The cats proved a useful antidote to the vermin that had for a time taken over the barn and outhouses, and they did their work well. Throughout their time at the cottage the family never had an occasion when a mouse or rat was found inside. The one thing missing was a dog, which Catherine was desperate to have. However, the time taken to look after the new baby and the other three children, meant that having a dog to look after was out of the question.

Peter marvelled at Catherine's patience, left with the responsibility of growing children in a home with so many shortcomings, and also with the task of looking after him. She had accepted the challenges of the cottage with a commitment that was often found wanting in his own efforts, despite the eagerness with which he had bought it. Catherine was constantly thinking about the improvements needed, and often became frustrated with Peter's apparent lack of concern. He knew that his interests and work off the moor inevitably affected the time he could commit to helping, and he knew that there were occasions when Catherine found this annoying.

But Peter, anxious though he was to improve the cottage, managed, to some extent, to deceive himself into believing that his commitment to other spheres was the key to his having a successful career, and consequently being able to provide more security for the family. His involvement in rugby, as well as his extra activities at school, drew him away from some of the jobs he could be expected to do in and around the cottage. It was not difficult for anyone associated with him, to see that he was too easily distracted by what even he recognised as his most unappealing quality, his own interests. Had it not been for Catherine's love for him, which meant that she shared equally with him in the joys of his successes and the disappointments of any failures, their marriage could not have been so successfully sustained.

Nevertheless, despite change appearing to be slow, the couple could credit themselves with some worthwhile internal improvements. The sitting room was bright and cheery, and it provided the comfort in which Peter and Catherine could settle of an evening, and a place in which the children could imagine themselves to be whatever they wished to be, as they played with their toys. The dining room now had character, and divulged, in an instant, a hint as to the history of the cottage to those who came through the front door.

Outside, Peter had eventually got round to persuading Jack and his son Tim, an apprentice builder, to build, at not too great a cost, an attractive porch at the front of the cottage. It gave welcome extra space, and provided a shield for the front door against the scurrying winds that crossed the moor. Peter had also used the walling skills he had learned, to create a small walled garden to the side of the porch and in front of one of the bay windows. He was helped in the digging and earth removing by the busyness of the children. These times, when he was being what could be loosely regarded as helped by the children, were among his most enjoyable, despite the occasional, 'What on earth are you doing, Gregory?' or, 'Put that down Katie,' or, 'It doesn't go there Sarah,' or, 'For heaven's sake, James,' as the toddler crawled through the dirt.

Father and children were often joined by the hens, which sought to pick over the ground, uncovering and devouring worms and insects. Photographs showed these as happy family times, and indeed they were. This was the sort of freedom that Peter had sought for parents and children when he had bought the cottage. Unobserved by anybody, adults and children could dig, lift, move, and place, to their heart's content, and then take pleasure in what had been achieved. Throughout, he could content himself with the thought that the keen moor air penetrated lungs unsullied by the debilitating dust of the towns, and was contributing to the healthy life his children led.

Once the porch was in place and the new garden was completed, the front of the cottage provided an attractive entrance. A stone-flagged path led from the gate up two steps to the stout wooden porch door. On the one side of the porch was the walled garden filled with roses and a variety of colourful flowers, and on the other a flagged area with a recently acquired wooden seat which was placed in front of the cottage window. Across the stone path was a grassed area, with three small trees providing some protection from curious passers-by, hiking or in cars, and the most severe weather. Then there was the drystone wall which enclosed the cottage and protected it from the sheep wandering on the moor.

At the rear of the cottage, Peter had agreed with his tenant that he could portion off a part of one of the fields for a back garden, and he had erected another stone wall, extended by a tight wire fence, to keep out the various stock that used the field. It gave the children a further area in which to play safely and, once the grass had been cut, an attractive place in which Peter and Catherine could sit, on the occasions when the breeze allowed, and have tea.

The support that Peter's aunt was able to give proved indispensable to Catherine. She would often come up to the cottage at short notice and take over the supervision of the children, allowing Catherine to go down into town for a while, or visit a friend without the hassle of the children. She also spent some time in the cottage with Catherine, helping with the children or just generally helping about the cottage. In so many ways she was like the grandmother she should have been, and yet the children did not know it. Peter did not find the situation problematic, as he could see that his aunt was content to be treated as such, and did not interfere in a way that suggested that she was more closely interlinked with the family than was generally known. Even after his mother's death, her approach did not change.

Despite the things that had been completed, both Peter and Catherine knew that there was still much to do, some of it critical. Their evening topics of conversation incorporated the obvious.

'Well, pure water is becoming essential. You'll never know how much I worry about using the tap water, even though I boil it all.'

'So that must be first on our agenda,' responded Peter. 'I suppose we also need to check out the septic tank, I'm not too happy with everything just leaking out into the field.'

'I agree, but I also feel that we need to sort out the kitchen and provide another bedroom. That'll be a major development, but we have to do it at some stage. There's also the issue of the barn and mistal, and to what extent we can profitably extend into them to make this the sort of house that we want it to be. It looks to me as though we're looking at something like a five-year plan.'

'And some more,' was Peter's impulsive response.

Most of the ideas for home improvement came from Catherine, whose daily life was spent on the moor and with the children. Peter could not but be impressed by her approach. But they both knew that their best plans were likely to be thwarted by the lack of money. Peter's salary slowly improved, but so did general living costs, and so there was rarely any to put by for major improvements. Their biggest investment, the porch, had been minor compared with what was now required, particularly as the young apprentice builder had done it as much for his training as the low fee he eventually charged.

Prospects seemed to be improving when Catherine came up with the idea of providing weekend teas for the many hikers who walked the moors. It meant hiring a young lady from a nearby farm to help Catherine with the baking of scones and the making of tea and coffee. Catherine had the additional job of creating an appropriate sign to attract customers, and, on a board cut out by Peter, she painted, in large letters, '*Ts To Your Taste*'. The board was hung on a post by the front gate, and the cottage was ready for business.

Peter was amazed how quickly the enterprise prospered. Before long, Katie and Sarah, young as they were, were recruited as waitresses, carrying the plates of scones and cups of tea to the various tables that spread throughout the garden at the back of the cottage. Nestled below the *Beacon*, those enjoying the scones and tea had wonderful views across the valley. Groups of twenty would ring to book tables on certain weekends, and the steady stream of smaller clusters of hikers meant the need for more help and the hiring of another neighbour, Jack's wife.

Such success could not last. The weekends became times of anxiety as well as tiredness, and the encroachment of so many unknown people onto their property sometimes gave them concerns. On one occasion, a family group settled themselves around the dining room table, assuming that this was part of what they thought to be the café. Too embarrassed to usher them out, Catherine proceeded to serve them, whilst Peter endeavoured to make sure that nothing disappeared from the dining room or was damaged. The willingness of inexperienced, young help could not make up for some sort of professional approach, either, and was also a worry that lingered.

That is not to say that the younger staff did not show initiative. Sarah's foray into the garden on one occasion with a plate of scones, which tipped off the plate onto the floor as she tripped over a stone, would have stumped many, but not her. Sarah simply returned to the kitchen, dusted down the scones, and returned to the task of making a more successful delivery, with no one the wiser or seemingly unhealthier. Such incidents were a reminder of the prospect of a visit from the health and safety advisers once they became aware that such a business was operating. With some sorrow, but in the circumstances good sense, at the end of the first summer season it was decided to close the venture.

The compensation was that Catherine, trained as she was as in physiotherapy, managed to obtain a part-time post, essentially Sundays, unless there was an emergency, at the local hospital. This meant that she was doing something for which she was trained, which she enjoyed, and from which she had a regular income. That the work was on a Sunday was also fortuitous, as it meant that Peter could be at home to look after the children. Henceforth, his real education as a father began.

CHAPTER 25

PETER'S BIG SHOCK

Peter arrived in the staffroom the day after the concert to hear the name Webster being bandied about in almost every corner. His expectation was that colleagues had been so impressed with the lad's performance that they were sharing their experiences at the concert with those who had been unable to attend. As he went up to a group that included Stan, John, and Maxine, John turned to him and asked, 'Have you heard about Webster?'

As the expression on Peter's face clearly indicated that he had not, John went on. 'Webster is being sought by the police in connection with a mugging in town last night after the concert. In fact, it could be murder, as the victim, an elderly chap, has apparently died as a result of a knife wound.'

'I don't understand,' was Peter's incredulous and shocked response. He was shaken to the core and he felt his face pale. 'How could such a successful evening have such a dreadful conclusion? Webster was terrific last night. Surely, he couldn't be daft enough to get involved in anything like that.'

'It's right, Peter. The mugging was reported on the local radio this morning as I drove into school, and young Tomkins told me about Webster being involved as I was walking along the corridor to the staffroom. The pupils seem pretty excited about it,' Stan added as he picked up a set of exercise books.

'What did he say?'

Stan paused. 'His story was that Makin and Skelworth had been arrested in the park, but the rumour among his pals was that Webster had been with them and had escaped.'

'So it's only a rumour? It's not definite that it was Joe?'

'No. But what's for sure is that the police are looking for a third lad. That was reported on the news. As for Webster, if the youngsters who know him think he was involved, they've probably got some reason.'

'We'll see. If Webster's in school today, which I'm hoping he will be,' said Peter, 'it'll show he wasn't involved. If he's not in school, where will he be and what will he be doing? No, I'm sure he couldn't have been involved.'

'Well, Peter, keep hoping. You've more faith in him than the rest of us.' Arthur couldn't resist the opportunity to have his say.

Peter was indeed hoping. He looked across at Maxine who had been quietly listening to what her colleagues were saying. He was looking to detect a ray of support in her eyes for Webster and for his belief in him. But he was disappointed. Maxine lowered her eyes and looked as though she was busy with something else. Even so, until there was official confirmation of Joe's involvement, Peter refused to believe that he would throw away any benefits he would be likely to accrue as a result of all the accolades he had won at the concert.

Peter found some comfort in the fact that colleagues who had attended the concert made time to congratulate him on the success of the band. They had been impressed with the playing and also the decorum shown by the pupils. There was no doubt that for some, the performance had been an eye opener and an indication of the hidden capabilities of some of their pupils.

Peter and the musicians enjoyed further praise in assembly, when, after the hymn and prayers, the head complimented the band and its success. 'Last evening, I was delighted to attend the concert at the town hall given by the school band. Those involved brought great credit to the school. There's no doubt that the standard they have achieved reflects the dedication they have shown and provides an example to all of us. All those that I spoke with after the concert were full of praise. I think the band, and Mr Delaney, deserve our congratulations.'

He then led the clapping of the whole school for the band and its conductor. But he knew, as did some of the staff and pupils, that the memory of the evening might be marred by the foolhardiness of Webster. The fact that Peter could not see the lad in assembly did not augur well.

No sooner had the head left the stage and reached the bottom of the stairs leading to his study, than he saw two policemen approaching the front door of the school. He stopped, gathered himself, and then opened the door and invited them in. He did not need to ask what they were about. 'Good morning officers. I assume you've come to see me. I'm John Holdsworth the head. Perhaps you'd like to come up to my study.'

As the head passed through the office, he said to his PA, 'Ann, can you ask Mr Delaney to come up straight away. Let Tom know he'll need to find a substitute to stand in for him'.

By the time Peter arrived at the head's study, the officers were seated around the small informal table, holding their helmets on their knees. They were just about to receive a cup of coffee that the head had made for them in the percolator that always seemed to be at the ready for visitors.

The officers were personable and, being local, showed a good deal of empathy with the school's situation in the way they spoke and sat. There was no threat in their voices or manner.

'You've probably heard that three youths were involved in an attack on a pensioner last evening. Sadly, it resulted in Mr Mann's death. During the attack he was stabbed. We managed to catch two of the boys in the park, both of whom said they had attended this school. Their names were . . . .' The officer took out his well-worn notebook and flicked through several pages. 'Ah, here it is. Trevor Makin and William Skelton.'

'Yes, they were here. They left a couple of years ago.'

'When we questioned them, they named the other lad as Joseph Webster, who apparently is still a pupil.'

'I'm aware that the boy is still with us. D'you know if he's in school, Peter?'

'Don't know, Mr Holdsworth, but if he was involved last night it's unlikely.'

While Mr Holdsworth picked up the phone and asked Ann to check to see if Webster was in school, Peter turned to the officers. 'Are you sure that Webster was involved? I'm asking because last night he was playing with the school brass band in the town hall.'

'What time did you finish?'

'About eight o'clock.'

'We have only the other two lads' statement to go on and we won't be certain until we have had a word with this Joseph Webster himself. If you finished around eight o'clock, he would probably have had time to get to the scene of the crime, which occurred at quarter past eight as near as we can time it at the moment.'

The phone rang and the head answered. 'Oh, I see. Thanks, Ann.'

He then turned to the officers saying, 'He's not been registered as in school.'

Peter's heart sank.

'If he was involved I don't suppose that's surprising,' said one of the officers. 'We wondered if anyone at school might know his whereabouts and be able to help us find him. As he's not at home, we've already been to see his parents—some woman that Mrs Webster—and not here, it's possible that he has friends that he could go to. It might help if we could have a word with any staff who know him well, and with some of his friends, to see if he's been in contact with any of them.'

'Well, we have Mr Delaney here. He conducted the band last night, and probably gets on with Webster better than anyone else on the staff. Any ideas, Peter?'

'No, I only learned about what happened when I got into the staffroom this morning. I wouldn't have thought he would contact any members of staff. I don't think he's close enough to any. It might be worth having a talk with a couple of members of the band. They may know something. Joan Jameson tends to be the one who knows what's going on. He also has a couple of friends that he hangs about with, Conway and Robinson. Again, they might know something.'

As one of the policemen noted the names, the other said, 'A detective inspector is coming in from Leeds to take over the investigation because the consequences of the attack have been so serious.' He went on, 'We trust that the school will do what it can to help us. It appears that the lad has not been home since yesterday morning when he set off for school. His mum and dad have no idea where he is or could be. Although we've arrested and questioned the other two youths, they say they've no idea where Webster is either, or, if they have, they're not prepared to tell. In fact, we don't think they know where he went after they split. The last they saw of him was as he ran off when he heard the siren. It's important we get hold of him as soon as possible.'

'D'you want to speak with Joan Jameson?'

'That would be helpful. There's always a chance that he could have said something or somebody knows where he likes to go.'

The head sent for Joan. While they were waiting for her, Peter, still wanting to believe in Webster, asked the question that had been burning into his brain throughout the time he had been sitting in the head's study. 'D'you really think he could have done it? I ask, because his commitment to performing well last night and his involvement in the concert were irreproachable. I can't imagine that he suddenly switched to attacking an old man.'

'You can never say what motivates youngsters when you've a case like this. We can only follow the leads we have, and at the moment he's in the frame.'

When Joan arrived she was asked if she minded answering a few questions. Mr Holdsworth explained that technically one of her parents should be present, but because of the urgency of the matter it would be helpful if she talked to the police. He said that he and Mr Delaney would be present. Joan had no objection. The police put several questions to her concerning the whereabouts of Webster and whether anyone else might know. Joan was unable to help and couldn't suggest who else might be able to. It was clear that the police were not going to further their enquiries through the school and so, replacing their helmets, took their leave with, 'Can we ask that if you get any information you'll ring us straight away? This is, as we know you understand, a very serious matter. The family of the poor victim is, not surprisingly, anxious that we do all we can to arrest the guilty parties and bring them to justice as soon as possible.'

Both Peter and the head had been deeply disturbed by what they had heard, but were helpless with regard to helping the police.

'How could Webster be involved in this after such a success at the concert?' asked the head, not expecting any sort of answer from Peter.

Peter continued to shake his head in disbelief, trying to match what he had heard about Webster that morning to the lad he had cultivated and tutored to play so well. Webster's standing in the school had risen sky high as a result of his performance and yet here he was, the other side of his personality commanding everyone's attention. Peter left the head's room, not attempting to hide his disappointment.

As he walked back to his class, his gaze inadvertently strayed through the large window that overlooked the school entrance. He was shocked to see a group of men and women milling around, some with cameras and others with notebooks at the ready. 'The press,' he muttered and turned on his heel to return to the head's study. He popped his head around the secretary's door.

'Anne, I think you should let Mr Holdsworth know that it looks as though the press are at the gate. It's obvious what they want, but, I must say, I thought that they weren't allowed to talk with children without a parent's permission.'

'You're right as far as I know. No names should be mentioned or photographs taken. I'll let the head know.'

She stood up, knocked on his door and entered. Mr Holdsworth came out in some haste once she had informed him about the crowd at the gate. He looked through the window. 'Good God. What a mess.'

Startled by what he saw, he returned to his study and picked up the phone. He became pensive and then replaced it, as though he needed time to decide what the best course of action was. Although he had been a headteacher for several years, Mr Holdsworth could at one time appear shy and nervous, whilst at another confident and determined. Some of the staff blamed this inconsistency for the variation in his approach to discipline. On occasions, they felt that they were unsupported when they were facing some of their most critical incidents, and yet, on others, the head acted with a surprising robustness. All, however, saw in him a compassion for the pupils and staff that enabled and encouraged most to perform well, and so contribute to the good reputation the school had in the locality. Peter was aware of the differing views of the staff and he himself recognised the dichotomy, but he felt that the head was right in being inclined to look for amenable solutions to problems. He recognised that the head was now faced with what must be the most critical incident of his headship, and that he was in some difficulty as to how to deal with it.

Peter was not mistaken. Back in his room, the head paced the floor with his right hand rubbing his cheek, as he tried to work out what to do. With the press at his gate, and the police anxious to trace one of his pupils in a murder enquiry, he decided to do the only thing he could, which was to pick up the phone and ring County Hall. With a pain down the back of his neck, presumably caused by nerves, and perspiration in the palm of his hands, he again picked up the phone, dialled the fateful numbers and asked to speak to the chief education officer. As the head knew, Mr Rose was not the most sympathetic of people.

'Hello, Mr Rose. There's a problem at the school which I think you should know about.'

'It's about this pupil of yours, I suppose,' came the gruff response. 'He seems to have brought all hell down on us. I've had the press here this morning asking questions and taking photographs. I've also been asked to do a radio interview. The sooner you come in and let us know what's happening, the better.'

'I'll come in once the situation at the school gate has been resolved. I've the press milling around and I'm not sure what I should do.'

'Tell them to go, man. And if they don't, get the police to move them on. They've no right to be disturbing the school. I'll send John Wilkins down straight away to give you a bit of support. I know he's in the area because he's visiting the local grammar school.'

Wilkins was the Local Authority adviser for the school, and a person who got on well with Mr Holdsworth, always being available to give advice.

'Thanks,' said Mr Holdsworth. 'If it's all right with you, I will be in County Hall by about half past two.'

314

'Fine. And all the best with this damned problem. Oh, on second thoughts, I think it better if I come to see you. I'll be there sometime this afternoon.' With that he put the phone down.

Mr Holdsworth had not expected to be comforted by Mr Rose, who was known as a no nonsense figure, but one who would, in his own direct way, provide support if he saw the need. In this case, he was thoroughly aware of the pressure that Holdsworth was under, and although he answered crustily on the phone he was anxious to see him and give him what backing he could.

The head took his cue from Mr Rose and went to the front gate to talk with the journalists. Not unnaturally, they pressed him for answers to questions thrown at him from all angles, but, as he knew nothing, he could not satisfy their hunt for a worthwhile story. Eventually, he impressed upon them, with the threat of calling the police, the need for them to leave and allow the children to get on with school as normal. Seeing that they were unlikely to get any further information from staff, and being aware that they could not approach any of the pupils, the group gradually dispersed.

Peter's lessons for that day, fortunately, did not stretch his thinking beyond ensuring that he distributed the right materials, gave the right instructions, and provided what help was required by individual pupils. His mind was fogged by the day's news.

In the staffroom, much of the conversation surrounded Webster. For some of his colleagues, his situation was the natural outcome of a life of disobedience and insolence, stemming from incurable personality traits. Others sought to find some reason for what had happened in his home life, and the lack of interest his parents had shown in him even when he looked for support. For example, their non-attendance at the concert was regarded as the height of disrespect for their son's achievement. These and other psychological implications were bandied around the staffroom, with the concept of attention deficit disorder figuring strongly.

Peter could add little to the discussions, though his dejected expression was obvious to all. He looked only to four o'clock and home time. He wanted the open space of the moor, the seclusion fostered by *The King's Beacon*, and that continuous friendly breeze that would clear his head. The moor would distance him from the worries of the day. Just as on other days when he had left school with concerns, the tranquillity of the last couple of miles would unclog his mind and bring him to thinking about the opportunities life at the cottage offered his family, rather than the follies of Webster.

On this occasion, however, his journey home did nothing to allay his worst fears for Webster. Although it gave him time to think of reasons why Webster may not have been involved in the crime, and that he might have stood aside as his friends carried out the attack, he could come up with nothing that dispelled the sight of the two police officers in the head's study, the gathering of the press at the school gate, or the arrival of the Chief Education Officer to talk with Mr Holdsworth.

Once Peter had arrived at the cottage, he was greeted at the door by an anxious Catherine, who was keen to learn what had happened during the day. He pulled her close to him and gave her a lingering kiss, as much to give himself some comfort as to show his love for her. He then made into the cottage, found himself a comfortable chair, and set about describing to Catherine the day's events. She understood his feelings, because, like any dutiful wife, she had lived through his hopes and fears about the concert day after day, and probably could have played every note. She had also spent her day worrying about what was happening in Weberton, as the news of Webster and his friends figured hourly on the news. In her usual way she asked questions in search of every detail and offered what she could in terms of support and probable outcomes, but knew that Peter's concerns would not disappear quickly. Despite his worries about Webster and his whereabouts, he was also deeply disquieted by the fate of the victim.

CHAPTER 26

WEBSTER LOOKS FOR HELP

It was as evening darkness was creeping in and the children had settled in bed that there was a knock on the door. Peter and Catherine looked at each other with surprise because this was a most unusual occurrence.

'Better see who it is,' said Peter, rising and going to the door.

What awaited him, he could never have foreseen. Standing before him as he pulled the door back was Webster.

'God Almighty!' he exclaimed. 'What are you doing here?'

The bright light of the porch dazzled Webster for a moment and he dropped his eyes. He looked up again appealingly as he blurted out, 'Can you help me, sir?'

'You'd better come in quickly.'

Once in the sitting room, it was not difficult to see that Webster had been living rough. His hair was tousled, the school blazer, which Catherine had bought and he had worn at the concert with such distinction, had mud stains on the arms and back, and his trousers were also badly stained. His shoes were caked with mud and bits of straw that he had obviously picked up from wherever he had been walking. His eyes were tired, and fatigue transfigured his face, emphasising the deep lines of anguish. Here was a very worried boy.

Peter turned quickly to Catherine, who had recognised Webster, saying, 'Can you sort him out? It doesn't look as though he's had anything all day. Perhaps something to eat and drink?'

Catherine nodded while trying to adjust to the unexpected developments. As she left the room to go to the kitchen, she said, 'Sit down, Joseph, and talk with Mr Delaney for a minute or two while I get something.'

Peter hesitated to ask questions as his bemused visitor slumped into a chair. He decided to wait until Webster had had some refreshment.

Catherine looked across at Peter with a perplexed expression when she re-entered the room and invited Webster to go up to the bathroom for a wash and clean-up. 'Come along Joseph. Let me show you where the bathroom is so that you can wash and tidy yourself up a bit. Anyway, how d'you feel?'

'A bit tired, miss.'

'I can see that, Joseph. You'll feel better when you've had a wash.'

Catherine left him to it and went downstairs.

Almost in a whisper, she asked Peter, 'What d'you think he's doing here?'

'Well, he asked me to help him when I was at the door, and so I suppose that's why he came. At the moment, I don't know what to do. We'll have to wait and see what he has to say. I suppose we should inform the police . . . .' Peter finished off circumspectly.

When he returned, Webster tackled the two ham sandwiches and apple juice that Catherine had set out on a tray for him with the eagerness of any boy who had not eaten for twenty-four hours or more.

Catherine and Peter watched, quietly and calmly to all appearances but with anxieties deeper within them. They were faced with a situation that they knew should be resolved by a simple phone call to the police, though how Webster would react between the time of the call and the arrival of the police was anyone's guess. But they hesitated. Despite the problems that Webster had caused in the past, there was no escaping the fact that in recent months Peter had begun to recognise the growth of a genuine relationship between the two of them. What was happening that evening took his thoughts back to John's staffroom comments about the positive impact on Webster of the boat project, and how Peter himself had begun to believe that Webster's involvement with the band would have a similar effect.

Fighting back a natural desire to ask what he was doing at the cottage, Peter and Catherine both sat patiently and waited until Webster had finished.

'Now, Joe, you need to explain what's going on,' said Peter.

'Terrible, terrible, terrible. I dun't know what to se.' Webster started excitedly, with little form in the story he began to tell.

'Relax, Joe. Take your time,' advised Peter.

Webster cooled a little and then went on. 'Well, sir, it's like this. After the concert, I went outside to meet two of mi' mates. They hadn't been to the concert but knew that I was in the town hall and so said they'd meet me by the fish and chip shop, you know, the one in West Street, where we could get some fish and chips for supper. I was feeling pretty good after the concert and was looking forward to telling Trev and Will about it.'

'Did you go straight from the concert?' asked Peter, conscious that the answer to such a question would have an important bearing on the conclusions the police would draw as a result of their investigation.

'Well, yes,' answered Joe with an expression of surprise on his face at the question, but also one indicating that he was trying to recall the details of the evening. 'Oh, wait a minute; I went back for mi' mouthpiece. I'd forgotten it.'

'Where was it?'

'In mi' trombone case, sir. I'd left it with'art thinking.'

'Have you got it with you now?' asked Peter anxiously, though his actual concern for the mouthpiece was nil as he sat in his own living room asking questions of a boy being hunted by the police.

'Yes,' said Joe as he took his mouthpiece from his pocket. Peter's anxious expression became more relaxed for a moment, as he urged Joe to continue his story.

'It seems that this bloke came out a t'Dragon Pub. 'E had 'is wallet in 'is hand and I saw mi' mate run up to 'im and snatch it off 'im. By the time he got back to my other mate, I'd joined them and we all ran off down t'street and across to t'park.'

Catherine and Peter noticed how Webster was very careful not to mention which of his pals had actually attacked Mr Mann, a trait synonymous with his usual loyal approach to friends in trouble in school.

Joe continued. 'We stopped to share up the money—I got a share 'cos they were mi' mates. The next thing we 'ear are the police sirens. We thought they might be looking for us and so we split. The next thing I know is there's shouting and swearing and it sounded as though mi' mates had been picked up. I wa' just behind some bushes darn by t'canal but well 'idden, and I 'eard t'police say there wer' three of us and so wea' wa' t'other. That wer' me.'

In his anxiety, Webster had slipped into his native slang.

'I heard Trev give mi name and a' knew a' wa' done for. I decided to get away as quickly as possible. I'd nowhere to go and then I thought of this place. I remember you once saying that t'*Beacon*, I think you called it *T'King's Beacon*, up there was a good place to find some quiet, and I thought it might be the safest place to head for. It's a good distance from Weberton and it's quiet and nobody need know I was there. So

I walked through the night and then today I kept 'iding behind walls or in ditches if cars came by. I gor' up to t'top and fan' that cave you'd showed us once when 'a whar' up 'ere for practice. It wa' just the job for whar' I wanted. I can imagine wa' it wa' like when t'king's men wer' watching for t'Roundheads. I could see t'road through t'valley and up t'ill. That *Beacon*'s a great spot. I can see how it gor' its name. I could see for miles. T'police would never a got me. I could also see t'cottage and remembered you said if 'ah ever needed help to come to you. So when I gor' up there and saw t' barn an' all, wi' t'door open, I waited till I saw you come home and then 'ah sneaked darn and managed to 'ide in t'barn till everything went dark. Then I cem' to t'door.'

Peter and Catherine exchanged glances. They took some satisfaction from the fact that Webster, once the bane of Peter's teaching life, had looked to them for support, an indication that the lad, like so many of his type, recognised in others genuine concern for those in difficulty. Peter had seen similar characteristics in other pupils. He knew of lads in school who would approach the likes of John and Stan to ask for help or advice but who would never go near Arthur. Some would say that it was because they were what might be called 'soft,' but to those who knew them well, John and Stan were the sort of people who could put the past to one side and give their full attention to the present. Peter and Catherine were in this situation now. They couldn't say it aloud, but their eyes told one another that they were in the middle of a predicament that they did not quite know how to deal with. But their first thoughts were to try forget the past and to understand and help.

'What do you expect to happen now, Joe?' asked Peter.

'I dunno. What d'you think?'

'Well, Joe. I have some very bad news for you.' Peter could see no reason to hide the fate of the victim of the mugging. 'The man you robbed, a Mr Mann, has died.'

Webster shot bolt upright in his chair with shock and then burst into tears. 'No, no, no, it can't be!' he exclaimed. ''E wa' just pushed.'

Peter went on to outline what had been on the news and how the police were making the incident important enough to bring an inspector across from Leeds. Although he wanted to help Webster with encouraging words, he couldn't.

'It's very serious, Joe.'

For an instant, Webster became his old self. 'It's more than bloody serious. I need to get away from 'ere pronto.'

He made as if to go for the door, but Peter managed to bar his way and persuade him to retake his seat. Now began a period in which he endeavoured, with interjections from Catherine, to help Webster fully understand his position as well as to see the futility of trying to run away. He went on to explain the significance of Mr Mann's death for anyone involved and that the police would be considering whether to charge the suspects with murder or manslaughter. As calmly as he could, he indicated to Webster the difference between the two and also that anyone involved in the mugging, whether they actually touched Mr Mann or not, could be charged with one of the crimes. Much depended on the evidence the police produced.

'Now, Joe, be honest with us. Did you get anywhere near the man who died?'

'No,' replied Joe with a look of absolute certainty.

'Were you involved in the mugging in anyway?'

'No. Ah just ran wi mi mates.'

'If things were as you say, you need to put the case to the police as soon as possible. I'm sure you appreciate the difficulty Mrs Delaney and I are in. We can't hide you, and neither can we avoid contacting the police. You understand, don't you?'

Webster nodded. He understood all right, but where did it leave him? He asked himself, *Do I just sit there and wait to be picked up by the police, or should I make a run for it? But then, where would I run?*

His thoughts were interrupted by Peter. 'Look. I've a friend at the rugby club who is a solicitor.' He was thinking of Roger Jepson. 'If you don't mind, I could give him a ring and ask him what's the best thing to do.'

Again, Webster acquiesced with a nod.

Peter went into the next room to the phone and fortunately made contact with his friend. He explained the situation, and then Roger asked if he could talk to Joe. Peter went back into the living room, glancing as he did so at Catherine with a look on his face that seemed to signal some sort of hope. He said to Joe, 'Mr Jepson would like to have a word with you.'

Webster was taken aback, but with some encouragement, he rose from his chair and hesitantly followed Peter into the dining room. Peter handed him the phone, which he looked at as though he never handled one before, which was probably the case. 'Hold it up to your ear and say, 'Hello, Mr Jepson',' whispered Peter.

Webster did as he was advised and, satisfied he had made contact, Peter left him to it.

Webster eventually returned to the sitting room to say that the solicitor wanted to speak to Peter again.

'Peter, my advice is to take the lad to the police station in Weberton straight away. I've spoken with him and convinced him, I think, that to give himself up now will help when he comes to explain what happened. I'll meet you at the station. In the meantime, you need to get in touch with his parents so that if possible they can also be present at the station. Is that OK?'

'Makes sense to me,' said Peter. 'See you in an hour or so.'

He went back into the sitting room and explained the situation to Webster. The lad was in a state of anguish. He had been in lots of trouble in his life and he had faced his punishment with a brashness designed to impress his friends. This was something different. Murder? Manslaughter? What had gone so wrong?

326

'No way I'm going to the police station. I didn't do anything, an' I shouldn't get the blame.'

Peter could see that he might have real problems getting Webster to follow Roger's advice. Rather than forcing the issue, he decided to encourage Webster to talk. 'What actually happened, Joe? Have you told us everything?'

Joe looked down at his feet, clearly discomforted by the question.

'Are you hiding anything, Joe?'

As Peter looked across to Catherine, more in desperation than anything else, she nodded towards the dining room, stood up, walked across the room to pick up Joe's tray, and then continued towards the sitting room door, clearly expecting Peter to follow. 'Will you just wait here, Joe, while Mr Delaney and I go next door for a few minutes?'

Webster resignedly shook his head in agreement as Peter followed Catherine into the dining room.

'Peter, I think the lad might be telling the truth. I'm not certain, and you know him better than I do, but I've been watching him closely for the past half hour and he's clearly worried, wants to be believed, and doesn't feel that he should take the blame. I wonder if it would help if I asked him a few questions. I used to get on well with him when he came up on those music outings and I know he appreciated the clothes I gave him for the concert. I think he sees me as someone he can rely on and talk to. With you, I suspect, he can't get away from seeing himself answering the questions of his teacher.'

'I'm happy to do anything that will help,' responded Peter, recognising that Catherine had a sensitivity developed through dealing with anxious patients whom she knew had such serious illnesses that no one could foresee the outcome of their treatment.

'You've told me often that in school, if he's caught, he rarely denies anything that he may have done, and so his present denials may indicate that he wasn't directly implicated.'

'OK. Let's go and try and see to what extent we can help this lad.'

When they returned to the sitting room, Webster was slumped in his chair, his face pale from tiredness and worry. In her typically quiet and sympathetic way Catherine, having seated herself in the chair by the side of Webster rather than directly in front of him, the more threatening position that Peter had taken, asked, 'How are you feeling, Joe?'

''Orrible, miss.'

'I'm really sorry Joe. Mr Delaney and I want to help all we can. What d'you think would be the best thing that we could do for you?'

Joe looked at her with a sort of surprised disbelief of a child who had never been asked this question before. For a moment, he was speechless, as though trying to sort out his thoughts, and then he said, 'Look, miss. All I want is for people to believe me. I don't know whether you can 'elp in that, but somebody needs to.'

'Well, look, Joseph. The best way we can do is for you to tell us what happened honestly, so that we believe you. If we trust what you've told us, we can speak with other people with more confidence and hopefully convince them that what you're saying is the truth. Are you happy to tell us the story again? Think about it carefully. While you're thinking about that, I'm going to make a cup of tea for Mr Delaney and myself. Would you like something else to drink? Perhaps a Coke or some apple juice?'

'Apple juice, please.'

Peter almost gulped aloud as, for the first time, he heard Webster say 'please.'

He and Webster remained quietly in the sitting room whilst Catherine went into the kitchen. Peter stood and replaced on the bookshelf a book he had been reading, anything to ease the tension, whilst Webster gave the impression through the concentrated look on his face of trying to work through the events of the previous evening.

Eventually, Catherine returned with juice, tea, and biscuits on a wooden tray. She passed the drinks round, offered a biscuit to Webster, who gratefully accepted it, and then sat down. Her whole manner was one of calm and, to all intents and purposes, one of normality. However, her mind was working overtime trying to establish a process of questioning that would encourage truth.

'Now, Joe, just tell me what happened as best you can. I'll try not to interrupt, but if I need to in order to be clear, I hope you'll not mind.'

Peter could do no other but admire the way Catherine encouraged Webster to feel more at ease, as indicated by the change in his posture.

He now sat more upright but leant slightly forward with his elbows resting on his thighs, as if keen to impress upon his listeners the truth of what he had to say.

'Onest miss, I did nothing but watch. I was on my way to join mi' mates when one of 'em ran at the guy and stole the wallet. It all 'appened just as I rounded the corner of West Street, where the chip shop is and where we were meeting. I swear that before I got to mi' mates, one of 'em had dashed across the road. I didn't do a thing until he kem' back. By that time, I'd got to t'chip shop. 'E dashed back and said, 'Let's run for it,' and so wi did. I went 'cause they were mi' mates and 'cause I thought the police'd think I war involved anyway. As you know, I've bin in trouble before.' It was well known that Webster and his family were on police files for minor offences as well as causing disturbances to neighbours.

'Why did you go up to them when you saw what one of them was doing? Didn't you think that he would come back across the street and that you would then get some of the blame?' asked Catherine.

'I suppose so, but it seemed simple enuff to run away. I never thought not to go 'cos I thought it wa' good fun.' This is where the old Webster surfaced. If there was trouble, he didn't mind being part of it. 'When we stopped, we wer' by t'park. We began to share out t'money from t'wallet. There was a fair bit, I'll tell you.' Webster could not avoid expressing and showing briefly on his face the satisfaction he had on getting hold of someone else's money. 'It was then that wi 'eard t'police sirens. Wi' looked at each and said, 'Split' and ran for it. I went round towards t'canal and t'others went in t'direction of George Road. I think that's 'ow they were caught. I wa' still near enough to hear Trev shout out mi name to t'police when they asked who the third lad wa'. It wa' then that I decided to keep going and not go home. That's why I'm here.'

'Now think carefully, Joseph. Did you go straight to the fish shop from the town hall?'

'Yes, I think so.' He screwed up his eyes in thought and then repeated what he had said to Peter. 'But 'ang on. I had to go back for mi' mouthpiece. I'd forgotten the damned thing.'

'How long do you think that took?' asked Catherine.

'Abaht five minutes, I'd say.'

'And then you went to the fish shop and saw what one of your friend's did?'

'Ye'.'

'Which friend was it, Joseph?' Catherine thought she might as well try the trick of the casual question in the hope of getting Webster to identify who had actually carried out the mugging. Needless to say, it did not work.

'Dun know.'

'Did you walk or run from the town hall?'

'I suppose I did a bit o' both. I'd arranged to meet Will just after eight, but the concert didn't finish until then and I'd the job of putting away mi trombone, music, and stand and leaving it to be collected in t'morning. I wa' quicker than most 'cos I asked Joan to put away some of mi' stuff, and I simply put mi trombone in its case and 'eaded for the fish and chips. It probably took mi five minutes after t'concert had finished. I then set off and saw what I've told you.'

'Is that the full story then, Joseph?'

'As far as I can remember,' was Webster's thoughtful response.

'How do you think the man died?' This was question that Catherine asked after a slight pause and with kindly eyes looking straight into the eyes of Webster.

'I haven't a clue.'

'Now you're sure? Did you have a knife with you? Did you get involved with the man in any way?'

'No, miss, 'onest.' I never saw any knife, and I never touched 'im.'

Webster said this with such obvious sincerity that, had Peter not known of his past deeds and shared the stories with Catherine, both would have been convinced that he was telling the truth.

'Is that everything that happened, Joseph? If it is, you've nothing to be afraid of and I think you should go straight to the police and tell them what you've told me. The longer you stay away, the more likely they are to think that you had most to do with the tragedy. If you explain where you were when the wallet was stolen and that you'd no idea that the man had died, they may view your case more leniently than they do at the moment.'

Peter had raised previously the issue of guilt by association and the likelihood of all three boys being treated in the same way, but now seemed neither the place nor the time to labour the point.

Catherine went on to add, 'I'm sure your parents will be anxious about your whereabouts as well, and they need to know that you're safe.'

To which Webster answered dismissively, 'Who, them? They don't give a toss.'

'I wouldn't be too sure about that, Joe. Parents don't always show how much they love their children, but when they're in real trouble, they often worry more than anyone would believe.

Now something very important. Are you sorry for what has happened?'

Catherine's question took Webster by surprise. He was not accustomed to being asked if he felt sorry for any wrongdoing he committed, as nobody ever believed he was.

'Why d'you ask, miss?'

'If you can show some regret, Joe, people will think better of you. They'll feel that you've learned something as a result of this experience and that you're unlikely to get involved in anything like this again.'

'I suppose I'm sorry then,' was Webster's non-committal reply.

'You'll have to do better than that.'

Webster shrugged his shoulders, puffed his cheeks, and blew air through the sides of his mouth as if to say, 'What do you expect?'

The talking went well beyond the time that Peter had promised to meet Roger at the station, and he was beginning to despair of the possibility of himself or Catherine being able to persuade Webster that a peaceable move to the police station was the wisest thing to do. He was at the point of looking for alternatives when Webster suddenly stood up, commanded the centre of the room, and said, 'Well, I suppose we'd better go.'

It was with great relief that Peter led the way to the van and headed for Weberton.

The journey was made in almost complete silence as both thought through the implications of the previous evening and tried to foresee the outcome. Though they did not know it, both were hanging on to a strand of hope rather like a tightrope walker tackling an unknown height in a heavy wind, knowing that disaster awaits if he slips. For Webster, the slip was represented by any inconsistencies in his story. He felt betrayed by his friends who had called out his name to the police and yet felt guilt about telling a story that he claimed to be true, which incriminated them.

At last, they reached their destination, and true to his word, Roger was waiting patiently outside. The three of them went into the police station and reported to the sergeant on duty. In no time, Peter and Roger were in the interview room. In the meantime, Webster was taken down a corridor, presumably, Peter surmised, to another room to await his parents.

On being questioned, Peter explained how he had come by Webster at his home, how he and his wife had gone through Webster's story, felt that there was a good deal of truth in what he had to say, and that he hoped the police would also recognise that the lad deserved to be listened to with sympathetic understanding. He also made the point that Webster had played wonderfully well in the town hall and that his success with the trombone was having a positive impact on his behaviour. Throughout his statement, he sought to convince his listeners to take Webster's explanation seriously.

Once he had finished making his statement, he was asked to sign it and was then allowed to go. As he left the station, he passed Webster's mother who looked to be in no mood for appeasement. The police had collected her from home and no doubt had had some tasteful words to listen to.

CHAPTER 27

CONSTERNATION AT THE COTTAGE AND AT SCHOOL

When Peter arrived home, he related to Catherine what had happened at the police station. He described it in as much detail as he could and responded also to her close questioning.

'It was strange being at the police station as a witness. They took me into a room, and then asked me how well I knew Webster, what I knew about his movements after the concert, and why he had turned up at the cottage. They noted it all down very carefully, and then I had to wait until it was typed up. I then had to sign it. I found it quite an ordeal.'

'D'you think they believe that Joseph is innocent?'

'They never gave a clue. They simply asked the questions and wrote down my answers.'

'Well, d'you think they believed you.'

'I hope so, otherwise I suppose I could be in trouble for misleading the police.'

'Did you speak with Mrs Webster?'

'Thank goodness I didn't have to. You should have seen her when she came into the station. She was loud-mouthing everybody for being disturbed at home, for arresting her son, and for bringing her to the police station. Later, I could hear her having a go at Joe. If the courts want to punish him, they only need to put him in a room with his mother for half an hour. Phew, what a challenge.'

'I've never met her, but, from what you say, she sounds a real Tartar. Poor Joseph. Anyway, did you see the other two lads?'

'No. I've no idea where they are.'

Wearying under the cross examination, Peter was pleased to hear the phone ring. It was Roger.

'Hi, Peter. We had an interesting time at the police station. Webster's mother's some woman. First of all she let the sergeant know what she felt about them arresting her son, and then gave young Webster a real rollicking. When the detective inspector arrived from Leeds, his name is Grossman by the way, she had a go at him as well.'

'I'm sorry I got you into this shambles, Roger, but the lad needed some advice. I was in a very tricky position when he turned up on the doorstep.'

'Well, you did all the right things, and this should help both his and your case.'

'My case? Why?' Peter's mind went into panic mode.

'Harbouring a criminal,' laughed Roger.

Peter could almost see the twinkle in his eye as he temporarily discomforted his friend. 'OK, ok. Thanks for that. Anyway, how did it go?'

'You'd certainly prepared young Webster well. He gave his side of the story very clearly and convincingly. The police took it down word for word, and then asked his mother to sign it, along with the boy. I simply observed in case there were any issues. As nothing cropped up, I'd a quiet couple of hours. Joe's due in the juvenile court for the preliminary hearing in a day or two. In the meantime, the police have let him go home with his parents but asked for regular visits from the probation officer.'

'What about the other two lads? Did you get the chance to talk to them?' Peter was aware that, in the other room, Catherine would be waiting for some more answers to her questions.

'It was impossible to do that or even to get a sight of their statements. We will have to await the first hearing to get any clue as to what they're saying. Fortunately, we'll be shown their statements, and, if there's any way we can use them to help young Joe, we will.'

'Lots of thanks, Roger. I'll be forever indebted. I know how difficult Webster is, but I think there's still hope for him.'

'I hope you're right. All the best and sleep well.'

'And you.'

With that Peter put down the phone and went back into the sitting room. Not unnaturally, Catherine wanted to know exactly what was said.

'The interest you have in reading detective stories seems to be emerging here, my dear,' said Peter provocatively. He recognised, however, that it would be unfair not to see in Catherine's questioning more concern for Webster than for her detective inclinations. Nevertheless, she had spent the time whilst Peter was away writing out in her usual careful handwriting the story as she saw it, hoping, she said, to identify some elements in it that might help in Webster's defence.

'As far as I can see, there's a possibility that Joe was not involved directly. His return to the town hall for his mouthpiece delayed his arrival at the fish shop. By the time he arrived, the other two lads had probably already had their fish and chips, become bored, and had the bright idea to attack their victim. Mr Mann, unfortunately, gave them an ideal opportunity; in the newspapers it said he had walked out of the pub with his wallet in his hand. Somebody needs to establish who the knife belongs to, that's if the police have it. Did the police say anything about it?'

'Not to me, and Roger never mentioned it. All we know is that a knife was used in the struggle. Again, we'll have to await the hearing to see what the police have.'

'Drat. I wish I'd asked Joe more about it. He must have known what happened to it,' murmured a perplexed looking Catherine. 'That could be critical evidence.'

She went on, as if to herself and just loud enough for Peter to hear, 'If it belongs to one of the other lads, it would strengthen Joe's story.' Then more loudly, 'We must establish the ownership of the knife, the actual time, as near as we can, as to when the boys bought their fish and chips, and how late Joe was for their meeting. Such little things, if they fit what Joe is telling us, could be crucial.'

'I see where you're going, Catherine, but I'm sure the police will look into all that. They've a duty to see that justice is done.'

'I agree, Peter, but can't you see that with the reputation that Joe has, the police could easily accept that he was present at the time of the attack, even if they prove that one of the others carried it out?'

'Well, yes, but we'll have little say in what conclusions are reached. We can relate what we know, which is based purely on Joe's account, and then it's up to others to gather the concrete evidence.'

'Hmm, perhaps,' was the only, but thoughtful, response that Peter had from Catherine. 'It's time we were in bed. Let's go,' and she set off for the stairs with pensive written all over her face. Peter's expression was no less so, trying to work out how all this might end.

Even in bed, the thinking did not stop, as Catherine offered a possible way forward. 'You know, the other two have probably ganged up on Joe. They're older than him, aren't they?'

'Yes. A couple of years or so, but he's always been mixed up with them. Remember that time on the swings. Joe was with them then. What I can't understand is how to put together the ever so honest and innocent Joe who was sitting here in the cottage, and the guy I have to deal with at school. Not everything fits . . . . Then again, it rarely does,' he added. Eventually, tiredness took over and both fell asleep with thoughts of how they might help Webster.

Next morning Catherine was still thinking about Webster and his plight. Having strong inclinations towards believing Webster innocent in the affair, even before Peter got out of bed, she again opened the discussion as to what was the best thing to do to help Joe. Peter was not totally in agreement with her conclusion that Webster must be innocent, he had had too many run ins with Webster, but he knew and admired her determination to tease out solutions to unexplained problems. She invariably resolved a crime long before the detectives when listening to the radio or watching television, and would often put down a book before it was finished, with the words, 'It's obvious who did it.'

As she was dressing, she turned to Peter, who was still meditating on the seriousness of the previous evening's events, whilst trying to look relaxed in bed with his hands behind his head, and said, 'I'm going to ring your aunt and ask her to come and look after James. I think I'd like to go out for a while.'

It was the unusual time and place of the statement rather than the information it contained, that led to Peter sitting straight up in bed, his eyes alert, and questioning, 'Why?'

'Well, I just need to do one or two things in Weberton. Don't worry. I'll get a lift with Maureen when she goes into town.'

Peter was sensible enough not to ask any further questions. He rose, dressed, said, 'Good morning,' to the children, led the morning prayer, ate his breakfast and headed for school. He tried to dismiss from his mind what Catherine was likely to be doing, but just hoped that it was nothing foolish.

When he arrived at school he was the centre of attraction. The staffroom was full of colleagues preparing for morning lessons, but there was only one topic of conversation. Everybody wanted to know the story of the previous evening's events. Peter's closest friends were the ones who heard the story as he wished to relate it, and then by Chinese whispers it circulated to others. The excited hubbub continued, the staffroom had never witnessed anything so remarkable, until suddenly a hush fell on the room as the head walked in for the morning staff briefing.

'Good morning, everyone,' he said brightly. 'I understand that some pupils have a visit to the town library at ten to learn of its inner workings. Is everything organised, Jane?'

'Yes, I've put a list of participants on the notice board. They'll be out for about an hour.'

'Fine. And the match this evening, Stan?'

'It's a home match. As it's a cup game, I'm hoping to get plenty of support and all staff are welcome. Kick off will be around half past four.'

'Thank you, Stan. Any more notices?' Members of staff looked at each other, all with the same question on their faces, *Isn't he going to say anything about Webster?*

The head made as if to turn for the door to leave, but then spun round on the balls of his feet, and with a cheeky, boyish smile on his face, 'I suppose you're all wanting to know about Webster?'

He had not needed to ask. Staff sat up in their easy chairs, others straightened and looked at him intently. By now his face was grave, and the way he gently rubbed his forefinger across the underside of his chin and pursed his lips indicated his genuine concern.

'Well, I don't know the full story, but I understand he turned up at Peter's yesterday evening. He was eventually persuaded to go to the police station. The police telephoned me to say that they had questioned him and had then sent him home until the hearing next Tuesday. I'm expecting another visit from the police this morning. I'm not sure what they want, but I should later in the day. What I'll be able to share with you I don't know. I also had a visit from the CEO yesterday. He was concerned about the publicity.'

Maxine turned slightly to Peter and whispered, 'He would be.'

'But he has offered his support and recognises that the incident has little to do with the school. I can ring him anytime and there is an adviser at our beck and call for a couple of days. He warned us to be wary of the press, by the way. In the meantime, it's important that we get on with our work. The children will, no doubt, have got some inkling of the evening's events, but it's important that we don't let it affect the school day. I'm sure you know what I mean.'

With that he left the staffroom, which returned to its lively state. Still chatting in twos and threes, staff began to make their way to their classes for registration.

As Peter passed down the corridor, he was intercepted by Tom, who quietly and unobtrusively told him that the head wished to see him.

'I'll do your registration,' he said, and left Peter to climb the stairs to the head's study.

The head's PA received him with her usual smile and, 'Sorry to hear about your exploits yesterday. Catherine must have been worried sick, especially with the children being about. Go straight in. Mr Holdsworth is expecting you.'

Peter went in and the head, rising from behind his desk, nodded to the seat by the small table, seeking to keep the conversation as informal as he could.

'Now, Peter, as I'm seeing the police later this morning, I wonder if you can fill me in on the details of last night and also give me your views on the whole affair.'

Peter proceeded to go through the story as best he could, trying, as Catherine had suggested, to keep it as consistent with the events as they understood them. He tried to avoid entering any opinions into his account of what had happened, but simply to set out the facts as he knew them. The head thanked him for what he had done for the boy. Indeed, Peter had recognised among the staff as a whole that morning, more sympathy for Webster than at any time previously. He gained some satisfaction from what the head and colleagues had said, which indicated that he had done the right thing. 'If I need to call you up to talk with the police I'll let you know. In the meantime, do you feel capable of carrying on with your classes? You must be mentally drained after all this.'

'I'm fine, Mr Holdsworth. I think it'll be best if I go back to class and get on with my work. The more I do, I suspect, the less I'll think about what has passed and what is probably to come.'

'Good man,' said the head as he rose. 'Before you go, Peter. What d'you think? D'you reckon he's telling the truth.'

'In all honesty, I'm not sure. He sounded very convincing last night, and Catherine concluded he wasn't involved in the actual mugging. But she doesn't know him as well as we do. I'm glad I don't have to make a decision on this one.'

'Thanks,' said the head, as he opened the door for Peter to pass through.

CHAPTER 28

CATHERINE THE DETECTIVE

As soon as Peter had left for school, Catherine rang his Aunt Grace and asked if she could look after James for the day. Katie, Sarah and Gregory had now started school, but James was still too young.

'I'd love to look after James, Catherine. What time would you like me?'

'About ten o'clock would be great.'

'Fine, see you then.'

Catherine knew that Grace loved the times she could spend with the children, especially on the open moor. Although she never spoke about it, the fondness she had for the children emanated from her close relationship with them. In quiet moments, her thoughts sometimes turned to her earlier life and she deeply regretted what she had done. It was in those moments that she felt the guilt that only a mother who deserts her child can feel. The flashes of thought quickly passed, however, the result of constantly putting them to the back of her mind as she tried to forget, and she again, almost instantaneously, resumed her role of aunt.

Catherine then rang Maureen, who said she would pick her up at half past ten. In the meantime, Catherine planned what she intended to do once she was in Weberton. She knew the importance of evidence, and she knew some of the ways she might collect it. Her avid reading of crime stories had provided insights that many a detective would have been proud of.

Before Aunt Grace arrived, Catherine became aware of cars drawing up to the cottage, and the jabber of voices. Looking through the window she realised that a small crowd of people with notebooks and cameras had assembled at the gate. She realised what was happening. The press had heard of Webster's flight to the cottage and they were here looking for a story. Without Peter at her side, she was now likely to be faced with questions about Webster without really knowing what sort of reply she should give. In fact, if Peter had been at home, it was unlikely that she would have been able to answer any questions; she knew Peter would have kept the porch door thoroughly locked.

It would not have been Catherine, however, if she had not gone outside and asked, 'How can I help you?'

Delighted, the journalists fired questions at her.

'How did you persuade young Webster to go to the police? What state was he in? What did he say? Did you feel he might be a threat to the family?'

Catherine did her best, in her anxiety, to give brief but truthful answers, in the hope that the visitors would soon be satisfied. For their part, the journalists wrote down their own interpretation of what she said, taking particular note of her comments in response to a question about the safety of her family. 'No, she never felt that her young children were at risk, and, throughout the evening, young Joseph Webster had behaved impeccably.'

The photographers snapped photographs of her and the cottage. The first part of the morning thus presented Catherine with an event well outside her experience, but one which did not faze her. She was not sure whether the journalists had what they wanted, but after about half an hour they were back in their cars and heading off, keen, no doubt, to look elsewhere for information before having to make the deadlines for their next editions.

Shortly after the press had departed, Aunt Grace arrived.

'Hello love, how are you doing?'

'Just had an exciting time with the press. The journalists have left only a couple of minutes ago, having asked me all sorts of questions about this lad Webster. As you know, he arrived here last night when the police were looking for him. No doubt there will be some coverage of what I said, with everything else the press have learned, and, dare I say, imagined, in the papers tomorrow. We'll see then how the press have interpreted what I said. Anyway, it's good to see you and thanks for coming.'

She kissed auntie on the cheek and led the way back into the house. 'I'm going into Weberton and Maureen will be arriving shortly to give me a lift. Can you take over while I go and get ready?'

'Of course,' replied Grace, as she went into the sitting room where James was playing on the carpet.

Catherine went upstairs and prepared herself for her visit to Weberton. Not only did she put on her 'in town' clothes, she also carefully placed in her handbag a notebook and pencil.

Maureen arrived in good time and they took their leave of Aunt Grace and James, Catherine hugging her son and whispering in his ear, 'Now be a good lad and look after Auntie.'

After a journey filled with conversation about Webster, the mugging, and the morning's events, Maureen dropped off Catherine in the High Street.

Once in Weberton, Catherine walked across to the scene of the crime, The Dragon pub. The police had it cordoned off as a crime scene, and were quickly moving on any bystanders. Opposite, and across the road in West Street, she could see the fish and chip shop. The distance between the two, she estimated, was at most twenty yards. A young teenager could be across and back in a couple of seconds, and then be ready to head towards the park. The corner of the High Street, from which Webster said he observed the attack and in which the town hall was situated, was a little further from the pub. Nevertheless, it would have given Webster a good view of what happened and also the opportunity to join his mates on their dash from the scene of the crime. So far, thought Catherine, Webster's story fits.

She then decided to walk briskly to and from the town hall. Timing the walk both ways with her wrist watch, she reckoned a single journey took her at her quickest, thirteen minutes. Assuming that Webster had moved rather more quickly, anxious to meet up with his friends, he could probably have done it in ten, but then she remembered he had returned to the town hall for his mouthpiece. 'Interesting,' she thought, as she made her way back to the fish and chip shop.

The shop was now open. It was not regarded by the police as part of the crime scene and so it was business as usual. Catherine knew the owner and her assistant from the days that they had frequented the place when living in Weberton, and so as she ordered her supposed lunch it was not unnatural for her to ask about the evening's events. As it was relatively early, she was the only one in the shop, and so Jackie, the owner, was more than happy to talk.

'Hi, Catherine. Good to see you again. Thought you had deserted Weberton. The last couple of days have certainly been exciting. You and Peter managed to get caught up in it all, I hear.'

'Yes. You can never understand how lads can be angels one minute and little devils the next. What happened down here?'

'A couple of the lads came in at about quarter to eight and had a portion of fish and chips each. I knew Will, but not the other chap, who I now know is Trevor Makin. They were fine. Will asked me how I was, and in his normal cheeky way asked me to give him more than the usual portion of chips. Everything seemed as usual. We were fairly busy when the commotion started outside. We all went to the window to see what was happening. It was then that I saw George Mann lying on the ground outside the pub, with one or two others around him. The two lads were still outside and had been joined by Joe Webster. As some of those across the street began pointing towards the lads, they started to run towards the park. That scamp Joe Webster had obviously joined Will and Makin, though he had not been in the shop for any fish and chips. It's not difficult to put two and two together. Fortunately, the police got two of them. The last I heard, was that they're still looking for Joe Webster. He's always trouble and I'm surprised Will gets mixed up with him.'

Catherine did not enlighten her on Joe's situation, and left it for Jackie to find out from the one o'clock news or some other customer, but went on, 'I suppose the police came in eventually and asked you some questions about the boys?'

'They did, but they seemed more interested in what we might have seen across the street. As I told them, I was serving, so I didn't see anything. The customers were no use either, as they were queuing with their backs to the pub. It was only when we heard a scream that we all looked through the window.'

'How long d'you reckon that was after the lads had had their fish and chips?'

Jackie looked quizzically at Catherine, as if to ascertain the point of the questions, but being eager to talk about the most exciting thing to happen in Weberton for years, she answered, 'Well, I can tell you exactly, because as soon as I heard the scream, the town clock struck quarter past eight.'

'Gosh. What an evening it must have been,' said Catherine as she collected her fish and chips and passed her shilling across the counter.

Once outside, she began to put two and two together. She concluded, *If the concert didn't finish until about eight o'clock, it's just possible that Joe could have made it to his friends by quarter past. But that assumes he packed up and was out of the town hall in about five minutes. If he ran he could have been here, certainly by ten past, which would have given him time to be part of the crime. But he had to go back for his mouthpiece, which would have taken extra minutes. There's also the possibility that he didn't get out of the town hall by five past eight.*

She worked through the pros and cons in her mind, recognising that whatever she did would have little bearing on the outcome, but anxious to satisfy herself about the truth of Webster's story. On the journey back to the cottage, she turned the evidence one way and then another, trying to fathom the truth. Maureen, oblivious as to what Catherine had been doing, but aware that she was distracted by her thoughts, concentrated on her driving and said little.

When Peter arrived home from school, Catherine was bursting to tell him about her day. First, she told him of the press interviews she had given, making sure to put him at ease by saying that she had said nothing other than he would have said had he been present. Then, she described her visit to Weberton, the questions she had asked, and the answers she had received. 'I recognise that it's all circumstantial, but I'm positive in my own mind that what I've learned today indicates that Joseph may not have been involved in the mugging. I can't say that he wasn't, but I'm sure others may have similar difficulties proving he was. It's a pity his so-called friends have put the blame on him.'

After Catherine had outlined her evidence, Peter agreed that it all strengthened Webster's case, but like Catherine, he was unsure who

352

else would believe it. He then offered further support to Catherine's findings on the timings.

'I know for a fact that the concert didn't finish much before eight. By the time Joe had packed away his trombone and left the building it must have been at least five past. How long it took him to get to the fish shop I couldn't say. But at least, it could give him some hope if you can get the right people to listen to you.'

'Would anybody else be able to give the precise time when he left the town hall? I know if he ran down the High Street, he could probably do it in less time than I ever could, but it's critical to know what time he left.'

'I suspect Joan might know. She's worth having a word with.'

'Well, perhaps the police will do that. Anyway, how was your day?'

'It was certainly interesting.'

Peter described the scene at the school gate when the press arrived for a second time and the head had to go out and ask them to move on.

'I wonder if some of them had been here at the cottage earlier in the day,' mused Catherine.

'No idea. But anyway, the head asked to see me and listened very attentively to the story as Webster had told it to us. He had a meeting with this detective inspector Grossman from Leeds, and then the detective interviewed me. He asked the usual questions; when did

Webster arrive at the cottage, what did he say, who did we speak to, how long was he with us before we managed to get him to the police station? He seemed more interested in establishing whether or not we had schooled Joe in his answers to police questions, as though we might want to interfere with the investigation. I have to say that I didn't take to him at first, but things improved as he realised that I wasn't trying to cover for Joe. I got the feeling that he's already made up his mind. It's interesting, as you said, that he doesn't seem to have asked Jackie the questions you asked. I think we need to find some way of having what you discovered brought to the attention of the police, but in such a way that they'll attach some importance to it.'

'You're right, Peter. How we do that I'm not sure. Perhaps after we've slept on it and had the weekend to think about it, we might come up with a solution.'

'I think it's important for me to speak again with Roger. I'll see him at rugger tomorrow and discuss it with him.'

'Good idea. I'm going up to bed.'

'I'll be up shortly,' Peter called to Catherine, who was already on her way up the stairs, as he made his way to the back door to go out into the garden to get some fresh air. One of the beauties of the moor, he said to himself time and again, was the freshness that could be breathed in and the effect it had on a tired mind and body. The evening was relatively mild, and the half moon was dipping in and out of the puffy clouds that were meandering across the sky. The stars blinked, also using the clouds first to hide and then to reappear, and the stillness, not always a feature of the moor, was captivating. He took deep breaths, feeling the cool clear air penetrate deep into his lungs, and felt an easing of tension as restfulness enveloped him. In but a short time, he felt sufficiently refreshed to go back inside and think about a strategy for the morrow.

Roger was the first to raise the issue of the mugging when Peter met him in the clubhouse after the match. Roger was a committee man and not a player, and so he had watched, cheered, and been disappointed by yet another poor team performance. As with all those who had been involved with the club for some years, the memories of past glories persisted and Roger needed time after such a display to gather himself. A defeat by 40 points by a team from just over the Pennines was not something to savour.

By the time Peter managed to get to him, having pushed his way through the crowded, smoke-filled bar, he had already had a couple of pints and was beginning to feel much better. Peter, naturally enough, put the match behind him quickly and was more interested in the case than in the match result. He was keen, therefore to hear what Roger had to say, and then to share with him Catherine's findings. They bought their pints and managed to find a quiet corner where they could talk in reasonable confidence.

Roger again went over what he knew of the case, adding what he saw as the different outcomes for Webster. 'At best, young Joe could be bound over and put on probation. At worst, if it were proved that he'd joined his two friends before the mugging, he could have a much longer term in a borstal. I'm not convinced, in light of the statements of the other two lads, that he can show that he didn't do the stabbing. If he did do it . . . . well,' he added uncertainly. 'Whatever part he played, if he was present at the mugging, he faces the prospect of a pretty severe punishment.'

'I understand,' Peter indicated with a nod, but then went on to talk about Catherine's visit to Weberton. He was coming to the conclusion that it was not possible for Webster to have been in two places at once, and that if the times could be proven, there would be a good case to make. Therefore, he explained the findings with conviction, emphasising the strong possibility that it might be possible to prove that Webster was not involved. Roger listened and became increasingly interested as Catherine's work unfolded. In the quietness of his own thoughts he dissected the new evidence, trying to work out how it could be used.

'I think,' he eventually said, 'we should go along to the police station and share this with the police. That'll give them time to check it before the hearing on Tuesday and may influence what case they bring against young Joe.'

'D'you think they'll listen?'

'They have to,' replied Roger as he got into his car.

When they arrived at the station they asked the sergeant in charge if it were possible to see someone about the mugging case.

'You're very fortunate. Inspector Grossman is in the office. I'll go and have a word with him.'

He returned in a couple of minutes saying, 'That's fine, he'll see you now.'

The sergeant took them along to Grossman, who was busy looking over the case papers. It was obvious that he was keen to resolve the problem for which he had been sent over from Leeds.

'Hello, gentlemen. How can I be of help?'

'Hello, Inspector. Can I introduce Peter Delaney.' It was right for Roger to take the lead as the inspector had already met him as Webster's representative.

'We've already met. I interviewed Mr Delaney in the school,' said Grossman as he rose and shook hands. He then pointed to two chairs, and Peter and Roger seated themselves.

'We wanted to talk to you about the hearing on Tuesday. I think there is some useful evidence that's come to light that could have a bearing on it.'

'Oh, I see. And what is it?' Grossman asked, but showing no more than a passing interest, as he shuffled his papers.

'It's about the timings.'

Roger went on to outline what Catherine had discovered while Peter sat and observed. He watched Grossman closely, and although the inspector continued to look mainly at the papers on his desk, with only the occasional glance at his two visitors, Peter sensed that as Roger outlined the evidence that Catherine had collected, he was taking it seriously.

'Who is this lady?' he asked after Roger had finished.

'It's my wife. She became so interested in what had happened and so concerned that Webster should be given a fair hearing, that she decided to do a little investigation herself. You've just heard what she found.'

'I need to speak with her. Where can I see her?'

Grossman was abrupt, but Peter put it down to his desire to solve the case as quickly as possible, and that he may have seen something of critical importance in what he had just heard.

'I could bring her here, or I could take you up to see her at our cottage. But it's up on the moor, about ten miles away,' said Peter, assuming that Roger would also be willing to make the journey.

'I'll come to see her now. A visit to the moor on a not too bad Saturday evening sounds just the thing after the day I've had. Lead the way.'

Both Peter and Roger were delighted at this response. Having seated the detective in Roger's car, Peter went across to his van, and then both headed for the cottage.

As he travelled towards the moor, Peter's mind went on what had become a usual ramble over the events of the last few days. *What is he going to make of Catherine; how far is he likely to believe what she has found out; what other information will he need; are we doing the right thing; and is it all going to help Joe or make things worse?*

These were the questions, but he had no the answers. But he had hope, and, almost incidentally, prayer, as he began to ask His Lord for what help He could give.

Catherine obviously saw the cars arrive, and she was at the door as the three men walked along the path. She knew Roger but not the third man, and was taken aback when he was introduced as Inspector Grossman from Leeds.

'Catherine,' Peter was the first to speak with a voice that could not conceal his excitement, 'the Inspector has come to ask about the investigation you did into the case of Webster and his friends. We've explained everything to him, but he wants to talk with you and hear it firsthand.'

'Oh, come in. Would you like a cup of tea?' Her stock question to visitors was the only thing she could think of saying as they entered the living room.

'No, no thank you. Perhaps later,' replied Grossman. 'All I want is to ask you some questions about what you did yesterday.'

Catherine was struck by Grossman's well-groomed hair, the keenness of his eyes, and the smartness of his suit. *So this is what a real detective looks like,* she thought to herself, while mentally revisiting the images of her television detectives.

'I'd love to share my findings with you. I'm sure that what I discovered throws doubt on Joseph being directly involved in what happened at The Dragon. My reasons are . . . .'

'Wait a minute. Don't get ahead of yourself,' interrupted the detective with a comforting smile. 'Now, talk me through what you did, but more slowly, and without including any conclusions you may have reached. It's my job to reach conclusions.'

Roger looked across at Peter, raised his eyes, and showed his amusement at Catherine's enthusiasm and Grossman's response.

Having regained her composure, Catherine spelled out what she had done and whom she had spoken to, clearly and concisely. The Inspector carefully noted this down in a small blue notebook, interrupting from time to time to ask for more detail. When Catherine had finished, he flicked through his notes, *Possibly to check that he has an accurate record*, thought Peter, then closed it quite deliberately before carefully stowing it along with his pen into his inside pocket.

'Now, I would like a cup of tea if that's possible,' he said, and eased himself more comfortably into his chair. Catherine did the honours whilst the men talked about things other than the case. Grossman was interested in rugby, on some weekends when possible going to see Headingley, and on others the Leeds Rugby League side, and so he asked about the afternoon's game at Weberton. When Roger and Peter moved off that topic as soon as they could, both being embarrassed by the day's score, the Inspector asked about the cottage and what it was like living on the moor.

'It's a great experience for the whole family . . . .' Peter was just about to wax lyrical about life on the moor, but was interrupted when Catherine walked in with the tea and biscuits. The conversation continued, with Catherine taking over to outline what had been done in the cottage and what was still needed. It was Roger's first visit too, since the early days when he had been commandeered by Peter to help with the clearing up and painting, and so he also listened with particular interest. Peter and Catherine answered the usual questions asked by visitors, such as how did they cope in winter, how did they get on with the farmers, how far was it to Binkley and so on. They also took pleasure in the positive comments their two visitors made about the beautiful situation, the obvious age of the cottage, the depth of the walls, and the general warmth that seemed to pervade the cottage, despite the lack of central heating. Catherine took pleasure in pointing out the improvements that had taken place in the sitting room, and then referred to the dining room and the discovery of the ingle nook fireplace.

'Would you like to have a look at it?'

'Yes, please.'

Catherine rose and took Grossman into the dining room, closing the sitting room door behind her.

When they were out of earshot, Peter asked Roger, 'How d'you think it's going?'

'Difficult to say. He's a wily character. He sometimes doesn't appear to be taking much notice, but if you watch his eyes you get a different impression.'

'I agree.'

The conversation ceased as Catherine re-entered the room. Grossman stood at the door, commenting on what he described as a fascinating place to live and the wonderful inglenook, before suggesting that it was time to get back. With a slight look of misgiving at moving on from what had become quite an enjoyable social evening, Roger agreed. Both he and Grossman thanked Peter and Catherine, the latter shaking hands with a warm and genuine handshake, as he said to Catherine, 'Thank you for all you've done. I can assure you that it will be taken into consideration.' With that the two of them were gone.

Peter and Catherine were left to look at each other and try to work out for themselves the likely outcome of the evening. Catherine stood, eyes looking straight at Peter, arms and fingers straightened in front of her, and legs slightly astride. She gave the impression of someone who believed in what she had just shared, and was ready to continue in that belief until everyone else she met also did. Peter, feeling pride in Catherine's ability to raise important issues about the mugging, but tired after such a pressurised day said, 'Look, no further talk, let's wait and see what happens.'

CHAPTER 29

THE MAGISTRATE'S COURT

The hearing was fixed for ten o'clock. The magistrate had asked for the three boys and their parents to be present, along with anyone who could provide a statement about the boys' characters, and representatives of the police, which included the arresting officer and Detective Inspector Grossman.

Peter was given absence from school for at least the morning, and, if necessary, for the afternoon, so that he could answer questions about Webster if required. He went to the court room along with the head, who thought that his own testimony on Webster's character could be of some value in the boys' defence. He recognised that, although Webster was a nuisance, there were aspects of his behaviour which, if cultivated, could help him overcome some of his worst characteristics. He had in mind Webster's attitude during the boat project and the impressive way he had progressed with his trombone. He knew that he may have to reveal some of the worst of Webster's antics, but saw this as providing a full and helpful picture of the boy, one which might well help the magistrate to decide on the best course of action for the lad.

Peter and the head entered the court building together. Neither had been in before, and when faced with several doors and a staircase were not sure in which direction to go. Fortunately, in one of the darker recesses, brightened by a couple of matching table lamps, they saw a counter, behind which was a receptionist. They approached, made themselves known, and asked where they should go.

'First, sir, you need to complete this form,' said the young lady as she handed each of them a sheet of paper.

It was a simple enough form, asking for names, addresses, the purpose of their visit, and a signature. After they had passed the completed forms back across the counter, she gave them a small identity card.

'Please wear this so that it's visible at all times. To reach the juvenile court room, you go up the stairs and through the second door on the right. Don't enter until the usher invites you in.'

On reaching the door it quietly swung open in response to the push of a uniformed official. He had spotted them through the small window, strategically placed in the door to allow him to see anyone seeking entry. Peter and the head went through, showing their badges when requested.

Peter was struck by the simplicity of the room. It had the feel of a rather uncared for classroom. Simple wooden chairs were arranged in three rows on the roughly worn wooden floor. On either side was a further row of chairs. At the front were two chairs facing a long table, which housed seats for the magistrates. All the chairs were of a similar type. To the right of the table was a small desk and chair, probably, Peter guessed, for a scribe.

Another official, dressed in a smart navy blue jacket and trousers, and a tie with the Weberton coat of arms, seemingly gliding he moved so quietly, approached them, and in a whisper asked them who they were. They again showed their identity cards. Then, with the same movement, he led them to seats in the back of the three rows. Already present and seated, were the three boys with their parents, Grossman, and another uniformed officer. Several other people that Peter did not recognise were seated around the room.

The room, unprepossessing but daunting because of its purpose, was cloaked in tension. Peter could almost touch it. He began to wonder how he would feel if he were called to provide some evidence. He sought to give the appearance of control, but, as this was his first visit to a courthouse, he was finding it difficult, and he was unsure as to how the hearing would be conducted. Although he was not directly involved, he was already sensing the nervousness that he was sure was already engulfing the three accused lads. His hands rested in front of him on his thighs in his interview mode, but the clasping and unclasping did not allow him to conceal his anxieties completely.

On a word from the court official, the people gathered in the court room stood. From a door behind the front table appeared what Peter took to be the three presiding magistrates. They sat behind the table. They were followed out of the inner room by a young woman clerk who took her place at the side desk.

Peter looked at the magistrates with interest. The one who took the central chair was clearly in charge of the proceedings. He was, like his two companions, dressed simply. He wore a suit and tie, and nothing that indicated his office or that was designed to intimidate the defendants. Tall and slim, he bore the appearance of someone desirous and capable of quickly understanding and resolving the matters presented to him. On his left sat a woman who looked to be about fifty years of age. She wore the look of someone who regarded her role as of great significance, clearly recognising the importance of seeing justice done. Behind what might have been taken initially as an unfriendly expression, however, were understanding eyes that suggested the desire to do what was best for the accused. To the right sat a rather rotund gentleman who gave the impression of having some status in the town, which had been rewarded by his having a seat on the bench. He wore a waistcoat that bulged over a stomach that provided a resting place when he was seated, for his chained gold watch, which he was looking at as he entered the room. Peter saw less sympathy in his face than that displayed by his female associate.

'Good morning boys, ladies, and gentlemen,' said the magistrate. 'We are here this morning on very serious business, matters that are the outcome of the death of a well-respected gentleman of the town.'

He looked with genuine sympathy towards Mrs Mann, who, accompanied by her son, was sitting at the rear of the courthouse.

'I would like to start by outlining the procedure of the court. I'll first ask the police officer to outline what he thinks happened on that fateful evening when Mr Mann died. When we have heard that evidence,' he added, looking at the boys, 'I'll then invite you in turn to sit with one of your parents in the chairs here, just in front of the table. I will ask each one of you what happened on that evening. I want you to speak clearly and slowly so that I and my colleagues can hear what you say. Please answer any questions we may ask honestly. After all of you have been heard, I'll ask anyone else present to hand in anything they wish the court to take into consideration; for example, someone who wants to leave us some information about you that they feel we should have regard to when deciding what action to take at the end of the hearing.'

All this was said in a quiet but authoritative voice designed to put everyone in the room at ease. Occasionally, at the end of a sentence he would pause and smile, confirming his intention to ensure that everybody had time to absorb what he had said, and was sufficiently relaxed to present their story properly.

'Now, are there any questions?'

Peter was impressed with what he was observing. The intimidation he associated with trials, that is the ones he had seen with Catherine on television, was not present here. Wigged and cloaked judges, impressive insignia and formality had been replaced by everyday clothes and an almost informal, unthreatening approach. The accused were no longer in the shadow of severe physical punishment and immediate incarceration. In the format that Peter was witnessing, juveniles were being treated as such. They were being encouraged to be involved in the process in such a way that they could say what they had to say, with the confidence that they had some sympathetic listeners. The anxiety that Peter had suffered as he took his seat did not disappear altogether, but it was eased. He hoped, indeed assumed, that the three boys, but particularly Webster, would be responding to the magistrate truthfully and in a measured way. He was confident that if Webster could tell his story without any inconsistencies, he would have a fair hearing, and may even convince those present that he was innocent of the mugging.

As there were no questions, the magistrate asked the police to present the case that had brought the three boys before the court. The uniformed officer moved to one of the two seats in front of the table, took out his notebook and read out his statement.

'On Tuesday, fifth of October, at approximately seven forty five, William Skelton and Trevor Makin bought fish and chips from the fish shop in West Street. They stood outside to eat them and were joined by Joseph Webster. A short while later, at approximately eight fifteen, we understand that Joseph Webster dashed across the street and accosted Mr Mann, who was just leaving The Dragon public house. The boy pulled Mr Mann's wallet out of his hand, and, in the ensuing struggle, Mr Mann was pierced in the heart with a knife. He fell to the ground and the boy ran back across the road, joined his two friends, and then the three of them ran off with what they had stolen. The police were alerted by a call from Mr Dolman, who had come out of The Dragon just as the three boys ran away. An ambulance was sent to The Dragon, but Mr Mann was found to be dead by the time it arrived. Police car number sixty-seven was on patrol in the neighbourhood of the park when officers spotted two of the accused and arrested them. In the process, Trevor Makin called out Joseph Webster's name, saying that he had committed the crime. Webster had run off in a different direction and was not arrested until the following evening, when he gave himself up at the police station in Weberton.'

'You say that Mr Mann was stabbed. Do we have a knife, sergeant?'

'No sir. We have not been able to locate it or discover who it belonged to.'

'Have you carried out an extensive search for it? Have any of the boys admitted that it was their knife?' The questioning went on for about ten minutes, with first one magistrate putting a question and then another, but the policeman was unable to add anything else of substance to his statement.

'Many thanks, officer. You can now return to your seat.'

The magistrate conversed with his colleagues, too quietly for anyone else in the room to be able to hear what was said, and then, 'Could Trevor Makin come forward with one of his parents and take a seat?'

Makin, dressed in jacket and tie and with a look of innocence on his face, moved without any hesitation to one of the front seats. His mother sat by him, holding his hand as only a loving mother can. The hint of red, lining her brown eyes, indicated that many tears had recently been shed.

'Now, Trevor. You don't mind me calling you Trevor do you?' asked the magistrate.

'No, sir,' was the clear sharp response. It struck Peter that Makin was seeking to show himself confident in his innocence and relaxed about the proceedings. Peter guessed that someone had spent some time preparing him for his ordeal.

'Well, Trevor. You heard what the officer had to say. Would you like to tell us what you think happened?'

'Yes, sir. Will and me had arranged to meet Joe at t'fish and chip shop. He was not there so we went in to get ar' fish and chips.'

The lad was seeking to speak as he had been prepared, but now and again slipped into his normal language, which was much more related to the street than he was currently wishing to reveal. Peter was struck by the thin face, the shifty eyes that never seemed to rest on any one spot, and the way his hands, held behind his back, twitched at critical moments in his testimony.

'When we came out, Joe was there and he asked us for some chips. Hang on a minute?' he asked himself quizzically, 'Joe wasn't there when we fust cum art.' 'E cum a bit later. Then 'e said 'look at that guy o'er ther by t'pub.'

As he was trying to sort out his story he again fell inadvertently into his normal language. His mother looked up at him, nudged him as if to say *Remember what you were told to say,* and then took out a silk handkerchief to wipe her eyes. The movement encouraged the makeup on her face to run a little, re-emphasising her appearance as a sympathetic and loving mother who was distressed at her innocent son being drawn in to such a dreadful situation.

'Come along, Trevor. Just take your time and remember the events as they happened,' urged the magistrate.

Gathering his composure, Makin went on. 'Well, Joe suddenly dashed across the road and took the wallet. The man resisted, and the next thing I knew was that there was a struggle and the man fell to the ground. We all beat it to the park as fast as we could as soon as we realised what had happened. Then the police came and arrested us. It was Joe, sir, onest, and Will an' me had nought to do wi' it.'

'Thank you very much, Trevor' said the magistrate. 'Now can I ask about the knife? Do you know what happened to it?'

'No sir, I never saw it.'

'Are you sure that it was Joseph that ran across the road?'

'Yes sir. Will and I were just finishing our fish and chips and thinking of going for a walk through town when it all happened. Because Joe was with us, we just panicked and ran.'

'Can I ask again about the knife, Trevor? Was it yours?

'No, sir. I never saw a knife.'

'Trevor, why do you think Mr Mann fell to the ground?' Trevor looked a little perplexed by the question. It was one for which he had not been prepared.

He hesitated, and then replied, 'I think Joe pushed him.'

'Thank you very much, Trevor. Now what happened in the Park?'

'Well, we went by t'canal and Joe started handing money out. It wa' then that we 'erd t'police car. We ran, but got caught. Joe went in t'opposite direction. I dunno war' he did.'

'You can go back to your seat now.'

Trevor's mother stood up with him and, taking hold of his hand again, took him back to his seat. She sat with her arm around her son, pulling him close to her and looking like the loving mother that such a good lad deserved.

Peter had listened to the testimony with some amazement. It varied so much from what the magistrates were to hear from Joe that he wondered what they would make of it. His concerns were increased when Will went before the magistrate and repeated what Trevor had said, emphasising the part that Joe had played in the affair. It seemed that a strong case was building up against Joe, that the story he had told to Catherine and Peter had been fabrication, and that Catherine's detective work had been a waste.

Finally, it was Joe's turn to go forward. His mother, looking, as she always seemed to, dishevelled and belligerent, went with him. Her current appearance belied what she looked like when younger. Whilst never a beauty, she once had a certain air that attracted the attention of several of the young men of the town. Knocking on the door of middle age, she was now somewhat past her best. A woman of about forty, she was of a size that matched the loudness of her voice. In a temper she was fearsome. Her oversized body, with large breasts and even larger backside, was supported by solid stumps of legs.

Webster's father, who had been sitting next to Joe during the testimonies of the other two boys, was altogether different. A smallish man of about five feet four inches, he had a thin haggard face that looked tired of what it was asked to do. His body, thinned from the effects of nicotine, indicated a heavy smoker. His occasional barking cough, which disturbed everyone in the courthouse from time to time, completed the picture of a man of little ambition, and one who accepted a life of tedium. Oddly enough, he had once worked behind the bar in The Dragon, and so knew the scene of the mugging well.

As Mrs Webster rather clumsily sat down she managed to manoeuvre her chair so that she was a little closer to her son. She had come to the conclusion that her troublesome son had been up to his antics again, but on this occasion it had consequences far beyond anyone's expectations. She felt it important to be with him to give what support she could. Throughout Joe's testimony, she fixed her eyes on the chairman as if in some way trying to influence him, as a dog passively stares at the bone in its master's hand, willing him to throw it.

Without giving any indication that he was aware of anyone else except Joe, the magistrate continued with the enquiry. He looked at Joe with a kindly expression and asked him to tell the court what had happened when the concert in the town hall had finished. It was evident to Peter that the magistrate had been informed about the concert and possibly Joe's part in it, and he took this as a promising sign. What he did not know was that as a councillor, the magistrate had actually been present and had enjoyed as much as anybody, Joe's rendering of *Panis Angelicus*. Neither did Peter realise that as the magistrate looked at Joe, he found it difficult to understand how he could play so beautifully one minute, and within half an hour commit the heinous crime of which he was being accused. Inevitably, as he considered the situation before him, the magistrate reflected on the many occasions on which he had been faced with a juvenile who posed a similar dilemma. Nevertheless, he knew if justice was to be served, Joe's trombone playing could not affect the outcome of the hearing.

Joe felt a nervous twitch in his stomach as he began his story. He recognised how important it was for him to get his account of the evening's events absolutely right, and was determined to do so without deliberately blaming anyone else. It was up to others, in his view, to make of his version what they could. It was not in his nature to point the finger at others, he did not do that when in trouble at school, and so why should he do it now? But he knew that if he told the whole truth that was inevitable. He was also aware of his mother at his side, and gained strength from his realisation that for the first time in a long time, she was displaying at least some motherly affection for him. He was also conscious that the movement of the chair reflected her support for him, despite his placing her in this wretched situation. It was her presence that gave him the will to state his case unequivocally.

To his credit, Joe went through his story clearly and, to Peter's ears, convincingly.

'After the concert I left the town hall and I went to meet Trev and Will by the fish and chip shop. I set off just after eight o'clock and then had to go back for mi' mouthpiece. It must have been quarter past eight when I got to the corner of the High Street and saw one of mi' mates run across the road and attack Mr Mann. We all ran off to t'park, where we were sharing up the money when the police came. I dashed off toward t'canal but the police arrested Trev and Will.'

He went on to describe his journey to Peter's and what happened afterwards. Throughout, he was unrushed and clearly outlined the story as he had told it to Catherine and the police on his first interview. In a rather bizarre way, the leadership qualities that he had exercised on the many occasions he had led his friends into misbehaviour of one sort or another, gave him confidence and presence. He sat straight, upper arms by his side, elbows bent, hands joined in front of him, and eyes facing up to those behind the table. He told things as he said he remembered them. Peter and the head nudged each other as they jointly recognised the qualities that Joe was displaying. When he had finished his story, the magistrate asked,

'Why, Joseph, is your story so different from that of William and Trevor?'

'I don't know, sir. What I've said is the truth, sir.'

'Do you know anything about the knife, Joseph?' asked the rotund magistrate.

'No, sir. Never saw a knife and had no idea that one had been used until later. All I know is that once mi' mates began to run, I ran wi' 'em.'

For a moment, Joe's terminology slipped, but it was not through any noticeable confusion.

'Why do you think the other boys say it was you who attacked Mr Mann, Joseph?'

'I've no idea sir. As I said, I came out of the town hall and by the time I joined Will and Trev, Mr Mann was on the floor.'

'If you know nothing of the knife, Joseph, why do you think Mr Mann fell?'

'No idea, sir.'

'Which of the other two boys did you see run across the road, Joseph?'

Webster hesitated. This was the question he had feared. If he gave a name he would be betraying a trust, something that was not in his nature. Eventually, he responded, if a little hesitantly, and with his eyes lowering to the floor.

'I'm sorry, but it was too dark for me to see, sir.'

'Are you sure, Joseph?'

Now, with more conviction, 'Yes, sir.'

'Well, thank you very much, Joseph. You can return to your seat now.'

After waiting until Joe and his mother were seated, the chairman said, 'My colleagues and I have now to consider what has been said here today. The matter is so serious that we would not be fair to the three boys if we sought to reach a too hasty decision as to the rights and wrongs in this case. We also need to read papers that we have been provided with by Detective Inspector Grossman.'

He looked in the direction of Grossman, and the eyes of those present followed his. Grossman looked slightly uncomfortable as the focus of attention, but he knew that the papers he had presented would have significant bearing on the outcome of the hearing, and would also have some place when the case went to a more formal trial in a few weeks' time.

Remaining reassuring, the chairman looked around and then asked if anyone had anything that they wished to be taken into consideration by the magistrates during their deliberations. The head took from his inside pocket an envelope which he passed on to the clerk to the court, who, throughout the hearing, had diligently recorded on her typewriter everything that was said. Others also passed papers on to the clerk.

The chairman then advised the gathering that each of the accused would receive notification of the court's findings, and that it was most likely that the case would go up to the Assizes at Leeds because of its seriousness and the limitations on the powers of the magistrates to deal with such a serious crime. In the meantime, the boys were bound over, a strict curfew was imposed that severely limited their freedom, and they were told that they would be responsible to a probation officer. The parents were warned that they had a responsibility to ensure that their children stayed within the law and, if required, appeared at the Assize Court at the appropriate time. With that, he and his colleagues stood and, as the people assembled stood in respect, retired back through the door through which they had come.

Peter and the head left together. The head stopped at the entrance and waited for a few minutes as he wanted to have a quick word with Webster's parents. Peter stood by his side as first Trevor and then Will passed by with their parents. Neither of the boys looked at Peter or the head as, with their eyes firmly glued on what was in front of them, they made for the causeway that led homewards. Before they had gone very far, however, Mrs Webster bustled through the exit, made as if to run after them, and then, with her face knotted and twisted with rage, screamed with an ear shattering voice, 'Ba . . . . rd liars.'

Fortunately, one of the court officials, observing Mrs Webster's haste to push her way through to the exit as quickly as she could, had sensed trouble and managed to block her way, advising her, 'Madam, please be careful. You are in danger of being accused of disturbing the peace.'

Mrs Webster turned towards him, clenching her fists more in exasperation than in threat, and again used that stare with which she had tried to transfix the chairman earlier. For a few seconds the atmosphere was extremely tense and no one was quite sure what Mrs Webster was going to do next. Then her ire seemed to cool, her fists relaxed, and her face took on a look of despondency.

CHAPTER 30

SUPPORT FOR WEBSTER

When the chairman opened the envelope that the head had passed to the clerk he found that it contained two letters. The first, typed, bore the insignia of the school, the date, and the heading, 'To whom it may concern'. It continued,

Dear Sir,

Joseph Webster

Joseph Webster is a fourth year pupil at Weberton secondary modern school. During his time at the school he has revealed two sides to his character.

On the one hand he can be a difficult pupil who annoys his teachers and wilfully breaks school rules. He often sees himself as a leader of other pupils who are also prepared to flout instructions and the school's procedures. He has been

suspended from school on two occasions, once for fighting with another pupil and once for serious damage in the school toilets. The school, along with his social worker, has tried hard to counter this aspect of his character. Indeed, his parents have been called in to school on several occasions to try to find a solution, whilst his social worker has visited the family on many occasions.

There is another side to Joseph Webster, however, which the court needs to be aware of. When involved in a project with which he connects, he can commit himself beyond his teachers' expectations. He demonstrated this by the work he did on the school's boat project in his early years at school and more recently by the way he has contributed to the school brass band. The progress he has made on the trombone has been remarkable; it has been achieved by his dedication and steadfastness. His approach and attitude have been the direct opposite to the Joseph Webster described in the earlier paragraph.

The court may wish to take into consideration these two aspects of Joseph's character. In the view of his teachers, he often acts spontaneously, without thought for the consequences, and to gain the approbation of his friends. However, all his teachers agree that he can be diligent, thoughtful, and capable of setting a good example to his fellow pupils when he becomes committed to a project.

In my own view, Joseph has some good qualities that the magistrates cannot neglect during their deliberations. On the occasions I have had to deal with him on a disciplinary matter, I have found him prepared to admit that he has done wrong and accept his punishment. Indeed, there have been occasions, and this is why I think he has a following, when he has actually taken the blame for something done by another pupil. His loyalty in this respect is commendable.

I do not know sufficient about the case in which Joseph is currently involved to be able to form a judgement, but I hope that what I have written above will be of some assistance in enabling the court to reach a just decision about the boy.

If I can be of any further help please let me know.

Yours faithfully

George Holdsworth

(George Holdsworth,
Headteacher,
Weberton Secondary Modern School)

The letter, though signed by the head, was in fact the outcome of discussions he had had with his senior management team. It was interesting that all of them could find something in Webster of worth and although, in general, they viewed him, as one of them put it, 'A damned nuisance,' there was a feeling that he might be telling the truth. It was this that had encouraged their support for the boy.

The note that Peter had passed on to the head, outlining Catherine's findings also contributed to the team's doubt as to Webster's guilt.

This second letter was handwritten and signed by Peter. It read,

Weberton Secondary Modern School
Weberton
Yorkshire

To whom it may concern.

Dear Sir,

I have known Joseph Webster during the period of time I have been teaching at Weberton Secondary Modern School. I have to admit that, during that time, I have found the boy difficult in class and occasionally about the school.

Joseph surprised me when he indicated that he was interested in joining the school band, which I had formed. Despite some reservations I accepted him and taught him to play the trombone.

I can only say that I have been incredibly impressed by his commitment and by the progress he has made. A regular at individual lessons and band practices, he has worked hard to overcome any difficulties and in my opinion has shown rare talent for a boy of his age. The contrasts that he reveals in his relationship with me are marked. He is far

less cooperative with me as a classroom teacher than he is
as a tutor for the trombone.

I have always found him to be honest, prepared to take
responsibility for any serious misdemeanours, and willing
to support his friends.

If I can be of any further assistance to the court I will be
happy to oblige.

Yours faithfully

P Delaney

Peter Delaney
(History Master,
Weberton Secondary Modern School)

These letters were added to the evidence that the clerk collected, and Peter and the head assumed that they would be taken into consideration when the magistrates discussed the case. Peter was aware that the serious and unusual nature of the crime could, and probably would, in earlier days, have led to immediate incarceration of the three boys until such time as they came before the Assizes for trial, but that recent thinking on the treatment of juveniles had led to a relaxation in how they were treated. Peter was pleased to see that this change had shaped the nature of the first hearing and in all probability predisposed the chairman of the bench to speak so amicably with the accused. For those present it was a welcome transformation, as had been the alteration in procedure that had enabled the likes of Peter and the head to attend the hearing.

CHAPTER 31

THE VAGARIES OF LIFE

It was the uncertainties of life that provided the solution to Catherine's and Peter's problems at the cottage, though not in a way they would have wished.

The first unanticipated event that impacted on cottage developments was related to Peter's involvement in rugby. Throughout his days on the moor, Peter had his links with the town rugby club, showing little consideration for the pressures it put on Catherine. He found no difficulty in justifying his participation to her. 'Why shouldn't I?' he would say. 'It's natural enough for me to want to play a game. I've played all my life.' That streak of selfishness that he recognised in himself, but never conquered, would impose itself again, overshadowing any guilt that might want to encroach on him for leaving Catherine on so many Saturdays with the children.

Peter played in the centre and had looked to make a speedy impact at his new club, Weberton. But it took him several weeks to break down some of the barriers to unknown newcomers and win a regular place in the first team. Even then, he found himself in a team that was going through a difficult phase in its history; although it could count a few victories, it lost some games by a lot of points.

Nevertheless, his days at the club led to friendships that served Peter and Catherine well. Peter's ready access to Roger had been a help in the mugging case, and it was his rugby friends who had willingly helped them in their move to the moor, and with whom they had both enjoyed many a social occasion. Indeed, it was after the usual social occasion following a match that Peter returned home very late. He found the door to the cottage locked, all the family in bed, and himself without a key.

He did the usual. He threw a handful of dirt up to the bedroom window to try to attract attention, but without success. His next thought was to climb on top of the bay window so that he could reach the bedroom window and knock a little harder. He convinced himself that this was a good idea, grabbed the top of the bay, and endeavoured to pull himself up. What he had failed to take into consideration, however, was that once off the ground, legs tend to swing, presumably for balance. His heart was in his mouth as his feet left the ground and he lost control of what they were doing. He felt himself tipping backwards as he might when tackled head on, and his feet swing forward for balance. *Crash!* His feet went straight through the bay with a deafening shatter as the windowpane disintegrated into fragments.

As it was midnight, he was gratified to know that there was not another house within a quarter of a mile, but there was no way he could escape the, 'What the hell was that?'

'It's me,' was all he could say in an apologetic voice, which did nothing more than ease Catherine's fears that it might be an intruder. What it did not do was calm her nerves after such an awful fright, or save Peter from the outburst that followed.

'What on earth are you doing? What the hell has happened? Have you no sense or consideration? Where've you been? The match finished hours ago. You've been drinking again with the rugby lot! The children are awake, James is crying, and I'm having to let a drunken lout into the house.'

The tirade went on whilst Catherine switched on the light and made her way downstairs to unlock the door.

Peter knew he was in the wrong and that he was deservedly paying for his late return to the cottage. He had had a few drinks with his teammates after the game, but that was the nature of rugby. You played and then had a pint or two while swapping stories of what might have been. He knew he was not drunk and that the fate of the window was simply the outcome of misjudgement.

Even so, he knew he was in trouble.

'Oh, my God,' Catherine said. 'Look at the window, or what's left of it. There's glass all over the floor. What are we going to do?'

In her exasperation, she took a swipe at Peter who fended off her arm. Tears welled up in her eyes. He understood her anger and knew he deserved all he was going to get over the next few days if not weeks. He hesitated to say a thing. What could he say? He had been unbelievably stupid, created mayhem, and had no excuses.

'Well, I sort of let the time drift by without realising how late it was. We were having a drink, talking about the match, and . . . . well, you know how it is.'

Catherine certainly did. She had been married to Peter long enough to know what a crowd of rugby players could get up to and how Peter somehow always became involved. On one occasion, when they lived in Weberton, he had returned home so late that, as he made his way up the stairs, she had met him halfway to announce that it was time to go to Mass. And, despite his protestations, that is what they did. The window episode was a different matter, however. The window had to be repaired, there was the nuisance of organising the repair, and there was a cost.

The morning found both Peter and Catherine in a more realistic mood. They hardly slept because of their anxieties and because both were seeking answers to questions which flittered through their minds without being given answers on how to solve the problem. From time to time, Peter would hear Catherine mutter sleepily, 'How could he do it?' but he knew that she was not really seeking an answer. As it was, he didn't really have one.

Not surprisingly, even after such a late and stressed retirement to bed, they rose early. Peter was contrite, asked for forgiveness, and not for the first time received it. Pragmatically, they endeavoured to work out a resolution to the problem of the window. The bay windows were ugly and reflected almost amateurish workmanship. From the very first time that Peter had seen them, he knew they would have to be replaced. It had been just a matter of when. He certainly had not foreseen the why . . . . beyond their ugliness.

'Maybe you've done us a favour,' said Catherine, still showing her angst. 'We've certainly got to do something and quickly. We could have the glass replaced. That's the simplest and cheapest job. But why don't we take advantage of your stupidity?' That was a word that Peter knew he was likely to hear quite a lot of. 'Let's have new windows put in that are more in keeping with the cottage. It'll cost a bit, but it only brings forward a job we were going to have to do anyway.'

She knew that Peter had no hole into which he could retreat. His breaking of the window put him at Catherine's mercy and left him with no option but to nod in agreement.

'In the meantime, I suppose we need to make some arrangements to have the window blocked for safety's sake,' she said. 'It's going to look lovely! Perhaps you'll learn something from last night. You can take responsibility for organising the repair and what else we decide to do.'

Their conversation was interrupted. 'What's happened? Has Daddy been naughty?'

It was Katie who, along with Sarah, had been disturbed by Peter and Catherine. They had come down the stairs and now joined their parents looking at the glass strewn across the floor. Their faces were a picture of amazement, possibly because they did not think that a grownup could do such a thing.

Catherine answered with, 'Well, yes. Daddy has been naughty. But shall we forgive him because he's going to ask the local joiner and builder to come across and repair it? Aren't you, Daddy?'

The noose had tightened and Peter had no option but to get the builders to give them an estimate initially for boarding up the window but also for the replacement of the bay windows on either side of the porch.

The builder, Dan, showed quiet amusement at the story of the breakage, especially by the graphic way that Catherine described it. He gave an affordable estimate for boarding up the window and showed them a variety of attractive window designs. Peter and Catherine eventually settled on windows that were chamfered rather than square like their predecessors and agreed on a style that they felt suited the look of the cottage. Another examination of the bank account suggested that they could just about afford the work and so the go-ahead was given.

The first job, however, was to board up the broken window with a strip of plywood. In Catherine's view, 'It adds a great deal to the character of the cottage. We now really live in a shack.'

Peter, like a child who had been caught by his mother stealing the last bun, decided to keep a low profile until such time as Catherine had found a reason to forgive him. He was helped by the discussion on new windows and how smart they looked as they were inserted. Little had he known when they first moved into the cottage what further help the rugby club would contribute to its improvement.

A second unexpected event was the death of Peter's mother. She had suffered with heart trouble for many years, and with the development of heart surgery during the 1950s saw an opportunity for a cure. Unfortunately, the operation was not a success and she never recovered from the surgery. Shortly afterwards, Catherine's mother, overcome with cancer, also died. She had suffered for several years. The doctors had treated her with cortisone injections, which possibly extended her life but did little to reduce the discomfort she suffered. She bore her pain and the likelihood of an early death with great stoicism, winning the admiration as well as sympathy of those who knew her. On her last visit to the family, she had looked desperately ill, her face drawn with pain and her hands shaking uncontrollably. Her offer to look after the children whilst Catherine had her baby was clearly never going to be fulfilled.

Catherine's joy of a new birth was muted by news of her mother's deteriorating health and death.

And then, within four years, both fathers died from cancer, smoking an indisputable factor in the tragedies. Catherine's father was the first to die, closely followed by Peter's.

And so, over a period of five years, the length of time that it took Peter and Catherine to have their four children, their four parents died, none reaching the age of sixty.

Inevitably, Peter and Catherine shared stories about their fathers and mothers. They remembered the days they had been supported through school and in their different activities, the guides or the brass band. The mood was lightened with some amusing memories and especially with those associated with the cottage. The one that both remembered well concerned an occasion when Catherine's father had journeyed to the cottage to visit them one summer in their early days of residency. He had enjoyed his stay, especially the meeting with his grandchildren. On his first night, however, he was rudely awakened by drops of water. It was rain that had penetrated the roof tiles and was dripping ever so slowly onto his forehead. Rather than wake Peter and Catherine, he persevered all night in his usual stoic fashion, moving his head from one side of his pillow to the other to avoid the drops. By the following morning, his pillow was drenched and when Peter, oblivious to what had happened, took him a cup of morning tea, he was miserably but uncomplainingly looking upwards towards the ceiling. Catherine and Peter could not help but be amused, and her father also saw the comical side of his situation. The story gathered legend status within the family as it was told and retold.

It lightened their grief on the sad evening of his death.

Catherine inherited what her father left. The money, though relatively little, brought the prospect of carrying out some of the developments they had hoped to initiate but which they never thought possible. Another significant outcome was that the Morris van was replaced with an up-to-date Triumph car, which had been Catherine's father's joy. Little came to the family from Peter's father's death, the outcome of his life as a miner. His rented miner's house provided nothing and his savings did little more than pay for his funeral.

It was shortly after these deaths that another tragedy befell the family. Peter's aunt was killed in a road accident. After her partner died, she had obtained a post as house manager with a hotel group in the northeast. It was while she was travelling between hotels in Cumbria and Northumberland that the accident had happened. An overtaking driver had crashed head on into the car in which she was the front-seat passenger, the force of the collision bursting open the car door and throwing her onto the roadside. It was an early morning call from the police that informed Peter and Catherine. They were asked to travel north to identify the body. The task fell to Peter, as Catherine was disinclined to travel with the children.

Peter was received considerately by the Northumberland constabulary. He was not shown into a morgue as he had expected, the impressions given him by similar events in the different series on TV he had watched, but into a small, darkened room with a bed. His aunt was covered by a sheet that the officer pulled back to show her face. Compassionately, the head was slightly turned so that Peter could not see the bruised side that had obviously been damaged in the crash. It was a soulful experience for Peter to see his natural mother in this state and one he was pleased that Catherine, who had grown to love his aunt, did not have to experience. The identification took only a second, as did the sign of the cross, before the sheet was returned to fully shroud the body that had been so supportive of Peter, Catherine, and the children.

Once outside the fateful room, Peter signed confirmation that the body was that of his aunt. 'What happened?' he asked the police.

'It seems that on the road between here and Carlisle, another car was overtaking and ran into the one your aunt was in. She was thrown out of the car when, we gather, her door flew open. The driver was also killed, but as seems to happen too often, the guy who caused the accident escaped with a broken shoulder. He's been charged with dangerous driving.'

'I'll never understand these guys,' murmured the crestfallen Peter. 'When is the inquest on my Aunt's death by the way?'

'When we've completed our enquiries. Probably in a couple of weeks. There's no need for you to attend, as you live so far away and now we have your identification statement.'

As Peter left the room and passed into the main office, the sergeant drew his attention to his aunt's belongings.

'On the corner table there we've put your aunt's belongings. There's underwear, a dress, and a stained coat. There's also a little jewellery. There's a ring, a broach, and some earrings. There's also your aunt's handbag. Shamefully, someone took the opportunity to steal its contents as she lay on the roadside. I doubt whether we'll ever know who.'

Peter was shocked by the news. He found it difficult to imagine how someone could behave in such a manner. But silently he agreed that little could probably be done.

'D'you want to take any of your aunt's things? It's for you to decide what to do with them.'

Peter could barely look at them, he was so upset by what he had encountered on his visit north. He followed his immediate instincts, saying, 'No, thanks. I don't think it will serve any purpose for me to take them. I'm sure we've no use for them at home, and I think it would only upset my wife if I walked into the house with them. They were very fond of one another. Can you dispose of them?'

'Of course.'

'Well, thanks. Let us know if there's anything else we need to do.'

With that, Peter took his leave. His sadness was genuine despite what had passed so many years ago, and he prayed his thanks for the help his aunt had given Catherine and him in recent times.

On his journey home, he brought back the many happy memories he had of his Auntie Grace. He remembered the holidays when he was young, the Christmas presents she had bought him, and the visits she had made to his home. As he knew nothing of his earliest days, he did not carry the pain he believed was borne by those who had been deserted when much older and who were more likely to understand what was happening to them.

It was late when he eventually arrived home, but Catherine was still up and waiting for him.

'How did it go?' was her first question.

'Not the most pleasant of things to do. After I'd done the identification, the police asked if I wanted to take away any of auntie's things but I said no. I hope I did the right thing.'

'I'm sure you did. I wouldn't have wanted reminders about the house, and I wouldn't have known what to do with them.'

Peter went on to recount briefly what had passed. Catherine listened quietly, sitting facing Peter in an easy chair. When he was done, she offered some supper, and then together they made their way up the stairs to bed.

The outcome of this sad event was that Peter, as the sole surviving relative of his aunt, inherited what she left behind. In a strange and unforeseen way, Peter's aunt at last made some tangible provision for a son with whom she never discussed what led to her deserting him so many years ago. For his part, Peter never asked and, in truth, was not really interested.

What he did know he had learned from one of his aunt's friends late in his teenage years. He learned that his aunt had left his natural father for a rather imposing young man who was thought to come from a well-endowed family. His aunt had been renowned in the local village as a good-time girl and had been noted for her partying. This did not fit well with her husband, who was of a much more serious disposition. When he began to object to her behaviour, Peter's aunt paid little heed. Her husband became increasingly morose and unhappy, traits that Peter was told were used by his aunt as an excuse to leave home and join her new boyfriend. Within days, she had left the village.

Peter's father, meanwhile, was devastated. He was aware that he could not look after the very young Peter on his own and after discussions with the family decided first to let his grandmother look after him and later to let his auntie's sister and brother-in-law adopt him. Shortly afterwards, evidently weighed down with grief and guilt at his failure to provide for his son, Peter's father disappeared without warning. The circumstances of the whole sorry affair resulted in Peter never meeting again with his natural father, but because of the closeness of the two sisters, he was regularly in contact with his natural mother and her partner, whom he called Uncle.

In the context of the times, what his aunt left to Peter was not insubstantial. There was a little money in a bank account as well as a small house in a nearby village. Peter's aunt had bought it for her retirement. It was in a row of similar houses overlooking the main road through the village. She had never lived in it or spent any money on its renovation. These things were for a future that was never to arrive.

Catherine and Peter went to look at the property, considering what they might do with it. It was a stone-built property in the middle of a row of six, sitting a short way back from the busy main road. A path led through the front garden, which was overgrown with weeds and untended bushes, to the front door. It was in a much better state than the moorland cottage when they first took it over, but it was obvious to Peter and Catherine that it needed money spent on it. The décor was tired looking and one of the downstairs windows was cracked.

As they walked through the bedrooms, the patchy marks on the ceiling raised their suspicions about a leaking roof, and this was confirmed when they went outside into the narrow road at the back and saw displaced roof tiles. The thought of having to repeat some of the work they had carried out in the cottage did not help to ease their worries about what might be involved in sorting out this element of their inheritance.

'Well, what d'you think?'

'We've a couple of options, I suppose,' said Peter. 'In theory, we could invest what your father left us, try to smarten it up, and then see if it could be used as a holiday rental. That was certainly on my mind before we saw it. But after all the work we've done and still have to do on the cottage, I can't see us really wanting to start something new here. It needs a new kitchen and bathroom at least, before we could dream of renting it. And then there's the roof. I'm more inclined to selling it and using the money to continue the restoration of the cottage.'

'Those are my feelings. Let's sell it and have done with it. I'm sure we have a better investment on the moor.'

Having decided to sell, Peter called in the estate agents, and thankfully the cottage was sold quickly.

The influx of the new money led to the prospect of major developments at the cottage. Again, the rugby club came to their aid. A teammate of Peter's, Baz, was an architect. More for friendship than money, he agreed to draw up plans for a sizeable kitchen, much prized by Catherine after its wretched predecessor, with a large double bedroom above. When Baz eventually brought the designs up to the cottage for their consideration, he had also planned for the replacement of the rickety dividing wall between two of the existing bedrooms by a much more secure structure. The intention was to provide the girls with reasonably sized individual bedrooms. Catherine was as delighted as Peter with what Baz produced, and both of them rejoiced in the prospect of their commitment to the cottage at last bearing fruit.

It was worth the kiss and cuddle that Peter shared with Catherine that night.

Work commenced fairly quickly outside with the kitchen-bedroom extension. Through the early summer months, the family saw the outline of the new building take shape as the ground was prepared for the foundations. They looked forward with eagerness to the day when the piles of Yorkshire stone would grow into walls, and the carefully treated timber into shaped floors, window frames, and rafters as the two builders from neighbouring cottages on the moor plied their trades. One was an expert in stoneware and the other in wood.

Much of the internal work was to await the summer holidays, particularly August, when the family had wisely planned a three-week holiday in Devon and Cornwall. During this period, the builders proposed to complete the interior walls and ceilings and take down the defunct kitchen wall. This would enable them to reorganise the bedrooms and to begin the installation of the new kitchen, ensuring that there was at least water and electric for cooking when Peter and the family returned. The intention was to have the basic work completed whilst the family was away, thus causing as little disruption as possible.

This summer plan looked an ideal solution to what could have been the tricky problem of how sleeping might be arranged during internal work, and how the essentials of life could be accessed if the old kitchen went out of action whilst the new one was still under construction.

CHAPTER 32

HOLIDAYS

The summer vacation arrived. With the extra capital they had inherited, Peter and Catherine decided to have their first real family holiday and make the long trip down to Devon. They made a booking in a bed and breakfast, not far from the sea.

On the planned day, they made an early start, wishing the builders well, and headed off the moor and south west across the country to their destination.

The accommodation turned out to be acceptable rather than luxurious, but, as Peter commented to Catherine, 'You get what you pay for.'

What was more disturbing, however, was that on the journey south James developed a sore throat and with it the tantrums of discomfort. Whether in the car, in a shop, or on the beach, he seemed inconsolable. Peter and Catherine were at a loss as to what to do with him. The patience of their host family was to be admired as they sought to help and advise, but the early part of the holiday was stressed by the little chap's response to his illness. The pain in his throat was sometimes severe and it was clear that he also felt it through headaches and sensitivity in other parts of his head and face. His throat was reddened, areas around his neck became swollen, and he had a high temperature. Everything pointed to mumps.

Catherine's hospital experience came in to play as she tendered to him, and ensured that he had plenty of warmish drinks, soft food and throat lozenges. Gradually, there was some improvement, the pain subsided and James became his normal jovial self. The second week of the holiday settled into a more restful phase for Catherine and Peter. The weather also improved, dispelling the overcast sky and the odd shower, and bringing in their place a rich blue sky that offered an open, free passage for the sun. The family was able to spend most of its time on the beach, where, as long as they were within safe range of their parents, the children needed less personal attention. Whilst Peter and Catherine relaxed, the four children developed their own entertainment, whether as individuals, pairs or a foursome. Inevitably, they turned to castle building, endeavouring to build a new, magnificent castellated city out of the sandy beach. One day they would stand back admiring their architectural achievement, and on the next, to their dismay, see it as a flat tide-washed ruin. Their disappointment was quickly alleviated by the prospect of the new challenge, to build an even bigger and better castle.

The beauties of Devon and Cornwall did not fail to impress. The boat-filled inlets, the welcoming beaches, and the rolling waves opened up a world so different to that offered by the moor. The children enjoyed the holiday attractions and the joys their new surroundings offered them, and the heat of the sun tanned their bodies as they adjusted to its burning rays. But by the end of the two weeks they were as ready as their parents to return to their home on the moor, and the life to which they had so successfully adapted. When the time to depart came, there was general excitement as to what changes they would find when they arrived at the cottage.

Catherine had booked an overnight stop in one of the beautiful Cotswold villages on the return journey. She knew nothing of Broadway, other than what she had read in guidebooks or heard from her friends. But it was about halfway home and offered a convenient place for a rest on the long drive. A couple of trips up and down the village high street and Catherine eventually located the bed and breakfast. Built in Cotswold stone and thatched-roofed, their home for the night looked ideal, even if only to have photographs to show to friends when describing what a 'wonderful' holiday they had had. What a shock for Peter and Catherine once inside. They were led up into an attic room in which all six of the family were expected to sleep. A double bed, two single beds, and two mattresses on the floor were cramped into the small room which had no other facilities. The shared bathroom was down a flight of stairs. One look was enough to convince Peter.

'Is this it?'

'Yes. As you probably know, the Cotswolds get extremely busy during the summer, and accommodation is tight,' replied the proprietor.

'Too tight for us.'

Peter seethed under his outward appearance of calm as he weighed his options. To Catherine, 'We can't stay here. It's not healthy for us all to be in this small room, even for one night.' Turning to the proprietor, he asked, 'Is this all you have?'

'I'm afraid so,'

'Why didn't you tell us this when we booked? We explained how many of us there were. Surely you don't expect all of us to bed down here.' The growing sternness in Peter's voice revealed his frustration with the situation.

Catherine, anxious to avoid an unpleasant argument, intervened to suggest, 'With some manoeuvring it might be possible to enable us to make better use of the space. After all, we're not going to be here for very long. By the time we've been into the village to eat it will be late for the children, and we could be away very early tomorrow morning. Perhaps it won't be too bad.'

Peter looked at her, then at the owner, and declared, 'If you've nothing else, we're moving on.'

'That's up to you, sir,' came the reply.

That was enough for Peter, who picked up young James and headed for the door. 'Come on, Catherine, we're not staying here.' The family trooped out of the house.

Standing by the car, Peter and Catherine discussed what they should do. 'The children are tired and so we have to find somewhere quickly,' said Catherine.

'You look pretty tired yourself, Catherine. But looking at the number of people milling around, some of them looking for accommodation, I don't see much chance of getting a room here. I feel OK. I suggest we go straight home. If I get too tired driving, we may find somewhere else on the way where we can get a room.'

'OK, if you're sure,' replied Catherine with a look and in a voice that implied a question. Peter nodded his assurance and Catherine went on, 'We'll go home, then. The children will probably sleep for much of the way, and at least it'll save us some money.'

Peter, foreseeing possible difficulties in arriving home a day early, said, 'At some stage we'll need to ring the builders to arrange where to pick up the key for the house, as we're arriving home early and they have the only key.'

Catherine agreed and pointed out the phone box at the corner, just below where they were standing. 'You might as well do it now.'

Peter went along and rang the builder. 'Tom, we've a problem here and we need to travel home tonight rather than tomorrow. Is everything OK? We should arrive around 9.00 o'clock. When we get there, from where do we need to collect the keys?'

'Hm, I don't think that's a problem. You'll be able to get in all right.' His cough seemed nervous and his, 'You'll be able to get in all right,' seemed rather open ended, disconcerting Peter a little.

'Where'll we find the key, then?' asked Peter again, seeking a definitive answer.

The builder mumbled something about there being no need for a key. Peter accepted what Tom said, but was puzzled that he had not been given clearer direction as to where he could pick up the keys. He was not too discomforted, however, thinking that he could call at the builders and collect the key if need be. He had interpreted the comment 'I'm not sure you need the key,' as meaning that the builder would have everything under control and would probably be at the cottage when they arrived.

How naïve can a father of four children be? After the long drive, during which the children and Catherine took opportunities to sleep, Peter reached Binkley and still feeling relatively fresh, tackled the moor road with his usual skill. When he had crossed the cattle grid and felt the pull of the cottage increase, he decided to pass by the builder's and make straight for home. If the builder was not at the cottage as Peter had assumed was the plan, he could easily return to pick up the key.

As they approached the cottage all looked fine. Peter had indicated on the phone that it would be about nine o'clock by the time they reached the cottage, and he had not been far wrong. The light was being slowly moved on by a darkening sky as the reddened sun began its dip below the far horizon. It was a wonderfully pleasant evening, with the red of the far sky for a time mingling with the approaching darkness, before being pushed inevitably from sight. Peter and Catherine looked at each other with eyes that said, *How lucky we are to be living in this wonderful place.*

Peter drew up in front of the gate, exited the car and, having eased his aching legs and back, made for the front door. It was locked. There was no sign of the builder or of a key. He was still wondering what to do as he wandered round to the back of the cottage to see if the back door offered a way in. Back door? He was staggered by what he saw. The new build was nowhere near finished, and much of the back wall of the cottage had disappeared.

The need for a key was clearly superfluous, and Peter now grasped the full meaning of the builder's comment, 'I don't think you'll need a key.' By now, Peter had been joined by Catherine and the children, all as shocked as he was. They clambered over what rubble was strewn about and, passing through a new wooden door frame that was already in position, entered what was to become their new kitchen. Without taking too much notice, and anxious to see the state of the rest of the cottage, they moved from the shell of a kitchen, through the dining room and on in to the sitting room. They found dust everywhere. The furniture was stacked on the far side of the rooms and the damp feel of an approaching autumn seemed to have infiltrated.

Catherine was the first to speak. 'What on earth is going on?'

'You tell me,' replied Peter. 'God, what's it like upstairs?' he exclaimed.

It took him a couple of seconds to climb the stairs and find out. The new bedroom was in the same shape as the skeletal kitchen below, though it hinted at better times to come. Catherine's and Peter's bedroom consisted of three-and-a-half walls, and a good deal of open air on the fourth side. The bathroom was also in disarray, as the builders had begun to link the plumbing with that of the anticipated new kitchen. The only habitable rooms throughout the whole of the cottage, were the children's two small bedrooms.

The rest of the family had followed Peter up the stairs. Catherine was in shock, whilst the children were seemingly more curious than disturbed. Peter and Catherine looked at each other and almost together said, 'We would have been better off staying in that bed and breakfast . . . . and at least for another month.' Despite what they were witnessing, they both laughed out loud, laughter reflecting more their amazement than their joy at what they had found.

It was Catherine's resilience that now came to the fore. 'Well, we have to sleep. Me and the girls can bed down in their room, and you and the boys can sleep in their room. Come on, Peter, let's get on with it.'

Taking the lead, she extracted bedding from what had once been an airing cupboard, and proceeded to make the beds. In no time all was ready, and comatose-like, all were found a place to lay, the boys in more comfort in their bunk beds, than their parents or sisters. Catherine then produced some sandwiches and biscuits from a small bag she was carrying. They had been prepared for the journey, but had not been touched. Catherine now used them to help sustain the family until morning, when it would be easier to assess the state of the cottage. Tired from the long journey, the family managed the unprepossessing circumstances well and slept undisturbed through the night.

Next morning the builders arrived, their ruddy cheeks bearing a cheerful smile. They had clearly decided that they would not be daunted by what even they could only have seen as a fateful return for the family.

'So, you made it all right last night. It was a bit of a surprise for me when you rang', said Tom. 'Thought you were away for another week.

Anyway, you managed OK. I reckon you had no difficulty getting in?' he added with a sheepish look that matched the moorland setting.

Unabashed as they were, Peter could do no other than explain why they had arrived when they did, and it became a communal joke between the four adults that they had found their own home no more welcoming than their bed and breakfast.

The agreed solution to the situation in which the family found themselves was for the builders to get on quickly with what they had to do, while Peter and Catherine sorted out as best they could, their accommodation. It was obvious to all that it would be several days before all the walls were in place and that any sort of normality could be restored to the cottage.

Fortunately, it was a day on which the sun shone with welcoming warmth, and so the children could spend their time outside, watching the builders, chasing the hens and the cats, teasing the cows with their feigned mooing, and pretending to herd sheep. In the meantime, their parents could get on with making the cottage as habitable as they could.

Peter and Catherine were making good progress in sorting out the furniture in the sitting room when, from the direction of the front door, came, 'Hello, anybody home?'

That sounds like Brian, flashed through both Catherine's and Peter's minds, *What's he doing here?* They looked at each other, initially startled, but then in a less unperturbed way, as if to say, *Well, what d'you expect.*

Every time we do any major revamp, you can expect Brian and Margaret to turn up.

Without even exchanging a word, both Catherine and Peter ceased what they were doing and looked towards the door.

'Hi, come in,' called Peter, as he made for the front door, which was unlocked and stood partially open. It was indeed, Brian. The amazed look on his face made no attempt to hide its question, *What on earth is going on?*

As he came through the door, his expression showing signs of increasing disbelief, he asked, 'Didn't you get our message? We spoke with the builder on Tuesday and said we were coming over to see how you are getting on. He said you were away but were due back anytime soon, and he was sure it was OK for us to come.'

'Brilliant—glad you were able to come and enjoy the delights of the moor with us,' Peter said, smiling both outwardly and inwardly.

The knack of choosing the most inauspicious times to visit seemed to be a God-given gift for Brian and Margaret. On a previous trip across the Pennines they had arrived on the day that the cottage's new well was being sunk. The money from Catherine's father had enabled them to hire a drilling firm which specialised in finding water. It had been particularly interesting for all the family to see the water diviner choose the best spot to drill. He searched as near to the cottage as possible to facilitate the laying of pipes into the kitchen and bathroom. As Brian and Margaret had approached the cottage on that occasion, they had been met with the sight of the upper rigging of the drill overshadowing the cottage.

No doubt they had some misgivings about arriving at such a time, but fortunately they never put into words the critical question, *If you are boring for water now, where is your water currently coming from?* The question was all the more pertinent as Margaret had just started feeding their new baby with a bottle. Because she never asked, she was never told where the water came from to fill the baby's bottle, otherwise Peter suspected that the visit on that day would have been a short one. *Thank goodness she doesn't ask,* thought Peter several times during what turned out to be an enjoyable day. *Today, fortunately, he could honestly say that pure fresh well water is on tap, but as to the rest . . . . ?*

The great thing about Brian and Margaret was that they always came with a sense of humour, as well as a sense of anticipation, each time they visited, because life never seemed to run smoothly for their friends. Today, they entered a half of a cottage and after having established the cause, settled, and settled as though there was nothing amiss.

'So what are you doing?' was Margaret's first open-eyed remark as she looked from one room into the next, trying to make some sense of what she was finding.

Catherine helped her in her quest. 'Well, we've had the chance to have some extensions done. They were supposed to coincide with our holidays so that the worst of it could be done while we were away. As you see,' she said with a genuine smile, 'someone miscalculated. Unfortunately, the work wasn't finished while we were away, and we came back last night to find this. Even if we'd known you were coming, it would probably have been too late to put you off. But now you're here, it's great.'

'So you didn't get our message?' Brian asked with almost a smile, suggesting that he was enjoying what he was seeing. 'I spoke to the guys, and they said it would be all right.'

'Well they were right. Would you like a drink? Tea or coffee?'

Catherine was quickly on the front foot and reinforced Peter's brushing aside any likely thoughts of inconvenience, or of their visitors immediately heading back to the car and Lancashire, by saying, 'The children are out at the back and Will, Mary, and Pat can go and join them. Let's sit and have a cuppa and have a natter. It'll be lovely to hear how you're doing. Then I'll get us some lunch.'

Together, Peter and Catherine made Brian, Margaret and their family feel thoroughly welcome, emphasising how helpful it was to have a visit on such a day, just as it had been when the drill had been in full action searching for fresh water. Brian and Margaret settled, their son and two daughters disappeared through the door in search of fun and games, and Catherine produced the tea and biscuits.

The situation was not ideal but, when good friends arrive, the only response is to make them welcome. This Peter and Catherine did as they made the Hurts comfortable, discussed how things were across both families, and then moved on to think about lunch. The option settled on was a trip down to the local town fish and chips shop, which proved to be an agreeable solution to children and adults.

The two men volunteered to go. Their journey took them across the moor and the iron grid designed to prevent sheep leaving the moorland, through the small village set on the side of the moor, past the small monastery, and then down the one-in-six gradient to the valley below. They crossed the river as they headed into the centre of town.

Much of the town was built of Yorkshire stone, though red brick and Victorian architecture also appeared in a town centre made especially attractive with its circular floral displays. As usual, its streets were busy with vehicles and people, mostly local, but with a good smattering of visitors. On their right, as they reached the traffic lights, the parish church stood. Straight ahead was the main street, with its memorial to those unfortunates who had died in the Two World Wars. The fish and chip shop was to the left, off the main road. Although it did not pretend to rival Yorkshire's famous Harry Ramsden's, it provided a decent lunch or supper. Peter did the ordering and the buying, and then the pair drove back to the cottage with lunch for the two families.

After lunch, Peter and Brian took the opportunity to have a walk across the moor, whilst Margaret and Catherine sat in the front garden enjoying the peace and quiet of their rural setting, well away from the chaos at the back of the cottage. The children returned to the rear of the house and played in the garden, where there was a swing and a slide. For their part, the builders, unfazed, continued their work, with half and eye out at Catherine's request on the children.

Peter loved these opportunities when he could wander over the moor with a friend and talk about anything that came to mind. On this occasion, the early discussion centred on the developments taking place in the cottage. 'A friend of mine at the rugby club is an architect and he's come up with the design. He's also overseeing, when he can, that is, what the workmen are up to. They're local chaps and despite the cock-up last night and this morning, they've always done what has been asked with care and skill. They reroofed the house a short time ago and also dug out the so-called septic tank to replace it with a proper system. They're the sort of builders who, together, can take on most jobs.'

'I suppose they're not too dear. Try to get somebody like that back home and it seems to cost the earth,' said Brian.

'No,' Peter replied. 'They seem to take into consideration how close the cottage is to their own homes, and also that friendship in a small village like this is pretty important. I couldn't complain about the price or the workmanship. Their present job is to complete the kitchen and bedroom above, and then knock through into the mistal. Our idea is to extend the sitting room and at the same time provide a sort of study in a room behind the current fire place. I'll show you when we get back.'

From a discussion about the cottage, life on the moor, and Brian updating Peter on what was happening in rugby league, their conversation naturally drifted to life in Lancashire and how things were going for Brian and Margaret.

'We're fine,' Brian indicated. 'As you've seen, Margaret and the children are well. We've made some improvements to the house. Even though we've been there since we were married, we've no intention of moving. Margaret's still teaching and I've now moved to a headship in a junior school.'

'Wow, that's a change from a secondary school,' cut in Peter. 'How is it?'

'I've got to say that I'm enjoying it. We have our problems, but I'm glad we're not dealing with the ones you are. What's the news on this guy Webster. His case has been all over the newspapers. He sounds a nasty piece of work.'

Peter outlined to Brian his own involvement in the affair and that he could not understand how the lad could go from being acclaimed a success at the concert one day, and then unmercifully vilified by the media the next. Peter said that the whole experience had been very demanding and had raised for him some important issues that he was still trying to resolve. 'I hope young Webster can also ask himself questions and find solutions to his problems. I really feel sorry for the lad, facing as he is a major trial and the prospect of an interminable period under lock and key, for a death that he claims to have had little part in. His story to me was that the whole episode centred round one of his mates taking a wallet from a chap coming out of the pub and that he wasn't involved.'

Peter went on to describe how Webster had turned up at the cottage and how he had to take him to the police station. He described his own anxiety on being questioned by the police as they sought to establish Webster's movements after the event. 'It's clear that during the incident, the guy, not surprisingly, had tried to resist and had been knifed. As far as I know they've not yet produced a knife, and so are unable to identify any of the lads as owner. None of the lads will own up to it being his. A disturbing factor is that the other two lads have both accused Webster of committing the crime, and so he's in real trouble. Unless they change their story he's got mega problems. Catherine's been all het up about it. She had got to know him because of his connection with the brass group. She did a bit of detective work and feels that there's enough evidence to throw doubt on whether young Webster was actually involved in the whole scam, never mind the actual knifing. She's taken it seriously enough to follow his movements, check times, and come to the conclusion that he couldn't have been present at the time of the robbery. In fact, a detective inspector came up to the cottage to ask her some questions. He took her evidence away with him for further study.'

Brian commented, 'I've known Catherine long enough to know she'd love to tackle a problem like this. She's like a terrier if she thinks something's not quite right. She'll pursue it, you can guarantee it. Remember when you lost your watch when we were at College? The meticulous way she tracked your movements through the day and, eventually, found it impressed all of us.'

The two friends continued their walk across the moor, Peter knowing which parts would provide Brian with the most interesting views. It meant walking eastwards up a slight incline to get to a position from which they could view the valley below. It was obvious that Brian was impressed by the scene and by the way the river snaked through the valley, controlling the route the road could take and the sites of the few villages below. Then they turned left in the direction of the *Beacon*, and the eyes of both men were drawn up towards its summit. They shared a point or two about what they could see and Peter outlined the story behind its name, *The King's Beacon*. This led him back to Webster and how the lad had sought shelter in the cave.

He then went on to spotlight the various farm holdings and who owned them. He also told Brian about his rights on the moor and, laughingly, how he had a stint that allowed him to feed five sheep and geese with followers. He explained the system, which brought a wry smile to Brian's face, along with the question to which he thought he knew the answer, 'And do you find that all the farmers are sticking to their allotted stints?'

'They're supposed to,' replied Peter, but the look the two friends shared suggested that perhaps he did not really believe it.

Eventually, the subject that was uppermost in Peter's mind resurfaced in the conversation.

'It's a tragic story, but I expect those who always doubted Webster will be saying, with some justification, 'He was always heading for a bad ending. He was the sort of lad that would always find trouble and now he has, the worst sort'. I suppose they have some justification. I have to admit the lad can be a real pain. You'll understand. I've no doubt you've had your problem kids.' As Brian nodded his agreement, Peter added, 'But they didn't see Webster at his best or see how hard he worked to play the trombone well. I know he could react to situations without thinking, spontaneously if you want, but even I'd accept that, with patience, there was a possibility that he could have overcome this problem. Have you heard of this so called attention deficit disorder?'

'Since I have been in primary schools I've come across one or two terms that have set me thinking. That is one, and I know it can cause serious problems. Another one is dyslexia, a disability to do with not being able to formulate writing properly. I know there's a lot of research in to it, particularly among kids in junior schools. It could be that Webster has something like attention deficit disorder, but I wouldn't know, and I'm not sure whether anybody has yet worked out a cure for it.'

That seemed to bring to a close the conversation on Webster. Brian and Peter began to concentrate more on enjoying their walk and what the scenery had to offer. The fine, sunny day seemed to have brought calm across the moorland. The sheep were settled to their munching, hardly making a sound, and, other than for the occasional skylark, the moor seemed devoid of life.

'You were lucky to find this place. Are you glad you made the decision to move here?' asked Brian, disturbing for a moment the tranquillity of their meandering walk. Peter didn't reply straight away, but cast his mind back to the days when he had made what could have been a fateful decision and when he had so disturbed Catherine with his proposal to buy the cottage. All that was now in the past. The family had settled to the moor and what it had to offer. Parents and children had grown closer together as a family as they successfully etched out a life for themselves in an environment, at once friendly and then unfriendly, and one hardly known to most of their friends. Despite the experience of the previous evening, and the disruption being caused by the new building work, how could he answer Brian without saying, 'Yes. We're very happy here.'

CHAPTER 33

CHILDREN

Children have the ability to educate adults. This is a fact of life. They can educate them into what to eat at meal times, at what time to rise in the morning, what television programmes are the best to watch, and how to respond to childish pranks. Adults tend only to admit to what they have learned when the children have headed off to create their own lives and start their own process of learning.

Certainly during their days in the cottage, Peter and Catherine learned a lot. In the weeks and months after his birth, their youngest demanded food at particular times of the day, made sure that he slept when he wanted, and also let Catherine know when his nappy needed changing. Catherine, an experienced mother, quickly learned the particular sequence and it was important for her to be ready if the bleating of the sheep was not to be further amplified by the cries of her latest born.

Even Peter had to accept that certain television programmes were not to be missed and that the 'Daleks', without his foreseeing it, were to begin to play an important part in the way he viewed life in space.

As they began to grow accustomed to their new life the children developed their own ways of showing their parents that they could cope. The eldest, Katie, generally assumed overall control, as far as she could exert it, usually being followed by willing disciples.

An early instance was the banana challenge, which was a typical experiment in group compliance, stemming as it did from the question, 'How can we slow down the cars and motor bikes on this dangerous corner in front of the cottage?'

The solution, devised by Katie and one fitted to young, inexperienced minds, was to try to cause cars to skid on banana skins and so make their drivers more cautious.

'If they make people slip, why not cars?' posed Katie, the rest nodding knowledgeably.

'Oh, it certainly would be a lot simpler for us to cross the road if we knew that cars were going to go slower,' said Sarah, agreeing with her older sister.

'Yep' chimed in Gregory in his usual thoughtful way, as he endeavoured to work out how they might do it.

The wheeze was part of being a member of the 'Red Indian Club', which had also involved chopping up anything stored in the barn, and, snatching the opportunity when parents were busy elsewhere, painting everything with 'Red Indian Club' signs, including the pram. Katie was the chief, the rest the tribe.

'First, we need a good supply of banana skins. We all like bananas don't we? So, let's ask mum to buy some.'

During the next few days, Catherine was taken aback by the regular demand for bananas from the children. They took an unforeseen pleasure in them, but it didn't worry their mother unduly as she recognised the value of fruit in the children's diet. What she did not know, was what the children were intending to do with the skins.

Fortunately, their ruse failed to achieve its purpose. Only one motor cyclist was caught and, cursing, almost fell off as he sought to take the bend Geoff Duke like, unaware of the trap that had been set for him in the middle of the road. In fact, his anxiety was probably caused more by his speed than by the banana skin. Several cars ran over the skins, but, to the children's disappointment, without skidding. They were disheartened, but undeterred, by the fact that their banana skin ploy had not worked as well as they had hoped.

'Perhaps a nail through the middle of the banana skin would provide the solution,' suggested the chief.

'Good idea,' agreed Sarah and Gregory, and even James, in his forever nodding mode, seemed to be in agreement.

'Let's go and get some nails out of the barn then.'

The children quickly processed in single file behind Katie into the barn, where Peter kept his tools. Standing on a piece of wood whilst being supported by Sarah, Katie reached up to grasp a box, which to her delight contained tacks of an ideal size for their bananas. Pushing the tacks through two banana skins to increase the chances of a slip, they returned to the road and carefully placed them where they estimated a passing car's wheels would be.

At last! What joy! A car, with banana skin flapping round the rear wheel, headed into the distance. To their happy minds, this verified what they believed to be great victory, and possibly the prospect of an unexplained puncture for an innocent driver.

The children's unconcealed delight at their first success alerted Peter to their antics. 'What are you doing?'

'We're slowing down the cars,' replied an excited Katie. 'We've put banana skins on the road, haven't we?' she asked as she turned towards her tribe.

'Yea,' came back the response, and Gregory punched the air.

Their joy was short lived. Peter dealt them a severe reprimand, explaining to them the dangers of such games. They were ordered to clear the rest of the skins from the road, collect others from the barn, and bin them. Undaunted, the children went off to think of other ways of resolving their problem, though their solutions offered nothing as exciting as the skins and each was abandoned, though, as always with children, not in total despair.

The youngest of the children, James, also developed an exploratory streak as he grew older. Time and again, he disappeared into the fields or onto the moor, and it took an organised family search with police discipline to find him. His small body swayed from side to side as he sought to keep his feet and stay upright on the rough moor, and his accentuated breathing issued a 'Pshew, pshew', as it responded to the effort he had to put in. He enjoyed disturbing the grouse, seeming unfazed when the startled birds burst out from under his feet, and made as if to chase the sheep as they skipped away from him and back in to their flock. When he was eventually caught by one of the family, he produced a beaming smile, bright eyes and stillness, as he pointed to the sheep or the hens he had been following. His hands and knees were usually covered in dung from a field or the moor, the result of his regular falls, but his shining eyes and ruddy face expressed the extent of enjoyment his explorations were producing.

Such activity entertained him whilst his age meant he could do no more than stumble from one destination to another. As he grew older, he found other answers to his desires. It became an almost regular feature of Sunday afternoons to hear crying coming from the roof of one of the outbuildings. James had learned how to climb the slope of the roof, sling his legs across the ridge, and then get stuck. He often refused to move for anyone except the dog, Sam, who had been acquired from a local dog's home so as to give Catherine an extra feeling of security when Peter was away. He was a mix of Labrador and Boxer, strong, yet soft. Sam was eventually trained to go up to encourage the youngster from the low roof if there was a call for help. When the dog reached him, James would hang on to it while pulling himself up, and he would then follow the dog down what always seemed to be, fortunately, the gentlest part of the incline.

Peter and Catherine never worked out how their son managed to reach the roof top, nor how Sam, on some occasions, managed to stalk him, as James manoeuvred across the roof sitting astride its ridge. Peter was not quite sure whether Sam was there to provide some sort of safety net, or whether he simply enjoyed being with James, but his excited barks and James' cries were the signal that help was needed. A ladder and a risky crawl across the slope of the roof were Peter's response if the usual trick with the dog failed. A screaming James, grounded, indicated that any immediate danger to the child was dispelled, whilst the dog engineered its own route to safety. These expeditions did not always pass without incident. On one occasion, a slate preceded the pair of them, sending Catherine diving for cover, and on another, James preceded the dog and was only saved by Peter's welcoming arms.

Such experiences were be multiplied as the children adapted to their surroundings and found ways of entertaining themselves. It was the openness of the moor which offered such optional activities, eagerly exploited. They became used to pigs, cows, and hens, as well as the horses which were kept for hunting and for point-to-point racing. They were introduced to the natural outcome of procreation, being awakened one morning by the painful mooing of a cow and seeing the hanging legs of the expected calf as it fought for exit from its mother's womb and for its own life. The children followed the actions of the farmer and the vet as they performed their separate functions, with eyes wide with curiosity rather than alarm, as the bawling newcomer made its entry into life.

The experience opened up an awareness of a topic they felt no embarrassment in talking about. It came as no surprise, therefore, when, a few months later, Sarah eloquently explained to the family at tea, how, 'Daddy's sperm goes into Mummy and then one of us is born'. This at a time when parents and teachers were involved in serious discussion in the local primary school as to whether sex education should be introduced into the curriculum before children had reached the age of eleven. Sarah was all of seven! Her sex education had been via her observation of the local bull with a cow and the questions she had asked the farmer, and a sex education lesson on television which she had watched when she had been absent from school with a bad cold. The experience and knowledge seemed to have done her no harm, and it helped Peter and Catherine through what they reckoned might have been a delicate subject for them when raised by their children sometime in the future.

There was little doubt in Peter's mind that the moor was providing a learning playground for the children that could not be replicated. They began to put on one side, to a healthy extent, the plastic toys of the town as they extended their familiarity with what became natural to them on the moor. The feeding of the cats in the barn became a daily excitement, with the eldest carrying the small bucket and the others dipping in with their hands, spreading a trail across the barn floor which was eagerly consumed by their four-legged followers. The hens also provided opportunities for new delights. Not only did they cluck around the children's feet as they spread grain, but they also laid eggs. The regular attempt at identifying which hen had laid which egg became a competition in which even the youngest child could participate.

As the different seasons revealed their secrets and provided more opportunities for excitement to the children, spring with its sprouting grasses, early summer with its gift of new flowers, later summer with its sounds of gunshot, and winter with its ready opportunities for sledging on the hilly fields, Peter and Catherine recognised in their children a growing understanding of human relationships, of the value of joint endeavour, and of the overwhelming control, exercised in its innocence, by nature.

Inevitably, there were memorable occasions shared by all the family. The first day when all the children went to school together was such an historic occurrence. Catherine was determined to take a photograph so that one day the children could be reminded of how they looked as a family of children, taking the steps to a future life that they could not foretell. In years to come, they might look back at the photograph and wonder what was, and what might have been. Would they have made the best of their opportunities, and would chance have provided them with more than anyone could have planned for; or would they look back with nostalgia, tinged with sadness, because of the route their lives had taken. No one knew the answers to these questions, but on their first day to school, no-one seemed to care. The excitement they were experiencing was their life as they knew it, and the future they saw was no more than a two to three mile journey across the river to their school.

That first day saw the children preparing excitedly within the cottage, collecting pens and pencils, checking lunch boxes and pulling on winter coats. The chatter was incessant, the names of teachers were bounced around, and some of the memories of the older children from their earlier years recounted. James, in particular, displayed both the enthusiastic anticipation and coy vacillation that any child of four would be expected to show on his first day at school. He had collected his bag and, helped by Catherine, had put in a small carton of juice, a sandwich in case he was hungry at mid-morning break, and other bits and pieces that he might need during the day. This was the last occasion on which he required such careful supervision, because, even by the following day, he thought of himself as a practised hand in matters of school. But today, he had difficulty concentrating beyond excitedly asking the other children, 'Who's going to be my teacher?'

As usual, Katie, the Chief, had the answer. 'It'll be Miss Briggs. She always takes the little ones.'

'Is she nice?'

'She can be really lovely. She shows you how to do things in class and then lets you play outside. But don't do anything wrong, because then she gets ratty and makes you stand in a corner.'

Catherine saw doubt creep across James' little face and, seeking to avoid his believing that he was about to experience the end of his world, immediately interrupted. 'Katie, don't say things like that. You know Miss Briggs is very kind. She'll look after you and tell you all you need to know, James. You don't think Mummy would let you go to somebody who was going to be ratty with you, do you?'

Thankfully, James was appeased and preparations for his great day continued.

This first day of the new school year was one of those early September mornings on which the moor seemed to relish giving warning of impending autumn. The wind was blowing, hair was forced back, and teeth were gritted. Katie was the tallest of the four. Dressed in a brown checked duffle coat, she led the way out of the cottage for the photograph. With her face cringed, her eyes half-closed, and her mousy coloured hair blowing in the wind, she braved the elements as she grasped her school bag close to her side. She stood in readiness for the photo, obviously hoping the others would join her quickly. She was closely followed by Gregory, who was similarly taken aback by the force of the wind. The strap of his school bag crossed the shoulder of his winter coat, and his fair hair stood straight, disturbed by the strong breeze. His short trousers gave no protection to his legs, though the red band around the top of his socks stretched up to his knees. James followed, hands in the air and open, as if to shield his face, but still with that smile that typified his best days of childhood. He, more than the others, exuded the excitement related to the start of a new school year, a year in which he was to meet new friends, and become adjusted to the drills of the classroom and its environs. Sarah appeared with mouth open as she screwed her eyes against the wind, and the contortion of her face said all that had to be said about the sharpness of the breeze. She had difficulty holding her school beret on to her head with her right hand, whilst at the same time seeking to hang on to her school bag with her left.

Once they were grouped, with the tallest at the back, Peter had the nerve to say, 'Smile', as Catherine clicked the camera. The children did their best and for a second and third time responded to their father's urging. Only when the film was developed a couple of weeks later, was his success confirmed, with one of the photographs showing four smiling children ready for school.

The school was in Binkley. The Local Authority had provided a minibus to pick up the children from the village each morning, to take them to school, and to return them at the end of the day. The driver and bus owner was a local man named Wilf. He drove with determination and at some speed on the moor road. As a result, small children could sometimes find themselves on a ride not dissimilar to one they might experience at a fairground, as they swayed from side to side at the taking of each bend, hanging on to the seat in front or to friends by their side, like children in dodgem cars. Wilf knew the road well and parents naturally put their trust in him. Indeed, on the occasions when an adult needed to be in town early and had no other transport, he or she might ask Wilf for a lift. Squeezed into the back of the van, they then experienced their children's morning and afternoon ride first hand, always pleased to alight with legs, body, and head still linked, as they made for their appointed destination.

Peter had arranged for the children to go to the local Catholic primary. It catered for children from Binkley and neighbouring areas and, in Peter's and Catherine's eyes, provided a good education. As parents, they looked to see their children's school helping them mature to become confident and articulate young people, able to make the best of their talents, to be at ease socially, and to develop a Catholic life that would guide their future. They had confidence in the young lady who was the head. She mixed firmness with understanding, had created a popular and successful school, and she made parents and children feel welcome.

As with most primary schools, it provided an ideal meeting place for new, young parents. As they delivered their children to, or collected them from, the school, they often found the opportunity to talk and establish relationships. They also met at the various functions that the school opened up, such as parents' meetings and social gatherings.

Not surprisingly, the school became a centre through which Peter and Catherine established some life-long friendships.

As Peter knew, primary schools offered many more opportunities for parents to connect with one another than did his secondary school. The close relationship that class teachers seemed to be able to build with parents stemmed, Peter believed, from the ease with which most parents could meet and talk with a teacher or the head at the beginning or end of the school day. In his school, such close links seemed more difficult to create. Peter recognised that size, and the more formal organisation, hindered such close contact, and wondered why the school did not see the value of overcoming such obstacles. He reckoned that the routines common in his children's primary school would have helped the likes of Webster and his parents to identify more meaningfully with the school's ethos.

Peter held the view that formal schooling, although critical, was not the only educational experience his children should enjoy. He looked to broaden their interests. Peter's background in music meant that he and Catherine sought to encourage the children's interest in playing a musical instrument. The recorder was the instrument for Katie. She practised at home under the watchful eye of her father, but enthusiasm soon waned and the slow progress came to a stop long before anxious parents had expected. For Sarah, the violin was the chosen instrument. She keenly followed the instructions of her teacher to good effect in the early days, but as with Katie, what appeared to her as stultifying practice gradually lessened the interest, the will, and the progress. Even so, she did improve, and had it not been for the unfortunate death of her tutor, she may well have repaid her parents' commitment. For the boys, to follow in father's footsteps as cornet players, seemed the thing.

At a certain time each day, the peace of the moor was disturbed by what could only be described as raucous blasts on the trumpet. It was not long, however, before the moor could settle down again into the peace and calm of its nature, as the trumpet went back in its case.

The experiences that Peter sought to introduce to the children, however, were hardly matched by the lessons that Peter was to learn from them during his most demanding week of parenthood. Catherine was asked to accompany a party of pupils from his school. They were travelling abroad for ten days over the half term holidays. There had been some miscalculations along the organisational stream and, a few weeks before the pupils were to go, it was discovered that an extra female adult was required to provide the right amount of supervision. As no member of staff was available, Peter offered Catherine, knowing that she could establish good relationships with the pupils and staff, and believing that her medical experience might come in handy. As a result, he was left with the children to learn the foolishness of his offer.

His plan was to accompany them on daily walks across the moor, to take them to stay with his aunt for the occasional day, and to make sure he had plenty of paper, water colours and children's books around the cottage for the children's entertainment. The television would also provide a useful aid.

He discovered, during that fateful period, that the plans of the parents do not always match those of their children. It didn't take long for him to realise that his ability to manage a class of thirty in his day job was ill preparation for managing four of his own, when one wanted to play snakes and ladders, a second wanted to play on the moor, a third wanted to chop wood, and the fourth, probably the most imaginative, wanted to dig a trench in one of the fields as a defence against any unexpected Vikings.

Persuasion, backed on occasion by a firm teacher's command, became the order of the day, though its success was variable. He had to cope with tears, resentment, and on occasion downright rage, as he sought to find solutions to the children's requirements. Even his nature ventures with the children across the moor did not always go any more smoothly. He found out where the quagmires were and how difficult it seemed for his offspring to avoid them. He also learned how sheep's droppings can stick to small feet and footwear, how children need to dress to make sure that they are properly protected against the changeable weather, and, when necessary, how to change soiled clothes. The need for regular washing of hands, faces, and feet was something he had never foreseen. Peter also recognised that the clearing away of childish things, whether it was toys, rubbish, or articles that he never thought to be in their possession, had almost to become a pastime. It was during this time that the ability to make sandwiches, more often than not with half cooked sausages, also became his prized asset. The children loved them, though many years later never failed to remind him of how sausages should be done on the inside, as well as be brown on the outside.

The experience stunned him into recognising that it was not only the different spelling of 'mother' and 'father' that was of significance, but that each word carried a depth of meaning of which he had previously been unaware.

Nevertheless, parent and children had the opportunity to explore life on the moor together. The children were never at a loss for questions and, as the five of them roamed across the soft grass and itchy bracken, stirring sheep to movement, and disturbing the wildlife, he enjoyed seeking to answer them. The more they explored the more amazed Peter was at what the children were likely to find and what they showed interest in.

'What's this called Daddy?'

'Oh, that's bracken and those are rushes. Can you see the difference?'

'Look at that Daddy, it's a butterfly.'

'D'you know what type it is?'

When, as he expected, he had no response from the children, he was able to point out, 'You can see from its colour that it's a green hair streak. You'll see that there are other different coloured butterflies that flit across the moor and have different names. If you see one, tell me.'

Peter was also able to distinguish the foxgloves and the cotton grass among the flora for the children, as well as slight differences in the ring and bell heather as they bent down to collect their bunch of flowers. The girls, in particular, were keen to fill their small tight fists with blooms that attracted them. For the boys, it was more exciting to run after the disturbed grouse that flew up in front of them, though their chances of ever catching one were as remote as their ever catching a sheep.

'Do you know what that bird is called?' Peter asked on one occasion, when one flew up in front of James.

'No.'

'It's what we call a grouse. When you hear the guns, those are the birds that are usually being fired at. But there are other birds on the moor. There are lapwings, plovers and curlew . . . . look, there's a curlew,' he said, as one flew across their path. 'And if you look here, you'll see holes used by rabbits and hares. There are lots on different parts of the moor.'

Peter also pointed out different insects as the older children cautiously moved blades of grass to uncover their hideaways. Some of these Gregory collected in a small bottle he had with him, and no doubt had the intention of carefully studying them on his return to the cottage.

It was with increasing pleasure that Peter joined the children on these moorland walks and saw them growing in their knowledge of the moor and what it had to offer. He knew that the detail of such delights was hidden from those whose only experience of the moor was a car journey, which brought from them 'oohs and aahs' as they flashed past some of its beauties. He could not help but be thankful for what Maxine, who had long departed in marriage, had done for him and his family when she sold him the cottage.

CHAPTER 34

THE ASSIZES

Eventually, the day dawned on which the Leeds Assizes were to open. Unlike in the magistrate's court, the full pomp and splendour of the English judicial system was revealed, as the Judge, in gown and wig, processed to the court house along with his entourage. The whiteness of the wig contrasted sharply with the red gown enclosing the tight trousers that made their way down to the knees and white socks. The socks continued the journey to the specially buckled shoes that rounded off the powerful image of English justice.

Peter was struck by the difference between this scene and the one that he had observed at the humble magistrates' court. That gentle approach, designed to put the accused at their ease, was now replaced by the full authority of the law in all its dignity. From the moment he stepped over the threshold of the court house, Peter became aware of the importance of the occasion in which he was about to be involved. The leaded glazed windows in which the national emblem, 'Dieu Et Mon Droit', and the initials 'VR', were delicately integrated, stared down from their superior position, reminding everyone who entered of the significance of the room they were in. The mosaic floor, upon which was inscribed Leeds City Police, provided further evidence of the legal purpose of the building.

As Peter pondered on these changes, Webster and his two pals were also trying to come to terms with what they saw before them. The arrangements for the trial were markedly different to those they had experienced in Weberton. The Judge sat alone at a high bench, overshadowed by the Royal Coat of arms emblazoned on the back of his high chair. To his right was a seat raised almost to the level of his; it was the stand into which witnesses went to give their statements and answer questions. At first sight, it meant nothing to the boys.

Directly in front of the Judge and the witness box were the tables and chairs used by the barristers, prosecuting and defending. They, too, when they took up their positions, were in wigs and gowns, the latter being black rather than the red of the Judge. Facing the witness box were the seats for the jury, enclosed by a low wooden rail. Unbeknown to the boys, it was strategically placed so as to enable the jury to observe the general demeanour of a witness and of the accused. The clerk of the court sat facing the Judge, to be ready for any call on his services, whilst the court reporter, recording the proceedings, faced in the opposite direction.

The most forbidding area of any court was the dock. It was here that the accused, in this case the three boys, stood or sat to listen to what was said about them and their actions, and from where they would be expected to answer any questions that the Judge might wish to ask them. The boys had already been told that they must address him as,

'Your Honour', and stand if spoken to. They had also been warned that, if required, they could be called to the witness stand to be examined by the Defence or Prosecution Counsel. The custody officer, who had led the boys into court, stood with them in the dock, alongside their social workers, to ensure that they behaved as expected and had some understanding of what was happening.

It would be fair to say that probably for the first time in his life, Webster began to feel intimidated by what he was involved in. He had naively believed that if he told what was for him the truth, admitted that he was one of the three boys identified as running away from the scene of the mugging, and cooperated with all those who had, for one reason or another, examined him, things would be all right. This was what he had experienced in school. Admit the blame, take the punishment, and life goes on. He was becoming overwhelmed with the feeling that what he was about to experience was going to be different.

Webster was confused by the pomp and ceremony with which he was now surrounded, and his previous nonchalance was undermined by a nervousness he had rarely experienced. He felt a horrible sickly feeling in his mouth, engendered by his growing fear as the seriousness of his situation took a hold of his thinking. His inner self shouted, *I should not be here, I am trapped; trapped by the lies of my friends and by all this paraphernalia that is going on around me. What can I do? What is going to happen?* In desperation, he looked around seeking a way out of his predicament. His eyes were as bright as ever, not from the bravado of the Webster everyone knew, but from panic. *I can't do anything. I'm stuck.*

At great speed, he retraced what had happened since he gave himself up to the police. But he could not think in a logical way and place events in the chronological order in which they had happened, as he searched for reasons as to why he was here.

What else could I have done to avoid this? he asked himself. He had been as honest as he felt he could with the police and the detective on the several occasions they had interviewed him. He was confused by some of the questions of the psychiatrist, but he was not aware that she had any concerns about what he had to say. His solicitor had asked all sorts of odd questions, but again, he felt he had answered them as fully as he could and with what conviction he could muster. Mr Delaney and his solicitor friend had seemed to believe him when he spoke to them up on the moor. In fact, the solicitor's parting 'Not to worry Joseph, everything will be all right,' was a recollection that flashed through his mind.

Nothing, he said to himself, '*absolutely nothing I did or said should have brought me to this place. I know I can be a sod and that I've caused lots of problems to people, but . . . .* and so his thoughts rumbled on haphazardly without his being able to explain his situation. *Trev and Will have sold me out, I know it. What do I do . . . . ?* and again his thoughts drifted, but this time to what he would do to Trev and Will if he ever got out of this situation. He could still be the same truculent, challenging Webster that he was in school. But here, nothing seemed to fit. Had his QC been aware of how the depth of Webster's anxieties was confusing his thinking, he too would have been nervous. He knew how important it was that Joseph, if asked, could re-tell his story with accuracy and conviction. If he faltered, it could have an unfortunate impact on the thinking of the jury.

Webster glanced around the courtroom, seeking to find something or someone with whom he could connect. Initially, and totally unintentionally, he found himself looking at Mrs Mann. Her black coat and matching hat accentuated the grief displayed on her face. Her tear-tired eyes looked beyond the dock and the three boys towards the bench, still, and seemingly sightless. Eventually, Webster picked out his mother and father in the public gallery. His mother, her hair pinned back in a bun, revealing some rather smart-looking earrings, was in a more stylish jacket and blouse than Webster had been accustomed to seeing. He looked at her with that same appealing question, *What am I doing here?* For the first time in a long time, she smiled at him, and raised her eyes in a look that seemed to say, *It'll be OK, Joe.* The usually imperturbable Webster could not hold back a tear as his heart went out to his 'Mum', and he was overcome with that comforting feeling of someone who at last knows he is loved.

The several witnesses who would be called to give testimony during the trial were kept outside the court room as part of the procedures designed to ensure that one witness was not influenced by another's testimony. The anxiety that Peter had felt in the early stages of the initial hearing were multiplied by ten as he sat waiting to be called. On this occasion, he was joined by Catherine who was also a witness. Both had been drawn in by Webster's Defence Counsel, and both wondered, sometimes by comments to each other or within the silence of their minds, how Joe was coping. Their understanding of, and concern for him, had heightened as a result of the awful tragedy, and had cemented that affinity with the boy that Peter had looked for in those early days.

By ten o'clock the general public had taken their seats in the gallery. Shortly afterwards, there was movement around the various tables as the lawyers and their aides organised themselves. The appearance of members of the jury signalled how near the trial was to beginning, and they were closely followed by the arrival of the accused in the dock. 'All rise,' was called and the Judge made his stately way to his seat at the bench.

It was almost eleven o'clock when the Judge began the proceedings by outlining the procedures in his court and confirming, with Prosecuting Counsel, what charges were being brought. Having dealt with the formalities, he looked across at the jury, six men and six women, and, in a much more affable manner, welcomed them, outlined the gravity of the role they were to play, and trusted that they would carry out their responsibilities honestly and objectively.

The three boys watched with some trepidation as the prosecution spelled out for the jury the nature of the case against them. Details of the attack on Mr Mann were outlined, providing a clear picture of the dash across the road by one of the boys, the robbery, the struggle, and the scene outside The Dragon after Mr Mann fell to the ground. The prosecutor went on to describe the flight of the three boys from the area after the attack. He described how the police had arrested two of the boys, he used the aliases A and B for Will and Trev, in the park. The third, C, who was Joe, had managed to flee, and it was on the following evening that he surrendered himself to the police in Weberton police station.

Turning to point to the three accused, he said, 'It is the prosecution's intention to prove to you that these are the three boys concerned and that one of them, Joseph Webster, was responsible for stabbing to death Mr Mann.'

He went on to say that the jury would need to consider three charges. These would be the charge of murder, the charge of manslaughter, and the charge of involvement through association.

'Two of the boys have admitted involvement but have accused the third, Joseph Webster, of actually carrying out the attack. Joseph Webster has denied any involvement whatsoever, and he claims that he only joined in when he saw his friends running towards the park. You may wonder why he felt the need to run,' he added pointedly. 'It is the prosecution's contention that he was directly responsible for the attack and that William Skelton and Trevor Makin were involved through association. You will be provided with sufficient evidence to enable you to come to the same conclusion.'

There were two Defence Counsels, one for Joe and the other for the other two boys. Will and Trev's Counsel said very little, other than to confirm that his defendants pleaded guilty to being present and running away. They had not, however, been involved in the robbery, which, he maintained, was the idea and deed of Joseph Webster. He was aware that if the prosecution proved its case, that is what the jury would find, and so, giving the impression of confiding in the jury, he said he was happy to follow the prosecutor's lead in relation to what evidence was provided.

Joe's Counsel spent time explaining that the prosecution case relied too much on the testimonies of the other two accused, and that the failure to produce the knife or establish who owned it, undermined their contention that Webster was the perpetrator of the dreadful crime.

'Furthermore, insufficient weight has been given to the timings of the crime. The defence will demonstrate that these were critical, thus providing you with enough doubt as to the truth of the testimonies of the other two accused to enable you to find Joseph Webster not guilty.'

As the case progressed, and this was over days rather than hours, Joe could not believe how much detail had been collected to put before the jury. For much of the proceedings his mind was in a spin, as he hardly understood the technicalities of what was happening around him. The intricacies of the questioning, the passing around of evidence, and the objections raised, permitted, or refused, left him as if covered in one of the black cloaks of the barristers with only a chink of light emerging to help him understand what was happening.

Prosecuting Counsel began the case by presenting the evidence which had been collected by the police. First, he called the officer who had carried out the arrest to describe what he had found when he first detained the boys. Then he called Inspector Grossman to provide further details of the investigation that followed. The QC led the detective carefully through the story, seeking to establish that all three boys had a part to play in the crime, but that the testimonies of Trevor Makin and William Skelton were sound enough to lead to Joe being convicted. Part of the police evidence was supported by a video clip, shown to the jury to indicate the relationship between the town hall, the fish shop, The Dragon pub, and the corner of West Street. Its purpose was to illustrate their proximity and the limited amount of time it would take for the crime to be carried out and the boys to link up.

A good many questions were directed at Grossman by Joe's Defending Counsel as he sought to throw doubt on some of the conclusions inferred, whilst it seemed to be in the interests of Will and Trev for their Counsel to sit quietly and to accept the story as being that portrayed by the police.

Joe's Counsel wanted to know, 'Was the time required for Joe to get from the town hall to the fish shop and The Dragon carefully checked?'

'Yes. We did several journeys at different speeds to see whether or not Webster's account was accurate. Although there were different outcomes, our view was that for a boy of his age, walking with purpose to meet friends, it was possible to be at the scene within ten minutes.'

'And what about his return to the town hall for, what was it, ah, his mouthpiece?'

'We took that into consideration.'

'I see.' Defence Counsel looked to walk back to his seat and then, suddenly, he turned to ask, 'Inspector Grossman, can you describe to us what a trombone mouthpiece looks like?'

'Well, I assume it's the bit of the trombone that has something to do with the mouth,' came a rather hesitant and less confident response.

'Do you know where a trombone player would keep it?'

The detective looked a bit nonplussed, giving Defence Counsel the opportunity to quickly interject, 'Thank you, Inspector. Now, you say you did very careful checks of the various timings. At what time did Joseph actually reach the corner of West Street?'

'Well, by our reckoning, it must have been just after ten past eight, giving him time to run across the road to The Dragon and tangle with Mr Mann.'

'I'm sorry, Inspector. I asked for the precise time.'

'Well, you can't always be absolutely precise in these matters, as I'm sure you appreciate.'

'I'm sorry, Inspector, but I don't appreciate. Either Joseph was there in time to be involved in the crime or not. From what you are saying, there is some doubt about that.'

Defence Counsel looked across at the jury as if to be sure that they had not missed the point he was making, and then back to Grossman. 'Thank you, Inspector, I have no further questions.'

The evidence of several other prosecution witnesses was also introduced. Mrs Johnson, the lady who had screamed, described her shock at seeing Mr Mann on the floor and how she had rushed back into the pub for help, just after, 'I saw the three boys on the other side of the road running away.'

When questioned further by Defence Counsel she admitted that, 'One of the boys was a little behind the other two when I saw them. I don't know which one,' she admitted, when asked to look at the three accused in the dock.

The paramedics, who had rushed to the scene, described the state of Mr Mann on their arrival, and the pathologist went into great detail to describe the wound from which Mr Mann had died. He confirmed death by stabbing, and was able to describe the type of knife that was likely to have been used. He went on to say that the knife had pierced the heart and had been delivered with some force.

Defence Counsel wondered, 'Were you able to compare your perception of the knife used with the actual knife?' to receive the response, 'No, not yet, the knife has not been found.'

'So we don't know to whom the knife actually belonged?' asked Defence Counsel with a rather astonished look at the witness and then the jury as if to ask, *What are we doing here if we don't know whose knife it was and who used it?'*

Because of the youthfulness of the boys, the court had asked for a psychiatrist's report. This dealt in some detail with the particular character traits of each of the boys. Prompted by the prosecution, the psychiatrist indicated, 'All three boys have some abnormality of the mind. All of them are capable of carrying out violent acts without any qualms, and my findings suggest that they would show little remorse.'

This was a damning indictment of the three boys.

When asked by the Judge, 'Are you implying that they do not feel any moral responsibility for what they do?' the psychiatrist was a little more circumspect but replied,

'I think that characteristic would be more likely to apply to Joseph and Trevor than to William, Your Honour.'

The social workers that were called indicated that all three boys lived in circumstances that may well have influenced their attitudes. They described the conditions in which they lived, the limited vision that their parents had for their future, and the groups they mixed with. Their evidence helped those listening to gain some understanding of the circumstances in which the boys had been brought up and possibly some sympathy for their plight. They referred to Trev and Will having left school and being unemployed. Other witnesses were called, several of whom had been on a bus and had seen the boys running towards the park, noticing them because they almost caused an accident A young girl testified to seeing the boys together in the park after the attack, looking as though they were sharing out money. She noticed them because one of them, whom she did not know, whistled after her.

And so the trial went on with the Prosecuting Counsel producing some damning evidence to support his case, that it was Joe who had been responsible for the stabbing. From time to time, as particular pieces of evidence were produced, the three boys looked at each other as if to say *Told you so*, but mostly, after the first flush of excitement at the start of the trial, they lowered their eyes as if to absent themselves mentally from the proceedings that were going on in front of them.

Joe's Defence Counsel, a tall imposing figure who moved about the court room with self-assurance, looked in the direction of the jurors at every opportunity, as if to draw them into his confidence and share with them some snippets of information that would have a significant bearing on the outcome of their deliberations. He felt he had some key witnesses that just might cast doubt on Trev's and Will's story and swing the jury Joe's way. He guessed that if the police could not identify the owner of the knife or produce any independent witnesses who had actually observed the mugging directly, he would be able to make a strong case for the defence.

His first witness was Jackie from the fish shop. Her testimony was critical in establishing the actual time of the attack.

'Mrs Slack, can you describe what you witnessed on the night of the mugging?'

'I was serving when two youngsters came into the shop and asked for portions of fish and chips.'

'Are the boys in the courtroom?'

'Yes. They are those two,' said Jackie pointing to Will and Trev.

'Carry on, Jackie, you don't mind me calling you Jackie?'

'Of course not. I know the time was about five to eight because we were having a quiet time in the shop. We tend to get busiest between programmes and we expected a bit of a crowd at about eight after Coronation Street had finished.' This caused titters in the public gallery and a stern look in that direction from the Judge. 'The boys came, took their order, and went to stand outside to eat their fish and chips. As expected, at about eight o'clock, lots of people arrived and I could no longer see the boys through the shop window. The next thing I heard was a scream from the direction of the pub, just as the church clock struck quarter past eight. The customers, me, and Joan, my assistant, all ran out of the shop and saw Mr Mann on the floor outside the pub and Mrs Bell disappearing back into the pub.'

'Did you think it possible that Mrs Bell had stabbed Mr Mann?'

Jackie almost laughed at the amusing thought. 'No chance. She would not have gone back into the pub and then come out again with two or three others, to try to help Mr Mann. We knew the three boys were involved, because they were running down the street.'

'Thank you, Jackie. Your witness,' Defence Counsel said, nodding to his adversary.

'Jackie, you say that you served the boys and they then went outside. How long d'you think it would take them to eat their fish and chips?'

'About ten to fifteen minutes, depending on their hurry.'

'So, by your reckoning, it would probably have been about five or ten past eight by the time they finished.' Jackie nodded in acknowledgement. 'So, by the time Joe arrived, they would be ready to set off on their walk through town.'

'I suppose so.'

'Had they at any time during your observation of them appeared aggressive or been looking for trouble, or were they behaving like any ordinary teenagers?'

'I would say they were pretty calm.'

'Thank you, Jackie. I have no more questions. You may step down.'

The thing about barristers is that they can ask questions in such a way that nobody really knows where they are leading until they eventually produce the question or statement that proves to be the telling blow. The relevance of the prosecutor's questions to Jackie did not seem to be leading anywhere, but the Defence Counsel knew he had to remain alert to any change in the arguments produced to pin the crime on Joe. He knew that the calmness of Trev and Will in the fish shop would linger in the minds of the jury for the remainder of the trial, and no doubt appear again to support the prosecution's case.

'I would like to call Mr Peter Delaney, Your Honour.'

'Mr Peter Delaney,' rang through the courtroom and then Peter emerged from the antechamber in which he had been waiting. He took the stand and then, with his hand on the Bible, took the traditional oath.

Defence Counsel started, 'Mr Delaney, please tell us as clearly as you can about your dealings with Joseph Webster, from the time of the concert in the town hall until his eventual arrest by the police.'

In response, Peter went through the events as the concert finished. 'By my reckoning, we finished just before eight o'clock. The band then packed away their equipment. I'd asked some of them to stay behind to be introduced to the Mayor.'

'Was Joseph Webster among that group?'

'I invited him, as he'd been a soloist, but he said he had to leave to meet his friends. I remember that Joseph left as soon as he could, first asking one of our musicians, Joan, a sort of leader of the band, if she'd mind packing away his equipment. He was keen, as I've already said, to join some of his friends in town. I didn't object, as I knew how well he had contributed to the concert, and that he was the sort of lad who wouldn't take kindly to having his request refused. Joseph was well known for his tantrums.' Immediately, Peter realised that such a description was not in the script, and so quickly added, 'and on this so successful evening, I didn't want to do anything that might show I did not appreciate how well he and the band had performed. As it was, he left in good humour, pleased, I think, with his own performance.'

'Can you be precise as to the time when the concert finished?' asked Counsel.

'Yes, it was at five minutes to eight. By the time the applause had finished and we were ready to pack up, it was certainly eight o'clock. You could add some time to that for packing away the equipment.'

'I thought you said Joseph asked Joan to pack away his equipment?' asked Counsel in a pre-arranged question and answer session. Peter knew exactly what he was expected to say.

'Yes, but that didn't include casing his trombone. Joseph was very jealous, as I think all musicians are, as to who touched his instrument.'

'So that would take some time?'

'Well, yes. It could take two or three minutes to put the trombone in its case, that's once Joseph had left the stage.'

'Do you know what time Joseph left the town hall?'

'I didn't see him leave, I was involved in a range of other matters, but it couldn't have been before five past eight. Then he returned for his mouthpiece, which would have added extra minutes.'

'Oh, yes, the mouthpiece, that essential part of the instrument that the Inspector seemed confused about.'

He paused slightly, giving himself time to look meaningfully again at the jury, as a sort of reminder of the Inspector's testimony. 'Where is this kept?

'In the instrument's case.'

'I could ask why it was that Joseph was keen to have it after the concert, but I suspect that has no bearing on what we are about. What I am interested in, is how long it might have taken him to retrieve it once he returned to the town hall.'

'Difficult to say, but we've to recognise that he would have had to go through the concert hall, climb onto the stage, retrieve his trombone case, open it, and then extract his mouthpiece. I'd have thought it would have taken several minutes.'

'I see,' said Counsel. 'So we have Joseph rushing back to the town hall as quickly as possible, finding his trombone, and then taking out his mouthpiece.'

He stood as if considering the implications of Joe's actions, with his forefinger stroking the underside of his chin pensively, and then, 'Could we say at least five minutes?'

He did not wait for an answer, but left the jury working out what it all added up to in relation to the time of the attack.

The Prosecuting Counsel spent time working with Peter through the timing of the different activities, intent on seeking to prove that Webster could have been at the crime scene at the appropriate time. He knew that he could still make capital out of what might be described as the missing minutes, but the church clock and the evidence of the fish and chip owner were crowding him as he sought to prove beyond doubt that Webster could have been at the scene in time.

'Mr Delaney, did you see Joseph come back for his mouthpiece?'

'No, but I know that he always carries it with him, because he is not allowed to take his trombone home.'

'So, if you didn't see him, you have no way of knowing whether he actually returned for it or how long it may have taken him if he had.'

Peter realised he was in a difficult position regarding the actual events and that his post-concert activities had got in the way of his being able to be precise about the activities of a number of his musicians, including Webster. The only answer he had was, 'I suppose not, but I think his story has been verified by one of the other pupils in the band, who takes some responsibility for overseeing the kit.'

'No more questions,' said Prosecuting Counsel, as he turned to his seat feeling that he had made a significant point.

The next witness was Catherine. Defence called her because of the meticulous way in which she had tracked and timed Webster's movements. It was as if she were the detective. Her evidence was very clear. The Defence Counsel opened the way for her to take the jury through the events, the times, and the evidence of the people she had spoken with. Her own acceptance of the possibility of Webster's story being true was evident in the confident way in which she declared what she had discovered.

'I went through Joseph's well publicised journey on the day after the mugging. I timed my walk down West Street, the return to the town hall, and then down West Street again. There is no way he could have been there before eight fifteen.'

Prosecution Counsel spent some time seeking to undermine the basis of her evidence. He had no doubt that the timings were key to the case, and that they needed explanation. It was this that Counsel was endeavouring to highlight for the jury. The questioning followed the pattern of, 'Are you sure of the time of the attack? Are you sure that the clock in the town hall was showing exactly the same time as that of the church? How do you explain one witness saying she saw three boys across the street? Why do you think the police have not given more weight to your evidence?' and so on.

Prosecution Counsel was well aware that he had to challenge Catherine's timing of events if he was to make it clear where guilt lay. To her credit, Catherine stood up to his questioning doggedly, remaining constant in her belief that it was likely that Joseph did not arrive at the crime scene before quarter past eight.

The public interest in the case had meant daily coverage of the trial in the press and on local news. National television also took an interest from time to time, and different witnesses gained a brief celebrity as their evidence was reported. The names of the boys remained anonymous and could not be revealed until after the trial. This did not mean to say that they felt any more comfortable in their plight. All three of them became morose, the outcome of their worries. Their isolation during the trial also played on their emotions, and the early nerves were replaced with their more normal characteristics of belligerence and cussedness. The social workers and the court officers found their behaviour increasingly challenging. On occasions, they refused to eat what was given, flew into tempers at the slightest provocation, and as soon as they saw one another spat expletives without consideration of who was present. It was only in court that they displayed the conciliatory demeanour advised by their solicitors.

Peter did not find it difficult to understand the pressures on the three boys, as they sat or stood through two weeks of the trial. He knew that for Joseph in particular, it was especially stressful, as he was the one being accused of the killing. Joseph could not release from his mind the abhorrence he had for his friends. He would have been happy to share the blame and take the consequences. He identified himself as a good mate, loyal and steadfast. But they had slipped the demands of real friendship and given his name to the police. He was aware that his reputation had gone before him, and before the trial had begun to believe that the police were not being fair to him. What he had not known before the trial, and had discovered once the evidence was being presented, was how thoroughly the police had checked his story and how carefully they had tried to pinpoint the various timings of events. The problem was, that they were seeking to convince the jury of their version of events. If the jury accepted them, and that he could have been at The Dragon at the time they asserted, Joseph began to realise he was in real trouble. *How is it all going to end?* he asked himself, time and time again.

The summing up of the Prosecuting and Defence Counsels covered the arguments that had been made, emphasising in particular the importance that the jury needed to attach to the time frame of the crime.

Prosecuting Counsel asked the question, 'If Joseph Webster is not guilty, then who is? It is beyond question that there was a death from stabbing and the three boys were involved. That two of them were prepared to point a finger at their friend is significant. Do you really believe that both would simply gang up on their friend, Joseph, simply to save their skins. Remember, all three were 'mates', as they describe themselves, and that they were such good friends that young Webster was hurrying to be with them. Remember, Joseph Webster has not given any indication as to whom he believes stabbed Mr Mann. As a jury, you need to put aside any feelings you may have towards Trevor Makin and William Skelton emanating from your disgust at their participation in a dreadful crime, and recognise that they, as the only eye witnesses to the crime, have identified Joseph Webster as the attacker. If you weigh all the evidence carefully, I'm sure you will reach the just verdict; that Joseph Webster is guilty of killing Mr Mann.' He emphasised the last phrase, wishing to leave the jury in no doubt as to what verdict he, and possibly every other right minded person, expected.

Defence Counsel concentrated on the time frame and the impossibility it would have been for Joseph to have arrived at the scene of the crime in time to commit this heinous act. 'The attempts of the prosecution to blur the timings of events have been thoroughly refuted by the precise detail of Mrs Delaney's testimony, the meticulousness of which has not been effectively challenged by the police or Prosecution Counsel. Joseph Webster's return to the town hall is crucial, and makes it impossible for him to have been at the scene before eight fifteen. To climb the steps into the hall, to get on to the stage, and then to find his trombone case and extract his mouthpiece, before retracing his steps and hurrying to the fish shop, make it most unlikely that he could have been at the scene by the time the police have indicated. They make it, I suggest, impossible. And once he has arrived, after such a successful concert, why should he suddenly spoil it all by wanting to attack Mr Mann? In my view, you've no option but to return a verdict of not guilty in relation to the killing, though I accept', and this was his bone to the jury, 'that you may feel that Joseph was one of the three boys observed sharing out money in the park. I accept that this could tie him in by association.'

The Judge sought to unravel the different arguments in the case for the jury. With the authority bred by his position and experience, 'You will attach a good deal of importance to the different times of events, I have no doubt,' he said, looking directly at the jury, 'and you would be right to do so. You need to be sure beyond reasonable doubt that Joseph Webster could have been at the scene of the crime at the time indicated by the prosecution. Of course, you may ask, at what stage did Webster decide to mug Mr Mann; when did he first make contact with his friends; did he carry out the mugging on his way to his friends; and what of the mysterious knife—how significant a piece of evidence would that have been if it had been produced? You will also consider, I'm sure, the psychiatrist's report on the three boys, and their propensity for violent behaviour. I have no doubt that you are already weighing in your minds the validity of the evidence of the other two boys, William and Trevor, who admit to being involved and have named Joseph Webster as the perpetrator of the crime. You have to ask, 'Was it in their own interests that they accused Joseph Webster?'

He went on, seeking to pinpoint for the jury those aspects that would have a bearing on their deliberations. Eventually, he pointed out that the jury needed to reach verdicts on four charges. The first was that Joseph Webster had murdered James Mann.

'I think you will probably agree that this is an unlikely outcome of your deliberations, as pre-meditation, which has not been mentioned in the case, would have to be demonstrated. The second is, that Joseph Webster is guilty of manslaughter, that is killing Mr Mann but not with prior intent. There is a third option, of course, which is that Joseph Webster is not guilty of stabbing Mr Mann but is party, through association with the other two boys, to the killing and robbing of Mr Mann. That of course leads to the question of who is guilty of the stabbing.'

He paused for a moment to give the jury time to consider, and then added, 'If you agree the third option, we are left wondering who actually did the stabbing, as no other person has been charged with that crime.' Another pause and time to reflect on the implications of such a verdict. 'The fourth charge you have to consider concerns William Skelton and Trevor Makin, who have been charged with, and have admitted, being the accomplices of Joseph Webster during the crime.'

After he had spelled out the jury's responsibilities, he asked the jury members to retire to consider their verdicts. Then, with the customary pomp that had been exercised throughout each day of the trial, he left the courtroom.

It was on the afternoon of the following day before the jury announced that they were returning to present their verdict. The court quickly filled with observers, the press, officials, Counsel and the accused, all eager to learn the outcome of the trial. Eventually, the Judge arrived, preceded by the customary, 'All rise'. He looked to the jury and asked the Foreman if they had reached a verdict.

'We have, Your Honour.'

The Judge turned to the three accused and asked them to stand and look at the jury whilst the verdicts were read out.

'And how do you find?'

'In the case of William Skelton, we find him guilty of crime by association. In the case of Trevor Makin, we find him guilty of crime by association. In the case of Joseph Webster . . . .', and here the assembled court seemed to stop breathing as it awaited the announcement. Peter reached for Catherine's hand and held it tightly. He looked across at Webster, who seemed to be awaiting his fate impassively. Peter wondered what Webster was actually thinking behind those still, passionless eyes. Was he still the belligerent boy that he had met those years ago, or was he cowering within, desperate not to show his fear.

The Foreman hesitated for a moment, as if entranced by the general feeling of expectancy that was running through the courtroom, and then announced, 'We find him not guilty of murder.'

Despite the tension, this verdict was not unexpected. No matter how shocked those present had been by the actions of the three boys, it was generally recognised that the crime had been on the spur of the moment rather than a premeditated act.

The court room fell into an expectant silence again, as the Foreman looked at his notes in readiness for his next declaration. For those closely involved in the trial and its outcome, these few moments seemed an eternity, and a reminder of how, in happier times, the announcement of the result of a competition seems always to be delayed a few seconds to allow tension and anticipation to build. For Joseph, it seemed like time without end as his thoughts about the possible outcomes danced across his mind.

Can they still find me guilty of something? If they do, what will the punishment be? What if they find me not guilty? What then? Will I still have to serve a sentence because of my involvement in sharing out the money in the park? And what will that sentence be?

The questions appeared and lingered as he awaited the judgement.

At last, the Foreman declared, 'And in respect of manslaughter, we find Joseph Webster not guilty.'

There was hubbub in the court room, as the press and the general public, seemingly taken aback, turned and shared their views with each other. The defence team fell into congratulatory mode. Some members of the press assumed that everything now pointed to guilt by association and dashed for the exit. Joseph looked at his mother, who was now smiling and exchanging congratulatory words with his father, and burst into tears.

'Order,' called the Judge, and as quiet returned he looked to the Foreman questioningly.

'We find Joseph Webster, William Skelton and Trevor Makin guilty of the killing of Mr Mann by association'.

The Foreman sat down, knowing full well that the verdicts created as many questions as answers. The case of the actual stabbing had not been solved. The jury had opened up the need for further police investigation. They had found no one individual guilty of the killing, but had come to the conclusion that it was an undisputable fact that, whilst one of the three boys had carried out the stabbing, the other two had in some way been involved. That Joseph was found not guilty of the knifing threw the blame on to the other two, and it was now up to the police to re-open the case and identify which one.

Everyone in the courtroom was sharing these same thoughts as the Judge looked up at the boys and asked, 'Have you anything you wish to say?'

All three shook their heads, trying to cope in their different ways with the outcome of the trial.

'I will delay sentence until the police have had some time to reconsider their evidence. You can rely on it, however, that there is likely to be a custodial sentence for each of you on account of your involvement in the whole affair.'

Whereupon, he stood and left the courtroom to the cry, 'All arise'.

The trial had been a chastening experience for both Peter and Catherine. Their growing familiarity with Webster had led to them having more and more confidence in their belief that they were helping him, and that he was beginning to see a value in having respect for others. The outcome of the trial, though not as disastrous as it might have been, demonstrated that the progress the lad had made was slight. He was still prepared to mix with the worst elements of the town, and felt no real guilt in getting involved in activities that were a blatant contradiction of the law. In their discussion on their journey back to the cottage, they did find some consolation, however, in what they regarded as positive outcomes. Webster had not been found guilty of harming Mr Mann, and he had owned up to his involvement in the crime, but without descending into accusing either of his friends of the attack on Mr Mann.

CHAPTER 35

VISITORS

By its nature, the moor attracted a wide range of people who saw it as providing the different pleasures and interests suited to their particular taste. Those looking for shooting game were prepared to pay sizeable sums of money for the pleasure of walking across the moor, seeing grouse stirred to flight, and then filling them with as much lead as they could muster. An old and once essential pursuit designed to provide food for those who hunted, to Peter's mind it now provided little more than an expensive pastime. He was far from convinced by the arguments that there would be no grouse unless bred by gamekeepers for sport or that the economy of those who lived on the moor would be sorely affected without the annual activity.

Other visitors were happy enough to use the moor for what Peter regarded as more suitable activities such as hiking. Dressed in light clothing in summer and heavier tackle, which often included Gore-Tex waterproof jackets, in winter, the hikers invariably wore woolly headgear and carried rucksacks of variable size, depending on the time of year and the need for extra clothing. Most wore boots, but occasionally trainers were also on display. How the trainers coped with the boggy land was a mystery to Peter, but those who wore them gave the impression of being comfortable walkers. Groups would often assemble at the edge of the moor by the cottage wall to consult their maps and sometimes a compass, before setting off either across the moor westwards or down the road and through the village.

On other occasions, the moor was seen as an ideal venue for competition. Cyclists were attracted by the challenge of the hills, the quiet of the roads, and the sort of route ideal for time-trialling. In their bright tops, spiky helmets, and classy bikes, they would gather speed down the slope to the cottage only to find that they had to brake sharply to round the severe bend outside the gate. It made good entertainment for the family, usually on a weekend.

The moor road was also used occasionally as part of the route for a national motor rally. The family was fascinated by the screeching tyres, the change of gears, and the roar of the engines as the drivers negotiated the sharp bends and steep inclines. They became even more enthralled when one driver missed the bend by the cottage completely and headed onto the moor, until his wheels became locked in the soft earth. Reverse, push, reverse, push, and reverse freed him to continue on his way, with a clapping, cheering family wishing him well.

The visitors that were less popular were those who were classed as treasure hunters. They used to arrive with the first dawn of spring, usually from one of the villages in the valley below. Their task was to collect a range of information or items and then return to the starting point. Those who had achieved the highest level of performance won the prize of the day. These innocent souls were members of clubs and societies that ranged from Rotary Clubs to School Parents' Associations and were invariably organised to raise money for some charity or other. Cheerful as they were, they rarely considered the nuisance they were to the farmers whose lives were spent on the moor, and those like Peter and Catherine who lived there to escape from the noise and bustle of the towns below. What these visitors failed to realise was that these same people whom they were disturbing not only enjoyed the tranquil days but also had to endure the different moods of the moor, the sometimes unrelenting rain, the harsh winds, the swirling mists, and the snow that could envelop all in a bleak silence.

On one occasion, the family was rudely disturbed by a series of paired visitors who had clearly been given tasks related to the immediate neighbourhood of the cottage. Some climbed the outside water tank, presumably to count the number of rings that made up the iron exterior or, thought Catherine, assess the amount of water it contained. They then proceeded to collect a number of leaves from the small trees at the front of the house and what appeared to be the wool from sheep. The strangest request came from one of the groups who asked if Peter minded if they took some hen feathers. It was only when he saw hens flying in all directions and squawking that he realised that they wanted to take them from a living bird. It was clear that they had misunderstood what was required by the organisers of the competition, but they set about their task with determination. Peter had no option but to step in and halt the activity to the chagrin of the treasure hunters.

The most prestigious of visitors that Peter and Catherine welcomed to the moor and the cottage was a group of American educationists. They were one of the few groups of the 1960s to make their way to Russia via western Europe, and had been invited to the school to meet with pupils and staff. As part of the arrangements, staff had been asked to entertain some of the visitors in their own homes on one of the evenings, provide them with dinner, and enable them to sample traditional English life. The Americans were staying in Binkley, just below the moor, and so it was no trouble for Peter to pop down and collect them. However, the Americans were sizeable people, and to squeeze four into his relatively small Triumph car was a challenge. The Americans were greatly amused by the car's size, comparing it with what they were used to back in the States, but with a bit of manoeuvring and seating according to size, the group managed to squeeze in, joking with one another as they did so.

There was still a little light as the car headed skywards to the cottage. As the town and its environs were left behind, the Americans expressed their fascination with the moor. They also began to fire questions at Peter, which followed a not uncommon theme. 'How long have you lived on the moor? Do many others live here? How do children get to school? Can it get lonely?' And as heavy clouds began gathering around the *Beacon*, 'What's the weather like?'

The questions continued throughout the journey, with particular interest being shown in the history of the *Beacon* and the way it dominated its surroundings. By the time they reached the cottage, their questions had gathered a new intensity typified by, 'Wow, do you really live here?' One American said, 'This is all I could have dreamed of when told I was visiting a country cottage.' And another said, 'This must be older than the United States.'

On entry into the cottage, the visitors could not contain themselves. They were welcomed by Catherine, but their initial interest was in the large inglenook fireplace with its roaring fire, the beams that crossed and supported the ceiling, and the thickness of the walls. It was some time before they settled to think about taking their coats and scarves off, looking curiously into different parts of the dining room, the open staircase, and the structure of the sitting room. This was a group who were touring Europe on an educational fact-finding mission, but at this stage, the facts associated with a seventeenth-century cottage were all they were interested in. Peter and Catherine felt some pricks of pride as the Americans admired the rooms and especially the fabrics and the furniture, which they felt matched the charming Old World look of the cottage. It seemed that the hard work and dedication that the couple had expended on their moorland home had borne a fruit that could be enjoyed not just by themselves but also by those they invited through its doors.

Catherine had prepared a splendid meal, which began, for the particular benefit of the guests, with nicely risen, crisp Yorkshire pudding with sage and onion gravy. It was eaten as a starter in the traditional Yorkshire way.

'I hope you will enjoy this,' she said as she sliced the pudding in its pan, placed it on plates, and passed around the gravy boat.

The visitors watched one another asking, 'Do you put it straight onto the pudding?' and then proceeded to follow the advice given by Catherine. The pudding was followed by roast beef, roast potatoes, runner beans, and cauliflower topped with gravy and a slightly sharp radish sauce. Peter had extended to a good Bordeaux red and a Pouilly Fumé. The sweet consisted of a choice between apple crumble and bread pudding, both with custard. An attractive selection of cheeses with cream crackers was then brought to the table. The meal was rounded off with percolated black coffee and home-made cake. There was no doubt that the visitors enjoyed their meal, constantly making comments about how tasty it was and how different it was to what they had back home.

Throughout the meal, there was plenty of chatter of a professional nature, with the Americans using the opportunity to quiz Peter and Catherine about the English education system.

'How old are children when they start school in England?' someone asked.

'Well, it varies,' responded Peter. 'Some start as young as three in what are called nursery schools. Others will be five. It depends on what's available in the area in which they live. Indeed, in some places, children younger than three are taken in, generally to help working parents. The parents usually pay a small fee when that happens.'

'And which school can they go to? Can they choose any school?'

'I suppose in theory, they can, but it's more common to go to a school within what's called the catchment area. Schools have stipulated areas from which they draw their pupils, but if there are places in other schools to which parents prefer to send their children, they can apply. Sometimes, they get a place. Sometimes, not. It varies from area to area and on the popularity of different schools.'

Catherine then added, 'There are also independent schools, of course, which charge a fee, and some parents prefer to send their children to them. Some of these schools also provide for boarders, you know children who stay overnight. I'm sure you'll have something similar in the States.'

There were looks of agreement around the table. 'Yes, it suits those who work abroad or are in the forces, or who simply want a different educational experience for their children. We've heard of places like Eton and Harrow and we also have schools, such as Phillips and Deerfield.'

'Don't forget St Paul's,' added another one of the guests, who obviously had some connection with the school and didn't want it to be missed off the list.

'There are plenty of other schools which offer boarding, of course,' said Peter. 'For some pupils, it's full-time, and for others, it's weekly, which means they go home at the weekends.'

'And at what age do children leave school?'

'Again, there's no simple answer. Officially, the leaving age is the term in which a youngster reaches fifteen. It can be Christmas, Easter, or summer. Some carry on to sixteen because they want to get some qualifications, and a minority go into what we call the sixth form and leave at eighteen or nineteen. Generally, those who stay on to eighteen go on to college or university, whilst the others tend to go into various kinds of work.'

'Fascinating,' said one of the Americans. 'As I'm sure you know, we've a few problems in the States. The question is not just about racial inequality but also about the comparative quality of education across different districts. Any American, no matter what their colour, who lives in a prosperous district has access to a decent education. It's the people who live in poor areas who struggle. Children in the poor, inner-city areas and the small, country areas of the South, where racism is still endemic, are the ones who suffer most.'

'Hang on a minute,' interrupted another visitor. 'You know it's not that simple. Different researchers come out with different views on the issue of who does best. I read somewhere that school funding has little effect on student achievement. A lot depends on their parents' expectations and their own desire to do well.'

'I agree that a student's family background is important, but I'm pretty sure that most pupils who come from a wealthy socio-economic background do better than those who don't; it's more to do with economic status than simply the desire to do well,' added one of the ladies in the group. 'How d'you expect a child from a poor area, where schools are deprived, to do as well as one in an area where schools can provide a much wider range of opportunities, can pay for the best teachers, and will certainly have good parental support?'

This exchange of opinions started a heated discussion among the Americans, which was only interrupted when Peter suggested that perhaps the issues were not that different in England.

'Here,' he said, 'the thrust of change seems to be towards providing equal opportunities for all children. Even so, those from poorer areas may still be disadvantaged. It will be interesting to see if what some would describe as "de facto segregation" disappears if the changes being discussed over here are ever introduced. Talk is of a reorganisation of schools designed to avoid segregation and give every child an equal chance. It's been traditional for pupils to be in what we call infants schools from age three to five, in junior schools from five to eleven, and in senior schools from eleven to fifteen, sixteen, or eighteen. It's at eleven that pupils currently get split, the so-called brightest going to grammar schools and the others going to secondary modern schools like the one where I teach.'

'Yes' said Catherine. 'An idea currently circulating is that children of all abilities should go to the same school. Lots of ideas are being slung around, and there's a possibility of different systems emerging in various parts of the country, rather in your style in the States. Of course, some people are totally opposed to such a change, wanting their children to go to what they consider the top school, a grammar school. But what's different?'

'I know what you mean. No matter how many changes there are, not much seems to change. But would there be just one school for the whole town?' asked an American.

'Here, in Binkley, yes. But it depends on the size of the town. In the largest towns and cities, there would be several,' said Peter.

'You see, that's the problem and that's the issue in the States, especially in a place like New York, where I live. I bet my bottom dollar that if there is more than one school, they'll be in different areas and that one will be thought to be more successful than the other. What does that do to so-called equality?'

'It's true, as Catherine said, that not everybody agrees with changing the system because it could lead to the disappearance of the grammar school. But to some, it would have the good outcome that families do not become divided. Thus, it avoids placing one child in one school and another in a different school, which can be a nightmare for some families.'

'So a key question for you, as it is for us,' chimed in one of the Americans, 'is how d'you ensure that every child has an equal chance?' It was a comment that gained acquiescing nods around the room.

'I think that's where we are at. I remember in the case of one of my friends,' added Peter, 'he passed his 11+ and went to the grammar school whilst his sister went to the local secondary modern school. Does that sound equality of opportunity?'

'It'll be interesting to see what the situation is in the rest of Europe, especially Russia,' said one of the Americans, which centred the visitors on what they might find in other areas they were visiting and brought the discussion about English education to an end.

The friendliness and openness of the Americans indicated that they were thoroughly enjoying themselves. They were prepared to discuss and even argue about the quality of their own system, listen in learning mode to the proposed developments in the English system, and predict what they might find elsewhere. The evening appeared to pass, as such pleasant occasions invariably do, very quickly. The compliments to Catherine's cooking flowed along with the wine.

For Peter, however, there was an issue growing more serious by the minute. Stationed where he was at the end of the table facing the window, he could see through the chinks in the curtains. He had deliberately left on the light by the front door so that he could keep an eye on what was happening outside. The clouds over the *Beacon* earlier in the evening had begun to deliver their threat and scurries of light snow had begun to dart across the road, carried by the growing wind. Throughout the meal, Peter could just see the snow was still falling. In fact, as the evening progressed, it looked as though it was increasing in intensity. As dinner finished and the guests retired to the sitting room, Peter took the opportunity to slip out through the front door, take his coat from its hanger in the porch, and with a torch make his way hurriedly up the road.

The snow was still falling, the flakes large and soft and forming a half-inch-thick carpet across the road. There were no tracks from passing vehicles, which was invariably a sign that the steep hills were already proving difficult. Peter continued up the slight incline to the place he knew the snow drifted, and his concern increased as he saw that the snow was gathering at its usual spot. Fortunately, the wind was not too strong, and as yet it was not a desperate situation, but if the snow continued to fall and his guests continued to enjoy their visit, things could be tricky. Once again, the moor was having its say.

As he returned to the cottage he heard one of the Americans saying, 'I've just looked through the window on my way back from the rest room and I saw a guy with a torch coming down towards the cottage. Do you know who it might be?'

Peter owned up, not by word, but by the showering of snow coming off his shoulders as he shook himself in the doorway. All this caused merriment but no obvious concern on the part of the guests, who

470

clearly knew little of life on a moor. The evening continued, the Americans gathered round the welcoming fire in the sitting room, and the conversation and drinks continued to flow.

Catherine began to share Peter's anxieties, and from time to time, their eye contact revealed their growing concern. A quiet moment in the kitchen gave them the opportunity to discuss the situation.

'Are you going to be able to get them back to Binkley?' asked Catherine.

'At the moment, yes,' he responded, 'but I don't know how late I dare leave it. On the one hand, we cannot ask them to leave, yet on the other we don't have the wherewithal to be able to keep them overnight.'

Catherine looked thoughtful and whispered, 'Well, two could go into our bed. We can put the girls in one room and use the other for the other guests, one in the single bed and the other on the floor. We can sleep in the sitting room.'

Peter looked at her with genuine amazement. 'You've got to be kidding. Nobody on this earth could see that as a solution. How can we ask them to share a bed? And then he added jokingly, 'I wouldn't mind sharing one with the blond girl. Have you chosen your partner yet?'

'I can't see any other solution,' said Catherine, and then mockingly she added, 'I fancy the one in red trousers.' In a more serious manner, however, she continued. 'I mean, they haven't come prepared for an overnight stop, and let's be honest, there's no guarantee that things will be any better tomorrow morning.'

'Please ask to go back to the hotel,' muttered Peter as he stared upwards as if to ask the spirits to intervene and encourage the Americans to bring the evening to a close.

But back in the sitting room, the entertaining continued for another hour before one of the guests stood and said, 'It must be time to go. We've had a lovely evening, one which we will treasure. If you are ever in the States, you must look us up.'

'It's been a delight,' Catherine responded genuinely. 'I hope the rest of your trip goes well.'

Peter agreed that it might be wise to make a move and head for the hotel. 'The snow's been falling whilst we've been enjoying ourselves. Let's hope that we can make it to the hotel without any trouble.'

By now, the Americans were registering some anxiety, but as they put on overcoats, scarves, gloves, and headgear, they continued to thank Catherine and Peter profusely for their hospitality.

Once outside, they realised the significance of what Peter had been saying. Their shoes gathered snow and the rising wind blew flakes into their faces. They piled back into the car, and Peter began the tortuous journey back to the hotel.

The skill that Peter had developed to descend, cope with the bends, and manage the sharp slopes with limited use of the brakes stood him in good stead. He relied almost completely on the smooth transition from one gear to another as he responded to the nature of the road and kept the car running smoothly, without acceleration or severe braking. He had to use his brakes occasionally—the steepness of the descent forced it upon him—but the steadiness of his speed through the choice of the appropriate gear and his use of brakes only on the straight enabled him to negotiate the bends and the steepest slopes.

There was some excitement as he felt the car begin to slide on one of the tricky bends, and for a second, the Americans stopped talking and seemed to be holding their breath. He managed to regain control, however, and proceed even more cautiously. His concern was more for his American guests than for himself, and he felt some slight exhilaration when overhead lighting announced that they were in Binkley. It was with great relief that he arrived at the visitors' hotel, shook them by the hand, and bade them goodnight and a good journey on the morrow.

He could not avoid the wry comment, 'I'm sure what you're experiencing at the moment will stand you in good stead for your visit to Russia.'

'We're looking forward to it,' replied one of the jocular American gents as they climbed the steps to the hotel entrance. 'Good night, and thanks again.'

Now for the return.

For Peter, it was time to consider his journey home. Fortunately, the snow had not yet reached an impassable depth. His expert driving and his winter tyres ensured he reached home safely.

Not surprisingly, Catherine was delighted to see him. She had been busy in his absence, carrying the crockery and what was left of the meal into the kitchen and clearing away the tablecloth. She had also done much of the washing up. As a result, they could settle for a moment or two in the sitting room to enjoy their final drink of the evening whilst complimenting themselves on what they saw as the success of the occasion before retiring to bed.

Next morning, the moor was mantled with snow of a depth that forbade driving. Peter's tracks from the previous evening had disappeared, and silence seemed to overshadow everything. For Peter and Catherine, the peacefulness of the morning offered a wonderful contrast to their anxieties of the previous evening. Peter had no hope of making it to school and so contented himself with a phone call to let the secretary know. He was not surprised to hear that it was likely that several other staff and many of the children would also fail to get to school.

He looked forward to an enjoyable day at home, to improving on his skill in making snowmen with the children, snowballing Catherine if she put her head outside the door, and to the warm fire as evening crept in.

Some snow clearing along the path to the gate took up part of Peter's morning. This was followed by play in the snow with the children. The old sledge was brought from the barn and provided excellent transport for the children as they used the slope in the middle field to get as quickly as possible from top to bottom. Before long, they had snow in their boots, clinging to their backs, and reddening their faces. Peter sought to ensure that all had a fair go and that young James could also enjoy a ride. As usual, Katie was in charge, deciding whose go it was next or which pair could go down together.

Catherine also joined in the fun for a time, starting a snowball fight by slinging one at Peter. The children quickly joined in. Once this early activity ceased, the more serious matter of a snowman was suggested. And so the family set about rolling the snow, creating the shape, and then discussing how Cedric the snowman should be adorned. An old hat, scarf, and real buttons for his supposed coat were used to give him the appearance of a man about town. One of Peter's old briefcases, attached to the snowman's arm, completed the image. The children loved it.

For Catherine and Peter, the scene brought the moor alive and confirmed their faith in the benefits of what it offered to them and their children. In the crispness of the morning, with the snow carpeting everything in a flatness reminiscent of the calmest of seas and the sun shooting its winter rays to create sharp shadows, the children were at play, undisturbed and natural in their moorland surroundings.

The snow not only brought to a halt all the traffic on the moor but also in the valley below. A further call to school to check on how things might be for the next day informed Peter that the head was likely to keep the school closed because of the dangerous road conditions. He had already sent the children home at midday and could see no improvement on the morrow.

Peter also learned that, because of the treacherous road conditions, the Americans had been blocked in their hotel and were unlikely to see little else of England before their exit in search of the rest of Europe and, as he understood it, education in Siberia. *They should be well prepared for the last* became his thought for the day.

CHAPTER 36

THE FARMERS DISCUSS RIGHTS ON THE MOOR

Peter continued to play rugby throughout the family's period on the moor. His training regime included regular trips to the club ground, generally twice a week through the autumn and winter months, to train with the rest of the team. On the other days, as a result of his desire to play as well as he could and to be as fit as possible, he often did some training on the moor. This usually consisted of a brisk jog from the farm, following a path called Longridge, which started along the wall of his land, and then continued further into the moor. He used to turn right along another well-worn path, a trail fashioned by the feet of countless sheep, before turning right again to head for the road and the completion of his workout. From time to time, he stopped to do some exercises, usually designed to strengthen his arms, stomach muscles, and his legs. He looked to improve the contribution he could make to the team's efforts by the likes of press ups, pull ups, and sit ups.

On his training runs or during his walks across the moor with his family, Peter could not avoid contact with sheep. They roamed freely, but within a flock, and seemed to know which bit of the moor was designated as their grazing. The different flocks never seemed to quarrel or dispute their territory. They were only a nuisance to Peter when they attempted to mount the wall round the front of the cottage and break into the garden. Fortunately, this was rare.

Peter knew that the means of controlling livestock numbers on the moor was by 'stint', written into the deeds of each property and Peter had such a 'stint'. When he had discussed the deeds of the cottage with the solicitor he had clarified what it meant for him.

Peter had come across the system when studying history. He knew that in the past, stinting was designed to ensure that there was a reasonably fair division of the use of the common land. It also provided a system through which the farmers could settle disputes; for example, if one farmer believed that another farmer was putting more stock on to the moor than his stints allowed, he could challenge him by having it discussed at a meeting of local farmers.

When he had asked Maxine, during his purchase of the cottage about his stint and how the principle of stints were respected on the moor, she was pragmatic enough to suggest that in practice it was unlikely that anyone knew. How many stints different farmers had, or how many sheep they had the right to feed on the moor was probably a mystery. As a result, she admitted that it was likely that the system was not operating in the way intended.

What Maxine had had to say about stints did not surprise Peter, as it did not surprise his friend Brian. Maxine did say, however, 'The farmers do have a meeting from time to time, and I assume that matters such as this are discussed. What conclusions they reach, of course, I've no idea.'

'They don't publish minutes of their meetings then,' joked Peter.

It was later, when Peter was talking with Jack and discussing the lease of the land, that the question of stinting arose again. Jack asked, 'What does tha' intend doin' wi' the' stint?'

Peter had given it little thought but, faced with the question, the answer seemed obvious. 'I suppose it makes sense for you to use it, Jack, as I've no stock.'

Jack was obviously pleased with the answer, but before he could turn to leave Peter commented, 'I'm intrigued to know if there are any disputes about the use of the moor and how the farmers usually settle them.'

'It's t' practice up 'ere for agreement on how t'common land should be used should be left to t'local farmers who already have stints, no matter how they gor'em. These meetings decide who owns what, how t'land's to be shared, and how any disputes settled.'

'How often do you meet?' asked Peter.

'Not regularly. Just when there's a problem. I'd reckon I've been to two in t'years I've lived up 'ere,' replied Jack.

It struck Peter that such a system, the gatherings of the local farmers, would have helped these non-unionised men develop the skills of negotiation. Fascinatingly, their discussions relating to the common land and its use, and the agreements reached, would bear the weight of community, despite the fact that such a meeting held no legal authority. It would be left to each individual farmer to guarantee that the agreements were kept.

When Peter asked, 'Does the system work well?' Jack took off his cap, scratched his head, put his cap back on at the right angle, and went on to say rather disparagingly, 'Tha's got t'undertand that t' stints are property that can be traded, loaned, sold or simply given away. That means that nobody really knows who owns what. I'm sure that some a' t'farmers claim well beyond what's their registered number a' stints. I also reckon that some register their rights more than once, and others claim more grazing than they should, especially if they 'ave what's called a right 'without number'. So far it 'ant bin a problem up 'ere.'

Peter began to understand that these informal and varying arrangements that had been allowed on the upland commons inevitably led to a good deal of confusion and vagueness. It was unlikely that anyone knew as to how many sheep, or for that matter geese, should be grazing on particular areas of common land at any one moment. It struck him that it would not be surprising to find far more sheep than agreed on the land and in some instances more than the land could properly support.

Peter learned, now that he was involved with matters to do with the moor, that it was not only he who was intrigued by this issue. There was growing concern nationally. Eventually, he heard that the Government had taken the decision to set up a Royal Commission to look in to the regulations concerning common lands and their use.

It was during one weekend in mid-summer that a paper was pushed through the cottage letterbox. It was from Mr Rissington, and from the quality of the English it had been written with the advice of someone more schooled in letter writing than one would expect from a person who had spent his life farming. It read as follows.

Rowland Farm

Dear Friends,

A recent report by the Royal Commission on Common Lands has led to the Commons Registration Act 1965. This provides for the registration of all common land and of town and village greens and the numbers of livestock that use them. It clearly applies to the use of our own moor.

As a result, there will be a formal meeting of local stint holders on Wednesday the 14th of the month at 7.00 p.m. at Orchard Farm. It will be important for you to bring with you any evidence you have of your holdings on the moor.

If you have any questions about the new Act you can refer to the Town Hall, where a copy has been placed for public information.

Please be kind enough to be prompt to the meeting.

Yours faithfully

Anthony Rissington

Peter read the letter with interest. He spoke to his tenant about the implications, not only for the two of them, but also for the users of the moor in general. Peter had rights, clearly recorded in his deeds to the cottage, and although he had passed these over to Jack as part of his tenancy, he believed himself to have remained the legal owner and so had a duty to attend the meeting. He was keen to participate in what he considered a significant historical event, a meeting replicating those he had read about and had taught about in his history lessons. In a sense, this was his main interest, and ensuring that his common rights were protected was only a secondary purpose.

As the day for what he regarded as a magical meeting approached, Peter could hardly contain his excitement. He had taught pupils about the significance of the village moot in Medieval history, and how this had given the freemen of the village the opportunity to discuss and decide on village affairs. *Am I about to participate in such a noteworthy event?* he pondered. To him, the meeting had a special significance, one that he felt was likely to be lost on many of his neighbours. This was because he believed that such gatherings, in their own small way, had helped develop a sense of local democracy across the country in a manner that he thought had been rarely practised in many other areas of Europe. He had often wondered to what extent these early seedlings had helped to prepare the freemen of England for the responsibilities engendered by the 1832 Reform Act.

At the appointed time, Peter made his way down the narrow lane that led to Rissington's farm. He did not know what to expect—*Who would be present? What form would the meeting take? How was it likely to affect the holdings on the moor and the number of sheep each farmer was allowed?* were the questions revolving in his mind as he pushed his way through the gate. No matter, his anticipation was high as he deliberated about the meeting in which he was about to be involved. He expected the experience to take him beyond the history books he had studied, and into a world he thought had passed. For him, mentally romanticising, this meeting offered the opportunity to play a part in history itself.

The unusually large front room of the cottage was crowded with the local farmers when he arrived. He was struck by the apparent sameness of the jackets they wore, their cloth caps, and the uniformity of the rugged weather-beaten faces. All had taken their boots off at the door. In what appeared to be small friendship groups of twos and threes they were exchanging their thoughts on grazing the common land, and expressing quietly their views on the new regulations. On the floor, in the middle of the room, were some old papers, with turned up corners, displaying hints of yellow streaks; papers covered with that carefully crafted script of earlier years. A few of those assembled were looking over the papers, occasionally pointing a finger and uttering a knowing 'Hmm'. There was none of the social additives that Peter would have expected had he been meeting with colleagues from school, the rugby club, or with friends socially. No one offered tea or a drink of stronger brew. This was a meeting for business, not a social gathering. Peter was the only person present who was not a farmer, but he felt none of the general animosity that he might have expected in some other gatherings, even though some of the farmers would not have known his business there.

Eventually, Mr. Rissington, this is what Peter had always called him, by what appeared to be general agreement assumed the role of Chairman and called the meeting to order. He was without a cap and in a smarter jacket than most. Peter was impressed by the almost instantaneous silence Rissington's voice commanded and the attention given to him. It became clear that Rissington was of long standing in the village, and this made him something of an authority figure. He commanded attention and others listened.

'We all know that we've to submit a record of our holdings to the appropriate authorities. What I suggest is that we each declare the extent of our rights and how many sheep we have on the moor. We can then total up and fill in the form. I'll sign it and then send it off.'

All nodded in agreement, though as Peter looked around he marvelled at the seeming belief that such a complex issue would be resolved so easily. He sat quietly and observed. He was fascinated by the general acceptance of what was proposed, the easy recognition given to Rissington, his role, and the general brusqueness of the proceedings.

One by one the farmers began to indicate how many stints they had and how many sheep they were grazing on the moor. Peter made his case, adding that he had loaned his stint to Jack. Others in the gathering looked at him quizzically.

'Is tha' sure?' one of the farmers asked in a doubtful sort of voice.

'It says so in the deeds' replied Peter, holding up the papers the solicitor had given him. Jack nodded his agreement.

As each farmer declared his rights, it was not long before it became obvious that there were far more sheep chomping on what the moor had to offer than expected. Questions produced answers such as, 'Well, wi've alus had this many, ever sin' mi' dad had t'farm,' and, 'When Jack left he said I cu'd have 'is stints,' and a third, 'Ah bought some stints off Bill Murgatroyd when 'e went o'er t'other side.'

T'other side was not identified, but it seemed to be an acceptable description for the rest of the group. Peter thought it might refer to the moor beyond the valley and hoped it didn't mean anything more sinister.

The actual stints marked on the aging papers bore no resemblance to what was actually happening on the moor. Although somewhat disconcerted, mostly because they did not know what the likely outcome of their discussion would be, no one showed any obvious surprise, though their general approach seemed to be summed up by a further interjection, 'Ah never agreed wi' stints in't fust place.'

It was not long before everyone present realised that the idea of reconciling the numbers of sheep with the actual stints was never going to work, and the attempt was abandoned. Nobody seemed to care, and there was no accusatory condemnation of anyone who was clearly grazing more sheep on the moor than he should have been. In fact, it seemed to be acceptable practice. As a result, discussion began to centre around how all this was to be resolved to the satisfaction of the Register.

'What wi' could do is add up t'stints wi' what wi' think wi' 'ave, see what wi' should 'ave according to t'paper you' 'ave there, and then mek' it fit', was one suggestion, though there was no indication as to how to, 'Mek' it fit'.

This was followed by, 'Let's just see how many sheep we're supposed to have, fill in t'form and send it off.'

'Hang on. Them darn in t'town hall will see that straightaway. Wi' ave to mek' it look as though we're doin' it proper.'

Peter watched with interest as various suggestions were made and were rejected. There had been no palpable tension in the room, other than at the stage when one farmer was challenged about the number of stints he was claiming, a claim well above what was regarded as an acceptable level. Gradually, the group swung away from trying to record anything like an accurate estimate of the numbers, and the main purpose of the meeting developed into finding a way to present unobservable facts.

'It won't be easy for anybody to check t'register, will it? Ha' can anybody do an accurate count o' t'number a sheep on t'moor at any one time.'

'Tha's reight, Jack. At different times o' t'year, we've different numbers a' sheep grazing. 'A' can't see how anybody can check 'em against any figures produced on t'form.'

According to the nodding heads of the gathering this was a fair assessment of the situation. The assembled farmers knew that, although nature had some control on their activities, it was not uncommon for them to collect their sheep from the moor at different times for different reasons.

The discussion went on in similar vein for a while, and it became clear to Peter that nobody wanted any change to what had become the traditional way of using the moor. Neither did they want any busybodies coming up from Binkley checking. Eventually, the farmers agreed that the solution was to complete the Register with the number of stints to which each farmer was willing to claim, pared down where necessary to what could be seen to be appropriate on the basis of the size of his holding. To help their calculations, it was agreed that they should ignore the bought or loaned stints.

'Does that mean I fill in t' form on that basis?' asked Rissington. 'It'll mean I have somehow to match t' notes I've been taking and the claims you've all been making to what's on those papers lying in front of us on the floor.'

'That's it, George. A' reckon we're all agreed on that.'

As he finished what he was saying, Will Gibson looked around for confirmation from his fellow farmers. Everybody was in agreement and no objection was raised. Rissington, who had started with the firm belief that he would be able to present a fair record of what was happening on the moor, now knew what he had to do. True to his status in the village, he accepted his responsibility. There was little doubt in Peter's mind that the difficulties would be reconciled, the form would be completed and the needs of the authorities satisfied. As to revealing the true nature of the grazing, that was another matter.

Peter had done nothing in the meeting other than respond when asked about his stint, and then nod towards Jack as a sort of verification that he had granted it to him. He had, however, thoroughly enjoyed what he had observed and could not help wondering to what extent the event he had witnessed reflected those moots of earlier days, and even the political bartering of the present. His knowledge of history suggested to him that moots may have been little different, but he wanted to believe that twentieth century politicians made use of more secure evidence before reaching important decisions.

After the meeting, he took leave of his neighbours, and with Jack headed for home.

'What did you think of the meeting, Jack?'

'Waste a time. I should ha' bin at home, lookin' after t'sheep.'

They both laughed and knew that things would continue as they had done for as long as the farmers wanted them to. For Peter, the history lesson was complete, and it would give him fascinating evidence to help him in teaching his pupils. Whether he could continue to talk about the merits of such activities in earlier times as representative of the beginnings of democracy, he would have to think.

CHAPTER 37

THE MOOR REVEALS MORE HISTORY

As Peter became more familiar with the moor and its surroundings, it revealed other aspects of its history. What he did not know was that his training runs took him past some fascinating historical artefacts. He was unaware that even whilst he was going through his paces, others were scouting the moor for what became archaeological finds of some significance. One was a Stone with a carved cup and ring motifs and the other was the remains of a Roman road.

The extraordinarily ornamented cup-and-ring stone, with its five full cup-and-rings, sat amidst a cluster of many other carvings on the same ridge. It had gone unnoticed by Peter, whose mind was on other things as he crossed the moor day after day, as had the Roman Road he had trodden without realising it. It was only later that he came across the story of the discovery and the guidance on how to find it.

A further discovery, but one strikingly more obvious, was the small monastery on the edge of the moor. It could be seen through the grove of trees by the family as they passed it on their way to town. When he learned that it was open for Sunday worship for those who could not get to the parish church in Binkley, Peter, Catherine, and the children occasionally took the opportunity to attend Mass in the chapel.

The chapel reflected its age. The narrow windows leaked the sun's rays during Mass and the well-worn statues, positioned in strategic places to catch the eye, reflected the light of goodness that their image sought to portray. Peter recognised that some were of an age when England was a Catholic country, preserved from destruction by the astuteness of the monks who sought to retain the old religion.

Inevitably, Peter's interest was aroused by the monastery's history. The chapel and surrounding buildings, with their Tudor windows and chimneys, were reminiscent of many that had survived from the sixteenth century. Peter had learned from his reading of a short history of the monastery, given in the booklet at the back of the chapel, that it was once the home and hunting lodge of a wealthy Catholic family. Its members had had an almost unbroken association with Catholicism. Their loyalty to the Church had been particularly significant during and after the reign of Elizabeth I, when the persecution of those who sought to avoid attending the services of the newly Established Church was often severe, and particularly so for Catholics who still subscribed to the old religion. The booklet described the early days of the Lodge, as it was called, and compared it with the homes of other recusant families who had continued to practise their Catholic faith, despite the stringent laws introduced by Elizabeth. The fact that the Lodge housed a priest, meant that there were opportunities for the local population to attend Mass and benefit from the Sacraments during the years of persecution.

This background was of particular fascination to Peter and he made use of it in his lessons when he sought to help his pupils understand the English Reformation and its outcomes. It fitted in well when he taught about the religious struggles during, and following, the reigns of the Tudors. It enabled him to localise a national event like the Reformation. He would explore with his class the lives of the famous such as Henry VIII, Cranmer, Thomas More, Edward VI, Mary and Elizabeth 1, and how their actions influenced the changes that took place. He would then endeavour to show how national events affected life locally, by referring to Weberton and its castle and churches, and how they responded to the changes.

When he reached the story of the Recusancy Laws, he was able to draw attention to the brief history of the monastery that he had collected from the back of the chapel. Together, the class would investigate what evidence they had, seeking to understand the methods by which religion developed as it had in England. This would bring them to the Commonwealth and the history associated with Oliver Cromwell and the Puritans. Inevitably, the story of *The King's Beacon* infiltrated his lessons, as did the threat of the new religions to Catholicism. He could not explain, however, why this chapel and several others in different parts of the country escaped the wrath of those Puritans who sought to destroy everything within them in the name of iconoclasm.

Wrapped in this background knowledge, Peter and Catherine always approached the chapel at the Lodge with admiration for those who had been prepared to risk everything in following their faith. It led to several discussions as to how they might have reacted if faced with similar circumstances.

A typical conversation on Sunday mornings, as they sat in the car on their short drive to the monastery, would be, 'I don't know whether I would have dared to go to church in those times. Is it any less worthwhile to pray at home and not put yourself at risk by going to a Mass?'

To Catherine's uncertainty, Peter would respond, 'But what about receiving the Sacraments? You can't do that at home. Without the Blessed Sacrament there doesn't seem a lot of point.'

'I see what you mean.' But then after a while, 'But what about those who live in places where for one reason or another there's no priest. They don't get the Sacraments, but they continue to believe and pray. Are they wasting their time?'

'I think that's a bit different. Those people are not making the decision not to go to Mass. They just can't. In this case, you'd be deciding not to go, and you'd be putting your own fears ahead of your so called beliefs. Is that the right thing to do?'

'Perhaps not, but I'm not sure I'd be brave enough to face up to the other option. Would you be?'

'How do I know?'

'D'you think it would be easier to get to church in a city or would it be better to live in a place like we do?'

And so the debate would go on, inevitably without any outcome, because neither Peter nor Catherine knew what they would do. They had read stories about the martyrs of different faiths, often empathising with their suffering, but they were unable to place themselves closely enough to the inner working of their minds to understand how they formulated the decision to challenge authority and risk all. Were the martyrs, like Peter and Webster, prone to spontaneous decisions, looking neither to right or left, and loathe to work through the outcome or full consequences of anything they decided to do? Or did they carefully reason out what they were doing? Did they recognise their dependence on a Supreme Being and hold to their faith, having weighed up the consequences of being caught and punished, being convinced that the risks were worth it? Such imponderables of the different faiths about which they knew were never far from the couple's thoughts, yet they never impinged on their beliefs.

Here in the twentieth century, Catherine and Peter recognized that the monks, their lives dedicated to their calling, had a way of celebrating Mass with a meaningful simplicity. It imperceptibly drew a more than usual pious response from the praying worshippers. And yet they were being challenged to consider further changes to the way they responded to God's calling. The Cardinals of the Church, through the Council Vatican II, were beginning to have a significant impact on the way Mass was celebrated; in particular the extent to which the congregation should become involved. English was to replace Latin, allowing the congregation to join in with some of the responses, and so feel much more involved in the Mass. Peter recognised that there were likely to be differences of opinion amongst the monks, just as there had been centuries ago, but he also recognised the willingness of most to keep in step with the changes and so adjust their practice to serve the requirements of the faithful.

CHAPTER 38

THE KNIFE

Peter was in the front garden, shaping the border of the path with some loose stones, when Catherine came running out of the house.

'They've found the knife. The police, the police have found the knife,' she repeated, excited beyond measure and repeating the information as if to convince herself rather than Peter.

'What's happened?' asked Peter as he jerked up straight with expectation.

Catherine continued. 'As you know, the police had to re-investigate the crime after Joseph was found not guilty. It was obvious that either Trevor or Will had done the mugging. According to the news, they have been crawling through all the evidence again and carefully examining the areas where the boys were known to have been. You'll remember they came up here.'

'How can I forget,' said Peter.

'Surprise, surprise. The knife has reappeared.'

It was a fact that the police had been embarrassed by the outcome of the trial. Grossman could not believe that Joe had been found not guilty, but he had to accept the fact. As a result, he had ordered another detailed examination of all the evidence. Several more trips had been made between the town hall and The Dragon in order to check the accuracy of the timings. The thoroughness with which these new investigations were carried out confirmed, much to Grossman's chagrin, that Catherine was right, and that Joe could not have arrived at the scene in time to be directly involved in the mugging. How the mistakes had been made he could not explain, but the fact was that the wrong boy had been accused.

The three boys had also been questioned again. Despite the intensity of the interrogation, which stemmed from the fact that the police knew that one of them was the guilty party, they had held to their stories. Makin and Skelton knew that so long as the one did not betray the other, and the knife remained missing, the police would have difficulty in proving who was guilty. It was also an oddity that, although they had betrayed Joe, they trusted he would not betray them.

The police tried the usual gambit of questioning the boys separately and strongly hinting that one had incriminated the other, but even this did not break the boys' determination to stick with their original description of the crime. The presence of a solicitor and of a parent ensured that they felt sufficiently supported in front of the police, and their previous experiences of police questioning, both in relation to this crime and to other misdemeanours, provided them with obstinacy beyond the norm.

It became increasingly obvious to Inspector Grossman that the solution to the case rested on the finding of the knife, and then proving to whom it belonged. So far, the boys had given no inkling as to whose it was or where it might be, and it was clear that they had no intention of providing that or any other helpful information. As a result, he had drafted in extra police to do an inch by inch search along the route taken by the boys. At the same time, the canal that ran through the town and bordered on the park was searched by police frogmen.

The interest in the case raised in the town was immense. It led to people who were going to work or simply for a walk scanning the pathways and gardens, as they were unconsciously drawn into the exercise. It seemed as if the whole town became involved in the search, determined to bring the criminal to justice and some respectability back to the town.

The police also did a check of the road up to the cottage, and two police officers spent a day searching the barn, outhouses and nearby field in the hope of finding something connected with the case. They even climbed *The King's Beacon* to visit the cave where Webster had hidden. Catherine, in her investigative manner, enjoyed walking with them and talking to them about this as well as the other cases in which they were involved. Her enquiries were augmented by cups of tea and biscuits, welcomed by the officers. Eventually, when they were satisfied that there was nothing that might impact on the case, with a cheerful, 'Cheerio,' they headed back to town.

With the head's permission, Grossman had also spoken to the pupils at the school during assembly to ask if anyone knew if one of the boys had a knife. He also asked the pupils to keep an eye out in case they came across something that could be useful to the police. He advised them how they could contact him, wisely adding that they should do so with at least one of their parents, and that a small reward was being offered by Mr Mann's family for any information likely to lead to the conviction of the boy responsible for the knifing. Unfortunately, the responses that he received failed to move the investigation forward, as they indicated that all three boys had knives at one time or other.

When it seemed that nothing more could be done and that the knife would never be found, the police had a call from a hiker who had been on the moor. As it had begun to rain, he had taken shelter in the cave on the *Beacon*, and whilst rummaging in the various corners had found a knife under a heap of stones. Like so many other people, he was aware of the Mann case and the interest created by the lost knife. As he thought it might be evidence, he left it where it was. When he got back home he rang the police.

'I hope you didn't do anything with it,' the sergeant on duty replied, 'and that you left it where you found it.'

'Well, I did. I knew the interest and so felt it better to report it than do anything else.'

At speed, the police were in the cave and inspecting the knife. It was a flick knife of the sort forbidden but still carried by some youths. It was soiled, the result of lying in the damp cave for several weeks. It was unlikely that it would still carry any fingerprints or blood samples, but Grossman was convinced that if the knife did belong to one of the boys, its reappearance would put them under pressure to tell the truth. Unusually, it had a multi-coloured casing which made it quite distinctive.

The cave and the surrounding area on *The King's Beacon* had been searched earlier. The knife had been missed and the only reason that could explain this was the failure of the police to carry out their search with sufficient assiduousness. Grossman believed it should have been discovered, particularly as it was here that Joe Webster had taken refuge during his flight from the police. He began to consider what action he should take against his officers who had been, seemingly, so negligent. But first, he had to have a confession.

The cave soon became a crime scene. The police were anxious to discover anything that might point to the killer, and all the circumstantial evidence seemed to indicate that this could be the knife used in the crime. If the knife was the killer weapon, suspicion was thrown back on Webster, as being the only one of the three to have visited the cave. There was no doubt that Webster could have hidden it. Whether he had used it was a different matter.

Inspector Grossman was convinced that he had the solution to his crime. It seemed that *The King's Beacon* had played another important role in the story of the Yorkshire Moors.

Back in the station, the three boys were shown the knife and questioned as to its ownership. It was clear from the look on Will's and Joe's faces, and the conviction of their declarations, that neither was the owner. In Trev's case, a reddish colouring in his cheeks and a lowering of his eyes were immediate signs that he recognised what he was being shown. Grossman had his man. It did not take long for him to extract a confession from Trevor and to be able to charge him.

'You recognise this knife, don't you Trevor?' he asked after giving the lad some time to think and to look at the incriminating evidence.

'I'm not sure,' came the hesitant reply.

'Trevor, it will not take long to show the knife to those who know you. D'you think they'll recognise it?'

Trevor's solicitor leaned towards him and whispered in his ear. What he said confirmed for Trevor that the game was up and he realised that he had no option but to make a full confession. With anxiety spreading across his face he dropped his eyes, and muttered, 'OK, it wa' me. 'Ah saw Mr Mann come out a' t'Dragon with his wallet for everybody to see. Ah said to Will, let's get the wallet. When Will med no effort to move I ran across t'road and snatched it. The old guy tried to pull it back and so 'ah took mi' knife out as a sort of threat. Afore I knew what wer' 'appening, the guy stumbled forrard and the knife went in. Onest, ah didn't mean it.'

He looked appealingly at Grossman who, without any change in his expression said, 'Carry on, Trevor.'

'Anyway, ah ran back to t'other side to Will, just as Joe cem round t'corner and that Mrs Bell screamed. We decided to run for it and Joe joined in. When we got to t'park, we thought we wer' safe, and so we stopped. Ah looked in t'wallet and fan thi'ty pounds. We decided to share it. It wa' just then when t'police arrived. Will and me wer' a bit slow and got caught, but Joe shot off in t'opposite direction.'

'How did the knife come to be in the cave up at *The King's Beacon*?' queried Grossman.

'When we 'eard the police I pushed t'knife into Joe's hand and told him to get rid of it for me. When we split he 'eaded for t'canal and got' away. I suppose 'e 'id t'knife in t'cave.'

'Are you sure that that is what happened?'

'Yes' said Trev.

Grossman looked across at Trev's solicitor. 'I need all this in a written statement. Could you help him put it together? Then he needs to sign it.' He looked again at Trev. 'If you had told us all this in the first place, life it would have been a lot simpler for a lot of people.'

It would certainly have been simpler for Catherine and Peter. When they heard how the knife had ended up at the top of the *Beacon* they could only look at each other with shock. They had trusted Webster, though they were never fully convinced of his innocence or guilt, but he had quite deliberately misled them about the knife. They found this difficult to accept. Catherine, in particular, expressed her sadness, and Peter, within the privacy and quietness of the cottage, had to console her, explaining that he too was upset, and also surprised by Webster's concealment of such an important fact.

As he put it to Catherine, 'I know that Webster's a shocker, but in the past he's always been prepared to accept responsibility for what he's done wrong. For some reason, he seemed to act out of character by not telling the full truth.'

Not wishing to lose his grip on the strengthening relationship he had created with Webster, and not wishing to think ill of him, he added, 'I've no doubt he saw it as staying loyal to his mates. We'll never know for sure, but I reckon there is something of that in it.'

Peter knew that Webster should have been more honest, but he was glad to find words that gave Catherine some comfort in the face of what had emerged with the finding of the knife.

It was a couple of days later at school, when he was discussing the story of the knife, that his friend Stan said, 'It's obvious what happened. Webster knew that if he told about the knife he would be pinning the blame directly on his mate Trevor Makin. We know that to blame somebody else is out of character for Joe. He couldn't admit to having a knife because he didn't have one. But neither could he say that Makin had one. So, it was simpler for him to say he knew nothing about a knife.'

Stan's explanation was so palpable that Peter kicked himself for not having seen it himself. When he related it to Catherine, she also saw that it made sense and excused, to some extent, Webster for not telling them the full truth.

The confession by Trev gave the police everything they needed. Along with the wallet that had been taken from the boys when they were arrested, they now had the knife and the name of its owner. They had a cast iron case to take to court.

The retrial was not as fraught for Peter and Catherine as had been the previous trial. The police and prosecution had sufficient evidence to prove that Trev had been the main perpetrator of the mugging, and they set out the new evidence with clarity and confidence. The prosecution produced the knife so that the jury could see it, and pointed out that Trev was the owner. Trev's confession was also produced as part of the evidence. This established that Will had been no more than a supporter in the crime, had remained by the fish and chip shop, and had not crossed the street or been part of the attack. It was now clear that Joe also had played no part in the crime until he had joined Will and Trev after it had been committed, and then run away with his pals. His involvement was limited to taking a share of the stolen money and trying to hide the knife. Once the jury had heard the prosecution case, they retired to reach a judgement.

The jury returned to the court room within half an hour. They had found Trev guilty of manslaughter and Will and Joe guilty of being willing participants in the robbery. The Judge, accepting the verdicts, said he would delay sentencing until further psychiatric tests had been carried out on the boys.

It was two weeks before the judge called the boys back to court for sentencing. He had had the psychiatrist's report and other information that he felt he needed before sentencing.

Looking at the boys as they stood in the dock, he asked 'Before I sentence you, have you anything you would like to say?' His tone was more conciliatory than it had been at any time during the trial.

The boys said, almost in unison, 'No, Your Honour.'

With that the judge gave sentence. 'Trevor Makin, you have been found guilty of manslaughter. I have taken into consideration your age and the fact that you did not intend to do more than steal a wallet, a dreadful crime in itself. Nevertheless, a good man has died as a result of your action. You will serve ten years, firstly in a juvenile detention centre and then in prison. William Skelton, although you were no more than an observer when the crime was committed, you are guilty of withholding important evidence, deceiving the police and taking a share of the gains from the crime. You will serve three years in a detention centre. And Joseph Webster, although you were not present when the crime was committed, but joined the other two boys and then hid critically important evidence from the police, you are guilty by association and will serve four years in a detention centre.'

The measure of the sentences surprised no one. The seriousness of the crime could not be overestimated. For Mrs Mann, the boys got what they deserved, but it in no way compensated for the loss of her husband. Peter and Catherine, although their sympathy for Webster, who had been drawn into the crime, remained, recognised that he had received his just deserts. Their hope was that the time he spent in the detention centre would do something to help him develop the sort of social responsibility that would help him avoid similar problems in the future.

CHAPTER 39

PETER MAKES ANOTHER IMPORTANT DECISION

It was on the moor, lit by a full moon, and full moons are said to carry some mystery, that the significance of Peter's decision really struck him.

Peter had invited some of his former pupils, members of the brass group, for dinner towards the end of the autumn term. He wanted to know if they had settled after school, what they were doing, and, incidentally, if they could pass on anything that might be useful to him in his teaching. He also wanted to know how many of them were still involved in any kind of brass group. Catherine ensured that they were well fed with filo pastry, salmon parcels, pork loin with red onion marmalade, oven roast potatoes and ratatouille, followed by mixed gooseberry and blackberry tart with vanilla ice cream.

After coffee the moon was shining so brightly that, late as it was, the visitors invited Peter and Catherine to walk with them across the moor.

Catherine politely turned down the offer because of the children, who were already in bed, but Peter willingly accepted. He loved his moorland ramblings and on fine evenings such as this he would often wander out alone to enjoy the quiet solitude. His former pupils also made it obvious that they were enthralled with the cottage and the moor.

'It must be wonderful to live up here. It's so open and quiet. How long have you lived here sir?'

'Let's see. I suppose it's about eight years. With everything we've had to do it seems a lot longer,' said Peter with a smile.

'I think if I had the chance to live up here I would never surrender it. It's beautiful. I know from the visits we made when we were in the school band, your children love it,' mused Alan.

For a while, conversation ceased, as though all the ramblers wished to do was absorb the moor—the freshness of its air, the freedom of its space, and its unmatchable tranquillity. Their youthful expectations seemed to assume that what the moor offered that night was what it offered every night; the calm of late autumn, the full moon casting such a beam as to open up a view of the moor distinguishable in every respect from that seen in the light of its master the sun, and the comfort of companionship.

Peter couldn't help but be affected by the same feelings and began to wonder, as he felt the softness give way beneath his feet, the softness that brought back memories of the many times he had enjoyed the same sensation, whether or not he had made the right decision. It was a decision that was destined to take him away from what had become his beloved moor. His desire for promotion had drawn him into looking beyond his present school, and he had just taken a new post which meant that the family had to move on. Beguiled by the views that his former pupils were expressing so enthusiastically, he began to ask himself whether or not the spell of the moor was too strong for him to break.

As the boys and girls continued their discussion, Peter listened rather than contributed, engrossed in his own private thoughts. *Were they reinforcing what he already knew, that his selfish desire had once again led to a decision without proper consideration for the lives of those dearest to him; were they right in believing how wonderful it must have been for the children to have such a playground; and were their comments on how hard but satisfying it must have been renovating the cottage a fair assessment of how he and Catherine felt?* Peter could not escape the answer, *Yes,* within his own mind. But he knew himself well enough to know that such a response would not deter and, indeed, had not deterred him.

As they laughed at the sheep turning away from the walkers, and usually bounding no more than two or three yards to return to what they obviously considered safety, Peter's former pupils knew nothing of his intentions. They were absorbed in their walk and in their conversation. They had matured into young adults, seeking their own way through life's difficult maze, and almost all were still playing. Peter was pleased to hear that one or two had made excellent progress. Three of them, Joan, Alan and Arthur, were now with highly rated bands and making names for themselves in a world that had once been Peter's. He wondered what they would think when they learned that all they were now looking at would be forsaken in the summer, when he and the family opened up a new way of life in the Midlands.

Even though he watched his guests with interest, he could not prevent his thoughts turning back, for a moment, to Webster, and how the lad's unthinking action on the evening of his triumph at the concert had led to his mistake of becoming embroiled with Makin and Skelton. He reflected on the visits he had made to Webster during his incarceration and the sadness of his plight. But he also gained a feeling of satisfaction from learning that Webster had been given permission to continue to practise his trombone, loaned as it was by the school. At least he had helped the lad find something to hang on to, and as far as he could tell, something that might help him to escape the pointless life into which he could so easily be dragged.

Neither could he ignore how the moor, despite its many foibles, had helped him and his family find a new life. He, too, recognised that the freedom of the moor, the joys offered by the sounds of the diverse life it supported, and the oneness that the children had established with their childhood surroundings, compensated for the hours of toil in and around the cottage. The ambition to make the cottage and the moor a home for Catherine and the children had been largely achieved, and, together, he and Catherine could look back with some pride.

But with little consideration of the consequences, he was about to uproot the family once again. *What is it that stirs me into this desire to look for change?* he asked himself so many times. *Is it ambition, the desire to be seen to have reached the highest echelons of my chosen career? Is the desire for change so deep within my psyche that the motivating drive will not let me rest, but subtly encourages me to see justification in my next unforeseen step, no matter what the actual consequences are for Catherine and the family? Is it related to what I perceive as frustration at a measure of incompetence in my superiors, which stirs me into believing that I can do better? Is it something to do with my background and its expectation of change? Or am I simply a more fortunate Webster, a person who also has difficulty in explaining why I do things that have such a significant impact on my life?*

Are all people like this, he wondered, *with some being more fortunate than others? Or is it just me and the likes of Webster? Or am I really a scheming, ambitious person who refuses to recognise it and simply hides it, even from myself, under a fortuitous cloak of good fortune?* He knew he could ask himself questions forever without finding the answers, but he had to admit that many of the important decisions he made were from the heart rather than from the head. They came from an urge that this was what he wanted to do, and were rarely the result of a carefully worked out plan that could be coldly justified.

In Webster's case it seemed that his ill-thought out actions almost always led to failure, whilst as for his own situation, the spontaneity of his decisions had so far worked in his favour. Peter still believed that the outcomes of Webster's misguided choices provided some sort of satisfaction for those who looked to feed their own desires for success off the shortcomings of others, rather like the stage comic whose jokes live off other people's misfortunes. Although the lad's successful sojourn with the trombone must have thrown his detractors into disarray for a while, his current situation gave such people ample evidence of his failure. Peter, dawdling a little behind the strolling group, genuinely felt sorry for the lad and he wondered what the future held for him.

Once the couple had agreed there was no option but to sell the cottage, the local estate agent was called in to discuss how best to go about its sale. The discussion ranged over the price, the means of advertising, and the different ways in which the cottage might be sold.

'Mr Delaney, it's almost impossible to put a figure on the cottage. It's so unique. The work that has been carried out has made it a very desirable place in which to live. As you know, there isn't another place like it. I've no idea how much someone will be prepared to pay for it. I would suggest that, rather than trying to fix a price, we go to auction.'

'I tend to agree,' said Peter, for once looking at Catherine for some confirmation. She nodded. 'We'd need a reserve price on it and so we need some guidance as to an estimated price and reserve.'

'I agree,' said the estate agent. 'What I suggest is that you should try to work out a price by adding how much you initially paid for the cottage to what you've spent on it. I can then probably gauge what inflation may have added to it. If we can do that, we should be near enough a fair price."

On the following day, Peter called in to the estate agents with the figures that he and Catherine had discussed. After the estate agent had looked at them and done some calculations on his desk calculator, he came up with a price. 'It seems to me that we should have an estimate of fourteen to sixteen thousand, with a reserve at fourteen thousand. I think it will go for much more than that in all honesty, but what do you think?'

'That's fine by me,' said Peter. 'I just hope the right people come along. When d'you think it'll be a good time to hold the auction?'

'I think we need a couple of months to get out the papers and give people the chance to look over the property. The weather will be better then as well. We have a lot of people already on our books. I'm pretty sure from what they've said to me about other properties that some of them will be interested in the cottage.'

With that, Peter left and drove back to report to Catherine. After he had told her the outcome of his meeting with the estate agent, she agreed with Peter that it was a good price and should provide a good amount of money with which to buy their future home. The date for the auction also gave Peter and Catherine time to search for a house in and around their favoured location.

The interest shown in the cottage was immense when it went on the market. Lots of so called prospective buyers wished to look over it, though Peter and Catherine reckoned that many were just sightseers. There were even rumours of one interested party flying over the area in a helicopter to survey what surrounded the buildings.

In the meantime Peter and Catherine made several trips to the Midlands to look for their next home. Catherine identified the area where she wished to live. As usual, once she had come to terms with Peter's wish to move on, she entered wholeheartedly into the venture. Perhaps it was her continuing recognition that any promotion that Peter gained would be of benefit to the family as well as to him personally. Or perhaps, like Peter, she had within her that itinerant spark which, from time to time, blazed into a desire for new experiences. No matter, she did her research and was convinced that she had found the right place for the family.

'It has lots of lovely houses and some very good schools.'

'How far is it from my school?'

'It'll not be as far as you're travelling at the moment. The other factor is that there's a hospital in the town, and I may be able to get a position there.'

'If you like it, let's go ahead and look for a house.'

And so for once, Catherine's choice became the target.

It was not long before a suitable house was discovered and then the bargaining began to try to reach a reasonable price. As the house was being sold by a company, it did not take too long to agree a figure. Without knowing the actual sale price of the cottage, Peter could not estimate the mortgage they may need, but with his increase in salary and the prospect of Catherine finding full-time work, this did not seem the major obstacle it once did. In fact, it would place them in a similar position to almost all their friends.

The prospect of a good sale for the cottage was going well. Interest continued and more people found their way to the cottage. At last, the auction day arrived.

Peter and Catherine went to the auction room nervous, but full of hope. Among those collected in the room were a number of local people whom they recognised, and who had obviously come to see how things might turn out. Peter dismissed these as not very serious bidders. There were a few strangers, but not as many as Peter had hoped. In fact, he could not recognise any of the many prospective buyers as people who had visited the cottage and had expressed an interest in it.

They were greeted by the auctioneer as they entered the auction room and were given seats in the front row, being advised that it was a good thing for prospective buyers to be able to see from whom they were buying. After a brief chat, in which the auctioneer commented with that confident sweep of the eyes of a man in control, 'There's been a wide range of interest in the cottage and I'm pretty sure we will have a good sale.'

These were the sorts of words that the young couple were delighted to hear and as the auctioneer stood to make his way to the rostrum they wished him good luck.

Peter's and Catherine's nervousness increased as the auction began. Both had attended the occasional auction as prospective buyers before, but neither had ever sold at auction. This was a new experience. They had had little to do with the production of the flyer describing the cottage, or of making sure that it reached those who might be interested in buying it. All this had been left to the highly respected local agency. On the basis of their discussions with the agent, Catherine and Peter had no doubt that the cottage would sell. Their only concern was for how much.

The auction started, slowly. The auctioneer's first request was for a bid just below the reserve price. Nothing. Peter sat unconcernedly, believing that bidders were biding their time to see how the competition was likely to respond. The auctioneer dropped the price to ten thousand, and then received his first bid. A further five hundred came in and then eleven thousand. It seemed that at least two people were keen on the cottage, and in auctions Peter believed that was all that was needed to keep the price rolling upwards. Then suddenly all went quiet.

The auctioneer cajoled those present by describing the benefits of the cottage, by indicating what a good deal it was, and how he had expected it to do much better. All to no avail. Eventually, he came across and sat down next to Peter.

'Nobody is bidding. I can't believe it. We have had so many people into the office to make serious enquiries, and yet I can't see more than one in the room. In fact, we have only got it to eleven thousand as a result of a bid from a complete stranger. What do you want me to do? Do I go back and try again, or do you want to sell for eleven thousand?'

'Can't do that,' said Peter, having the cost of their new house in mind. 'Go back and see what you can do. I can't afford to sell below the reserve price.'

During this conversation the hubbub in the room increased as first one, and then another, turned to a neighbour to comment on what was happening. It was as if nobody had foreseen such an outcome. By now, both Catherine and Peter were becoming increasingly apprehensive. They had put in an offer for their new house and they were facing the possibility of a no sale on the cottage. The high hopes of the morning were sinking, apparently with little prospect of being able to resurface.

The auctioneer returned to the rostrum, took up his gavel and started again. 'I've given you a little time to think about the cottage, and I would like to start the bidding again. Can I have a bid of eleven thousand five hundred?' Up went a hand.

Twelve thousand?' He had another bid.

Thirteen thousand?' On this figure time seemed to stand still before at last, more hope, another bid.

But that was it. Silence. The auctioneer looked at Peter and Catherine. Peter shuffled his feet, nudged Catherine and her response confirmed his own thoughts. A shake of his head brought the auction to a close. The cottage was not sold! What would Peter have given to have his former headteacher in the auction room at that moment?

The auctioneer joined Peter and Catherine. He was at a loss as to what to say. They all agreed that the auction had been a disaster. In the confusion caused by the no sale neither the auctioneer nor Peter was able to grasp the initiative and suggest what should be the next move, other than to agree that it would be a good thing to talk next morning.

Catherine's and Peter's disappointment was tinged with embarrassment as they left the room, passing one or two friends who expressed their sympathy on the way. What were they to do now? Like a becalmed boat waiting for a fresh wind to give new life, Peter sat quietly in the car as he drove back up to the cottage. As he passed the different indicators of the many journeys he had made along that road, he sought to revive Catherine's as well as his own spirits. 'Well, at least, we didn't give the place away.'

'That's true,' Catherine replied, pushing back a tear in her pretence of brushing back a lock of her hair which had fallen across her forehead. Fully aware of her deep disappointment, Peter said nothing more. For the rest of the journey both wrestled with the implications of the failed auction.

Throughout the late afternoon and evening the same mood prevailed, with neither being able to come up with either a reason for the failure to sell or a solution to their problem. 'The only thing we can do is pray and hope,' said Peter as they settled in bed to try to sleep.

An then a remarkable thing happened. The family had hardly risen next morning when there was a phone call. The chap at the other end of the line wanted to know what had happened at the auction. 'No sale,' answered Peter, wistfully looking across the moor through the back window.

'Hmm. What did you really want for it?' came across the line.

'The reserve was fourteen thousand,' answered Peter, no longer concerned to keep quiet about what he thought to be auction secrets in a conversation he thought to be pointless. Nevertheless, he wondered what this guy was doing on the phone.

'Hmm' again. 'Tell you what, I'll give you the reserve price.'

Peter could not believe his ears. Here was the best bid he had had and it was not at the auction. He tried to keep his cool, answering, 'OK. You go in and see the estate agent at nine o'clock to confirm, and it's yours'.

Once off the phone, Peter gleefully went across to Catherine, gave her the news and took her into his arms. She could not hold back the tears, some of joy at the sale of the cottage and some of sadness at the thought of leaving it, as Peter whispered again and again, 'We have a buyer,' as though the relief was too much to bear. It meant that their own move could be confirmed and that a new phase in their life was to begin.

Even so, the nostalgia for the moor remained; the mist creeping away before the morning sun as *The King's Beacon* took its stance to survey the surrounding countryside. The variety of sounds from the chorale of birds and animals of the moor as they rose to life were memories of the spring mornings that would linger. The long summer days announced by a sun, still hidden behind the horizon, yet colouring the early morning sky with a deep, rich red, would be another reminiscence that would be recalled in future days with affection. Even the worst of the snow, the wind and the rain would do little to dampen the fondness with which mother, father and children would look back at those early family days, and neither could they dispel the feeling of nostalgia. The experiences presented by life on the moor below *The King's Beacon* inevitably bred independence in the minds and attitudes of the children and determination in their parents. As Peter looked over Catherine's shoulder, he visualised the changes that had taken place in the dining room, in the sitting room and the upstairs, and how significant had been the impact of the new building. It was in this and in so many other ways that the *Beacon*, the moor, and the cottage, would leave their mark on all the family for ever.

Lightning Source UK Ltd.
Milton Keynes UK
UKOW040921061112

201723UK00002B/2/P